Table for Two

Dara Girard

ILORI
Press Books, LLC

Large Print Edition

Table for Two (Large Print Edition)

Copyright © 2003 by Sadé Odubiyi

ISBN 13: 978-1949764307

Cover and Layout Copyright © 2018 by ILORI Press Books
Cover Design: WMG
Cover image airbrushing by ILORI Press Books
Cover image © Foto2rich/shutterstock

This is a work of fiction. Names, characters, places, and incidents either are the product of the author's imagination or are used fictitiously, and any resemblance to actual persons, living or dead, business establishments, events or locales is entirely coincidental.

ILORI PRESS BOOKS LLC
PO Box 10332
Silver Spring, MD 20914
www.iloripressbooks.com
Originally published by BET Books in 2003

Other Large Print Books by Dara Girard

THE FORTUNE BROTHERS
A Tempting Proposal
A Seductive Arrangement

NOVEL
Remember My Name

This book is dedicated to my family,
who know the importance of a good meal.

Dear Reader,

Before I wrote category romance novels, I started my career in mainstream romance. Ten years ago, I decided to write about a character that was a complete contradiction: An overweight, insecure woman who's a successful self-help instructor. And her love interest? An anti-social guy who loves food and owns restaurants. I didn't realize at the time that romance heroines were supposed to be beautiful and confident. Okay, I'll be honest. I didn't care because I loved this story.

The characters intrigued me. I loved that Cassie's rival for Drake's affection was a fitness guru (the chocolate scene between the two women still makes me laugh). I liked Drake's sly brother Eric, his impish sister Jackie and Cassie's sassy best friend, Adriana. I had a blast writing this story. It wasn't the first novel I'd written (not by a long shot, it was probably book number fifteen and that's not counting the plays, essays, articles…you get the point), but it was the first novel when I realized my true passion—creating stories.

For years I'd focused on publication, but suddenly I realized publication was just icing on the cake—creating was divine. Suddenly, I didn't care if I became the most prolific unpublished writer around.

Which seemed likely because the moment I put my manuscript in the mail it returned to me like a boomerang. I was disappointed but not defeated. I was gloriously stubborn and ambitious (if not a little insane) and didn't stop writing and submitting. After a year of effort I finally got 'the call' and a year later *Table for Two* was published.

It has flaws and I've learned a lot since I was a young writer with a dream, but I wrote this story with love and joy and I hope that still comes through.

All the best,
Dara Girard

Chapter One

*C*assie Graham knew the moment of impact would be painful. She was certain it was impossible to have more than six feet of well-muscled male fall on top of her without suffering a few lasting bruises. She landed with an undignified *ooof!* on the grassy turf of the park with any belief that grass was softer than concrete forgotten. The impact knocked off her glasses, turning her world into an impressionist painting of hazy trees and buildings. She briefly wondered if all the nineteenth-century masters were just myopic.

"Are you all right?" the man asked. His voice was unusually kind, which it had no right to be since she was the cause of the collision. His concern made her feel even more foolish.

Cassie glanced up and two meltingly rich golden brown eyes came into focus, gazing at her like a medieval charm that had the ability to put someone under a spell. She was not sure if it was the expression or the color that brought heat to her face, but something made her cheeks grow very warm. She opened her mouth to say that she was fine and assure the poor man that there was no reason to worry, but words caught in her throat when she glanced down and realized that he was half naked. He was shirtless, proudly displaying his Brazilian nut skin in the summer heat. He hovered above her like a large cat, his solid arms on either side, trapping her as if she were some unfortunate prey. She knew that she was in no danger, but the image of his powerful arms and torso made her wary.

"Is she okay?" an impatient male voice asked.

Another spoke up. "Where did she come from?"

Cassie transferred her gaze to stare at the blurry faces of a small semicircle of mostly half-naked males. She briefly shut her eyes and groaned. Could the day become any more humiliating?

"I'll handle this," the man above her said. He tossed the football to one of the men. "Start without me."

The first man stared at the ball and began to protest. "But—"

"I said start without me," he repeated, his voice firm.

The group of men mumbled among themselves and left. Cassie kept still. Perhaps if he thought she was hurt he would not be angry.

She heard the man softly swear as he moved off her with the agility of the athlete he obviously was. Cassie breathed a sigh of relief now that she was free of him and his speculative gaze. Suddenly, his hands were all over her, expertly searching for broken bones or torn flesh. She gasped when his sensitive fingers slid down her side like a series of butterflies. She sat up, grabbed his hands, and bit back a giggle. "Stop that! I'm very ticklish."

He smiled, flashing brilliant white teeth. "That's good to know." He had a pleasantly deep voice like marmalade on toast. She also recognized a soft musical lilt that suggested an island birth. It reminded her of her extended family back home in Jamaica.

"Can I have my hands back?" he asked in a teasing tone.

Cassie saw that she had her hands wrapped around his wrists. He had large worker's hands. She wouldn't have expected them to be so gentle. She quickly released them, embarrassed. "Oh, sorry."

"Are you sure you're not hurt?"

"Nothing that a bowl of asparagus vichyssoise can't cure," she said without thinking. She instantly regretted such a gauche statement, knowing that she should have said, *No, my body does not feel as if it had been crushed by a car,* and left it at that. She opened her mouth to retract what she'd said, but he didn't let her.

He stretched out next to her, resting on an elbow, and said, "Garnished with chive oil and asparagus tips."

She paused, surprised that he would be knowledgeable of one of her favorite dishes. "Naturally." She decided to test him some more. She narrowed her eyes, wishing she could distinguish his features and read his expression. However, at the moment all she could decipher was a beautiful voice and flashing smile. "Then there would be a shrimp, avocado, and mango salad."

He shook his head. "No, you've already had avocado." He reached up, gently pulled a strand of grass from her hair, and twirled it between his fingers. "How about chicken with olives and preserved lemon with an Old World Pinot Noir?"

Her heart began to pound from both his touch and his words. Could it be? A man who loved food as much as she did? She bit her lip, wondering if she should continue but unable to stop herself. "And for dessert? It must be something chocolate."

He thought for a moment, then snapped his fingers. "Chocolate and banana pie."

She grabbed her chest and stared up at the sky. "A man after my own heart. I have died and gone to heaven."

The man watched her return her butterscotch gaze to his face, the expression lovely and wistful. He doubted she knew how adorable she looked with her red blouse and khakis stained with dirt and her dark brown hair springing from its braid. She had a pleasant round face the color of cocoa, and a mouth that looked as if it would taste like sweetened raspberries. He licked his lips at the thought. That was something he would definitely like to find out.

He stared at her, searching his mind for something else to say, when she suddenly looked worried and began hunting through the grass.

"What's wrong?" he asked.

"I'm looking for my glasses." She felt around in the grass, trying to find her frames. She hoped she would not hear the crunching of someone stepping on them.

"Oh." He didn't feel the obligation to mention he had them safely in his grasp since she was offering him a very enviable view of a nicely formed derriere.

She raised her voice. "Damn, where are they?" Her hands curled around an object that felt like her glasses, but it turned out to be a twig. In disgust, she threw it away.

"Ow!" a distant voice cried.

She glanced up and saw a hazy form, rubbing its forehead. "Watch what you're doing," an older man ordered.

Cassie squinted, trying to see the man. "Oh, I am so sorry." Whether the older man accepted her apology or not she couldn't tell. He just walked away, muttering something about the dangers of careless people.

She could hear her companion softy laughing behind her. On any other occasion, she would have found the sound pleasurable, but at that moment it irritated her. She turned to him and saw he had stretched out like a lazy animal of prey that had completed a very successful hunt.

She frowned at him. "I'm glad you find this so amusing. If you were a gentleman you would help me find them."

"I'm afraid gentlemen don't exist anymore. The world is full of rogues." He held out his palm.

Cassie glanced down and saw her glasses, dwarfed in his large palm. She reached for them, but he moved them out of her grasp.

She folded her arms and glared at him. "I see you revel in your rogue status." She narrowed her eyes. "You've had them the entire time and watched me look for them?"

He sat up, resting an elbow on his knee. "Yes," he said without apology. "I like watching you. You look sweet and vulnerable forging through the grass like a blind mole."

"I'm hardly blind." She lunged for the glasses; he moved them out of her reach. She ended up wrapping her fingers around his hand and falling across his bare chest. Up close, she could see the contours of his muscles. She resisted the urge to skim her hands across them, wondering if they would constrict under her touch. For a man who enjoyed food, he kept his body in top condition. Unfortunately, she couldn't say that about herself. Her decidedly round figure hinted at her love of a good meal. No amount of kickboxing or aerobics could alter her shape. She quickly pushed herself off him, aware of how heavy she must feel against him.

"I'm sorry," she gasped.

"No need to apologize," he muttered, trying to recover from the feel of having her against him, the touch of her breasts against his chest.

She held out her hand. "May I have my glasses?"

"In exchange for a trade."

She was immediately suspicious, not trusting the deepening tone of his voice. "Of what?"

"A name."

He was flirting with her. She recognized the intimate teasing and suddenly felt relieved. If he had been solicitous or worried, she would have become flustered, but a flirt was someone she could deal with. Besides, if he was secretly laughing at her she would never know since she couldn't see his face clearly.

She sent him a mysterious smile. "I'm not sure that's a fair trade. A person's name is quite a valuable possession."

She didn't realize how enchanting she looked with her eyes sparkling and her mouth quirked in an inviting expression. She didn't notice the man's eyes darken or the secretive smile that touched the corner of his mouth that meant her fate was sealed.

The man rose to his feet and offered her a hand. For a moment, he saw hesitation cloud her eyes, but he did not want her to hesitate or think too much about the attraction that hummed between them. He lifted her up in an effortless pull. She stumbled against him, placing a hand on his chest to balance herself. Her touch was quick and soft, but he felt as if he'd been branded. His attraction for her was so sudden and fierce that it scared him and he backed away as if she'd slapped him.

Cassie decided to laugh at her clumsiness. No doubt, the poor guy had not expected her to weigh so much. "Not used to a real woman, huh? I'm afraid these curves come with a heavy price." She expected him to smile at her joke, but he didn't. He continued to stare at her. She licked her dry lips. "Your friends are probably anxious for you to join them. Could I have my glasses back please?" Her tone was firm. She was ready to end this encounter for both their sakes.

"Not yet." His voice was odd, as if he was considering something.

She could feel her temper replace her embarrassment. "Listen, I am not in the mood for your games."

"I am not playing any games."

"Then what are you trying to do?"

"I'm still trying to find out what a man has to do to elicit a name."

Cassie now regretted that she could not read his expression. They were close, but he was a whole head taller than she was. She couldn't understand his need to prolong the encounter. She placed a hand on her hip, ready for any challenge he had to offer. He would not intimidate her. "You want a fair exchange? Then give me something I couldn't resist." Hoping to catch him off guard, she quickly reached for the glasses but he moved them easily into his other hand.

"Hmm." He tapped her glasses against his chin. "How about strawberries dipped in chocolate fondue served with a light dry wine?"

She paused. The man was good. She tilted her head to the side and narrowed her eyes in playful accusation. "You've been reading my diary, haven't you?"

He slowly smiled. "No, otherwise I would already know what your name is."

"My name is Cassie and it just so happens that the other day I wrote that the first man who offered me strawberries dipped in chocolate would be the father of my children."

He thought about this, then nodded. "We'll have three of course."

She grinned at his solemn tone. "And just what is the name of my children's father?"

"Drake Henson."

"Drake Henson." She tasted the name in her mouth, then nodded in approval. "Yes, that will do."

"And all our children will enjoy food as much as we do."

"I'm not sure. As you can very well tell, that's a fault of mine."

His voice lowered and she could feel his eyes skimming her figure. "From where I'm standing, I see no faults at all."

Cassie swallowed. It had to be the heat that sent the trickle of sweat gliding down her back. It was a hot day after all. "That's where you have me at a disadvantage. I can't see you at all."

"Hmm, I suppose our delightful companionship will end once you discover I have no teeth and one eye."

"Don't be ridiculous. I'm not that blind. The fact that you have teeth is something I can see."

"Here." He put the glasses on her face. His fingers brushed against her cheeks, sending jolts of awareness through her body.

"Thank you." She glanced up at him and froze.

She had indeed crossed paths with a mythical charmer. His eyes were the color of hot amber, gazing at her intensely, which made her wish she had stayed on her cottage cheese diet just one more week. He wasn't classically handsome. His jaw was too harsh as if life had not always been kind, and although he did not look older than thirty-six, gray was fighting through his black hair with vicious determination.

He was dynamic. A ball of sexual potency. A man that should be served on top of a banana split and eaten with great enjoyment. His smile was more sensuous than wicked, more inviting than taunting, and it drew her like a beacon. His long eyelashes half shielded his eyes as he casually stood watching her. His jeans hung low on his hips, leaving plenty to admire of his upper torso. She must be hallucinating from the fall and the heat, he couldn't be the man she had been so boldly flirting with.

She had flirted with a lot of men, but something about this one made her feel uneasy.

She took a quick step back, dusting off her trousers as an excuse not to look at him. "I'm sorry I ruined your game."

"You didn't. I still caught the ball." His wicked grin turned smug. He took a step toward her, his voice lowering. "Umm... since you like to eat..."

"Yes," she readily agreed, annoyed that he felt the need to mention that. She could easily bury her face in banana cream pudding right now. "Yes. I do and as I said, it shows. I don't have the athletic aptitude of some. It's a good thing I didn't land on top of you. I could have flattened you like a Swedish pancake." She expected him to laugh. People usually did, but he frowned instead. Cassie sighed. Didn't the guy have a sense of humor? "I'm sorry for this... this inconvenience, but I really must go."

"No, wait." Drake grasped her arm as she turned, but immediately let go when she looked up at him startled and annoyed. He couldn't understand why the warm, sexy woman was now looking at him with something akin to dislike. Where had he gone wrong? He knew if she gave him a chance, he could explain it. "Give me a minute. I want to talk to you. I'll be right back. Wait here."

He was a man obviously used to obedience. Instead of waiting for her to agree, he turned and walked to his companions.

Cassie stared at him, watching the easy grace with which he moved, how the muscles in his back worked like a well-oiled machine when he folded his arms. He started to talk to his companions, and one man in shorts and a shirt that read Sports King glanced in Cassie's direction with disbelief. She didn't want to imagine what Drake was saying about her. Probably congratulating himself on such an easy conquest. She glanced away and saw an old woman who looked like a colored negative. Everything was pink. From her pompadour hair, high-heeled shoes, and upscale clothing to the poodle she was walking. Cassie started to laugh; she needed to laugh. Wasn't life absurd?

The woman briefly looked in her direction, shaking her head in a tut-tut manner, and walked away. Cassie sighed, sobering. Who was she to laugh at anyone? She knew she looked a mess. She was a normally tidy person and could only imagine what she looked like. He must be secretly laughing at her. A chubby woman offering to have his children over chocolate-covered strawberries. How amusing. She shrugged. She was used to it, but today she had better things to do than be a source of entertainment. She glanced at the group once more, then turned and fled.

* * *

She grimaced at her reflection as she stood in the restroom of the Golden Diner. Granted the lighting was poor, but she still looked worse than she had imagined. Her blouse was stained; dirt was on her cheek and clung to her glasses. Her hair was similar to that of a porcupine. The man definitely didn't have a sense of humor. When she had seen her reflection, she laughed so hard the woman at the sink next to her stared at her with a worried frown.

Cassie washed her face, tried to attack the grass stains that stubbornly decided to cling to her clothing, and then combed back her hair. She looked at her reflection again. It was an improvement, although a small one. She put on some lipstick and left to meet her friend.

They usually met at the Golden Diner for lunch. The place was called a diner because of its easygoing atmosphere; the word golden was added because of the prices. Only successful professionals could afford to frequent the cozy DC restaurant. It was imperative to look one's best, which was why her friend Adriana gaped in horror as Cassie approached the table.

"You're filthy!" she cried.

Cassie tossed down her purse and sighed. "There is no need to exaggerate."

Adriana had been her best friend since grade school. Both knew how it felt to survive the wilds of the rich suburbs while living with island parents who wanted to keep traditional ways. On a number of occasions, Cassie had organized Adriana's escapes so that they could attend parties, and Adriana, in turn, found ways to handle Cassie's overly critical mother. Their backgrounds were similar— good schools and good families—but in appearance they were opposites.

While Cassie had grown from cute chubby kid into cute chubby adult, Adriana had metamorphosed into a tall, svelte woman. She had dark brown eyes and purple-black hair that fell to her shoulders in silky curls, and a sensuous mouth that had men panting when she used it appropriately. She was not beautiful, but interesting, and that was enough to gain men's attention. Today she looked casually elegant in cream trousers, a white blouse, which offset her coffee skin, a pearl choker, and large gold hoop earrings.

"Why are you dirty?" she amended.

"I accidentally walked into a football game and was tackled."

Adriana winced. "Sounds painful."

"It was." To both her body and her pride.

"Hi, ladies," the waitress greeted. The young woman wore what the Golden Diner considered a uniform: Purple fluorescent top and skirt, clunky black shoes, and cap. She held a tray expertly in one hand as she tried to adjust the cap that was falling over her eyes. Cassie's stomach grumbled, reminding her of the grapefruit she had eaten for breakfast.

"What happened?" she asked, staring at Cassie.

"Long story. If you're willing to feed me, I might tell you all about it."

"I'd love to hear it, but I don't have the time." The waitress placed a plate of food in front of Adriana. Cassie glanced at her friend, confused that food would already arrive when they hadn't yet placed their orders.

"I ordered for us. My treat," Adriana explained as the waitress placed a grilled chicken sandwich, French fries, and coleslaw in front of Cassie.

She groaned, remembering Drake's breathtaking physique, and stared at the curvaceous woman in front of her with a brief stab of envy. "Great! The perfect food for a woman on a diet."

Adriana paused with a French fry midway in her mouth. "You had better not be."

"I'm not. Just thought about it." There was no need to mention the cottage cheese diet.

Adriana thoughtfully munched on her fries, then shook her head. "I don't believe in diets."

"That's because you don't have to."

"The problem is you're living in America. In another country you'd be a prized possession."

Cassie rolled her eyes. Somehow, they always came to this conversation. Adriana was convinced that she would be a beauty elsewhere. The problem was she wasn't elsewhere. "Yes, I'd make a perfect sacrifice. I'd keep the fire burning."

Adriana frowned. "Not funny."

"I'm sorry." She wasn't, but said it anyway so that she could drop the subject. She took a bite of her sandwich. Unfortunately, the bite was too big, which she usually did when annoyed, and she ended up maneuvering her food so that she wouldn't choke.

"So why were you walking into football games?"

Cassie swallowed with difficulty, then took a gulp of her drink. "Timothy sent me flowers," she explained. "Red roses to be exact."

Adriana swore.

"Exactly," Cassie agreed. "You'd think after a year he'd get the hint, but he always was a slow learner. He refuses to believe that we're really divorced and that I'm completely over him."

"Yes, of course." Adriana held her nose in the air and affected the tone of a snotty socialite. "How could anyone get over Timothy Milton the Third, heir to the Milton Furniture chain, Ivy league graduate, and all-out ass—"

"That's enough," Cassie said before her friend warmed to the subject "Although I agree with you, it only makes me sound jealous calling him names all the time." She didn't think it necessary to talk about the number of choice words she had used when the flowers had arrived.

Adriana tapped her foot, her brows furrowed. "I'll never forgive myself for not shooting him when I had the chance. You know how I feel about controlling the rodent population. You have to get rid of them before they reproduce."

"It was a shame the rat poison didn't work," Cassie teased.

Adriana shook her head mournfully. "You didn't use enough."

Cassie laughed. "I deserved what I got anyway. I was so flattered when he chose me over you that I didn't think." She had met him after she had survived a crash diet that caused her to lose her hair.

Consequently, she had gained the weight back and her hair grew back as thin as new grass—she felt like a Chia Pet. As a result, she had eagerly accepted his attention. Timothy had looked so handsome and refined that first night she had met him. Any woman's dream—her ultimate nightmare.

"I wasn't surprised that he had good taste. Most jerks do. So what did you do with the flowers?"

"Set them on a grave site."

Adriana nodded in approval. "Too bad it's not his own. Are you sure you don't want me to have my brothers talk to him?"

Cassie knew what her friend meant by talk. Adriana had two older brothers who were very skilled in primitive rhinoplasty and orthopedic surgery. They had developed their skill on playgrounds and back alleys when their classmates made the unwise decision to tease them about their accents or foreign manners. Cassie and Adriana were spared from any teasing because of that.

Cassie shook her head. "When I want him physically harmed, I'll let you know. I can handle him."

"When you can't handle him, let me know." Adriana pointed a manicured nail at her. "So have you gotten your seminar speech all set? I can't wait to hear it."

"You're still coming?" Cassie asked in disbelief. She squirted ketchup into her plate. "You've already heard what I am going to say at least a hundred times."

Adriana waved that fact away in a dismissive gesture. "So what? First, it's great for business." Adriana owned several lingerie boutiques and Cassie's seminars sent women running into them. "Second, I love to hear you speak and watch the way you capture an audience. Sometimes I forget that you're the same woman."

Cassie swirled a fry into the ketchup and smiled with triumph. "Ah, then Cassandra has succeeded."

Adriana frowned. "I don't see why you have to be two different people."

"It's the illusion that counts." She swept her hand through the air. "The presentation is of the utmost importance. Nobody would look at me now and think I could teach them how to be seductive." She stared down at herself. "Especially not now. They would expect me to do a comedy routine. Cassandra is more convincing. I just—" She stopped and stared at the entrance of the diner.

A man stood there like a giant shadow with a sliver of sunlight peeking behind him, giving shape to his massive form. When he stepped into the light—tall, virile, and real, like a shadow transfer-ring from one world into another—he glanced around the restaurant as if he was looking for someone. Instinctively, Cassie knew who that was.

She squeezed into the corner of her booth, her heart pounding so quickly she was afraid it would leap from her chest and run. "I have to hide."

Adriana stared at her, baffled by her friend's be-havior. "What is wrong with you?"

"That man by the door," she said in a panicked whisper. "I don't want to see him or rather I don't want him to see me."

Adriana turned. "There are three men by the door."

"The guy in the blue T-shirt."

"Oh." Adriana turned again. "Oh, my God!" She looked at Cassie as if she'd lost her mind. "I can't believe it. You've snapped."

"Don't be silly," Cassie scolded.

Adriana leaned forward, resting her arms on the table. "You're hiding from that! That's like running away from a winning lottery ticket."

"Be quiet!" she demanded.

Adriana looked suddenly concerned. She reached out to feel Cassie's forehead. "Perhaps you're suf-fering from heat stroke."

She slapped her friend's hand away. "Possibly," she agreed. "Look, I've made an idiot of myself enough today. I'd prefer to stop now while I still have some of my pride to salvage."

Adriana glanced over her shoulder. "Well, you're out of luck, sweetie, because he's coming this way."

Cassie searched for a means of escape, then slid under the table just as two well-built legs stopped in front of the table.

"Excuse me," Drake said politely, confusion evident in his tone. "But wasn't there someone sitting with you?"

"Yes," Adriana replied, trying to appear as if nothing was out of the ordinary. "She just left."

Cassie scooted over to Adriana's side and nudged her friend's leg in warning not to give her away.

Drake sighed in frustration, then asked, "Do you know where she went?"

"And why should I tell you that?"

"That's a good question." He slid into the booth. Cassie shut her eyes in prayer as his legs barely missed touching her knees. When she opened her eyes, she stared straight into his lap. She briefly wondered if he was well built all around. Was the lower half of him as sensitive as his hands? She placed a hand on her forehead to block out the image and the sensation that followed it.

"Let me introduce myself. I'm Drake Henson. I think your friend was the woman I bumped into a few minutes ago."

"Bumped into?" Adriana scoffed. "She said it was more like a tackle."

Cassie pinched her for giving her away; Adriana kicked her in response.

"Great, so you do know her. One of the guys thought he saw her come in here." He sounded satisfied. "Could you tell me how I could reach her?"

Adriana was silent for a moment, then said, "I'm sorry, but if she wanted you to have that information she would have told you herself."

"I didn't get the chance to ask her." Cassie saw his leg bounce up and down with impatience. "Could you at least tell me where she is?"

Again, Adriana paused. "I'm not sure." She reached into her purse for something. Cassie guessed that it was her lipstick. She was going to use her secret weapon, a mouth that had men drooling. She knew Drake didn't have a chance. She felt vaguely sorry for him. "I don't think that would be fair."

"Hmm, I see." Cassie couldn't read his tone, but he didn't sound terribly disappointed, more pensive and curious. For some reason, that annoyed her.

He stretched out his legs and Cassie stiffened in horror as one softly brushed against her bare arm. A jolt of heat shot through her body as his leg rocked back and forth against her. Cassie fought the urge to lean against him and delight in the feel of his hair whispering against her skin. Adriana's plan was working; he clearly thought her arm was Adriana's leg. He suddenly stopped the distracting activity and drummed his fingers on his thigh. "So what is your name?"

"Adriana."

"I'm Drake."

"Yes, you told me."

"Right." There was silence, then, "Well, thanks for your time." He abruptly slid out of the seat.

"No problem."

There was more silence; then he left.

A moment later, Adriana tapped the table in a strange pattern of beats.

"What are you doing?" Cassie asked.

"Morse code. He's gone now, you little coward."

"I know that." She wasn't sure she wanted to move. She felt as if the feel of him had melted her into the floor. She took a deep breath and crawled back into her seat. "You would not believe what he was doing. The man is an incurable flirt. He was flirting with you."

"What are you talking about?"

"He thought he was rubbing against your leg," she explained. "But it was really my arm." She glanced down at her plate, noticing that some fries were missing. Also her friend's lipstick didn't look as if it had been touched up, but Cassie guessed she had done a subtle job of it and didn't want Drake to drool, just be distracted. "So much for charming. He was trying to hit on you. What's so funny?"

Adriana sobered, but her eyes continued to dance with humor. "You crawl under a table when a gorgeous man looks for you; then he rubs up against your arm, and you ask me what's funny?"

"Laugh away. I'm afraid I can't see the humor in this situation." She picked up her sandwich.

"Personally, I think it smacks of romance. A gorgeous man searching for the woman who has captured his heart."

"Don't get carried away. It doesn't take much cunning to know that you'll find a fat woman in a restaurant."

Adriana's smile fell. "You're not fat."

"Oh, I forgot. What is the politically correct word of the day? Big-boned, oversized, rotund?"

Adriana ignored her and held up her drink. "He is so adorable. I'd never seen a man so shy."

"Shy? He's as shy as van Gogh was mentally stable. It was all an act to flirt with you."

Adriana shrugged. "Doesn't matter. You didn't want him anyway, right?"

Cassie nodded. "Right."

Adriana lifted an eyebrow. "Cassie, you really should try to sound more convincing when you lie."

Cassie made a face and finished her sandwich.

* * *

From another booth, someone watched her and smiled. He put down his menu and let a relieved sigh escape. He had been worried for a minute. First, she had been late for her lunch with Adriana. Then that man had come after her. Who the hell was he? He loosened his grip on the table; he wouldn't get angry. Everything would be okay. The man obviously wasn't a concern since Cassie had hidden from him. He allowed his smile to widen. Good old Cassie, she knew to whom she belonged.

Chapter Two

*D*rake was annoyed. It was a usual emotion after he'd failed to get to know someone interesting. And Cassie was definitely interesting with her wide, teasing eyes, a mouth that softened easily into a welcoming smile, and a body that showed men what womanhood was all about.

He sat in the bar with his brother, Eric, and Eric's friend Malcolm, drinking beer amid the noise of a televised game. He usually enjoyed Eugene's Bar, shouting at the TV, and throwing back a cold one, but now he just wanted to be alone to think. To think about Cassie and why she had run from him. He took a drink of his beer and slammed it down as various thoughts crowded his mind. Yep, there was no doubt about it. He was definitely annoyed.

Why did she feel the need to hide from him? He remembered her friend's face when he had asked her where Cassie was and she pointed to the table. She looked as baffled as he was. At first he thought it was a joke, but when his leg brushed against a silky soft arm he knew it wasn't. Why hide? Hadn't she felt what he had?

"Drake, are you going to finish your pizza?" Malcolm asked, wiping crumbs off his *Sports King* T-shirt.

"No."

Malcolm was a skinny guy with a gigantic appetite and a mouth to match. Drake didn't really like him, but acknowledged that he didn't like most people. He found them arrogant, obnoxious, or boring and his natural tendency to be an introvert didn't help, so he tried to be tolerant of his brother's friend.

Malcolm took a large bite of pizza. "What's wrong with you?"

"Nothing." He glanced down at the table, wishing Malcolm didn't have the habit of talking with his mouth full.

"He's thinking about that woman he bumped into," Eric clarified with his usual insight. Drake was always surprised how his younger brother could read him so well. Especially when he wasn't able to do the same. No one could mistake them for brothers. Eric was of a slighter build and lighter complexioned with a serious face that could be intimidating. His gold-rimmed glasses gave him the solemn look of a professor. He looked myopic, but he didn't miss a thing. However, their smiles were the same—broad and a little wicked. He flashed one now. "Don't worry about it. Did you get her number?"

He shook his head and lifted his beer.

Eric's smile dimmed. "A last name?"

He finished his beer and again shook his head.

"A birth sign?"

"Nothing."

Eric stared at him in shock. "You mean you were talking to her all this time and all you found out was that her name was Cassie?"

Drake sat back in his seat, irritated by his failure. "Yep."

"The way you two were staring at each other, I thought you were trying to create your own summer heat. What were you two talking about then?"

"Food."

Eric kissed his teeth in disgust. "Food? How did you manage to do that?"

"It just happened naturally."

Eric swirled his drink, then took a gulp. He looked at his brother as if he were a promising student who'd failed a class. "That's the problem with you. You don't know how to talk to women unless it's related to work."

Drake raised his hand to signal the waiter to bring him another beer. It would be his third, perhaps his fourth. It didn't matter, because he wasn't driving. "Trust me. When I was talking to her, I wasn't thinking about work."

"You're hopeless."

"Wait a minute." He rested his arms on the table and looked at his brother's serious face with a smile tugging on his lips. "When did you become an expert on women, Mr. Casanova? Tell me the last time you had a date."

Eric adjusted his glasses in consideration. "The last time I've wanted one."

Drake accepted the beer the waiter handed him with a quick nod and took a healthy swallow. "So that would be in the fifth grade when you gave Margaret a bag of candied hearts."

Eric grinned, not offended by his brother's teasing. "I think you're confusing things. That was what you gave your date at your senior prom."

Drake's humor faltered. He hadn't been to the prom or any of the other high school functions. He had wanted to go. He had dreamed of asking Brenda Timmons, taking her to a fancy restaurant, then making out at one of the after-prom parties. He hadn't been able to dream long. He was poor and had to take care of two younger siblings. Whatever money he earned went to them. Nobody expected much from him. Many predicted he would end up a wino. Fortunately, that hadn't been the case. Now he was going to see his old classmates again in two months at his twentieth high school reunion and he would have the chance to prove them wrong.

Eric banged the table with his glass, awakening Drake from the melancholy mood that had hit him. He shrugged good-naturedly. "Okay, so you made your point. I'm not an expert, but I've had more success than you. It's obvious you need to work on your technique."

Drake clasped his hands behind his head. "Things were going great," he said, reviewing the moment in his mind. "I honestly don't know where I went wrong. We were both talking about great meals."

Malcolm leaned forward, feeling safe to join the conversation. "No surprise there. I'm sure she's familiar with every meal around the world. Don't tell her you own a few restaurants. Hell, she'd probably eat you out of business."

Drake's eyes flashed. "What do you mean by that?"

Malcolm delicately cleared his throat, not wanting to get on Drake's bad side. It was not a pretty place. "I'm just saying she's a big woman."

Drake's eyes didn't leave Malcolm's face, like a missile aiming for its target. His voice lowered dangerously. "And your point is?"

Malcolm's eyes slid away. "I don't have one."

He let his gaze fall. "I didn't think so."

Eric hit his brother on the back to ease the tension that hovered over the table.

"Look, we all miss opportunities. I'm sure there's someone out there for you."

"And here she comes," Malcolm said, leering at a shapely woman with caramel skin and spice-colored hair. She had entered the bar and was now speaking to the bartender. Her tiny fluorescent green skirt hitched up her legs as she leaned on the counter.

Drake saw her and turned away, letting his hands fall to his sides. "Oh, her."

Eric leaned forward. "Kristin is someone you can handle. She likes you."

"That's only because I ignore her."

"Then stop ignoring her."

"I'm afraid that would take too much effort."

"At least practice on her. Most times, you're like a statue. This will give you a chance to talk, interact, practice your moves."

"I don't have any moves."

"Then make them up."

He stood. "I call this one 'making an exit.' "

Eric grabbed his sleeve and pulled him down. "Try again."

"Hi, guys," Kristin said, sliding into a seat next to Eric, while she flashed a brilliant smile in Drake's direction.

Both Eric and Malcolm said hello. Eric sent his brother a pointed glance that was as eloquent as a nudge.

Drake sighed. "Hi, Kristin."

"Hi, Drake. What have you been up to?"

He wrapped his hands around his mug. "I've been working on this new recipe for brown rice. See I—" He stopped when he saw Malcolm shaking his head and Eric doing a sawing motion against his neck signaling him to cut it out. "Never mind. How are you doing?"

"Just fine. I just got my nails done. Do you like them?" She rested her hand on his. Her nails were bright red with gold tips. They made him think of claws tainted with the blood of its victims. He moved his hand away. "Very nice."

"For what they cost me, I hope they look more than nice."

Malcolm spoke up. "You want compliments, baby? You'd better come to me."

They began to flirt. Drake didn't care. He had done as much socializing as he had rationed for the day. He stared down into his beer glass, wondering where he had gone wrong with Cassie. If things had gone right, he would be sitting here with her.

"Drake, you don't look happy," Kristin said, breaking into his thoughts. He glanced up; her lovely dark eyes showed concern.

"Women troubles," Malcolm explained.

"Is that possible?"

"For him it is."

"Lay off," Eric said.

"Oh, poor Drake." Kristin leaned toward him, exposing an ample amount of cleavage. Drake was amazed and disgusted—disgusted that in his present state the invitation was tempting. "You know you can talk to me any time."

He stood. "I think I'd better go."

Eric opened his wallet and stood too. "Same."

* * *

"I don't know how you can hang out with those two," Drake said, squinting from the glare of the sun a few minutes later. "You have nothing in common."

"Malcolm amuses me. I find his simplicity refreshing."

"What do you see in Kristin?"

"What's not to see?"

"An intelligent thought perhaps."

Eric wiped some sweat from his forehead. "True, but she's interesting in other ways."

"Don't tell me you've slept with her."

"Okay, I won't."

Drake looked at the sky. "I don't believe it."

"What's not to believe? She was willing and I was curious."

He shook his head, then finally asked, "Was it any good?"

"I don't tell." Eric took a flyer from a volunteer advertising a new store and scanned it "But she really wants you and just uses me as a substitute."

"And you don't mind?"

"Hey, if a woman wants to take out her sexual frustrations on me, I'm here to serve."

"That is warped."

"No, just sex." He tossed the flyer in a trash bin. "It usually happens that way. Women are drawn to your distant, brooding looks and turn to me for comfort." He straightened his glasses. "I comfort them. It all adds up."

"A true Sir Galahad. I'm glad to have been of service to you all these years. How does it feel to be a scavenger?"

"Hey, you got the looks, but I've got the brains and they've served me well. Started with Greta Rodgers my sophomore year. She was a senior and my first."

Drake remembered a quiet girl with big glasses, and decided not to ask. "What about marriage?"

"Now that's a nasty subject to bring up."

"No, it's not, Peter Pan. Don't you want to grow up?"

"In case you've forgotten we spent most of our childhood as grown-ups. Don't fault me for want-ing to have fun now."

"I don't." Drake shoved his hands in his pockets. "I want to marry and have kids."

"Kids? Why? You spent most of your time rais-ing us."

Drake shrugged. It had been hard, and at times he thought of giving up, but the struggle had ultimately made him strong. Coming home to see his brother and sister waiting for him had made him feel whole. He knew a wife and kids would give him that feeling again. "So you don't plan to marry?"

"I didn't say that. Actually, I already have the type of woman in mind."

"Oh."

Eric kicked a pebble out of the way. "Aren't you going to ask what type?"

"A woman who looks like Kristin, with the manners of Malcolm and the intelligence of a Teletubbie."

Eric scowled. "Actually, I intend to marry a very educated woman, with refined manners who appreciates jazz and good food. We'll eventually have one child."

"Reaching for the gold, huh?"

"I've got money. There's no reason I shouldn't find her."

"What about convincing this refined woman's family?"

"I'll make sure she's desperate."

"Your deviltry is troubling."

Eric shrugged. "What about you? What kind of woman do you want to marry?"

"Cassie. She's beautiful, funny, sweet, and she makes me feel... good. I actually flirted with her."

"You flirted with her? Wow. She is a miracle worker. Did you say 'waa-waa' too?"

"Are those a new pair of glasses? I'd hate to break them."

"All right, I'm sorry. I just don't believe there's only one woman for you. For anyone. You'll eventually forget about her and find someone new." His brother stopped in front of his apartment building. "Come on up. You always get this way when you've been drinking."

"No, I don't."

The two brothers argued about this on the way to his floor, then stopped and stared at the bundle wrapped in a yellow and red blanket in front of Eric's door.

"What the heck is that?" Drake asked.

Eric lightly kicked the bundle. "Something I've unfortunately continued to feed. Wake up, Jackie."

A small, female head popped out of the bundle and glared at them through almond-shaped eyes. "Where have you been?" she demanded.

"You forget your key again?"

She stood, barely reaching Eric's shoulder. "I was in a hurry. Come on, I'm hungry."

Eric opened the door. "You know we did her a disservice. Because we took care of her, she's going to expect some poor chap to do the same."

"That's not true. I only expect that of you two." She turned to Drake. "So what are you going to cook?"

"He's not cooking. He's drunk."

"I'm not drunk. Just pensive." Drake turned and hit his head against the base of a hanging plant. "Why do you have to hang these things so low?"

"They aren't low. You just need to watch where you're going."

"Your place looks like a damn jungle," he grumbled, surveying the many small indoor trees, plants, and vines that occupied the apartment. It was all cleverly done, but today the greenery irritated him.

Eric headed for the kitchen. "Please file the rest of your complaints down the toilet while I find something to eat."

* * *

"So why are you unhappy?" Jackie asked, wolfing down the grilled jerk chicken and brown rice Eric had prepared.

Drake pointed a fork at her. "If you don't slow down, you're going to get the hiccups."

"I'm not going to get the hic-ups."

Drake grinned. "I love being right."

"Oh, shut—up." She took a large gulp of water and held her breath until they subsided. "Now answer my question."

"No."

Eric spoke up. "He met someone and it didn't work out."

"Then it wasn't meant to be. You two think you can control life, but life happens to you. You can't lose the one you were truly meant to be with."

They were quiet a moment and then Eric said, "You just broke up with Richard, right?"

"Yep."

Drake looked stunned. "How did you know that?"

"She's always philosophical after a breakup," Eric said.

"What do you do, study us?" Drake asked.

"How else is the middle child supposed to entertain himself?"

"Ignore him," Jackie said. "What I am saying is true. You won't have to change for the person you're meant to be with. It will just happen and it will be perfect."

Eric nodded. "Good advice. So what did Richard want you to change?"

"He thought that I would look good with a nose job and weave."

Drake leaped from his chair. "That bastard's a dead man."

Eric leaned back in his chair looking cold and vengeful. "Why kill him, when we can bring him to financial ruin?"

"Cut it out, you two." Jackie grabbed Drake's shirt and nudged Eric with her foot. "I knew he was shallow from the beginning."

Drake sat, his scowl still in place. "He insulted you."

"Not really. You two have to promise to leave him alone. I've seen him with Betina Hart—man-crusher number one. When she's done with him, there'll be nothing left. So promise you won't do anything."

They nodded. Satisfied, she kissed them and left.

"She has a point," Eric said, watching Drake take dirty dishes over to the sink. "It wasn't meant to be. Now go along about your business, so that I can get some work done."

"Right."

"Besides, why worry about another woman when you've got Elizabeth?"

Drake only smiled.

* * *

Drake tossed off his apron with triumph. Elizabeth— his beloved stove—had again worked her miracles. After creating raspberry tarts, he was beginning to feel better about his failure. Besides, he was finally going to do something about his social grace.

He glanced at his watch. He still had a few hours before his class. His family didn't know it, but he enjoyed taking courses at the local community center. He'd learned how to play piano, choose antique furniture, and take photographs. He was making up for the lack of education he'd acquired in school. Back then he had spent most of his time either working or asleep. Since he was an unobtrusive student, teachers let him pass. Therefore, he had ended up with a degree and not much else. The adult classes helped him to socialize. He usually hid in the back of the class, but occasionally managed to tag along if a group went for drinks afterward.

The course he was going to take was one he eagerly anticipated, "Attracting Anyone Anytime: the

Art of Social Grace." He knew the instructor couldn't work miracles in the three days scheduled, but figured he could learn some much needed tips.

* * *

The memory of Drake entered Cassie's mind as she changed into Cassandra. It usually took her two hours to transform into the woman of mystery that kept her audience captivated. She heavily outlined her eyes with a smoky gray pencil and sprinkled glitter on her bare shoulders. She glanced down at the turquoise dress she wore that floated about her ankles like a mist. She usually wore a choker, but tonight she tied a gossamer scarf artistically around her neck. She stared at her reflection, always amazed what makeup and clothes could accomplish. She looked like a woman who could capture any man's attention and place him under her spell. The perfect companion for a sorcerer with hypnotic eyes. Cassandra was bold, sexy, fearless, and quite capable of going after anything or anyone she desired. She smiled wickedly as she applied a deep purple lipstick. Good old Cassandra.

"Cassandra" had come about by necessity for a shy girl who lived inside herself. Being the clown worked for a while, but made dating difficult since she always felt she had to provide the entertainment. One day at a party, she pretended she was someone else and was amazed by the response of men. The men who had seen Cassie as a pal suddenly saw her as a desirable woman, and to her disbelief they were entertaining her and it was empowering. Through college she perfected her technique, taking cues from her heroine, Elvira, Mistress of the Dark, then wrote a book called *The Shy Girl's Guide to Romance*. To her surprise the book sold well as did its sequel for men, *The Way of the Wallflower*, and *The Fear of Ridicule*. Her success led to conferences, lectures, and seminars. She loved the attention she commanded, watching as people hung on to her every word. It was wonderful being the mentor she hadn't been able to find while growing up. She enjoyed working with people and helping them find their potential.

Cassie glanced at her computer, which frowned at her in the corner of the living room. She had a contract to write a new book on keeping romance alive, but her mind was blank. Since her own romantic life was such a disaster, she was having a hard time giving advice to others. She was too busy thinking of a book called *How to Resist Killing Your Ex*. Her divorce had hurt her ratings, so this next book had to be successful or she might have to find herself a new publisher or a new career.

She sighed, resigned. She just needed to relax and the ideas would come. Perhaps the seminar would revive her. She could think about all the things Cassandra would do to her mysterious sorcerer.

Heat rushed to her face as her mind filled with ideas her mouth would never utter. She pushed the thoughts aside. She had to focus. She slipped into her silver high heels and popped in her contacts. The day was over and the night was now hers.

* * *

The seminar was held in the Acton Center, a converted brownstone on one of the side streets in Dupont Circle. It was popular with both artists and academics alike, offering large and small rooms for speakers to share their knowledge. Cassie had reserved a medium-sized room on the second floor that boasted a view of the lighted garden out back, with rows of comfortable chairs, and a warm, relaxing atmosphere so that her audience could feel comfortable confiding in her.

When she reached the second floor, she saw Adriana in a black bow-back chair waiting in the hallway with a cup of tea. She jumped to her feet when she saw Cassie.

"You look wonderful," she said. "This is a definite improvement."

"Anything would be an improvement to this afternoon." She moved to one side; Adriana did the same. "Why are you standing here?" she asked, wondering why her friend was blocking her path.

"I just wanted to make sure that you were prepared."

Cassie lifted her bag and shook it. "I am always prepared."

"Even for surprises?"

"Especially for surprises. What do we have? A desperate bride, an old sweetheart, a best friend hoping to confess her love?"

Adriana straightened her friend's scarf and smoothed back an unruly strand of hair. "No. Him." She pointed to a man in the corner of the room who was stretched out across a row of chairs. He was dressed in complete black with a baseball cap over his face.   Cassie frowned. "Is he dead?"

"Why don't you go and find out? I'm not sure, but I think he's gorgeous."

Cassie was not impressed. "You call that a surprise?" For some reason good-looking men liked to attend her seminars either to get more tips on the art of being a heartbreaker or to find shy women who wanted a good time. She didn't know which. Because her seminars were rather expensive, people who attended knew they would meet someone with money to spend.

She walked to the podium and put down her bag, delighted that a number of seats were occupied. She might not make the New York Times, but she could still fill a classroom. "Adriana, since you seem interested, why don't you wake him up? You've attended enough of my seminars, you could give him some tips."

"He's not my type. Besides, he might be in the wrong room."

Cassie sighed and walked up to the man, who was fast asleep. She couldn't help smiling at the fact that he slept like a mummy with his arms folded across his chest. His staff—which took the form of an umbrella—lay on the floor next to him. His dark trousers were made of fine wool, his black cotton shirt clung to an impressive chest, and a Rolex smiled smugly up at her from his wrist. If his body spoke for his face, it would be impressive too. She touched his shoulder. "Excuse me, sir, but the class is about to start." When he didn't move, she shoved him, and when that failed to wake him, she pinched him—hard.

The man jackknifed into a sitting position, his cap falling to the ground, and glared up at her. His eyes immediately widened and his sensuous mouth spread into a familiar grin that made her skin tingle. "I've been awakened by the starry heavens," he said, his voice coating her like syrup.

Cassie gasped, taking an involuntary step back, and crashed into the chair behind her. The golden eyes didn't leave her face. It seemed that tonight Cassandra would be dealing with a sorcerer after all.

Chapter Three

*D*rake stared at her as she spoke, with anticipation, desire, and hunger threatening to consume him, forcing him to fight the urge to take her in his arms. She was so close—a tree branch stretched just out of reach to a drowning man. And he was definitely drowning. His little bowl of sweet butterscotch was now a river of silky cocoa crème, covering him beneath her waves. He closed his eyes for a time, delighting in the fantasy of her completely enfolding him. He opened his eyes and now saw her as a tantalizing vision of the night, seeming to become the starry sky in her blue dress and smooth shoulders that shimmered underneath the lights.

She moved with a slow allure—a present-day Circe, luring men to her island to practice her witchcraft—and he would be the first ashore. He squirmed in his seat, aware of the tightness that gripped his lower body as thoughts of her naked in his arms altered his focus. He wondered what kind of passion she kept hidden under that sleek dress. He shifted again, promising himself that he'd discover the answer another time. Tonight he had only one goal—to find out if her lips tasted like sweetened raspberries.

* * *

She was dying—slowly and painfully—of embarrassment. He was here, Drake the Sorcerer was here, watching her (as she stammered through the introduction), like a cunning rogue waiting patiently for the right moment to pounce and collect his treasure. Whatever that might be. No matter how she tried to ignore him, his eyes were like magnets that kept drawing her to him. Perhaps he didn't recognize her and was just riveted by her performance. There was no other explanation for such an intensely heated stare. She had to remember that she was Cassandra, not the wisecracking Cassie who could be intimidated by a pair of intense amber eyes. No, he didn't recognize her, she concluded, gathering her courage like a talisman against a magician's spell. She was somebody different. Cassandra was a woman of mystery, seduction, and power. He would be at her mercy tonight. Of course, later she would find out why Adriana looked so smug.

The session was going remarkably well despite her halted beginning, and she was discussing her

favorite subject about the importance of first impressions when a deep voice spoke up, cutting
through her speech like a low thunder.

"What about second impressions?" Drake asked.

Cassie paused, coming out of the cocoon of
words that had kept her mind occupied from him.
She leaned against the podium and said, "I'm sorry,
could you repeat that?"

"You keep talking about the importance of a
good first impression, but what if you made a bad
first impression? How can you make a good second
one?"

Cassie licked her lips, trying to give his question
the thought it deserved although she couldn't imagine how it would be a problem for him. "I always
thought it was best to be honest. Just say you made
a bad impression and would like a second chance.
Or come up with something clever."

"Hmm." He nodded, seeming to digest her
words. "That sounds complicated. I think I'll need
practice."

To her horror, he rose from his chair and came
toward the podium. She swallowed with difficulty
as he stopped in front of her. She expected him to
grin or smile, but he just continued to stare at her
in his all-encompassing way.

She broke his gaze by glancing at the audience. "You should turn sideways so that the class can see you," she advised, trying to maintain a professional tone, although her insides were shaking.

He lifted a brow and did so.

Cassie cleared her throat and stared at her audience hoping to get help from that direction. She didn't want to handle him alone. "Would someone like to volunteer to help him?"

A number of eager female hands shot up, but Drake defiantly shook his head. "Sorry, but I prefer to practice with the best." His eyes met hers. "You are the best, aren't you?"

She recognized the challenge. "The very best," she said. "So the problem is you've made a bad first impression?"

"Yes," he agreed. "I came on too strong and I'd like to correct that."

"That shouldn't be hard to do." Cassie brushed her hands against her dress, wishing he didn't smell so good; she could picture herself floating on the mere scent of him. "Just say something that would assure me or the woman that you weren't yourself."

He grasped her shoulders and turned her to face him. His eyes danced with mischief. "Tell me when to begin."

She took a deep breath, convinced she was going to regret this. "Begin."

"Hello, Cassandra. I'm sorry our first meeting was not successful, but I promise you, like fine wine, I improve with time." She opened her mouth to tell him his statement was fine, but he shook his head in disgust. "No, too trite. Let me see." He gathered the end of her scarf and ran it through his fingers, the movement as gentle as a feathery kiss. "I'm sorry that our first introduction was poor, but in the presence of such beauty a man loses his head and his senses; however, given a chance they will be restored."

"That's very poetic," she said quickly, embarrassed by how breathy she sounded. His voice had a disconcerting way of invading her senses. "I think that would work." She hoped he would take the cue and return to his seat.

He didn't. Instead he let her scarf go, lowering his eyes for a moment. "Or I could just be very straightforward and say..." He captured her eyes, his deep gaze sending her a secret message she did not want to interpret yet could not deny. "I would really like a second chance to make a good first impression."

Cassie could only stare, not trusting herself to speak. He does recognize me, she thought in a panic. His eyes were too knowing. But that was ridiculous. He had been flirting with Adriana only a few hours ago. He was a rogue with a rogue's habit of mischief, and she could feel that mischief challenging her to harness it.

"Honey," a woman called from the audience, "if she doesn't let you I will!"

The class laughed, breaking the moment, and Drake returned to his seat, winking at Cassie as he did so.

Cassie gathered her scattered wits and completed the presentation. It was a resounding success leading to a series of questions afterward.

Once she had answered everyone's question, she told them the restaurant where they would meet for their next class. She gathered her things, hoping she could catch Adriana before her friend could escape. She glanced around the now empty room filled with the shadow of seats.

"Looking for someone?"

All the hairs on the back of her neck stood at the sensuous tenor of a voice. It wasn't an unpleasant sensation. She didn't need to turn around to discover the owner of the voice. She shoved some papers into her bag and snapped it closed.

"I was, but she has obviously left me."

"That's good to hear," he said, tapping his umbrella on his shoulder. "Because we're going for coffee. I have a few more questions to ask you." He grabbed her bag and turned off the lights.

She switched them back on. "I'm glad you enjoyed the presentation but there's no need to take me for coffee. I always have time for questions."

He shut the lights off again. "I prefer coffee," he said quietly, his tone hinting that he intended to win this battle of wills. He gently but firmly took her arm and led her out of the room. A part of her rose up to object his high-handed manner, but another part of her found him amusing and felt indulgent.

They walked to a cafe two buildings down. Cassie loved how DC bustled and glowed at night. The lights from the stores greeted late shoppers with tantalizing smiles; restaurants opened their doors, tempting potential clientele with savory aromas and soft music. The sky was clear black overhead with a few twinkling stars and the air was cool, with the tender scent of rain. As they walked, Cassie noticed the covert glances sent in Drake's direction. She knew people couldn't help themselves, he moved through the crowd like a dark mist, emanating grace and a strong presence.

He shoved his hands in his pockets. "You definitely have a lot of admirers," he said proudly.

Cassie stared at him, stunned. Was the man legally blind? "Me?" She tapped her chest to make sure she had heard correctly.

He nodded.

"They're all looking at you."

He shook his head. "No." He slanted her an amused glance. "They can't believe that a piece of the sky has come down to join them."

She laughed. "This coming from a man who looks like a moving silhouette. Don't you know you're not supposed to wear black at night?"

He tugged on his shirt. "I think it suits me."

"Just be careful crossing the street."

He sighed wistfully, laying a hand on his chest. "She cares about me. I'm touched."

Cassie didn't reply as he held open the door of the cafe.

The cafe was not crowded and it hummed with jazz that complemented the peaceful light that filled the air. They chose a booth near the window.

Cassie ordered tea and he surprised her by ordering hot chocolate.

He read her expression and smiled. "I thought getting coffee sounded more mature than hot chocolate."

"Uh-huh. I bet you just get it for the whipped cream."

He grinned, holding up his hands in surrender. "Guilty." He held her gaze a moment longer, until Cassie turned away. Why did he look at her like that? What did he have to ask her? And why did his gaze make her feel like either ripping off her clothes or running for cover?

Silence fell between them. Cassie pretended to read the menu, which had—at the most—seven items to choose from, while Drake stared out the window at the street and the few cars that rolled past. Cassie was determined that he should be the first to speak. She stole a glance at him above her menu. He had a prominent profile that spoke of strength and an air of command. She wished she could read his thoughts.

His eyes suddenly caught hers. "Do I pass?"

She dropped her gaze to the menu. "I don't know what you mean."

"Hmm. I suppose a gentleman wouldn't admit that he caught a woman staring at him, but since I'm only what I am, I can't help being curious."

She stared at him, her heart constricting. Did he really remember her from this afternoon and was he referring to their talk about gentlemen and rogues? No, it couldn't be. She was Cassandra—bold, mysterious. Not Cassie, no one had recognized her as Cassie before. She tossed the thought aside. "I was merely lost in thought."

"I hope I was in it."

She didn't reply, not bold enough to admit the truth.

Their orders arrived soon after. Drake's hot chocolate was placed before him, heaping with whipped cream. He ran his finger through it, then licked it off. It was a simple gesture, but for a moment Cassie couldn't take her eyes off his tongue as it swirled around his beautifully long finger.

"Tastes good," he said, satisfied.

She swallowed. "I bet it does."

He held up his spoon. "Would you like a taste?"

Of him, certainly. "Yes... no." She shook her head to clear her thoughts. He would not get her stuttering again. "Oh, sorry, um... What was the question you wanted to ask?"

"It can wait." He sat back in his seat and studied her for a moment. "I'm sure you're curious about me. Why don't you ask me a few questions?"

She rested her chin in her hands and watched him with mocking eyes. "Are you always so arrogant? How do you know I'm curious about you?"

"The fact that you're here says a lot."

"It says that I'm interested in your questions, not in you."

"Hmm." That was true enough, but he didn't believe that. He took a sip of his drink, his mind racing with ideas of what to say next. If he wasn't careful he was going to screw up again. He could sense that she was aware of him. Her eyes were perfect mirrors into her thoughts, but she wasn't ready to admit it yet. He sighed, suddenly wishing women came with manuals. He glanced down at his drink. "Okay, then let's say that I hope I can generate some interest."

She shrugged, dismissing his statement as harmless flirtation. "Why did you decide to take the seminar?"

He seemed shocked for a minute, then replied, "The same reason everyone else did."

Cassie sipped her tea and placed it down delicately. She couldn't help him if he wasn't willing to be honest "Right," she said, doubtful.

His lip twitched. "You don't believe me."

"I didn't say that."

"You didn't have to. I can recognize when you think I'm lying."

"I don't think you're lying. I think you're being evasive. I can't help you if you're not honest."

He patted his shirt in an absent, searching gesture. "I am being honest. I used to be shy as a kid. Then when my life got shifted out of balance only my family became a priority. I never..." He paused, searching for the words. "Had the chance to socialize."

"What shifted out of balance?" she asked, curious as to what made his family a priority.

"My life." He left no room for more inquires.

Cassie recognized a Do Not Enter sign when she saw one. She tried to think of something else to say. "Yes," she said lightly, hoping to fill the now awkward silence. "It has a crazy habit of doing that."

"Hmm." He glanced out at the traffic. "So... sometimes I don't say the right things."

What a bunch of bull. She wondered if he used that pitiful story with every woman he met or if he had fashioned it just for her. He definitely was not shy or had any trouble socially. He wouldn't be as successful as he was if that were the case, and something about him besides his appearance suggested that he was very successful.

"You'll have no problem," she said coolly. "I'm sure there are plenty of women willing to forgive you your social gaffs."

He picked up his mug and watched a group of preppy teenagers go by. "Why don't you believe anything I say?" He held up his hand before she could protest. "And don't deny it. That will just annoy me."

"Okay, I admit I find it hard to believe that a man like you would have any trouble getting women."

He was silent a moment and then met her eyes across the rim of his mug. "I don't want women. Just one in particular."

The hairs on her arm began to tingle at his assessing gaze. "And who would she be?" It was none of her business, but she couldn't help asking.

"The woman I plan to marry."

Of course! He was a man on the prowl ready to shackle the first woman who was willing. Why hadn't she seen that before? Wasn't that how Timothy was able to catch her? "Oh."

He noticed the note of disappointment in her tone. "Why do you say 'oh' like that?"

"Doesn't matter."

His brows furrowed. He watched the elegant manner in which she poured hot water into her cup. It had taken him years to master the grace she so effortlessly possessed. "Don't you believe in marriage?"

"It's great for others, but I've done it before and don't plan on doing it again."

He wrapped his hands around the mug and rested his elbows on the table. "What happened?"

Her eyes were cold when they met his. "I don't discuss my private life with strangers."

"Forgive me, milady," he said gravely.

She was immediately contrite. "Look, I—"

With a shrug, he brushed away her attempt to explain or apologize. "Don't worry about it. I know when I've stepped on a land mine. Hell, I threw a grenade at you a moment ago."

She relaxed, calm in the knowledge that he understood. "Not quite a grenade, more like a brick wall."

"Hmm." He drummed his fingers on his mug with impatience. "This sure puts an interesting spin on things," he muttered.

"What?"

"You don't believe in marriage and I do," he explained, his face closed in a serious mask.

She didn't understand why this was of any importance to him but she hoped to help him understand her point of view. "I believe people can love each other and be committed."

"Where?"

She frowned. "You know what I mean."

He looked at her enigmatically. "So people can be committed, just not married?"

"Marriage changes things."

"It should." He pushed the salt and pepper shakers together. "Two people belong together. They become a family in the eyes of the law."

She picked up the items and shook them at him. "People belong to each other without the law. Love binds them together."

"Love is a dangerous and illogical foundation for any relationship." He'd seen love turn his father into a weak, miserable man. "Commitment is all that matters and marriage is that ultimate commitment."

"Marriage gives lip service to commitment. Love is its truth."

"You are a romantic."

"And you are a cynic."

"I'm a realist."

"On what planet?"

He took the objects from her and placed them against the wall. "I think we should drop the subject." He signaled the waiter to request the bill.

"Very wise," she said, sorry that their time together had ended so badly.

"Hmm." He opened his wallet and shuffled through his bills. "I can be when I put my mind to it."

Cassie fiddled with her scarf. "Of course you have nothing to worry about," she said, trying to salvage the evening. "There are plenty of women out there who want to get married."

He placed the money on the table and stood. "Hmm." Unfortunately, the one he had in mind didn't.

Cassie slid out of her seat. "I am sorry to have made you angry, but I can't help expressing what I think."

"I'm not angry. I always enjoy a good debate with the misguided." He opened the door for her.

"The misguided?" Cassie closed her mouth, refusing to rise to his taunt. She took a step forward, then hastily stepped back, bumping into him. "It's raining," she said, answering his confused stare. The rain fell in a light drizzle.

Drake casually lifted his umbrella and pulled
Cassie close. A secretive smile softened his lips.
"Better?"

Her heart lurched madly, excited that he truly
was not angry with her. Timothy would say 'I'm not
angry,' then sulk for days. She didn't question why
that was important to her. "Much better."

"So where do I take you now?"

"Actually, my building isn't far from here." She
felt so many conflicting emotions that she had the
urge to run in the rain, escaping all the feeling this
man brought to her. "If I made a mad dash—"

"Which direction?" he interrupted.

She pointed and he slid his hand down her arm
and captured her hand in a warm, solid grasp.

"Drake?" she asked in a hurried whisper, wanting
to understand what was happening between them.
"Yes?"

He sounded so ordinary that her anxiety began
to ebb. "Never mind."

He squeezed her hand in reassurance. "Hmm."

"Oh, I love a good rain," she admitted, delighting
in the giddy feeling that enveloped her. The night
seemed so unreal, the man a fantasy. That was how
she would remember the evening. Cassandra had
battled with a sorcerer and won.

"Hmm," Drake replied. "In that case." He moved the umbrella so that the rain fell on her. She grabbed his arm and pulled the umbrella close to her. She glared up at him. "I didn't mean that I liked to get wet."

He grinned down at her, but soon his expression stilled and his eyes smoldered with a desire that held her captive, for she knew the same expression was in her own gaze. Suddenly, the world consisted of only them, a big black umbrella, and the soft sound of rain.

"A warm summer rain and a beautiful evening," she said quietly, not recognizing her own voice. "Can it get any better?"

He lifted her chin and gently touched her lips with his thumb. "Do you want it to?"

She hesitated but he found answer enough in her eyes and captured her mouth with his own.

He did not expect the impact of her lips to send a shot of desire that tightened his groin in painful pleasure. He brought her body close to his, wanting her to know how much he wanted her.

Cassie was at first startled by his desire, but realized it mirrored her own. The kiss was overwhelming and reassuring, terrifying and exciting. It sent her mind reeling with questions she didn't want to answer. Her only impulse was to enjoy the moment, the feel of his arms around her waist, his commanding mouth moving over hers and devouring her with gentle mastery, demanding a response that she willingly gave with surprising boldness. She quickly darted her tongue into his mouth, eliciting a groan of deep masculine pleasure that had her reveling in her own prowess—the sorcerer was at her mercy. Soon their tongues were twirling around each other and they clung to each other trying to stay afloat in the stormy wave of desire that threatened to encompass them.

A deep grumble of thunder diverted their attention with angry fervor and opened the sky to release a torrent of rain. They broke apart and stared at each other in awe—now both soaking wet, the umbrella lying next to them unnoticed. The feel of rain awakened Cassie from her dream and the reality of what had occurred.

Before she could speak, Drake flashed his devastating grin and placed a finger over her lips.

"I was right," he said.

"About what?" Her voice was barely a whisper.

"You taste just like sweetened raspberries."

Cassie wrapped her arms around herself. "Drake, this was a mistake—"

He took her arms, draped them on his shoulders, and slid his hands around her waist. "No," he said deeply, his mouth hovering above hers. "It wasn't. Don't let fear deny you this moment." He kissed her again. This time slowly as if enjoying a fine dessert. "Hmm, that's better," he said, feeling her respond to him.

She smiled tremulously. He was right. Tonight fear would not take this fantasy away. Not when so many nights had been filled with a bitter emptiness. She would treasure tonight like a precious stone in her memory. "Do I really taste like raspberries?"

"Yes. What do I taste like?"

Cassie brushed her mouth against his, then licked her lips. "Hot chocolate."

"Hmm." He brought warm lips to her neck. "Figures."

"Drake," she protested, trying to pull away from him, "we can't do this here; besides, it's raining."

"I thought you liked the rain," he muttered against her neck.

"I do when I'm under an umbrella."

He scooped up his umbrella and placed it over her head. It was useless now that they were both wet, but still a kind gesture. He pulled her close again, the heat from him seeping through his wet shirt. "Seems I got carried away."

"Do you do that often?"

He considered the question. "No." He lowered his head to kiss her again, but she moved away.

"We're not starting that again," she said.

He sighed dramatically. "Yes, milady." He rubbed his forehead, desperate to find a diverting topic. "Class reunion," he mumbled.

"What?"

"That's the reason I'm taking your course. I have a class reunion in two months."

She stopped and stared at him. "But you'll be fine! You'll have nothing to worry about."

He shook his head and nudged her to walk again.

She continued to look at him in disbelief. Twice Drake had to save her from colliding into a person and a pole. "Don't tell me you were the ugly duckling."

"No, I was too invisible to be considered ugly."

"Well, your classmates are in for a shock." She undid her scarf and retied it around her waist. It had become a soggy piece of cloth around her neck. "So what was her name?"

"Who?"

"The cheerleader you had loved from afar, but who ignored you and broke your young heart."

"Brenda Timmons. She didn't break my heart and she wasn't a cheerleader, but she was kind... considering."

"Considering what?"

He shoved his hands in his pockets. "Did you go to your ten year reunion?"

"Do I look like a masochist to you? My twentieth is a few years off and I won't be going to that either."

"You don't think I should go?"

"Oh, you definitely should go. You'll have fun. I, on the other hand, have no need to see the beautiful people, who are of course now more beautiful, the smart people who are now millionaires, and the outsiders who are now in psychotherapy. They would all see me and tell me how much I haven't changed."

"Is it that bad?"

"Would you like to still be invisible?"

"Most times. I like to be left alone."

"Then why are you going back? To prove something, right?"

He frowned. "Sounds pathetic."

"No, it's human nature to see how we measure up. You know, you haven't asked me your question yet."

"Oh, right." He shrugged. "Forgot about that."

Cassie watched as his muscles moved underneath his shirt. She wondered if the rain had caused it to shrink, molding itself to his fabulous form. She didn't dare look down at her dress. She could feel it clinging to her like an eager child, exposing many of the aspects of her physique it was designed to hide. Drake had obviously noticed this because his hungry gaze roamed over her figure and it didn't take much insight to know what he was thinking.

"Aren't you going to ask your question?" she asked, trying to divert his attention.

"Are you seeing someone?"

She blinked. She hadn't expected that. "No."

"Why not?"

"Are you seeing anyone?"

"No."

"Why not?"

"Can't get a date."

She laughed until she realized he wasn't joking. "You're serious."

"Yep."

"I'm sure you can get a date."

He was quiet a moment, then asked, "Are you free to attend a barbecue this weekend?"

His words brought her back to reality, tearing at the seams of her fantasy. She felt her spirits fall; she knew their acquaintance could not last beyond this night. "No."

He lifted an eyebrow, his eyes hopeful. "How about dinner and a movie on Friday?"

She shook her head, determined not to weaken. "No."

"Lunch and bowling on Wednesday?"

"No, sorry."

He rubbed the back of his neck, shaking his head in frustration. "Like I said, I can't get a date."

"It's not that. It's not you." She sighed, wishing this didn't have to ruin her memory of the evening.

He softly swore. "You're going to give me the 'It's not you, it's me' speech.'"

"I'm doing you a favor."

He looked at her, appalled. "By stepping on my ego?"

"No." She stopped in front of her building and glanced up at the seventh-story window where her apartment was. It looked dark and lonely, but it would not encourage her to change her mind. "See,

I know the game, but that's okay." She took a step toward the door, but Drake seized her arm.

"Game? What game?"

"The game that men and women play."

He tugged on her arm. "Enlighten me."

Cassie grabbed the hem of her dress and wrung out some excess water. "Many men want to go out with me after a riveting seminar, trying to build up their confidence. I'm safe and comfortable. A non-threat, you could say." She let the hem go and stared at him. His gaze was still fashioned on her legs. She lifted his chin with her forefinger. "But you don't need a practice run. Go for the real thing."

He moved a strand of wet hair from her cheek. The gentle caress was electrifying. "I am. Trust me." He said the words slowly in a captivating tone that sought to bring her back to the intimate level she was trying to escape.

She grasped his hand. "Stop that."

"Why? I like your face."

"Drake," she said desperately, "you're a classic case. You used to be shy, awkward, and invisible in school, but now you're successful and you ooze confidence, but inside still feel awkward. So you flirt with different women to give your ego a boost, and that is all you're doing now."

He wasn't paying attention. His fingers were gliding over the glitter that still clung to her shoulders. "You're beautiful," he whispered in awe. "Do you sprinkle this on other parts of you?"

She grabbed both sides of his face, forcing him to look at her. "Drake, please pay attention. This is unnecessary. It's not about me. It's about you and Adriana."

"Who?"

She let her hands fall. "The woman you met at the Golden Diner. She told me about you. Now I don't blame you for being intimidated by her. She's elegant, attractive, and smart. But you don't have to worry, just be yourself and everything will work out. Be bold."

Drake pinched the bridge of his nose as if in great pain. "What are you talking about?" He waved his hand. "Wait. I don't want to know. I think we've misunderstood each other, but we'll work it out." He had to go home and think. He knew that if he stayed any longer he would lose his patience and effectively stop her from talking for a while. He brushed his lips against hers. "Remember that for now," he said and left, becoming invisible in the crowd.

"You forgot your umbrella!" she called.

She heard a smug voice full of promise rise above the raincoats and umbrellas. "Don't worry, Cassie. I'll get it tomorrow."

Chapter Four

Cassie. He'd called her Cassie. He'd known all this time who she really was. She shook her head. It didn't matter anyway. He was just a flirt testing his wings and she had to remember that when she saw him the next day.

She turned the key to her apartment and heard the familiar groan of door number 712 as it opened a crack.

"Hello, Mr. Gianolo," Cassie called.

He remained hidden behind the door. "You're late," he said in a harsh Detroit accent.

"I know. I had a busy but successful night."

"A man?"

"Maybe."

He paused. "You're wet."

"It was raining."

"Didn't he have an umbrella?" he demanded.

"Yes, and we used it, but we still got wet."

The door opened a bit farther, revealing a rough older man in worn jeans and a brown shirt with pale blue eyes and a small round nose. "Name?"

"Drake."

"New boyfriend?"

"No."

"Fine."

"Don't forget your soup." She pointed to a container near his door. Everyone in the building knew he and the widowed Mrs. Hill had a flirtation going.

"Thanks." The door closed.

Cassie smiled as she pushed open her door. Since she had moved in, Mr. Gianolo had made it his business to check up on her. He was a widower with his two grown children living in Michigan. He said watching over her gave him something to do; plus he didn't like the idea of women living alone. Cassie didn't mind his meddling. She had gotten used to the sound of his door opening, his quick, rough questions and ultimate acceptance.

The phone rang with an urgent cry for attention as she tossed down her bag. She kicked off her soggy shoes and picked it up, knowing who it would be. "Hello, Adriana."

"Don't hello me," she ordered. "What happened?"

Cassie feigned innocence. "Where?"

"You know where. Did he say anything to you?"

Cassie touched her wet hair and sighed, saddened that her fantasy night had to be ruined by such realities. "The man is obviously very shy about asking you out so he's gathering his courage by asking me out first. Could you wait a moment? I need to get changed."

She laid the phone down, changed into a pair of jeans and a sweatshirt, and returned to the phone.

"That makes no sense," Adriana said when Cassie returned to the line.

She plumped up a pillow and fell into the cushions of her couch. It was old but comfortable. "It makes perfect sense." Cassie drew up her knees to her chest. "It's sort of like those Hollywood stars who marry very ordinary women until they can afford trophy wives."

"Drake's not like that," Adriana argued. "He honestly likes you."

She rested her chin on her knees, her voice lowering. "Yes, his kiss would suggest that."

Adriana pounced on the statement. "He kissed you?"

"Yes."

"On the mouth? You know the forehead doesn't count."

Cassie stretched out her legs. "It was on the mouth."

"I just knew he had it bad." Her friend sounded triumphant. "Cassie, I am so happy for you."

Cassie stared up at the ceiling, exasperated. Why didn't anyone understand what was truly going on? "Adriana, please listen carefully He doesn't know what he wants. He flirted with me, then you, now me again."

"He was never attracted to me."

"He was trying to feel your leg. How more attracted can you be?"

"Wait, you've got it all wrong. He—"

A sudden beep interrupted the line. "One minute, I've got another call." She switched over. "Hello?"

"Hello, Cassie." Her ex-husband's smooth voice oozed over the line like an oily vinaigrette. It made her stomach turn.

She rested her head back and groaned. "What do you want, Timothy?"

"Did you get the flowers?"

"Unfortunately." She lifted her head. "Timothy, perhaps because you've never been divorced before you don't understand the protocol, but you're not supposed to send roses to your ex-wife with a note that says 'I love you.'"

"You do if you want her back. I love you and I miss you."

"Uh-huh." She didn't believe him. Timothy was a consummate actor when he wanted to be. Cassie wiggled her toes, wondering what new shade of nail polish she should use.

"I just want—no need—a chance to talk."

A nice mauve. She tucked her feet underneath her. "How's Debra?"

"Who?"

"Oh, dear. Is she out of the picture already? I thought that since you put so much effort into hiding her from me, the relationship was serious."

"We broke up," he said abruptly. "But that's not important. I—"

"Of course it's not important," she agreed in a sweet tone. "Don't worry, you'll find another. In the interim try to catch a disease or something." She switched back to Adriana.

"Who was that?" Adriana demanded.

Cassie tugged on her wet hair and stared at a soggy strand. She had better condition and blow-dry it before it turned into cornhusk. "The jerk."

"I think you should tell Drake about him."

At the sound of his name, Cassie let the strands fall and slap her on the cheek. She would have to think of how she would handle him tomorrow. "He doesn't need to know about my personal life. Besides, he likes you."

"Cassie, he knew you were under the table."

She felt blood leave her face. "He knew?"

"Yes."

"How would he know that?"

"Probably because I pointed to the table when he asked where you were."

"You didn't."

"I did."

He had known she was under the table. He knew that his leg had been brushing against her. Oh, God. Her face burned with embarrassment and guilty pleasure. What was she going to do with him?

"So what is your plan for tomorrow?" Adriana asked.

"After killing you? I'm not sure."

"Come on, Cassie. I did it for your own good."

"Said the vet to the neutered dog."

"Give the guy a break."

Cassie grasped a strand of hair again. "Right leg or left?"

Adriana sighed. "Try to be serious."

"All right. I'll seriously see you tomorrow." She hung up.

* * *

Eric slammed shut the ledgers he was reviewing and glared at his brother. "What's wrong?"

Drake didn't look up, too absorbed by the papers in front of him. "Nothing. Why? "

They were in the back office of the Blue Mango, one of Drake's older restaurants. The light from the morning sun shone on the cool gray elegance of the room.

Eric narrowed his eyes. "Because you're in an extremely good mood today."

Drake was unable to control a quick grin as he ran his fingers down a list of items. "How can you tell?"

"You haven't scowled at anyone yet. You actually said good morning to a busboy. It makes me nervous. What is going on? Discover a new recipe? Was Elizabeth extra kind to you?"

Drake rested his chin on his fist and looked up. "I kissed her."

Eric fell forward. "You kissed your stove?"

"No. Cassie. I kissed her last night and she liked it."

"How did that happen? Did you track her down?"

"I didn't have to. She's teaching a class I'm taking."

"What class?"

His gaze shifted to the window. "Social graces."

"Amazing." Eric sat back. "It could almost make one believe in fate. When are you going to see her again?"

"Tonight. But there's one little problem."

"What?"

"She thinks I'm attracted to her friend."

Eric lifted a brow. "You consider that a little problem?"

"She's just misinformed. Sure I said hello to Adriana in class and talked to her awhile, but I wasn't flirting. Cassie thinks that I'm practicing on her. Something to do with being shy as a child."

Eric shook his head. "A psychology major, beware."

Drake grinned. "I'm not worried. I know a little psychology myself."

"I'd wish you luck, but you already seem to have it. Oh, by the way, I spoke to Patrick the other day. He said you shot down his latest brilliant idea."

Patrick was the manager of Drake's other restaurant, the Red Hut. "I don't shoot down brilliant ideas, only illogical ones."

"He's beginning to feel undervalued and restless. He might leave."

Drake shrugged, unconcerned. "That's his choice."

Someone knocked on the door.

"Come in."

Lance, his manager, poked his head inside. He ran an agitated hand through his thick brown hair; his green eyes offered pity. "That girl is back."

Drake rested his arms on the table. "You mean that annoying one with the short hair, big eyes, and huge gold earrings?"

Lance nodded. "That's the one."

"Don't know her."

A tall, dark-skinned girl pushed her way into the room. Her manner didn't seem to fit her appearance. She had a few more years to grow into her body and her hair was cut into a chic bob, emphasizing her brown eyes. She wore a tailor-made white shirt and blue trousers and looked as if she'd stepped off a movie set as a boarding school extra. "I just need five minutes of your precious time, Mr. Henson."

Drake sat back in his chair and tapped his fingers on the desk. The girl was aggravating, but he had to admire her tenacity. "Three minutes starting now."

"Mr. Henson, please let me work at the Blue Mango. I will work for free if necessary. I know you said that you don't have any positions available, but I'll make one up. I'm very creative, you know, and you'll be so pleased with me you'll wish you had thought of it yourself. I love your restaurant and I had such a wonderful time when you let my cooking class tour here. I want to follow in your footsteps. I notice that occasionally you allow students to intern here and I would do anything to seize that opportunity."

"Pamela, I'm sorry but I can't help you. Try the Docks. I'll get the phone number for you."

Pamela shook her head, her large earrings hitting her cheeks. "Don't bother. You're not getting rid of me that easily."

"Pity."

He stood and escorted her to the front door and held it open.

She stopped and stared at him. "You may be tough, but you're fair. I'm not giving up on you yet." She sauntered out.

"Why don't you just give her a chance?" Eric asked as Drake watched Pamela race across the street.

"Because I'm already mentoring a kid."

They heard the sound of shattering glass.

Eric grinned at Drake's groan. "And that would be him right now."

They both went into the back dining hall, where they saw Cedric Diaz sweeping up glass. His ponytail was held back by a red rubber band, his trousers were wrinkled, and his off-white shirt was beginning to resemble his olive skin. He looked particularly uninterested in what he was doing. Lance came up to them, followed by his assistant manager, Trent.

"He has to go," Lance said under his breath.

Drake rubbed his chin. "He needs time."

Lance ran a hand through his hair, staring at the mess. "I know you're trying to help him, but he doesn't care about the job. He comes in late, argues when corrected, and doesn't uphold the image we are trying to reflect. Just look at him."

Drake didn't want to. Cedric had a real attitude problem that wasn't going to take him far, but he didn't have a father and his busy mother was terrified that either gangs or death would take her son. Drake knew the fates of some former classmates who never reached adulthood and others who were spending their time in jail. He realized Cedric's life would never be easy, but he wanted to give him an opportunity he never had.

He patted Lance on the shoulder, appreciative of his patience. "Just give him a little more time. He'll straighten out."

Trent spoke up. "He doesn't deserve to be here. We weren't hired to be babysitters."

"No one is asking you to babysit."

"I am not being paid to excuse the mistakes of some overgrown kid with an attitude problem. This is a restaurant, not a job corps for delinquents."

Drake's voice was soft. "If you don't like your job you can leave it."

There was a terse silence. Then Trent said, "Fine." And stormed out back.

"I'll try to talk to him," Lance said.

Drake waved his hand. "Forget it. I don't like staff that argues with me in public. Continue working."

Lance sighed and left. Eric shook his head. "You should have tried to reason with him."

"Why?"

"Because he's good. The reason restaurants run well, are a direct result of our managers. Besides, he has a point."

"So?"

"You could have explained—"

"No. If people don't understand why I do something, that's their problem. I didn't get to where I am by explaining every action I make."

"Just don't lose people based on ideals. If Cedric doesn't shape up, you'll have to get rid of him. And that will be his fault, not yours." He patted his brother on the back, unable to stop a smug grin. "And now I'll leave you to find a new assistant manager since that is your fault and not mine."

* * *

He was a silhouette in blue jeans. Cassie watched Drake enter the restaurant, oblivious to the eyes of appreciation that followed him as he approached the large round table. He seemed to move in rhythm to the soft music that floated around them. She watched him walk up to the man who sat next to her studiously checking his notes. He said in a low voice, "There's a chair over there waiting for you. It includes a free drink," and slipped the man a five.

The man pushed the money in the pocket of his plaid shirt, gathered his notes, and stood. "It's all yours, buddy."

Drake sat down and smiled at Cassie's stunned expression. "Well, that was bold!" she said.

He scooted his chair closer, brushing his leg against hers. "I always take the advice of my instructors, especially if it works."

"I suppose you're aiming to be my most improved student."

He searched her eyes. "No, I'm aiming much higher than that."

Unable to think of a satisfactory response, Cassie began the discussion. However, keeping her mind focused proved difficult. She knew Drake wasn't trying to drive her mentally insane on purpose, but the fact could not be ignored. He was distracting. Just his voice made her lose track of her notes any time he asked a question. She was too aware of how he watched her, how his arm brushed hers when he moved, how his scent seemed to draw her to him, how his face remained serious when everyone else was laughing.

She silently breathed a sigh of relief when the remainder of the class arrived. She placed the group into couples to interact. After fifteen minutes, she told them to switch partners.

The exercise helped people relax in a social atmosphere, learn to conduct small talk, and utilize body language. Cassie tried to remain impartial, going around to all of the couples, listening and observing them, but her eyes somehow always found where Drake sat and strayed to whoever he was talking to. When the exercise was over, some students left while others continued their discussion. Cassie was invited to join a group for a meal, but she declined and gathered her things.

Cassie overheard two women who had been paired with Drake.

"Oh, my God," one groaned, buffing her nails. "The man is so stuck-up."

The other slipped into a bright sweater with embroidered giraffes. "Stuck-up? He's so boring he makes grass growing look good. Yesterday, you'd have thought he was some sort of seducer. What a disappointment."

"So true. All I know is that I never want to be paired with him again."

Cassie was amazed and too curious to keep her mouth shut. She came up to them. "Are you talking about Drake?"

The woman briefly stopped buffing. "You mean Drake the fake?" She laughed at her own wit. "He certainly fooled me."

"What happened?"

The first woman put her buffer away. "You mean besides him sitting like a statue?"

"Or talking about the benefits of tomatoes?" the other added.

She glanced at her buffed nails. "At first I didn't know why a guy like that would need this class. Now I know."

The other nodded, adjusting her sweater. "A toad—"

"In prince clothing."

Cassie cringed. "I'm sorry."

The woman in the sweater shook her head. "It's not your fault. You've got your work cut out for you."

They both headed for the bar.

"Can I add my two cents?" a little voice asked behind her. Cassie turned and looked down into a cherub face surrounded by frizzy red hair.

"Certainly."

"I think he's obnoxious, arrogant, spiteful, and mean I told him about my great-uncle Walter's funeral up in New York and how my second cousin was found sleeping with the widow of Mr. James Masters and the family scandal that happened afterward but he didn't show one ounce of interest. He actually yawned, he didn't even care about the fact that my mother's third husband ran off with the deacon's wife from Second Story Baptist Church. Now I've always been told what a great storyteller I am and though my stories tend to run long sometimes, okay not just sometimes, but most times, but I'm working on it which is why I'm in your class, which I love by the way. I love your clothes and your confidence I have confidence it's just that sometimes I get carried away while in conversation I'm sure you know all about that since you did that talk about 'sharing the floor' I really am not as bad as I used to be did I ever tell you—"

"You have obviously been working hard," Cassie interrupted, afraid the woman was getting her second wind. "But I suggest you learn to breathe between sentences. Remind me tomorrow to give you more tips. I am sorry your partner was so unpleasant."

"Such a shame since he's so good looking but I've found that most good-looking men are jerks it's as if—"

"You're forgetting to breathe again." Cassie smiled kindly to soften the criticism. "We'll talk about it tomorrow." She turned and searched the restaurant for Drake. She found him at the bar, smiling for the first time that evening, at something the bartender said.

She came up behind him and heard him compliment the bartender on his selection of drinks. She tapped him on the shoulder. "I need to talk to you."

He spun around and looked at her, a gleam of interest shining in his compelling eyes. "All right."

She took a step back. He was like an eclipse. She had to remember not to look directly at him or suffer something infinitely worse than blindness.

"Is that the one?" she heard the bartender ask.

He nodded, his gaze not leaving her face. "Yep. This is the one. This is Cassie."

"Nice to meet you, Cassie."

She pulled her eyes from Drake's. "Oh... uh... thank you."

The bartender smiled, then attended another customer.

"What did you tell him about me?" Cassie asked as Drake led her to a table.

"Take a wild guess," he said as she slid into the booth.

She glared at him. "What is wrong with you?"

The warm liquid eyes turned to stone. "What do you mean by that?"

She hastily apologized. "That came out all wrong." She glanced around the restaurant as if she could find the right words floating around her. "What I mean is, why do you give the impression of being an obnoxious jerk when you're not?"

He rested his arms on the table. "Would you like to order something?"

"No. Drake, you haven't answered my question."

"I'm not sure if it's a question or an accusation."

"It's not an accusation. I know you're not a jerk."

He nodded grimly. "Thank you."

"I'm not criticizing you. I'm just trying to understand what went wrong. Your three partners complained about you."

He shrugged. "I have a few complaints myself."

"You have to be cordial, inviting."

"I was."

A woman in a green silk dress and high heels that could be used as ice picks approached the table and smiled at Drake. "Excuse me. Do you have the time?"

He glanced at the band on her wrist and frowned. "Why don't you check your watch and find out?"

The woman blushed, covering the watch with her other hand. "It's broken."

His frown deepened, confused. "You want it to do something besides tell time?"

"Uh, no. Uh... thank you."

Drake watched her leave. "What a strange woman. She has a fully functioning watch and asks me for the time."

He turned to Cassie, who had her head buried in her hands. She moaned.

He leaned forward. "Do you have a headache?"

"Yes. Don't worry about it," she said when he stood. "It will eventually go away."

He sat back, doubtful. "Are you sure?"

"No. Do you realize that you just humiliated that woman?"

"I just made her aware of her mistake."

She stared at him, exasperated. "She hadn't made a mistake. She was trying to flirt with you."

"Why would she be flirting with me when you're sitting right there?"

"Because I'm not a threat."

"What the hell does that mean?"

Cassie didn't wish to explain that most women didn't see her as competition. "Never mind, I just want to know why you didn't get along with your partners. I'm beginning to see why, but I still don't understand. You were fine with the bartender."

"That's because I didn't have to flirt."

"How come you can flirt with me and not other women?"

He dropped his gaze to the table. "The reason's simple."

"What is it?"

He looked up. "I want you."

"Don't say that," she ordered, heat touching her cheeks.

"Why not? I'm being honest. The other people didn't interest me."

"Drake, you could like them if you gave them the chance."

"Are you suggesting I act like I care when I don't?"

"I'm suggesting you act civil."

He reached across the table, grabbed her hand, and brought it to his lips. "How can a rogue act civil when what he desires is close enough to touch?"

She pulled her hand away. "This is a classic case of a student having a crush on a teacher."

"There's nothing classic about it. I wanted you even before I knew you were my teacher." His voice deepened as he slid next to her. "However, I like you as my teacher and I'm eager to learn."

"You just feel comfortable with me."

His finger trailed the sensuous line of her jaw. "I think you're beautiful."

Cassie turned away, dismissing his words. "Drake, do you really want to go to your reunion?"

His eyes lit up. "Would you like to go with me?"

"No. I'm only mentioning it because you're going to have to break out of your comfort zone and be friendly to people who bore you or don't interest you."

He rested an arm behind her head and sighed, resigned. "I know that."

"Then why don't you practice? That woman sitting near the stage has been eyeing you for a while. Why don't you go up to her and—"

"No."

His refusal was so swift and definite, Cassie sat back in her seat, bewildered. He must be more awkward than she thought.

"I know she looks intimidating because she's gorgeous, but—"

"Gorgeous? She looks like she had her last meal during the Irish potato famine."

Cassie poked him hard in the side. "Don't be rude."

"I know her type. You take them out to dinner and they order the most expensive meal, then proceed not to eat it."

"You don't know if she's like that."

"She hasn't even touched her grilled salmon with rice pilaf and spinach."

Cassie squinted at the woman's plate. "Are you sure that's spinach?"

"Yes, it's definitely spinach. Lightly garnished with strips of carrots and walnuts."

"I love sesame spinach."

"I should make it for you. Actually, I make an excellent spinach lasagna with—"

She held up her hand to stop him before her mouth began to water. "Wait a minute. We've gone completely off the subject."

"Hmm." He toyed with the soft hairs on the nape of her neck.

"Stop that."

His fingers stopped moving, but his hand stayed in place.

"Okay, so that woman doesn't interest you," she said. She searched the room, trying to ignore the warm feel of his hand. "How about—"

"How about I kiss you right now?"

"Drake," she scolded.

He turned and whispered in her ear, "The only woman I am interested in is sitting right beside me, and my only goal is to capture her attention. So why don't you teach me how to do that?" He flashed one wicked grin, then left.

* * *

At home, Cassie stepped out on her balcony to stare out at the sky. One more day. She only had one more day to deal with this painful temptation and then he would be gone forever and she would be free.

Mixed among the sound of cars and the hurried crowd below came a deep melancholy voice of a man proclaiming his love to the night sky. He had a booming voice that would do well on the stage and she found herself listening to him in spite of herself. She glanced up and saw another tenant leaning out on his balcony. His name was Glen Randall and for a time, he had hinted at wanting more than friendship, but she had subtly dissuaded him. He was an English teacher at a prestigious local high school. At times they went out together to fight the loneliness of being newly divorced.

After Glen completed his verse, Cassie shouted up to him, "You must read more prose, my good friend. Too much poetry will poison the mind to think only of despair."

"Night wanderer, be so kind as to leave me in peace."

"No. I must save you from yourself."

"You speak as one who has been made love to."

"Your imagination works overtime," she scoffed. "I haven't been made love to in a long time."

"Not with the body, but with the mind. You glow."

"I sincerely hope not. Nobody would get any sleep."

He chuckled softy. "You and I were meant for another time. A time of chivalry and romance. A time when a woman accepted the praise a man freely offered. Catch." He tossed down a purple carnation.

She smelled the flower and smiled up at him. "Thank you."

He mimed tipping his hat, then disappeared into his apartment.

Cassie walked inside, sniffed the flower once more, then stuck it in a little vase. One more day and he would be gone. With those comforting thoughts she went to bed.

Drake didn't come to the third seminar. Perhaps her words had finally sunk in and he felt embarrassed for trying to pursue her. She was sorry. She would have at least liked to say good-bye and give him some tips for his reunion. Maybe they could have been friends. She shook her head. Friends? Who was she fooling? He was a wizard with a plan and she'd made a narrow escape. She should be ecstatic; she wished she were.

"I can't believe he didn't show up," Adriana said in somber tones at the end of class.

"It was for the best," Cassie said, trying to be philosophical, although a part of her was upset.

Adriana blinked rapidly. "But you look so nice."

"I didn't dress up for him." She paused. "Are you crying?"

"I'm trying not to. I'm so disappointed it didn't work out. You two would have made the perfect pair."

"I don't see how that's possible." Cassie handed her a tissue, used to Adriana's sentimental tears. "Don't worry about it. I certainly won't."

"I was just so happy to see someone recognize how wonderful you are."

"I don't need a man for that."

The threat of tears subsided. Adriana tossed the tissue away. "That's not what I'm saying."

"He's probably embarrassed about yesterday. He made some bad impressions on people."

"I know. I set those women straight."

Cassie stared at her with a worried suspicion. "You didn't."

"Of course I did. I couldn't have them going around ruining his good name when all three had the social skills of kindergarteners. One acts as if she's got gold in her—"

"Adriana."

"The other is plain dull and that redhead never stops talking. I said that Drake was intelligent, handsome, and fun and it was their fault for not noticing."

She studied her friend a moment. "Are you sure you're not interested?"

"He's not my type." She tapped her chin. "Perhaps something happened. I know there's a reason he didn't come. You could look up his information in your registration and ask him why."

"No." Cassie picked up her bag and turned off the lights. "The chapter of Drake Henson is now closed."

Adriana looked disappointed but didn't argue. "Fine. I'll call you later."

* * *

Cassie arrived home feeling eerily depressed despite congratulating herself for avoiding a close call. With a little more pressure he could easily have caught her in his trap. But now he was truly gone. She glanced at his big black umbrella in the corner and thought of the night they had shared a kiss in the rain. What a memory he would be. Oh, well, it was over now. She popped a bag of popcorn in the microwave then flopped down on the couch to watch TV. She began *The Attack of the Killer Tomatoes*, but her mind wandered to what Drake might have said about the benefits of tomatoes so she changed the channel. She was enjoying a soppy drama when the phone rang.

She absently reached for it. "Hello?"

"I'm sorry I couldn't make the class, but I had business to take care of. Did you miss me?"

Cassie sat up; popcorn spilled everywhere. "Drake? How did you get my number?"

He hesitated. "Does it matter?"

"No." She glanced down at the mess. She sighed and began picking up the popcorn and putting it back in the bowl. *Relax... it's no big deal*, she warned herself. "Drake, don't feel guilty about not showing up. The last day was basically a review. Do you want a brief description of what was discussed?" She sat on the floor and held her breath.

"No, I called to ask you to lunch."

Cassie closed her eyes and wrapped the phone cord around her hand, divided between the impulsive need to say yes and the practical need to say no. She decided to tease him instead. "Dinner, lunch, barbecue. Can't you think of any activities that don't involve food?"

"Oh, sure, especially one in particular." He paused. "No, wait, that could involve food too."

She grasped the cord until it bit into her hand. "Drake, we need to get something clear."

"I agree. That's why I'm treating you to lunch." He gave her the name of a classy restaurant and told her the time.

"But what if I'm busy?" she objected.

"Of course you're busy. You'll be seeing me." He hung up.

She growled into the phone, then dialed Adriana's number. "You've got a date tomorrow with Drake." She gave the time and place then replaced the receiver and unplugged the phone, determined to escape the sorcerer's spell.

* * *

Early the next morning, Cassie went to the gym dressed in a colorful leotard, which made her feel as if two cantaloupes were strapped to her chest, and a long T-shirt to hide the fact.

She wasn't alone in the gym. There were a number of avid health addicts, displaying their beautiful bodies as if they expected a film crew to pop up and take photographs. She noticed one beautiful female body aptly displayed in black leggings, a thong, and a sports bra on the stair climber. She passed by the weight room to go into the aerobics class. People were already stretching in front of the large mirror on the main wall.

Cassie headed toward the back as always. It had taken her weeks to get the courage to join the class, afraid that she would stick out like a Twinkie in a box of ladyfingers. Fortunately, no one paid any attention to her, since they had their own weight issues to deal with. She made a face in the mirror (she hated exercise) and then began to stretch.

"Ah, she blesses us with her company," a pleasant masculine voice said. "I haven't seen you the last few classes."

She turned and smiled at Glen. "I've been busy." She had spent her time eating her way through writer's block and then trying a new diet.

"What's his name?" he asked with a knowing look.

"It's not a him, it's an it. My book."

"I see."

She stretched her hamstring. "I told you I'm not ready for a relationship."

"So you did." He smiled sheepishly. "I guess I'm still hopeful."

Before she could reply, the instructor spoke. "Okay, ladies and gentlemen, let's burn some fat!"

Cassie soon regretted missing the last few workouts. The complicated new steps made her feel out of breath faster than usual, but she congratulated herself for coming. It helped her to put everything into perspective. Drake's presence in her life was like a blimp on a screen—quickly seen and quickly forgotten... No, she was wrong. She would never forget him. But he was gone now.

She tried to think of ideas for her book, but the cheery voice of the instructor had her contemplating the benefits of homicide. Nobody's endorphins could make anyone this happy so early in the morning. She nearly collapsed with relief when it was over.

Cassie grabbed her towel and wiped the sweat that soaked her chest. She felt like a baked chicken.

"Today was a killer," Glen said, wiping his face with his T-shirt. Cassie glanced in appreciation at his firm stomach muscles.

"So that's why I felt light-headed," Cassie teased. "I must have died."

He laughed. "Perhaps."

She tossed her towel over her shoulder and headed for the exit.

"Are you free next Friday?" he asked.

She narrowed her eyes. "Why?"

"There's a poetry reading at Baden's bookstore, and I thought perhaps we could go. James Sheffield will be there."

She loved the work of James Sheffield and going out with Glen was always pleasant. He would be a nice change to... "Sounds wonderful."

He playfully tugged on her towel. "Good. I'll see you then."

* * *

She felt like dancing back to her room in spite of her exhaustion. Finally, she was back to men she could handle. Thank goodness Glen was different from Drake. He was safe, humble, gentle—although Drake had also been gentle, but that wasn't the point. Glen had seen her gain weight after her divorce and struggle through aerobics. He knew the real her and liked her anyway. He didn't play games or offer pitiful stories, although at times when he talked about his ex-wife she was sure she heard the sound of violins in the background.

"It's about time!" Adriana said, pushing herself off the wall next to Cassie's apartment.

Cassie frowned at her and opened the door. "What are you doing here?"

"You know why I'm here. You're going to have lunch with Drake."

"Make yourself at home, I'm taking a shower." She went into the bathroom and shut the door. Adriana was not going to persuade her to go to lunch with Drake. She had taken all night and this morning to put Drake into perspective. She would not have a man occupying her thoughts as Timothy once had. She quickly showered, then sat on the couch next to Adriana, who was flipping through a magazine. She turned on the TV.

"Now, Cassie—"

"Have you eaten?" she asked as a commercial for pancakes popped on the screen.

Adriana sat forward, determined to win this argument. "Cassie, you're going to lunch."

Cassie shook her head, her lopsided ponytail coming undone. "No, I'm not." She flipped through the channels, amazed that she had so many stations and nothing to watch.

Adriana grabbed the remote and turned it off. "What are you afraid of?"

She glanced down at her jeans and T-shirt. Right now she looked like a before picture for a weight-loss plan. She turned to her friend, who looked fabulous in a yellow summer dress and dangling earrings that looked like flower baskets. What was she afraid of? She was afraid of being captured under the spell of a magnetic man who would soon grow bored of her. She was afraid that she was somehow already under his spell and that if she ever saw him again he would only succeed in deceiving and hurting her. "You wouldn't understand."

"I always understand," Adriana argued, settling into the couch. "Explain it."

Cassie glanced down and tugged on the hem of her shirt. "I vowed I would never be enthralled about a man ever again like I was with Timothy, and one night I came very close with Drake. It was like a magical dream and in away continues to be. But in the light of day, the illusion will be shattered."

"Forget about illusions." Adriana threw up her hands in frustration. "You need male companionship."

"I have Glen." Cassie glanced up. "We have a date actually."

"Glen!" Adriana fell back in disgust. "Brokenhearted Glen!"

"I wish you wouldn't call him that."

Adriana stared up at the ceiling and groaned. "Anyone can see that he is still in love with his ex-wife."

"No, he's just devastated by the divorce. He's a real nice guy and knows all about dating, weight loss, and dieting."

Adriana sent her a cool glance. "He sounds like the perfect girlfriend."

Cassie poked her friend in the ribs. "Hey, not every man has to have the inclination to have something pierced."

Adriana ignored the reference to her taste in bad boys. "You're going from one extreme to another."

"Not true."

"From arrogant to self-effacing."

"There's nothing wrong with wanting a man with humility, kindness, and vulnerability." She pointed to the carnation. "Look what he gave me."

"Not a good sign." Adriana sighed. "When's your date with Glen?"

"Next Friday."

"Fine. Then today is free." She pointed at Cassie, her eyes narrowing in determination. "You're going to go to lunch with Drake and that's final. I don't care if I have to drag you. Now let's get you ready."

* * *

Cassie dressed in a blue knit top and floral chiffon skirt. Adriana pulled her hair back and applied makeup. She begged Cassie to wear her contacts, but Cassie opted to wear her glasses so that Drake would realize the real her. After helping her get ready, Adriana left for an appointment, leaving Cassie to battle with her emotions. One date wouldn't be so bad, she thought. They would be cordial and then never see each other again. Besides, he was looking for a wife and she definitely was not on the market. She could update him on what he had missed from the last class, and then there would be closure.

She ran down the stairs too excited to wait for the elevator and stopped when a familiar figure moved from the entrance wall to greet her. He was tall, classically handsome with skin the color of rum and a smile just as intoxicating, dressed in khaki trousers and a red shirt.

She gripped the railing and stared at him. Her excitement crashed at her feet.

Chapter Five

A mixture of fear, awe, and resentment consumed her. Fear that he wouldn't leave her alone, awe that he had ever felt the need to marry her, and resentment that she cared.

"Timothy, what are you doing here?" She had meant to sound disapproving, but her question came out in a breathless rush.

He flashed a two-thousand-dollar smile. "You look pretty. Where are you going?"

Cassie let go of the railing and folded her arms. "You haven't answered my question."

He grabbed her shoulders and pulled her close. The motion was tender, but she remained stiff in his arms. "You smell good." He toyed with an earring. "Going on a date?"

She drew away from him, her resentment overcoming her fear. "That's none of your business."

He rested a foot on the step and straightened his cap. "Of course it's my business, you're my woman."

"Been sniffing glue again, I see."

"You always did have a wicked tongue." He touched her cheek; she stepped away. Nonplussed, he shrugged. "I know you're trying to make me jealous. That's all right. I know that women need to do that sometimes to feel special. I completely understand."

"I don't need to make you jealous to feel special. As a matter of fact, I don't even think about you."

He sniffed, unconvinced. "Yeah, right." He tugged on her shirt. "You know, this top is a little tight. Have you been gaining weight again? I bet you have." He pinched her cheek. "Just can't stay away from the sweets, can you?"

She glared at him, not wanting to say anything that would show how his words really bothered her. She steeled herself for the put-downs she knew would come.

He didn't disappoint her. He stepped back and measured her outfit and face with cold eyes. Eyes that used to turn her legs into hot butter, eyes she had thought reflected desire, but only showed possession. "Hmm, you really must like this guy. You're wearing glitter and eyeshadow." He folded his arms and leaned against the railing, a malicious grin crossing his face. "So how long do you think you can fool him before he figures out how you really are? That you can't pass a cheesecake without taking a taste or that you try and fail a new diet at least every three months? Does he know that you and your mother never speak because you're a constant embarrassment to her?"

Cassie wanted to leave, but her legs wouldn't move. "That's not true."

"Oh, but it is, darling."

The word *darling* cut through her paralysis. She pushed past him, refusing to subject herself to his vicious tongue anymore. "I'm not listening to any of this." It was a lie of course. His words repeated in her mind like an echo.

"Fine, Cass," he said softy, mockingly. "But I know all about you and still want you. You can't say the same about him."

* * *

Cassie hurried to the metro, making her way through the crowded platform and squeezing onto the train, trying unsuccessfully to push Timothy's words from her thoughts. But they clung like sticky tape and continued to reverberate in her mind, covering her thoughts until they were all she could think of.

She pushed through the heavy glass doors of the restaurant and saw a woman devouring a twenty-four-dollar salad under the cool glow of the dining hall, the sound of bubbling water from the large shimmering waterfall on the distance filtered through the low hum of voices. The plush purple seats and turquoise carpeting spoke of quiet elegance and an enjoyable dining experience. Cassie saw Drake at a table look impatiently at his watch. A server came up to him and he waved her away in a quick, brusque manner.

She remembered the night he was dressed all in black as though a walking silhouette. Now, in its place, she saw an ardent, wealthy businessman who was entertaining himself with a funny woman he had accidentally crashed into. Their kiss two nights ago had been part of a fantasy she did not wish reality to tread on. She did not want to spend the afternoon trying to convince him why he thought he was attracted to her or giving him tips for his reunion. She didn't know what he imagined her to be, but she knew that she would only end up disappointing him.

"May I help you?" the maitre d' asked with eager attention.

"Oh, no. I was just leaving." She glanced in Drake's direction once more and silently thanked him for his attention that for a while had made her feel more alive than she had in months, then turned and left.

She returned home, tossed her bag on the couch, and slipped out of her shoes, half relieved and half disgusted with herself. She would not cry or feel sorry for herself, she thought, building an inner resolve. She had to accept life as it was. She would not worry about Drake. He was fine. He would realize that she wasn't coming, shrug, and eat a delicious meal. Perhaps he would even catch the eye of some sleek beauty sitting at the bar, use some skills he had learned from her class, and forget about her. She was used to being forgotten. Her mother had made a habit of it.

Angela Graham despaired of her middle daughter's struggle with weight. On family trips her mother would take her other children on outings, but leave Cassie in the hotel with the caretaker and her studious father. Her father was more absent-minded than forgetful of her presence. He would pat her on the head occasionally, as he would a beloved pet, and would then add to her problem by secretly offering her sweets, which she ate with fervor.

Her attempts to be close to her mother by losing weight always ended when the weight snuck back like a bad rash. The only time she thought they had a chance of forming a relationship was when she had married Timothy. At last she seemed to do something right, something her mother approved of. They had never talked on the phone so often or spoken of getting together so frequently. However, that camaraderie began to fray when she told her mother about Timothy's hurtful remarks. Her mother told her that she was too sensitive, that Timothy meant well. When she divorced, her mother stopped speaking to her altogether. Cassie admitted that she didn't miss her. She'd already felt inadequate and didn't need someone else to give voice to her thoughts. Timothy was right. Drake knew nothing about her and now he never would.

She grabbed a pint of French vanilla ice cream from the freezer. It was two-thirds finished due to her binge when Timothy's flowers had arrived. However, it would suit. She threw in some colored sprinkles and peanuts, wrapped herself in a gold chenille throw, and turned on the TV. There was a rerun of a seventies comedy she'd never really liked,

but she watched it anyway, not wanting to do anything that involved thinking.

She had finished the carton and a handful of
cookies when someone pounded on the door demanding entrance. She wrapped the throw tighter
and raised the volume on the TV. She didn't feel
like talking to Adriana and having to tell her how
the date went or in her case didn't go. She didn't
want to explain why she hadn't gone and then have
her friend lecture her on what a jerk Timothy was,
as if she didn't know.

The pounding continued. "Cassie, I know you're
in there. Open the door."

She paused with a cookie halfway to her mouth.
She knew the voice, knew the command, but didn't
want to see him. She buried herself deeper into the
cushions as if she could disappear.

"Fine," he said casually. "I'll just talk to the manager."

Her manager was a nosey gossip who would give
her no peace if a strange man demanded entrance
into her place. "Wait!" She rushed to the door,
unlatched the locks, and opened it.

She had expected him to be angry. So the fact
that he stood on her doorstep, looking very tantalizing in a classy gray suit, wearing an expression

that was both annoyed and worried, for an instant made her want to run into his arms and confess all. Nevertheless, she refused to weaken and rested her hip against the door.

His gaze was sharp and determined. "What happened? If you're sick you could have called and told me."

She boldly met his gaze. "I'm not sick."

A slight hesitation crossed his face. "Then what's wrong?"

She shrugged, not willing to explain herself. "Nothing."

"Then why didn't you meet me for lunch?"

"I changed my mind," she said simply.

He knew there was more to the story than that. Behind her, he saw an empty ice cream carton and a bag of cookies. Her dress shoes sat in the corner and she was wearing makeup and dangling earrings. She had meant to come, he concluded, but something had stopped her. He wouldn't leave until he found out what. He held up a large bag. "I brought lunch."

Seeing the determination in his eyes, she decided to combat it with flippancy. "Ah, the man thinks my weakness is food and who am I to prove him wrong?" She held out her hand to take the bag.

"May I come in?" he asked out of courtesy. They both knew he was coming in no matter the reply.

She reluctantly moved aside to let him pass. Drake stepped in and glanced around. Her apartment had a modern look, but instead of it being full of neutral colors, she had gone to the other extreme—purple and lilac with big red pillows on the couch. A silver bowl full of tiny shells sat on her coffee table and various brightly colored paintings hung on the wall. There didn't seem to be a central theme, but it worked.

"You have a nice place," he said.

Cassie fell on the couch. "Please stop with the pleasantries. There's nothing more trying than a rogue playacting the role of a gentleman."

Drake took off his jacket and threw it over the back of the couch, then removed the empty ice cream carton and bag of cookies from the table and went into the kitchen. He spread out the cartons of food on the counter. She had organized her kitchen nicely, but her chopping board was old and she needed a better knife set. He made a mental note to pick them up for her. He poured two bowls of shrimp and corn chowder, buttered the bread, placed it on a tray, then returned to the living room, where he found Cassie wrapped up in the corner of the couch looking bored.

"Here," he said, handing her the tray.

"Thank you." She took a sip of the soup and focused on the television. Drake waited a moment to see whether she would give her opinion of the meal. After a few seconds he realized she wouldn't. Annoyed, he returned to the kitchen.

Cassie watched him go and sighed. She was being petty, but the only way to deal with him was to be glib, nothing more serious. She finished the soup and placed the tray down. He had been kind and couldn't help it if he imagined himself attracted to her. When he didn't return to the living room, she went into the kitchen and found him halfway inside the stove.

"What are you doing?" she demanded, alarmed.

He hit his head and swore. He scrambled out and glared at her. "What does it look like I'm doing?"

"Committing suicide."

He held up a scrub brush. "I'm cleaning your stove."

She kneeled in front of him. "Why?"

He frowned, believing the answer obvious. "Because it's filthy."

Cassie grabbed the scrub brush from him. "Listen, dear. All you have to do is feed me. This other stuff is overdoing it. Hell, even my ex-husband only cleaned himself. Wait, I think he once cleaned the toaster, but I fainted, so I'm not sure whether that was a dream or not."

Drake glanced at the toaster, pensive. "I can do that too, if you want."

"I was joking." She stood and headed for the sink. "You need to learn to laugh more."

He grasped her hand as she passed him. He gazed up at her with mesmerizing eyes. His voice was low. "I'm willing to learn, if you're willing to teach me."

Her heart began to dance. Oh, boy.

A loud whirring sound erupted in the air, breaking the spell. Suddenly, the refrigerator started vibrating and moving from the wall.

Drake leaped to his feet, pushed Cassie behind him and stared in shock. "What the hell is going on?"

Cassie went up to it and kicked it. It shuddered, then quieted. "It does that sometimes."

"That's dangerous."

"Not at all. I know how to handle it."

He still looked unsure. "You have to get rid of it."

"No way. It has character and keeps me company."

He took her chin. "If you're that lonely, I'll move in with you."

She laughed, but knew he was only half joking. "Come on, let me show you something."

He went to the sink and retrieved the scrub brush. "Let me just finish this first."

She snatched the brush from him. "No, you'll get your clothes dirty. I'll finish it later."

He took the brush back. "I sincerely doubt it."

"We are not going to have an argument about this."

"Good." He disappeared into the stove again.

Cassie sat down on the floor next to him, resting against the cupboards. "Boy, are you stubborn!"

"Why didn't you meet me for lunch?"

"I already told you," she said, watching the sleek muscles work in his back. She wished his trousers weren't so loose so she could see the muscles there as well.

"Yes, but you lied."

"I did not."

He sighed. "Okay, then let me rephrase my question. What made you change your mind?"

"Common sense."

He was quiet.

"I'm not what you're looking for, especially if you want to marry. My ex-husband could tell you that." She rested her head back, trying not to remember her encounter with Timothy. "I'm too much woman for most men."

Once again Drake didn't respond as she expected. He threw down the scrub brush with such force that the boom echoed throughout the kitchen. He swore and sat back on his heels, pinning her with intense eyes. "That bastard called or came by and made you change your mind about me, didn't he?"

"He didn't make me do anything," Cassie protested, stunned by his vehemence. "I'm just telling you the truth."

Drake didn't hear her, he was scrubbing the oven again, too busy cursing Timothy under his breath and creating various scenarios of what he would do if he ever saw him.

"Drake," she sanctioned after hearing a rather vicious scenario.

His tone was hard. "What?"

It was clear he was in no mood to be scolded. "Never mind."

He completed cleaning the stove, washed his hands, then headed for the living room. "What did you want to show me?" He sat on the couch.

Cassie placed an album on his lap and opened it.

"This is my family," she said. "This is my mother." She pointed to a striking woman stretched out on a garden lounger. "This is my father." He stood next to her mother with a smile barely touching his somber face. "These are my two brothers and sister." She gestured to two kids, posing like models for a magazine, and one young man with his face turned away. "And this is me." She tapped the image of a girl smiling shyly at the camera, hidden behind her father. "Now all you have to do is figure out what is wrong with this picture. And please don't worry about hurting my feelings. They need to get trampled on every once in a while or they feel deprived."

Drake felt his stomach clench. He frantically searched the picture trying to find what she wanted him to respond to. She had presented him with a test. Instinctively, he knew he was going to fail.

"I need to make a comparison first," he said, turning to the next page.

Cassie anxiously watched him, wondering what he would say that would end their acquaintance. That would give her the fuel and stamina to throw him out of her life forever. Impatience threatened to consume her as she stared at him. Her anxiety soon turned to bewilderment—he was enjoying himself.

He went through her album as if he had discovered an antique volume. He carefully turned the pages and lightly ran his hands over certain photos, mostly pictures of her, at times asking questions about the other people in them and nodding absently when she replied.

Not once did he mention how out of place she looked. He didn't say, "Wow! This is your mom?" or "You don't look anything like your family" or "You were a big girl." Instead, he commented on the different trips and the things they did as a family, sounding almost awestruck.

"This is a great album," he said, bending over a picture that celebrated her sister Melody's sixteenth birthday. "I don't see anything wrong with it. Thanks for sharing it with me. No one has ever shown me their family album before. You have a wonderful family."

"You could conclude this from a few pictures?" she asked dryly. She knew she was being unfair to him, but couldn't help it. He annoyed her by being purposefully obtuse. She wanted his true reaction. He could mask his feelings so well. "My mother is disgusted with me. My father ignores me, as do my siblings, Melody and Lewis, unless they want something, and I haven't seen or heard from my older brother, Clarence, in years. My mother calls only to complain."

He closed the album and laid it on the table. "That shows she cares."

Cassie tapped her foot. "What are you, an orphan? Any parent is a good parent?" She held up her hands before he could reply. "No, wait. I bet you had the perfect parents and that's why you can't imagine how I can whine about mine. You're convinced I'm overreacting because you believe in marriage and family and all the wonderful things it brings. Without love of course, just a sense of duty and commitment."

Drake's expression didn't change, but his amber eyes darkened like a hot flame. He glanced away before she could read the expression, but she knew she had hurt him. Somehow, she had hit upon a wound that he had carefully hidden and that she had now forced open to bleed. Remorse struck her. Many words of apology came to her lips, but she didn't know how to apologize without embarrassing him.

She reached for the album, eager to end the afternoon. The man made her feel and say things she always ended up regretting. "Thanks for lunch."

He rested a hand on her arm, stopping her. "Is that my cue to leave? Because I'm not."

"Why?"

"I don't want to," he said simply.

Cassie chewed on her lip. "I'm sorry about what I said."

He removed his hand and offered her a quick forgiving smile. "Don't worry. My shoulders are wide."

Not that wide, she thought. She'd never seen such a flash of pain cross through someone's eyes—tangible enough to cause her heart to constrict.

"I know I failed your test," he said. "But I'm not leaving until I know what's going on."

"Nothing." She scooted away from him. "I'm just not interested in you. Besides, I'm seeing someone," she added hastily.

"But the other day you said—"

"I know, things change."

Drake shrugged, unconcerned. "I'm not surprised. You're an attractive woman. Of course you'll have casual dates, but I doubt you'll need them anymore."

Cassie feigned a cough to keep from laughing. He spoke as if her social life were filled with a man every night. Poor disillusioned man. "Drake, I'll say this once more. I'm not interested."

He sent her a black layered look. "If you weren't so scared, you'd be on me like sweet on a sugarcane."

She sucked in a sharp, astonished breath. "That's not true."

"All right." He drew her close, his eyes professing a test of his own. "Then resist me."

Her heart shuddered unexpectedly. "What?"

"You heard me." His voice was calm, his gaze steady. "Resist me." He removed the throw. "Try really hard." His fingers sensuously stroked her arm, causing the hairs on the back of her neck to become alert. "Very hard." He teased her lips as he cupped one of her breasts, gently massaging it with his large hand, his thumb brushing her hard nipple with tantalizing mastery. His hot lips slid to her neck and shoulders, trapping any amount of protest in her throat. She shut her eyes, savoring the feel of his hard body pressed against hers. She heard the thud of his heartbeat and smelled the musky scent of aftershave, contributing to the heady sensation in her mind. She wanted to bask in the sense of being safe, being beautiful, being wanted. "I'm waiting," he whispered, his breath warm against her skin.

"I can't," she admitted, both ashamed and freed by her honesty.

Pleasure deepened his tone. "I know."

She turned her head away. "You don't understand." And for a moment she was glad. She wanted him to be completely unaware of the truth that would separate them, but she was certain he already knew what it was.

Drake brushed his lips over her now swollen ones. "Tell me then."

Cassie stared at him for a moment, amazed at the heat of emotion that darkened his eyes. Her gaze slid away from his, then returned. "I'm the black sheep in the family."

Some of the fire diminished as he considered this. "And that means?"

She wanted to shake him. "I'm the heaviest one and I really don't want to be a circus act."

He blinked. "What?"

"The fat woman and her gorgeous companion."

"What are you talking about? Who's gorgeous? I'm an ordinary guy and you're not fat."

She lifted the label on the back of her shirt. "Would my dress size convince you?"

He halted for a moment, trying to process what she had said. His jaw suddenly tightened and his eyes flashed with anger, but his voice remained calm. "Are you going to tell me that this is all about your weight? That you hid from me and then left me waiting in a restaurant because of your size?"

"Don't make it sound ridiculous."

He moved away, shaking his head in disbelief. "I can't help it, because it is. I thought perhaps your hesitation had to do with your ex-husband or another bad experience, but this makes no sense. What next? You'll worry about the shape of my ears or whether or not my teeth are crooked?"

Cassie wrapped the throw around her again. "There is no reason to be sarcastic. You're the one who seems to want a relationship. The issue was going to come up eventually."

Drake clenched his jaw tighter, unable to believe he was having this discussion—not when she looked so warm and soft cuddled up on the couch.

He stood and began to pace to release energy. He couldn't understand the absurdity of it all. "How could it come up, when it doesn't even matter?"

Fury almost choked her. "Doesn't matter?" Cassie stood and poked him in the arm as he passed her. "Of course it matters! Don't pretend to be blind. That's even worse than admitting your true feelings. I know I'm funny and I know I'm cute, but I also know where I have to shop: the big beauties and luscious ladies section. My bras cost more than some outfits. Being with a big woman is expensive, you know." Once again he didn't laugh at her humor. She rolled her eyes. "Drake, I like you, but will you please honesty look at me?" She let the throw fall from her shoulders. "I clean up quite well, but there's one fact that's hard to hide. Trust me, I've tried."

"So if I gain a few pounds you'll be okay?"

"Don't be silly."

"You've based your entire argument on looks. Because of the way I look you don't want to go out with me."

She held her head for a moment. "Haven't you listened to a word I've said?"

"Words? You've been speaking gibberish."

"Okay. Then let me try, thickheaded man. I'm very fluent. How will you feel when you tell people about your girlfriend and you have to show a picture of me? Or when we go out to eat and people stare, wondering what an athletic guy like you is doing with a woman like me? You're not used to the stares, but I promise you they'll come. How will you feel when your family asks to meet me?"

He stopped pacing and folded his arms, piercing her with a stare that left her paralyzed. "Proud. I will feel proud that a beautiful woman of class, grace, and wit is mine to claim."

She was too stunned to think of a ready reply.

Drake took that opportunity to continue. "I have no problem with your size," he said, appreciating her figure in one sweeping glance, making her face burn. "If you have a problem with being a nice healthy woman, then deal with it."

Her tongue returned to her. "A healthy woman," she scoffed. "What a lovely euphemism for fat."

He arched one black brow and began to pace again. "You're not fat, you're confused."

"Confused?"

He nodded.

She poked him in the arm. "What planet did you fall from?"

"One that's infinitely more rational than yours."

"You think I'm some shallow, naive woman who's blown this completely out of proportion, right?"

"I don't think you're shallow or naive," he said carefully. "But I know you're blowing this out of proportion."

"I see." She'd make him pay for that. She would show him how dating her would really be. Since he felt comfortable with her, he assumed everyone else would be the same. Perhaps like her, he was involved in a fantasy of his own and while they were the only ones in this dream, inviting others would restore his sight. An idea formed in her mind. She would show him what it was really like to date a full-figured woman and how much their personalities differed. She began to feel powerful, knowing that she would win this battle. "Aside from the fact that you'd never be able to handle me, I like my men more outgoing."

He stopped pacing. "I can adjust."

"You can't change who you are."

"I didn't say I'd change. I said I'd adjust."

Cassie toyed with one of the buttons on his shirt. "Okay, you believe that we don't need to worry about my size, right?"

He grasped her hand. Her fingers against his chest had begun to distract him. "Not we, you."

"Fine. I'll give us a chance," she said easily, all signs of her previous anger gone. "I'm willing to try new experiences. My friend Kevin is having a party next Friday. I'm going. Would you like to join me?" She hadn't planned to go but she would now.

Drake let her hand go and stared at her warily. She had become too agreeable. That meant she was up to something. Fortunately, he was always ready for a challenge. "Sure."

"Great. Pick me up at nine and dress casual."

* * *

"You're taking her to a party?" Eric asked, staring at Drake in shock. "You hate parties. You either close up like a fly trap or end up talking about food."

Eric stood near the mirror with Malcolm, while his sister, Jackie, sat on the bed. They had come over for lunch and now they all looked at Drake as if debating whether they should commit him to an institution or not.

"So?" Drake replied, unconcerned. "She likes them and I can compromise." He laid out two shirts, trying to decide which to wear.

"You can't even dance."

He picked up a charcoal-gray shirt. "I can move."

"In rhythm?"

Drake glared at him, then began buttoning his shirt.

"You should have told us this before so that we could give you the perfect excuse to cancel."

"I don't plan to cancel."

"You're going to hate it."

"Eric, leave him alone, "Jackie scolded. "Cassie must be some woman to make him go through all this trouble."

"She is something." Malcolm snickered. "A whole lot of—"

Malcolm's statement was aborted when Drake shoved him against the wall, his hand grasping his collar, all of Cassie's accusations rushing back into his mind. He had enough trouble with Cassie believing such nonsense. He would not allow others to lend credence to her claim. "Would you like to discover the wonders of wearing dentures?"

Malcolm held up his hands in surrender and Drake let him go.

"No more snide remarks, understood? It's not wise to talk about somebody's woman. Especially when she belongs to me."

Malcolm tugged at his collar, glad that his head and neck were still attached. "Yes."

Jackie stared at her brother, shocked by such a vehement show of emotion. "Is she a big woman?"

Malcolm snorted, but said nothing.

"She's healthy," Eric said.

"She's beautiful," Drake elaborated. "And kind. You'll like her."

"Perhaps we could have her over for dinner," Jackie said. "I'd love to meet her."

Eric sighed, annoyed that they were all missing the main crucial point. "You are assuming she'll want to go out with him again after tonight."

"He'll be fine," Jackie said with confidence.

"When's the party?" Eric asked.

"She wants me to meet her at nine."

He glanced at his watch. "You realize it's only one-thirty, right?"

"I just want to be prepared."

"Oh, in that case you should have started this morning. At this pace I'm not sure you'll be ready on time."

"Leave him alone," Jackie said. She shooed Eric and Malcolm out of Drake's bedroom and shut the door. She leaned against it and studied her brother

as he tried to straighten his collar. "You're nervous."

"I'm not nervous," he growled.

"Then why have you misbuttoned your shirt?"

He glanced down and noticed that one side was
longer than the other. It certainly explained why his
collar was crooked.

He sighed and unbuttoned the shirt. "I just have
a lot on my mind."

"You really like her, don't you?"

He began to smile. "What is this, high school
confessions? 'Do you like her like her? Or just like
her?'"

"Drake, I'm being serious."

"So am I."

Jackie picked up the remaining shirt off his bed
and placed it in the closet. "Did you tell her about
us?" She tried to sound disinterested, although the
subject was important. Drake rarely discussed his
family with anyone.

"No, not yet," he said, assuming the same tone
as he tucked in his shirt. "I will eventually." His
voice lowered. "She comes from a good family."

His sister closed the closet door with a flourish
and held her nose high. "So do you."

He laughed at her assurance. "I guess so."

Jackie stretched out on the bed, picking up the picture he kept on his side table of Eric and her. "Have you slept with her yet?"

Drake stared at Jackie's reflection in alarm. "What kind of question is that?"

She replaced the picture and bit back a laugh at his expression. "Get that Victorian look off your face. I do know about sex."

"Yes, but you shouldn't be talking about it with your brother," he grumbled, feeling his ears grow warm.

"Why not? Eric and I were worried that you were studying for the priesthood. You've spent so much time taking care of us you didn't carve a life out for yourself."

They were his life, he thought. Seeing them succeed from what little he had been able to offer them had made his life complete. He would never admit that of course. "My life's just fine."

Jackie lay on her stomach, holding her chin in her hand. "So I guess the answer is no," she said, disappointed.

He picked up a pillow and threw it at her. "Get out of here."

Laughing, she darted out the door.

Drake stared at his reflection. He would do fine tonight. He was used to having to prove himself to get what he wanted. And he wanted Cassie. He'd just have to make sure she realized that she wanted him. He turned from the mirror. Somehow he knew tonight would be one he'd never forget.

Chapter Six

*C*assie was working on expanding the outline for her book and thinking about what she would wear for the party, when the phone rang.

"So are you ready for our date or do you need a little more time to prepare?" Glen asked.

She groaned and covered her eyes. She had completely forgotten about the poetry reading. "I'm so sorry, I overbooked. Could I take a rain check?"

There was a brief pause; then he laughed. "I forgot how popular you are. I'll file your rain check."

She sighed, relieved. "Thanks for understanding."

"Why don't you come up and let me treat you to lunch instead?"

It would be a perfect reprieve from her work. "I'd love to. I'll be right up."

The door was open when she reached his apartment. The rich smell of tomatoes and peppers wafted into the hallway and called her to the kitchen. She loved Glen's place, its simplicity and subtle class. He grew flowers on his balcony, had a bookshelf of old volumes only a true lover of literature would read, an old TV in an all-wood cabinet, and woven throw rug. She found Glen in the kitchen chopping vegetables.

"What are you cooking?" she asked, glancing at the bubbling pot.

"Minestrone."

"It smells delicious." Cassie peered over his shoulder. "Do you need help?"

He quickly shook his head and moved to block her view. "No, I'm just chopping onions. I'll be finished soon."

She turned and rested against the counter. "How do you chop without tearing up? Those don't even smell."

"I refrigerate them first."

"I'll have to try that."

The soup was as good as it smelled. They sat at his old wooden table and chatted about poetry and life, then rescheduled their date—fortunately, Sheffield was performing next Thursday. Cassie promised she would go.

"Rita wants to remarry," Glen said, cleaning up the bowls.

"I'm sorry." She knew it must be hard to realize your ex was really over you. If only she had that problem.

"It's not that I want her back. It just makes me wonder what she sees in that guy. Louis, that's his name. He's a bouncer at a strip club of all things. Sure he's attractive, but he's so uncouth and doesn't treat her as well as I did. Or at least tried to."

"Who knows what people find in each other? Perhaps this guy fulfills a need. Bad boys can be enticing, just ask Adriana."

"I guess so. I loved her so much." Glen sighed and Cassie could hear the musicians taking out their violins. She knew it was time to leave before she was presented with a sob story.

"Thanks for lunch." She kissed him on the cheek. "And no poetry for two days."

He smiled grudgingly. "I'll try. Take care."

* * *

It was humiliating, Drake thought, standing in front of Cassie's door. He was nearly forty years old, but he felt as awkward as a kid on a first date. He was successful, he dealt with people every day, he could handle a simple party. He would find a way to get out of dancing, but he would ultimately prove to Cassie he was the man for her. Proving himself was something he did very well. He took a deep breath and rang the doorbell.

Cassie glanced at her watch and swore with feeling. It said 8:35. He was early and she hadn't finished pinning up her hair. Didn't the man know the importance of giving a woman time to prepare? Glen of course would be sensitive to that fact. She could already picture Drake glaring impatiently at his watch, waiting for her to answer the door.

Fortunately, she was already dressed in an outfit that emphasized every curve and roll on her body. He wanted a night with a full-figured woman and he would get it. She called it her hippo-in-a-tutu dress because of its revealing qualities. It lifted her ample chest and the material moved restlessly against her shape. He probably wouldn't want to leave the apartment.

"One moment," she called around the pins in her mouth. She quickly finished her elaborate hairstyle, then answered the door.

Drake looked handsome in his silhouette uniform—dark trousers and a charcoal shirt. The sense of quiet power swirled around him. Yes, she thought, feeling her heart quicken its pace, if she wasn't careful she would easily fall victim to him.

His eyes roamed over her figure, darkening as it made a path to her feet. He suddenly shut his eyes and held his hands together as if in prayer.

"What are you doing?" she said, wondering if her plan was already working.

He opened one mischievous amber eye. "I'm thanking God you decided to wear that dress tonight. You look sensational."

Cassie sighed, exasperated, and pulled him inside. "Have you been drinking?" she asked, shutting the door.

He lightly touched her cheek. "If I say yes, do we get to stay home?"

Trying to chastise him was as fruitful as kicking a wall. "No."

Drake slid his arm around her waist. "What material is this? Velvet?" He trailed a finger up the back of her dress until it reached her bare skin.

Shivers of delight followed his touch. "Yes, it is. You're early, you know."

"I know. Can't blame me for being eager." He clasped her hand, led her to the couch, and pulled her down beside him. "I didn't want to give you the chance to change your mind. Plus it gives us the chance to make out for a while." He leaned toward her.

She drew back, resting a hand on his chest. "I still have to get ready."

"You look perfect." He rubbed his thumb lightly over her hand. He suddenly sighed and let her hand go. "I have a confession to make."

Cassie held her breath. Now he would admit that it was all a game and ask to bow out of the evening. "What is it?"

"You look more than perfect. I thought tonight might be a trick." He flashed a sheepish grin. "I thought that you would show up in overalls or something dreadful and dare me to take you to the party." His eyes melted into hers. "But now I see that you're as serious about this relationship as I am and I'm ashamed that I thought you were up to something."

"Drake—" she began helplessly.

"Let me finish." His gaze fell. "I'm so used to people wanting me to convince them that I should have a chance that I'm worthy of..." He shook his head, frustrated that he didn't have the right words. "I should have known that you're not like that." He glanced up. "I realize it is hard getting into another relationship after a divorce, but I don't care what other people say. We can make it work."

Cassie tried not to grimace as a headache of guilt hammered its way through her conscience. If only his words were true. It was a shame he was so deluded. Perhaps he hadn't been exposed to many women. Well, tonight he would get an education. Since she had no words to say, she only smiled.

"Here." He pulled a small, golden box from inside his jacket.

She ran her hand over the box. "What's this?"

"Chocolate-covered cherries."

Cassie growled at him. "You're not helping my problem."

He lifted his eyebrows, becoming the picture of innocence. "What problem?" He took the box and opened it.

"Hey, I'm supposed to open it."

"Sorry, but you're too slow and I want to see if you like them."

She laughed. "Why? Did you make them yourself?"

For the first time, he looked very uncomfortable. It was terribly satisfying to see his arrogant veneer slip. She didn't give him the chance to reply; instead she reached for the box. "Let's see. Which one should I choose?" She wiggled her fingers over the selection of chocolates, prolonging the moment of anticipation with wicked enjoyment. "So many to choose from. I don't—"

Drake seized one and popped it in her mouth.

Outraged, she glared at him; he smiled.

She had the childish impulse to tell him how horrible it tasted, but when she bit down into the rich chocolate and fruit mixture, it instantly engaged her taste buds in an enviable feast she could not deny.

Cassie shut her eyes a moment, sighing in pleasure.

When she opened them, she saw him watching her. His face looked impassive, but his eyes were uneasy. She found it vaguely unsettling how quickly she was beginning to read him. "It's delicious."

He tried to hide his pleasure with a casual shrug, but she'd caught the corner of his mouth kick up in relief.

"Here, have another one," he urged, bringing another candy to her mouth.

She stood. "Tempting, but we have to go."

He ate the chocolate and picked up another.

"Hey, those are mine," Cassie cried, grabbing the box. Drake sucked the remaining chocolate on his finger. "Sorry, I didn't realize I was so good."

She groaned. "Do you ever tire of yourself?"

"Only when I'm being annoying, which is rare."

She laughed, placing the box in the refrigerator. "Oh, good. You do have a sense of humor. I was beginning to worry." She turned to leave.

He blocked her exit from the kitchen. "You know, there's no reason why we need to be on time."

The suggestion was extremely tempting. One night alone with him without anyone to comment or judge. One night when they would completely belong to each other. She thought of his sensitive fingers and delicious mouth and steeled herself against the memory. She would not indulge; she had to resist.

She squeezed past him, barring herself from his enticing scent and presence.

"Still running, Cassie?" he asked in a soft voice.

She slipped into her high heels. "In these shoes?" she teased to cover the truth. "Not a chance." She grabbed a shawl and her purse and opened the door, eager to get the night over with. "Let's go."

* * *

Kevin Jackson was a rich playboy with a glutton's appetite for women. Cassie had become a friend of his when he had asked her out after one of her seminars. She had declined because she was seeing Timothy at the time, but Kevin had been persistent and soon they became friends.

The Jackson estate was an hour's drive out of the city and sat among one of the exclusive suburbs of Maryland. Situated on ten acres of magnificent grounds, it rose like a monument, exuding elegance, grace, and privilege. The drive past the private lake and row of trees always left Cassie in awe, but Drake looked bored as he parked the car and handed his keys to the valet. He sighed wistfully, watching him drive off. She tugged on his arm.

"Your beloved car will be okay," she assured him.

He looped her arm through his. "Are you sure that kid has a license?"

"It was revoked last year, but he was able to get it back. Joke," she said quickly, when he looked ready to run after his car.

He sent her a cool glance. "Hmm, I'll remember to get you back for that one. Come on. The doorman can only hold the door open for so long."

Cassie's excitement soared when they entered the grand foyer. Its fourteen-foot ceiling looked down into a lavish circular greeting area. Her hands trembled as they walked toward the ballroom. It wasn't the ambience that excited her, it was the ratio. Just as Cassie hoped, there were at least five beautiful women to every man present.

"Impressive," Drake said, as they walked down the main hall with its burgundy carpet and extravagant vases and paintings. She didn't think to ask if he was talking about the decor or the women. Gorgeous women lined the walls as if they were live mannequins, and their eyes lit up at the sight of another man.

They entered the sitting room, which greeted them with low lights, the careful hum of voices, and jazz. The bar was in the form of a large waterfall; couches looked like art pieces—beautiful to look at but uncomfortable to sit in.

Drake released her arm. "Let me get you a drink."

Cassie grabbed his hand. "No, let's mingle first. There are so many people to meet."

He sent her a suspicious glance, but nodded, silently cursing himself. He could already feel an icy trace of panic inch up his spine as he watched the group of strangers. He caught many of them staring at him, no doubt waiting for him to trip on the carpet or crash into a vase. He would be cool; he would be calm, despite the fact that he enjoyed crowds as much as malaria. He needed to be civil.

He took a deep breath and smiled at a woman near the window. She smiled back and winked, licking her lower lip in an erotic invitation.

"Ow!" Cassie cried, pulling her hand from his. "Your grip is like a vise."

"I'm sorry. Are you okay?"

"If I develop gangrene and my hand falls off, I'm coming after you."

He cradled her hand in his. "Here, let me see."

She snatched her hand away. "I'm okay."

He shoved his hands in his pockets, feeling like an idiot. "Let me get you something to drink," he said, desperate for something to do.

"I'm not thirsty."

"Are you hungry?"

"No."

"Perhaps I could—"

"Drake, I'm fine. If I need anything, I'll be sure to tell you."

He nodded and glanced around the room like wary prey—a deer trapped in the forest with wolverines.

Cassie laughed, "Will you relax?"

"I am relaxed."

"You're so stiff that if I poked you, you would topple over. At least take your hands out of your pockets."

He did so and his elbow hit a woman's wrist; bright red wine fell down the front of her peach dress.

"You clumsy bastard!" she cried.

Drake turned. "I'm sorry. Look, I'll pay—" He reached into his back pocket and elbowed a woman in the stomach.

She hit him in the back of the head with her handbag. "Hey, watch it!" She readied herself for another swing when Cassie grabbed the bag.

"That's enough," she said. "It was an accident."

The woman glared at her. Cassie would have found the gaze intimidating if it hadn't been clouded by alcohol. "This isn't about you," the woman said, her words coming out in an angry slur.

"I believe it is since he belongs to me. Why don't you calm down and sober up?"

"Why don't you take your fat behind back to the zoo where Kevin found you?"

"Only if you'll return to your street corner," she said sweetly. She seized Drake's arm before he could do more damage and led him into the hallway.

"Did she hurt you?" she asked, turning his face so she could see the back of his head. "God only knows what she had in that bag."

"No, I'm fine." He paused. "Did she hurt you?"

Cassie shrugged. "Sharing witticisms with a drunk always makes for pleasant entertainment."

"Cassie, I'm serious."

She ignored the tone and shook her head. "Now I know why you keep your hands in your pockets. You're a dangerous man. Especially with those elbows."

Drake rested against the wall and stared down at her. "You're laughing at me, aren't you?"

She bit her lower lip and shook her head.

He stared up at the ceiling. "Go ahead. I like to hear you laugh even when it's at my expense."

She couldn't laugh at him. Not when he looked so dejected. She took his hand and pulled him from the wall. "I know what will relax you. Come on, let's dance." The look of horror that crossed his face broke her resolve. She burst into laughter.

When she'd sobered, she noticed he was smiling. "Finished?" he asked.

It was the smile that did it. He smiled so rarely it was always a gift to her. She impulsively hugged him. "Drake, I'm so sorry. The night will improve, I promise."

He wrapped his arms around her. "You can be as sorry as you like." He brushed his lips against her hair. "I liked what you said to that woman."

Cassie rubbed her cheek against his chest. This position felt better than it should, but it was their last night together so she might as well enjoy it "What did I say?"

"That I belonged to you."

It had been a slip of the tongue, but even as he repeated her words they sounded right to her. She pulled away, remembering why they had come. It was not so that they could become closer. "Yes, that's right. Well... let's meet people."

Drake sagged against the wall and lifted a dark brow. "Is that a requirement?"

"Yes."

They returned to the main room, where Cassie surveyed the crowd to see who she could leave Drake with. She saw a woman with rich auburn hair talking to a dark brunette; both were sitting on a bright red couch in the shape of lips.

"I know those two. Let's say hello." She dragged Drake along before he could reply and weaved her way through the crowd, stopping in front of the pair. She flashed a wide smile.

"Vicki, Mandy, hello there," she greeted.

They stood and the three women exchanged air kisses.

Vicki, the auburn-haired woman, was small with the energy of a hummingbird and her gold lamé outfit seemed to flitter with every movement. Mandy was cool as ice water and entertained a bored expression.

"I'd like to introduce you to Drake Henson," Cassie said, pushing him toward the pair. She watched their eyes turn predatory. "He's a—" She hesitated, realizing that she didn't even know what he did for a living. She glanced at him for assistance, but the smug smile he sent her made it clear that he wasn't going to help her through the awkward moment "A lover of wine and women," she improvised.

"That's good to know," Vicki murmured, looping her arm through his with the practice and conceit of many years.

"Yes," Mandy agreed, taking his other arm.

Cassie could almost sense him withdrawing into himself. The last thing she needed was for him to make a rude comment and ruin her plan. She had to give him a topic that was of general interest.

"Vicki makes a delicious cheesecake," she said. As she hoped, Drake's interest was piqued and they began talking about various desserts. Satisfied that her strategy was working, Cassie thought of a means of escape.

"Oh, I see someone I must talk to," she said, waving vaguely in another direction. "Take care of him for me, I'll be right back."

Drake seized her arm before she could leave. "Is that a promise?" he asked in a low, insistent voice.

"You'll be fine."

"That wasn't my question."

"Yes, of course, I'll be right back," she said lightly, hoping he couldn't feel the blood rushing through her veins.

"Then let's seal it with a kiss." He kissed her quickly but effectively, leaving her lips wanting more as he drew away.

"What are you doing?"

He flashed a wicked grin. "Being bold." He turned to Vicki and dismissed Cassie with a wave of his hand. "You'd better go before you miss your friend," he said in an ironic tone.

She nodded absently, then disappeared into the crowd. She went straight to the bar, smiling at the large waterfall structure. She was going to succeed. She was going to get rid of him and all the tempting feelings he brought with him. She ordered a martini, rested against the counter, and stared at the guests—beautiful, successful, and happy. She saw a woman slap another across the face and grab for her hair before two men broke up the pair. Okay, almost happy, she amended. Timothy had been happy here. These parties had given him plenty of opportunities to be with the women he dreamed of. It was any man's fantasy, women of all types eager and able to have affairs and not burden one with the need of marriage. She frowned at her drink. But Drake wanted marriage. She shrugged and took a sip. He would be cured of that soon enough. With so many people in the world, why tie yourself down? She took another sip of her drink, congratulating herself on her plan. Men were so predictable. She'd written a book on attracting them, hadn't she?

"You have a mean streak, don't you?" Adriana said behind her, in a knowing voice.

Cassie spun around, amazed to see her friend. She looked exotic in an orange mandarin top and loose dark green trousers, gold balls twirling from her ears. "What are you doing here?"

"Mike's band is going to play in the great room."

Cassie grimaced. "Ugh, but he can't sing."

Adriana lifted a glass to her lips. "That's okay, I didn't come to hear him sing."

Cassie rested her drink on the counter, shaking her head. "I don't see how you can be interested in a man who is as intellectual as a nail."

"Intellectual men bore me." Adriana shook her glass, causing her ice to spin. "Enough about me. Why did you invite poor Drake here?"

"Poor Drake seems to be enjoying himself. There's enough eye candy to make any man happy."

"Or give him a toothache," Adriana challenged.

"All good things in moderation."

Adriana took a swallow of her drink, then set it down. "You're not being fair to him."

"Not fair?" Cassie poked her friend in the arm. "Do you know that he said I have an obsession about my weight?"

Adriana smiled in admiration, looking around the room. "Where is he? I feel like giving him a hug."

"I am sure he is getting his share of hugs already," she said dryly.

"I love your dress, by the way. I bet it backfired."

"What are you talking about?"

"You thought he wouldn't like it because Timothy didn't."

"You are an annoying know-it-all," Cassie grumbled into her drink.

"I try." Adriana checked her new manicure—metallic gold. "He's not a chubby chaser if that's what you're afraid of."

Her eyebrows furrowed. "A chubby what?"

"A chubby chaser. It's a new term I heard on a cable channel." Adriana enjoyed picking up Americanisms. "You know, a man who sets out to date full-figured women."

"How comforting," she said in a sarcastic drawl. "Rolls turn them on, I suppose?"

A deep voice interrupted Adriana's response. "You two ladies should be mingling," Kevin said, planting a kiss on each woman's lips. "Eat, drink, and be merry." He was a good-looking man with the easy confidence that came with such knowledge. His crisp blue shirt and trousers were pressed to perfection.

"That's what I love about you, Kevin," Adriana said in a bored tone. "You're so original." She didn't like Kevin, but tolerated him for Cassie's sake and because he had the power to give Mike the needed exposure for his band.

"I leave originality to people who don't have lives." His eyes focused on Cassie. "You look gorgeous, my dear. Do I have the pleasure of keeping you all to myself tonight?" He took her hand. "Come and keep me company."

Cassie smiled, ready for a night of flirtation. "Feeling lonely in this crowd of gorgeous women?" She playfully patted his cheek. "Poor boy."

He sighed wearily. "One does get bored after a while."

"Cassie is already someone else's company," Adriana said.

Kevin's eyes sharpened, but the expression was unreadable. "Settling down again already?"

Cassie swung the end of her shawl. "I'm just breaking him in for the right woman."

"Babe, you can break me in anytime. Come on." He began to draw her away.

Adriana seized her other hand. "This isn't a good idea," she whispered.

"He's harmless."

"Like a barracuda."

Cassie winked. "I like an element of danger."

Adriana frowned. "What if Drake comes looking for you?"

She glanced at her watch. "It's early yet. He'll be too busy to know I'm gone."

"Cassie, please don't sabotage this."

"Don't worry. I've got everything under control." She kissed her friend on the cheek and let Kevin lead the way.

He led her to the lavish sunroom. The moonlight seeped through the large windows and touched the plush couch and love seat, polished the Mexican tiles, and made the leaves on the bushes gleam like opal. Other couples embraced each other in the shadow of the room; Kevin and Cassie's presence didn't seem to interrupt their ardor.

"Perhaps we should go somewhere else," Cassie suggested, feeling uncomfortable.

"Ignore them," he said, pulling her down on a love seat close by.

"I can't."

"All right." He clapped his hands. "Everybody out." The room was immediately emptied and Kevin rang for dinner.

A waiter soon arrived with plates of food and then disappeared, leaving them alone in a companionable silence. Cassie offered Kevin something to eat, but he said all the food was for her and poured himself a drink. He casually chatted while she ate and she found her mind wandering as she enjoyed an asparagus and shrimp potage. Drake would love it she thought, thinking about his love of food. She imagined the conversation they would have guessing what ingredients were used. What did he do for a living anyway? She took another potage and frowned. What did it matter when this would be their last night together?

Kevin watched her from under half-closed lids, holding his bourbon close to his chest. "You don't look happy, Cassie," he said suddenly.

"But I am."

Kevin put his drink down. "I don't believe you." He took her hand and held it between his. "Your eyes look sad."

Cassie smiled gently. "How could I be sad with you trying so hard to make me happy?"

"I'm sorry you didn't come alone, but I'm not surprised. Timothy was a fool to let you go."

"Timothy was a fool, period."

His hand inched up her arm. "I'll always be here for you."

She laughed nervously, pulling her arm away. "What are friends for?"

"There's a chance to be more."

His mouth was on hers before she could refuse. His lips, while not forceful, were definitely demanding and eager to elicit a response. One she could not give him. She pushed away from him and covered her mouth. Kevin offered her an indulgent smile, resting his hand on her knee. "Don't tell me you weren't expecting that."

Cassie moved her knee. "I wasn't."

"I was a bit rushed that time. Let's try again."

"No." She drew back, stunned. "Why are you acting this way?"

"Because I want you."

"You can't be serious." First Drake, now Kevin? Some celestial spirit was having a lot of fun messing with her life.

"You've known I've wanted you since the first day."

She glanced at her watch. "I'd better go."

"You can't actually be rejecting me," he said in disbelief.

"How could any woman reject you?" she teased. "I'm merely halting an uncomfortable situation."

He kissed the curve of her neck. "I'm not uncomfortable."

She grabbed his chin. "You will be if I'm forced to hurt you. I don't like hurting my friends."

"What would my punishment be?" He grinned. "Chains, whips, handcuffs?"

"An attack at your ego."

He winced. "Ooh, you are cruel." He sighed and drew away. "All right, a man can take a hint."

"Good, now don't pout. You're just drunk."

Kevin bit his lower lip and glanced away. "I'm not as drunk as you think," he said quietly.

"There are plenty of women to take my place."

He sent her a gaze so intense she swallowed. "No one can take your place, Cassie."

His serious tone worried her, and she tried to make light of the moment. "Yes, it's a big place to fill." She patted him on the head its if he were a little boy and slipped out of the room. "Try to find a woman you can handle."

* * *

Adriana couldn't wait to hear Mike's band play. He was such a lively, vivacious performer and always transferred that energy to her at night. He was not an intellectual, but his love of life and his passion for music made her feel alive. She liked people like that. Cassie was the same, so full of humor and compassion. She hoped Cassie had left Kevin's clutches and would join her soon.

"So we meet again," a familiar voice said.

Adriana turned and stared up into Drake's serious amber gaze. He didn't smile, but his face looked relieved to see her. "Adriana, isn't it?"

"Yes. How are you?"

"You wouldn't like the answer." He stared over her head. "Have you seen Cassie?"

Damn. She knew he would go looking for her. "Briefly. She comes alive at these parties. It's hard to keep track of her."

His mouth kicked up in a quick grin. "I know. She's in her element, but I'd really like to find her. Do you know where she might be? I've checked under every table."

She smiled. "No, I haven't seen her."

A woman with bright orange lipstick spoke up. "You came with the woman in the velvet dress, right? She was hard to miss."

Drake nodded. "Yes."

"She went off with Kevin."

Adriana sent the woman a fierce glare, then looked at Drake. "It sounds worse than it is. They're friends."

The woman continued, "Kevin loves his friends. He probably took her to the sunroom so that they could—"

"See the stars," Adriana cut in. "Cassie is quite fond of them." She stared at the woman and forced a smile. "Thank you, you've been so helpful," she said, her voice underlined with sarcasm. The woman got the hint and left.

Drake folded his arms and stared at the empty stage. "You look worried."

"I'm not."

"What do you expect I'll find in the sunroom?"

"Two friends having a good time."

He let his hands fall. "Relax. I trust her."

"I'm glad." She grabbed his sleeve before he turned. He looked at her, questioning. "I'm glad you're in her life."

He squeezed her shoulder in reassurance to combat the uneasiness in her eyes. "Don't worry. I have no plans on leaving it."

* * *

The night echoed the laughter and enjoyment of the party, but Drake didn't feel any of it. Every nerve was alert. He wasn't worried, he assured himself as he walked to the sunroom. Cassie wasn't the type of woman to toy with a man. However, he hadn't been able to assess Kevin yet and that bothered him. He clenched his fist as he passed the first window of the dome structure and heard Cassie's laugh. He turned the corner and saw her in Kevin's arms.

He took a step back as if he'd been struck and spun away from the scene that would now be seared in his memory. He had suspected Cassie was up to something and before the night was through he would figure out what it was.

Chapter Seven

Cassie escaped into the garden, blaming the unfortunate events in the sunroom on too much drink. Kevin had never behaved that way before, and they had flirted much more freely than that on other occasions. She was just glad to have escaped without irreparable damage to their friendship. She allowed herself to enjoy the tender feel of the warm evening, the happy flash of fireflies, and the sweet smell of lilies and magnolias. The moon winked at her from its inky black bed and offered her its condolences for what the end of the evening would entail.

She sat on a stone bench and stared at the fountain— a structure of a lion roaring. Cassie found it fierce rather than majestic, but let the sound of running water calm her. Suddenly, a ghostlike cloud of smoke arose from the hedge behind her. Curious, she went around the corner and saw Drake, lying stretched out on a bench like a black jungle cat, smoking. The way the gray smoke swirled around him gave the illusion of an apparition— an elusive wizard ready to disappear when the mood struck him.

"I didn't know you smoked," she said.

His eyes touched hers, then turned away. "Only when I'm annoyed."

"And why would you be annoyed?"

He exhaled a cloud of smoke and glanced up at the sky as if pondering the question. "I suppose that's similar to asking a zebra thrown into a pack of hyenas why he'd be upset."

"You mean you didn't enjoy yourself?" she asked, surprised. A secret part of her was thrilled, another part dismayed.

He took another drag of his cigarette and continued to study the sky.

The silence didn't alarm her; perhaps he'd been bored. "I was sure you would," she said, wondering what could have ruined his evening. "Vicki and Mandy are intelligent, successful, wealthy—"

His eyes trapped hers. "And why would that be of any importance to me?"

She hesitated, seeing her plan fraying at the edges. It wasn't supposed to be like this. "I just thought you'd find them interesting," she managed, hoping to sound innocent.

"I did find them interesting." He straightened. "The same way a microbiologist would find a slide of bacteria interesting. Don't worry. I was very civil." He dropped his cigarette on the ground and crushed it under his heel. It was a quick controlled movement, but she could tell he was angry. "They laughed at my nonsensical jokes, asked about my watch, my car, my clothes, thrust various body parts into my field of vision, and then began to grope me. Trina saved me; I remember her name because she repeated it at least twenty times, and chatted until my ears rang. A woman named Sheila, who wore an outfit that left little to the imagination, then tried to feed me. Afterward, some woman whose name I forget admitted I'd make a good father for her children and asked if I'd donate sperm."

Cassie bit her lip, trying not to laugh. "You're making this up."

"I'm afraid I'm not that imaginative," he said coolly.

She sat down next to him. "How did you get away?"

"I told them that I was poor." He flexed his fingers. "Of course a few said that I had excellent potential, but I told them I was a hopeless case and was devoted to my benefactress who had given me this watch—" he flashed the object—"for services rendered. I then disappeared here."

"You can't say that you had a boring evening," she teased lightly, hoping he would see it all as a joke. "A lot of men would love to be in your shoes."

Drake eyed her reflectively. "You mean a lot of men would enjoy their dates dumping them so that she can make out with the host?"

"I wasn't making out with anyone," she said, shocked. "Where did you get that idea?"

He flexed his other hand, his voice dangerously neutral. "Cassie, I didn't lie to you, so don't lie to me."

"I'm not lying."

"Then why were you kissing Kevin? No, let me guess. It was some sort of social ritual I'm not aware of. I admit I haven't been out much."

She placed a hand on her forehead, as a horrible realization struck her. Her stomach dropped. "Oh, God. You saw us."

"Yes." He folded his arms, his manner a little too relaxed. "I'm sure there's a reasonable explanation."

He was furious. His voice was cool, but the anger seething from it was iron hot. Unfortunately, he had every right. She had felt the same emotions when she'd seen Timothy with Debra. She worried her shawl with nervous fingers. "Actually, there isn't one. Kevin just got out of hand. I didn't know his intentions until too late."

"So you didn't encourage him?"

"Of course not."

Drake hesitated. She could almost feel the tight rein he kept on his anger. "Then what were you doing alone with him in the sunroom?"

"Eating."

His eyes flashed. "You needed me conveniently out of the way so that you could eat alone with him?"

"No! He wasn't part of the plan."

He paused. "What plan?"

Cassie closed her eyes, wishing the night had never happened. "Didn't you like any of the women?"

"What plan?" he repeated in the same flat tone.

She opened her eyes and sighed. "Let's forget..." Her words trailed off when she spotted the hard gleam in his eyes. She knew they weren't leaving until she explained. "I figured you would forget about me once you saw the other women," she admitted, her voice low with shame. "Kevin caught me at the bar and persuaded me to go with him to the sunroom. I admit it was a mistake. I'm not at all interested in him in that way and I would never do that to you. Never." She released a bitter little laugh. "I know only too well how it feels to be dumped for someone else." She ran her hand along a bush. "You were supposed to have a good time. A very good time." She plucked one of the leaves and forced a smile, eager to change the mood. "Did you know one of the women you mentioned is a famous dancer at—"

"I was supposed to come here, be so over-whelmed by these vultures that I'd forget about you? That's how you think I'd treat you?"

Cassie maintained her plastic smile. "Hey, you wouldn't be able to help yourself. Like me at an ice cream shop."

"That's the type of man you think I am?"

Her smiled faltered. "Well, uh..."

"Is that what your ex-husband would do?"

"This has nothing to do with Timothy."

"Hmm." Drake lit another cigarette, inhaled, then exhaled and rested his elbows on his knees.

Cassie hung her head, the lovely evening sudden-ly feeling cold. She didn't realize her shawl had

fallen around her waist until Drake casually reposi-
tioned it around her shoulders.

"I'm sorry," she said in a quiet voice. "I know it
must have looked bad and I can understand you
wanting to leave right now and never see me
again."

He studied his cigarette. "You're not getting rid
of me that easily."

"I wasn't trying to get rid of you."

He put the cigarette to his lips. "Yes, you were."

"I was trying to expose you to all the options out
there."

He slanted her a dark glance. "How old do you
think I am? I've been around plenty of women and
slept with lots. Okay, maybe not lots, but enough."
He stubbed out his cigarette and stood. "I've had
enough of this conversation. Let's dance."

She stared at him, stunned by the suggestion.
"But you can't dance."

He pulled her to her feet "Fortunately, you can
teach me."

* * *

He was a smooth dancer, his energy raw, his
movements compelling. Cassie felt herself follow-

ing his lead and coming under his spell. She fought
it.

"Now, it's your turn to relax," he whispered.

She glared up at him. "I thought you said you
couldn't dance."

He fingered a loose tendril around her face. "I
can't."

"Then what do you call this?"

"Foreplay."

Her gaze fell.

A man tapped Drake on the shoulder. "Do you
think I could cut in here?"

"Sure," Drake said. "If you think you can dance
with broken legs." He spun Cassie away.

She stared at him openmouthed, then said, "That
was uncalled for and downright rude!"

"Don't lecture me," he softly warned. "I'm not in
a good mood."

She turned away. The night was a bigger mess
than she could have imagined. Not only had the
other women not impressed him, but he probably
thought she had used him. Though she'd never see
him again, she didn't want him to hate her. "Drake,
I was only trying to help," she said, desperate to
explain. "I thought—"

"I know what you thought and you were wrong."

She stopped dancing. "Let's leave. You probably can't stand the sight of me."

"Cassie, shut up and move. I'll drag you across the floor if I have to."

"You wouldn't be able to."

The corner of his mouth quirked in challenge. "Try me."

She began to move. In his current mood she wouldn't trust him not to do something. "No."

After a while she heard him make a low grumble in his throat that was eerily close to a growl. Its cause came up to them.

"Hey, babe," Kevin said. He gestured to Drake with a jerk of his chin. "Is this your latest?"

Drake let go of Cassie so abruptly, she staggered back. He turned to Kevin, his voice low but dangerous. "Cassie is not a babe, chick, or hon. Nor is she one of your call girls to pick up and fondle when you feel like it. Now I don't mind her having male friends that treat her with respect, but the next time you mistake her for one of your bimbos, even if she is foolish enough to find herself alone with you in a Jacuzzi as tempting as a money-filled wallet, you'll be kissing my fist. Understood?"

Kevin's jaw twitched in anger, but when he spoke his voice was humble. "Understood. Sorry, Cassie, I didn't mean to embarrass you."

Cassie smiled. "It's—"

"Apology accepted," Drake interrupted. He took her hand and walked away.

"What was that for?" she asked as he handed his ticket to the valet. "Kevin has always—"

"Treated you like a stupid idiot put on this earth for his enjoyment? You deserve better than that. And I'll make sure you get it."

The man was too serious, that was his biggest fault. She knew that Kevin didn't mean anything by his behavior, he called everyone babe or something similar. Cassie thought it best not to talk Drake out of his strange sullen mood. She did not know what to say and he didn't look in the mood for the "Let's still be friends" speech. She also did not want to distract him as he drove through the city like a participant in the Indy 500. Buildings and traffic lights blurred past her like some futuristic ride at an amusement park. Drake gripped the steering wheel occasionally loosening his grip to change gears with unnecessary vigor. He seemed oblivious of how fast they were going.

When he finally turned into an underground parking garage, Cassie let a sigh of relief escape her, pleased that they had arrived safely and that she hadn't heard the siren of a police car in the distance. But as he slid into a parking space she remembered she didn't have underground parking.

"Wait a minute, this isn't my place," she said, getting out of the car.

He turned on his car alarm. "No, it's mine."

"This is not a good idea."

He flashed a bland smile over the hood of his car. "Funny, I felt the same way about your party, but I went anyway." He grasped her elbow and led her to the building. "Come on."

Cassie chewed her lower lip and hummed a song while going up the elevator, then tapped a beat on her leg as he put the key in the lock. Drake paused with his hand on the door. "I don't have any ex-girlfriends hanging on my walls, so relax."

She nodded. The request was illogical. It was like asking an unanesthetized patient to lie still while coming at the person with a giant metal object.

He opened the door to reveal an expensive, beautifully decorated condominium, which afforded a spectacular view of the city lights.

"You have a very kind benefactress," she said, impressed. "Do you think I could do her any favors?"

He took her purse and placed it on the table. "Yes. Make me happy."

"Sorry, that's not one of my talents." She stared at a glass bowl. "So, what do you do for a living?"

"I thought I explained that to you."

Cassie sat down, relieved that he still had the ability to joke. "You must be very good."

"You'll find out soon enough. Would you like a drink?"

"No." She'd had enough food and drink for one evening. She was sure her dress was stretched to its limit. If she breathed too hard, it would burst into pieces.

"Okay." He sat down next to her. "Let's get a few things clear." He tossed his jacket on the back of the couch and rolled up his sleeves. "You seem to have the impression that I like playing games." His magnetic gaze held her captive. "I don't."

"I never—"

Drake pressed a finger against her lips. "I've given you a chance to explain and now I deserve a chance to respond." He gently tugged her shawl off her shoulders and placed it next to him. "I obviously have not made myself clear, but tonight I intend to."

Any reply Cassie had was thoroughly kissed from her mouth. She had expected an angry, punishing kiss that would repel her as Kevin's had, but she was wrong. The engaging touch of his impatient lips sent a shock wave through her entire body. She met the current of desire willingly, unable to deny herself this sorcerer whose very eyes drowned her in a pool of pleasure. She grabbed the lapels of his shirt and brought him close, feeling his hard body against hers. He smelled like the night—musky, cool, and mysterious.

"You taste better every time," he whispered.

"It's my specialty." She licked his lower lip.

"Why did you fight this so long? I should shake you for refusing us this."

"You can shake me later. I like what you're doing right now."

"The bedroom," he muttered against her mouth. He did not want to take her on the couch, although at the present moment that was a distinct possibility.

They stumbled toward the bedroom, leaving various articles of clothing in their wake as they eagerly undressed each other. Drake hooked his foot behind her and Cassie fell backward onto the bed; he covered her like a monsoon—reckless and consuming. She wrapped her arms around him, placing kisses on his shoulders and neck while his hands caressed her body like a gentle wind finding its way through a forest—light, searching, arousing. She felt the expanse of his back, her fingers roaming like a river over his muscles. His skin was hot, seeming to imprint itself on hers, claiming her for the night and other nights to follow. The hair on his chest sent soft, thrilling currents of desire as they brushed against her breasts.

Cassie closed her eyes, captivated under his spell, for as the night progressed she felt beautiful—her body was not a temple of shame, but something this man worshipped with his zealous mouth and his greedy hands. No amount of words could have convinced her as his body had.

As quickly as the pleasure came, fear followed, filling her with doubt. What if she disappointed him? What if Timothy had been right about her lack of sexuality?

"Drake?" she asked in a hurried whisper.

"Hmm," he grunted, spreading her legs open with his knee.

"I may not be good at this."

The tremble in her voice caught his attention. The moonlight reflected in her eyes. They were big and full of apprehension. He rubbed his knuckles against her chin. "You'll be fine."

"How do you know?"

"A man does not have to drink an entire bottle of wine to know it's excellent. A sniff or simple sip will do." He slowly let his tongue trail a warm, wet path up her neck; her toes curled. "And from what I've just tasted, I know you'll be delicious. I want you to trust me. I'll take care of everything." He pressed a tiny kiss on her forehead. "I'll be right back."

She swallowed and nodded.

He disappeared into the bathroom, leaving Cassie to hope that the night would be good as he so confidently predicted it would be.

"Ready for me?" He turned on the lights.

Cassie buried herself in the covers. "Are you crazy! Turn them off!"

Startled by her outburst, he did so. "What's wrong with you?"

"I just want the lights off."

"Why?" he asked, bewildered.

"Do you want me or not?"

"You know I want you." He lifted the covers, slipped in beside her, and held one breast, teasing the nipple until it became hard. "I just wanted to see you, love. Is that wrong?"

Yes. "No. I guess not."

His lips touched her nipple with tantalizing tenderness. "Next time then."

She arched her body, feeling the moisture increase between her legs. She rubbed her body against his. "Isn't this good enough?"

"Yes." The mere feel of her filled him with dangerously possessive thoughts. He did not and would not share her with anyone. Kevin would do well not to tamper again with what wasn't his.

His hand skimmed across her belly. He loved the fullness of her form, the rolls and curves. He loved her softness and the comfort it offered. Tonight he had wanted to teach her a lesson, but the lesson had been his to learn. He realized how deep his feelings for Cassie had become. The knowledge brought a painful vulnerability coupled with a frisson of fear. It coursed through him as he entered her. He briefly shut his eyes, gathering his control. It was dangerous to desire a woman this much. It made a man weak. He couldn't afford to be weak.

He felt her tighten around him, her silken walls a sanctuary, and slowly his fear subsided. She wanted him. He was where he should be. There was no need for dominance or surrender. She knew she belonged to him and that he would take care of her.

He kissed her throat, hating the darkness around them. He wished he could see her. But the night kept her a mystery, reminding him that she was still out of reach. That he still had to prove himself so she would trust him.

He groaned as her lips trailed a wet path of kisses across his shoulder, pushing aside all his thoughts. They disappeared when she flicked her tongue against the sensitive skin behind his ear. He lost his battle with control and succumbed to his passion.

Cassie welcomed it. Tonight her wizard worked his sorcery. Never had ecstasy felt this tangible. It overwhelmed her body and mind. His ardor surprised her, but she was not afraid. He was a man of fire who shouldn't have such a disdain for love. His beliefs were a contradiction to his very nature. He was meant to love and be loved. But she wouldn't think of such things. Now she would enjoy the magic of being in his arms.

Under the cloak of night, their souls met, clinging to each other even as their love making ended.

"Drake?" a small voice asked beneath him.

"Hmm?" he grumbled, his body limp with pleasure.

"Can I breathe now?"

"What?"

"I love the feel of you, but you weigh a ton."

"Oh, sorry." He rolled off her, pulling her to fit into the curve of his body. "How's that?"

Cassie took a deep breath as though she'd just avoided suffocation. "It will do," she said primly. She felt him chuckle.

She traced a line from his ear to his jaw. The moonlight polished his skin a silky onyx. She let her hand glide down his arm. "You're a wonder."

"Why?" His voice was heavy with masculine triumph.

"Because you're a gentleman masquerading as a rogue."

"And you're a wench masquerading as a lady. Ow!" This because she punched him. "It was a compliment."

"Then you should work on them."

She tried to move away, but he wouldn't release her. "You can be angry with me close as well as far," he said, trapping her with one leg.

She nipped him on the shoulder. "You're a beast."

"Waiting to be tamed by Beauty."

"She isn't here. Let me go and I'll get her for you."

He laughed and Cassie admitted she did like the sound of his laughter. It was warm, inviting, and real. But what had just happened between them? What did this mean? "Drake?"

"Go to sleep, Cassie."

"But—"

"We can talk tomorrow."

With that sleepy promise, she finally allowed herself to relax against him, letting herself drift off to sleep. Holding her close, Drake fell asleep a few moments after.

* * *

When Cassie woke, the moonlight danced around her head at a dizzying pace, and for a moment she tried to figure out where she was—why her body ached as if it had been squeezed through a grinder. She felt a solid arm shift around her waist and remembered where she was and the night of lovemaking. Unfortunately, the memory was cut short when her stomach clenched and a wave of nausea hit her. She stumbled into the bathroom—unable to marvel at its elegance and impressive size—and lunged toward the toilet before she embarrassed herself. Her head felt as if an anvil had struck it and her entire body screamed in pain.

She raised herself to the sink and splashed her face with cold water, trying to combat the heat that consumed her like a desert summer. Another wave of nausea hit and she doubled over the toilet again. Once the nausea subsided, she rested her head against the rim and struggled to think of what to do next. She knew she had to leave. Whatever was wrong with her, she didn't want Drake to see. Timothy hated to see her sick and she wouldn't have Drake looking at her with the same disgust in his eyes.

She quickly changed into her dress, tears streaming down her face due to the pain that accompanied every movement. She called a cab and wrote Drake a note explaining that an emergency had occurred. She left it on the coffee table, then crawled toward the door, which seemed to move and shift every time she thought she was getting closer. She shut her eyes and held her head for a moment, hoping her stomach wouldn't rebel if she tried to make a mad dash to the door. However, one attempt to stand proved her legs refused to cooperate. She shut her eyes once again, gathering her strength. When she opened them, two powerful legs stood in her path.

She squinted up at Drake. Through the pain that racked her head she could see that he was furious. His eyes glowed with yellow fire.

"Playing hide-and-seek again?" he murmured satirically.

"Don't," she pleaded in a fragile voice. "I have to go."

"Why don't you get up and walk then?" He lifted one shoulder. "I'm not going to stop you."

Cassie was too weak to answer the anger and hurt that echoed in his tone. Her only goal was to get out before she disgraced herself and destroyed the beautiful night they had spent together.

"Good." She continued on her hands and knees as if walking were a preposterous idea.

"What are you doing?" he asked, seizing her arm. When she cried out in pain he immediately let go. He knelt in front of her and cradled her face in his hands, forcing her to look at him. "What's wrong?" he demanded, concern making his words harsh.

"I'm okay." She stood and took two small steps toward the door.

"You're not okay."

"I know." She swayed against him and they both fell against the wall. Drake swore.

"Did I hurt you?" she whispered.

"No. You're burning up. Why didn't you tell me you weren't feeling well?"

"Because I... Oh, no," she groaned in an ominous tone.

"What?"

"I'm going to be sick."

He rushed her to the bathroom just in time for her to empty her stomach completely. It later felt like a vise, her tongue and mouth like a sewer system. Drake tenderly washed her mouth and face with a damp cloth, wiping away the hot shameful tears that fell down her face.

"I'm so sorry," she mumbled. "So very sorry."

"No apologies, love." He brushed a tear away with his thumb, then tasted it. "Even your tears are sweet."

"It's not funny."

"Sorry, I was trying to make you feel better."

"It didn't work," she said, the flow of tears increasing. "I feel awful."

"It's all right. We all get sick sometimes."

Why now? she fumed. She must look dreadful and she probably disgusted him, but he was too kind to say so. She could not look at him. She rested her head against the toilet bowl, squeezing her eyes shut. Tonight she was aware of every aspect of her body, every roll, every curve, every clinging fat cell. She felt dumpy, worn, and revolting; her dress like sausage wrapping. Now he would think she was a reckless party girl who threw up like a drunk tee-nager at night. When the truth was that she'd never gotten drunk in her life.

"I'm taking you to the hospital."

Cassie could hear him standing up and tossing the rag in the sink. She kept her eyes shut, hoping to convince him to listen to reason. "No, please. I'll be fine in a minute. I just want to go home. Adriana can help me."

He didn't hear her. He had disappeared into the bedroom to pull on a pair of jeans.

"After the hospital," he continued, "I'll take you back home and take care of you." He knelt in front of her and held her shoulders so that she was no longer slumped against the toilet. Her eyes re-mained closed. "Do you think you can walk or do you need me to carry you?"

Her eyes flew open and she gaped at him. Did he think he was Superman? Able to leap tall buildings? Able to lift cars and large women? It was bad enough that she'd embarrassed herself, she would not worsen the situation by having him struggle to carry her down to his car.

"I can walk," she said. And she would if it took the last breath in her.

On unsteady legs, she allowed Drake to half walk, half carry her to the elevator. She rested against the wood-paneled wall, watching Drake push the G button to the garage level. She let her eyes trail to his condo door and a sense of ending crept over her as the elevator door closed, as if the curtains were closing at the end of a great performance. The fantasy had finally finished.

* * *

Damn it! He slammed down the phone, resisting the urge to rip the entire structure from the wall. Where was she? Why didn't she answer the phone? Three times he'd gathered the courage to call and three times she wasn't there. She was probably out with some guy, some guy who wasn't good enough for her. He took a deep breath. It was his own fault; he shouldn't have tried to get in touch with her, not yet at least.

He sat on the couch and rubbed his temples, fighting the headache that was racking his skull. No, he could not blame her. Cassie was too sweet to know what she did to others. That man on the other hand was an entirely different issue. Others had come and gone and this one would be no different, but he had to make sure. He looked at the various IDs scattered on his worn coffee table. He picked one up and frowned at the picture. Seemed he'd have to be Clay again.

* * *

"Food poisoning," Drake snorted as he helped Cassie into bed. "I'm not surprised. I half expected that we'd all need to be quarantined after that party."

Four hours after leaving Drake's place, they were back with the doctor's diagnosis and a prescription. He pulled the blankets up to her chin.

"Don't be mean," Cassie chided in a groggy voice. "It could be the flu."

"Are you feeling better?" He touched her forehead. His fingers were cold from the cool evening.

She felt drowsy and the world had a bad habit of spinning at odd times, but her stomach had quieted. "Yes, much."

"Then it wasn't the flu." He tucked the blanket around her until she felt as if she were inside a papoose. "You'd be feeling worse if that were the case."

"I suppose in your spare time you study the symptoms of gastrointestinal disorders versus influenza?"

He squatted next to her, grinning broadly. "Hmm. You're being sarcastic, that's a good sign."

"I wish you had taken me home. I hadn't planned on turning your place into an infirmary."

Drake rose to his feet. "Would you like some tea?"

"No."

"Then sleep."

"Don't go yet," she said when he raised his hand to turn off the lights.

His eyes darted to the door, then returned to her face. "Okay." He folded his arms. "Is there something you wanted to say?"

"No."

He leaned against the wall. "Then I'll just be here until you fall asleep."

"You could sit down."

"No, I'm okay."

She frowned. "Where are you going to sleep?"

"I'm not very tired. Don't worry about me."

He was lying. He looked exhausted. Of course, he had to be, she concluded. He didn't want to sleep in the same bed with her. She wished he hadn't brought her back; now even the memory of the night before would be soiled. She could tell by the restless way he moved his hands and shifted from one foot to the other that he was eager to leave.

"You can go," she said, sorry that she had asked him to stay. "I'm all right now."

"Are you sure?" His voice sounded concerned, but his eyes looked relieved.

"Yes."

He turned off the lights, leaving Cassie to stare into the darkness. Tonight she had accomplished her goal; he was no longer blind to the truth. They weren't meant to be. She just hadn't expected it to hurt so much.

* * *

Drake was exhausted but he couldn't sleep. He was afraid that if he shut his eyes the nightmare that had haunted him since his teens would return. He opened the fridge and grabbed a drink and a bag of plantain chips and then turned on the TV to keep himself from thinking. Cassie had really scared him. He had never felt such a sense of helplessness since he'd seen the viciousness of disease take his parents away from him.

He angrily flipped through the channels, then tossed down the remote. He shouldn't have been such a coward. He should have stayed with Cassie until she fell asleep, comforted her. But seeing her look so weak and fragile ripped at his insides until he felt as if they were bleeding. God, how she must despise him.

It wasn't just her illness that disturbed him. It was his reaction to it—the desperate need to do something, be something that would end her suffering. Looking at Cassie reminded him of how his father must have felt watching his mother die. In his mind he could hear the echo of his father's pleas, smell the musky stale scent of death stealing life, see the peeling brown wallpaper of the bedroom, and watch his strong father bent over his mother's prone form in the small bed weeping like a child. Those thoughts had passed through his memory and all he could think of was escape.

Perhaps that was why she had tried to leave him. Perhaps somehow she had sensed his weakness. He shook his head. No. She didn't know enough about him to come to that conclusion. He stood and shut off the TV. He had to do something proactive or thoughts would devour him and eat away at his conscience. He looked at the list of suggestions the doctor had given him. He would be the man his father hadn't been. Slowly the demons disappeared until another question only Cassie could answer rose in his mind.

Chapter Eight

*C*assie opened her eyes and saw the sun peering through the closed blinds, spilling onto the carpet. Her nose twitched at the calming scent of peppermint tea. She stretched and saw a picture on the side table—Drake with a young man and woman. She wondered if they were his family since they all seemed to share the same smile. She'd probably never find out since today she would be leaving. She saw her handbag on the dresser and took out her contacts and put on her glasses, ready to face the inevitable.

Feeling chilly, Cassie grabbed Drake's maroon terry robe that hung behind the door. It was too big, falling past her hands and dragging on the floor, but infinitely comfortable and warm. It smelled like cinnamon, and crumbled recipes filled the pockets. She walked through the living room and saw Drake in jeans, stretched out in a garden lounger on the balcony, smoking. She opened the sliding glass door and the crisp morning air slapped her face.

"It's too cold to be half dressed," she said.

He glanced at her, then out at the city, which hummed with its morning activities. "I like it. You didn't sleep long."

"No, I usually don't." She hesitated. "You're annoyed," she said, nodding to his cigarette.

He studied her for a moment, stubbed out his cigarette, then said, "Let me get you some tea."

"Look, I—"

He held up his hand. "Tea first."

She followed him into the kitchen and halted. It was gorgeous. The walls were painted a bright yellow, bronze pots hung overhead, a marble-top island stood in the middle, and tall, pinenut cabinets lined two walls. A bowl of exotic fruit sat on the large counter. To the side was a breakfast nook with a country table and chairs. He pulled out a seat, gently pushed her paralyzed frame into it, then prepared the tea.

"Could I have some toast as well?" she asked carefully, wondering how far she could push his hospitality.

"Sorry, but you're strictly on a liquid diet today. Doctor's orders." She pouted when he handed her the tea. A small rueful smile touched his mouth. "Don't worry, I've stocked my cupboards with broth and we have more Popsicles than anyone could hope for."

She paused, unsure she had heard him properly. "We?"

He pulled out a chair and sat in front of her, his eyebrows raised in wonder. "You didn't think I'd let you enjoy this liquid diet all by yourself, did you?"

She lowered her eyes, embarrassed that he felt the need to go through all this trouble. She took a quick sip of her tea. "You don't have to do that."

"I know." He reached for the carton of cigarettes that sat near the tin of tea bags. He took one out and began tapping it against his palm in an absent gesture.

"Aren't you going to smoke that?" Cassie asked after a while.

"No, the smell might make you feel queasy."

"It won't," she assured him, not wanting him to feel put out. "I feel fine."

He frowned down at the object as if it were offensive. "It's a stupid habit anyway."

"You only do it when you're annoyed."

"Hmm."

"And right now you're annoyed."

He tapped the cigarette against his palm and sighed in irritation. "Are you ready to talk?"

"About what?" She wasn't trying to be dense, but she wasn't sure which aspect he wanted to talk about. The fact that the possibility of them having a relationship was similar to a shark dancing or the fact that last night she had almost puked on him?

"Why you felt it necessary to crawl out of my apartment when you felt like death."

"I didn't feel like death," she muttered with resentment.

He continued to stare at her. His eyes intense but unreadable.

She tugged on the cuffs of his robe. She didn't know how to begin. She didn't want to begin. "I'm sure you think me rude, wearing your robe like this, but I was cold."

"Cassie, you're free to wear whatever you want, especially me, but that's not the point. Answer the question."

"It's so embarrassing," she hedged.

He waited, his tapping becoming more impatient.

She took a long swallow of her tea as if it were stiff bourbon, then placed it aside. "Timothy hated to see me sick," she explained in a rush. "He would call me a fat, disgusting slob and leave the house until I got well. He hated weakness, and sickness was a weakness. I didn't want you to see me that way."

Drake sat back and glanced around the kitchen and then returned to her face. "I hope you don't think you're flattering me by comparing me to him," he said in a bland tone.

"I'm not comparing you."

"Then why did you try to leave?"

"I just didn't want to disgust you. You already had a horrible night. I didn't want to make it worse."

He twirled the cigarette between his fingers. His voice grew husky. "Actually I had a very enjoyable evening."

She felt her face and body grow warm. How could he still look at her with such wanting in spite of what happened? "You know what I mean."

"Right." He put the cigarette back in the carton and pushed it away. "You mean if I had been sick you would have been disgusted at the sight of me."

"Don't be ridiculous," she snapped, surprised he would come to such a conclusion. "I would have taken care of you."

He nodded, then put his hands together in a steeple. His eyes roamed over her face speculatively. "Okay, then explain why you would take care of me and I wouldn't take care of you."

"You're blowing this out of proportion. Don't worry about it."

His eyes flashed fire, but his voice remained cool. "Right. Excuse me." He grabbed his carton of cigarettes with such force that some shot of out the box and landed unnoticed on the floor. He headed for the balcony.

"All right, I apologize," she said quickly, when he grasped the sliding door handle. She could feel the anger that he kept carefully in check. "I misjudged you."

He stared out the window. "Yes, you did." He slanted her a glance. "You seem to do it very well on a continual basis."

"I don't do it on purpose." She took a step toward him, but her foot got caught in the hem and she tripped and grabbed the table to keep her balance.

"Sit down before you hurt yourself," he ordered.

"I won't hurt myself. I just forgot how long your robe is."

"Was Timothy's robe shorter?" he drawled.

"I never wore his robe."

He nodded and opened the door.

"Try to see it from my side. I know at first I wanted to, uh..."

"Get rid of me."

"No, free you. But after we—"

"Had sex."

She placed her hands on her hips. "I am perfectly capable of finishing my own sentences, thank you."

He closed the door. "You're welcome. Go on."

"After we had sex, I wanted to impress you and when I got sick it was because of me, not you, that I had to leave. I didn't want to taint the picture of who I was."

"So if I ever get sick instead of shattering the illusion you have of me I should leave."

Cassie threw up her hands, exasperated. "You're misunderstanding me on purpose."

"No, I'm not. You're leaving out one important element."

"What?"

"I care about you. God only knows why, but I do."

"That's impossible." Men had wanted her, needed her, but never cared about her. The man didn't know what he was saying.

"No, it's not impossible. And believe it or not you care about me too."

"I hardly know you. I don't know what you do for a living, where your family's from, or anything personal." She shoved her hands in the large pockets of the robe and held out a crumbled piece of paper. "I mean, what is all this about? I don't know anything about you."

Drake stared at the label of the cigarette carton. "Probably because you tried so hard not to show any interest before."

"Well, I'm asking now. What do you do for a living?"

He looked up and shrugged. "I own a few restaurants. Two here in DC. The Blue Mango and the Red Hut."

She silently groaned in dismay. Restaurants—food— extra calories. "Impressive." She searched her mind for another question. "What is your middle name?"

"I don't have one."

"I thought everyone had a middle name."

"What's yours?"

"Annette."

His brows furrowed. "Annette is what you use to catch a fish."

She marched over to him and poked him in the chest. "Are you making fun of my name, Drake?"

He held up his hands. "I wouldn't think of it."
He began to smile. "Hey, let's go play Ping-Pong.
Wait, the table needs Annette."

She playfully swung at him.

He grabbed her hand; she trembled from his
touch. "Relax, Cassie. I would never hurt you."

"I know."

A dark thought entered his mind. He narrowed
his eyes and tightened his grip. "Did he ever hurt
you?"

She emphatically shook her head. "No. Never."

He kissed her knuckles. "Lucky him," he murmured, beginning to suck on her pinkie.

"Drake!"

"Hmm?" He took her hand and led her to the
couch. He sat down and pulled her onto his lap.

"This isn't going to work," Cassie said, trying to
wiggle off his lap. "Do you know how much I
weigh?"

He flashed a wicked grin. "Do you want me to
guess?"

"No."

"I didn't think so," he murmured against her
neck. "Please stop wiggling or I'll be forced to take
you right here and now. I'm not sure you're ready
for that."

She swallowed, feeling light-headed. She was sure it was from the lack of food, not from his words. No one could survive on peppermint tea. "You know you won't be able to hold me like this for long. Your legs will fall asleep. Perhaps you'll lose all muscle function."

"I don't care if they fall off." He kissed her behind one ear, then the other. "You're not going anywhere." He kissed her on the mouth, sucking on the lower lip.

"Drake?" she whispered.

"Hmm?"

"Could you do me a favor?"

"Anything," he breathed, ready to taste her lips again.

"Could you please let me have a slice of toast?"

He paused and shut his eyes as if in pain. "Cassie, you know I can't."

"Please." Her eyes begged him. For a moment, he felt himself weakening. He shook his head, steeling himself against her charms—her beautiful pleading butterscotch eyes and pouting raspberry mouth. "No, if you get sick again I wouldn't forgive myself."

She toyed with the curls at the base of his neck. "I'd forgive you."

He unwrapped her arms and held them in front of him. "You're a dangerous woman."

"Come on," she urged. "Just one piece of toast with butter and cinnamon and sugar sprinkled on top."

He shook his head sadly. "I can't."

She let her shoulders slump. "I don't think I like you very much anymore."

He lowered his eyes. "I'm sorry about that." He said the words so solemnly that she knew her joke had missed him again.

"Drake, I was just teasing."

He didn't look at her. "You can leave now if you want."

There was a moment of silence and then she said, "I don't."

His eyes met hers, filled with amusement. "That's what I figured."

"You big fibber!"

"Hey, I know how to tease too. We all have our talents."

She wiggled off his lap and surged to her feet. "I'll get you back for that."

"Ah, does the lady speak of revenge?" He kissed the back of her hand. "I accept the challenge."

He strolled into the bedroom, before she could reply to his outrageous statement.

Cassie darted into the kitchen and opened the fridge. There were only drinks and Jell-O present. She opened the cupboards and saw cans of soup. Where was the real food?

"Looking for something?" a deep voice asked behind her.

She gasped and spun around. Drake stood there fully dressed, swinging his keys in one hand.

"Just making sure we have everything," she said, swinging her arms in an attempt to look innocent.

He nodded gravely, but his eyes danced. "What would you like me to get for you?"

She rested against the counter and folded her arms. "Is that a trick question?"

He laughed. "No. I mean from your house. Are there books you want to read?"

She let her arms fall. "I thought you were taking me home today."

"I'm not," he said, walking to the hall closet He pulled out a black windbreaker and slipped into it. "So what would you like?"

He was doing too much for her. Soon he would become resentful. "Look, you've been really kind, but I think—"

He shut the closet door and rested a hand against it. "You aren't going to annoy me by arguing about this, are you?" He flashed a bland smile.

Cassie shook her head, sensing the temper that kept the smile in place. "No."

"Good. Now what would you like from your apartment?" He picked up a pen and paper from the hallway table.

"I have a book I'm supposed to be working on. It's on a disk."

"That's fine. I have a computer. Anything else?" He soon regretted the question when she gave him a list of items. Drake studied the list, then said, "Perhaps, I should just bring your entire apartment."

"Oh, could you?" she asked sweetly.

He stuffed the note in his jacket pocket. "You're high maintenance. I should have known better. Most beautiful women are."

She wrapped his robe tighter around her. "It's just a facade really. I'm truly horrible inside."

"I disagree. I've been inside you and you're anything but horrible."

Cassie opened her mouth, but no words came forth.

"Good, I've left you speechless." Drake handed her his cell phone number. "Call me if you need anything else." He glanced at the list. "Though at this point I think that's impossible."

She began to feel guilty. "Perhaps I shouldn't have—"

"I'm joking." He tweaked her chin. "You need to work on your sense of humor."

She smiled, amazed that in this odd circumstance she felt so happy. "Thanks for everything."

He opened the door. "This isn't everything. It's just the beginning."

Cassie watched the door close, then turned. The man was a complete puzzle. She glanced around the condo, curious as to what items would give her a clear picture of the man Drake was. He didn't have an extensive music collection, a few classical and reggae tapes; his bookshelf was filled with business manuals, cookbooks, and travel guides—Italy, Greece, Barbados. He'd highlighted certain cities, writing in the margins what restaurants and dishes to try. Pushed in the corner of the bookshelf was a dog-eared copy of *The Fear of Ridicule*. How could a man who had succeeded at so much still have that worry? She held the book close to her. She would be kind and gentle with him. She sat on the couch and shook her head, sighing. The guy was smart. He had been able to put a word to all the mixed feelings she had. She did care about him.

* * *

Drake heard the door next to him creak open as he placed the key in Cassie's door. A rough voice followed the sound. "Get away from there before I call the police."

"It's all right," he said. "I'm just getting Cassie's things."

The door opened wider. "What have you done to her?"

Drake paused, taken back by the strange question. "Nothing. She's staying at my place."

The man was silent a second. "Then what are you doing at her place?"

"Getting her things."

"Why isn't she getting them herself?" he demanded.

"She isn't feeling well." He shook his head, amazed that he felt the need to answer. But the man obviously cared about Cassie, so he couldn't blame him.

"I see. So what is your name?"

"Drake Henson.'"

"Do you have some ID to confirm that?"

The guy was definitely weird, but fortunately he was in an indulgent mood. "Yes." He took out his wallet.

The middle-sized man came out into the hallway scratching his thinning pepper-black hair. Drake handed him his driver's license. The man studied it for a while before handing it back.

"She's done worse." He stared at Drake through pale blue eyes. "What do you do for a living?"

He replaced the license and his wallet. He was becoming impatient, but kept his voice mellow. "I own a few restaurants."

"Names?"

"The Blue Mango and the Red Hut."

He grunted. "My name is Mr. Gianolo and Cassie is important to me. She follows my advice on whether someone is worth her time or not. What are your intentions?"

Drake folded his arms, prepared for any reaction that followed his statement. "I intend to marry her."

Mr. Gianolo's face spread into a toothy grin, making him look both young and old at the same time. He slapped his hands. "Hot dog! I should have known. You're one of those quiet serious types, not like her playboys and poets. I've been waiting for this day. Come inside for a drink, young man."

Drake ran a hand over his graying head. He hadn't been called a young man in years. He began to protest, but Mr. Gianolo had already disappeared inside the apartment.

"Sit down anywhere," Mr. Gianolo called from the kitchen.

Drake chose a tweed couch with pillows in the shape of footballs. Mr. Gianolo came out of the kitchen with a tray. He handed Drake a beer and a bowl of peanuts.

"Don't have nothing fancy. Haven't gone shopping yet."

"This is fine."

"Where did you go to school?"

Drake told him; Mr. Gianolo nodded. "A man of education and manners. A rare breed. You should have seen the first bum my daughter married. And my Cassie's first husband wasn't no good either."

"Ever met him?"

"Nah, saw him a couple times though. Carries his ego in a separate bag." He paused. "He just came by."

"What? Right now?"

"Yep, heard his footsteps. He has a distinct pounding sound. You won't catch him now," he said as Drake stood. "He's already gone."

They talked a little more and then Drake said good-bye.

As he approached her apartment, he saw a bouquet of flowers in front of Cassie's door that hadn't been there before. He picked them up and read the note: *To my dearest love, Timothy.* Drake scowled. He went into Cassie's apartment and promptly threw the flowers in the trash bin. He replaced Cassie's cutting board and knife set with the one he bought and began taking off messages from her answering machine. The first three were from Adriana, who sounded frantic, and then a male voice came on.

"Hey, babe—hon—girl—I mean Cassie. Have a hell of a headache. No hard feelings. Take care of yourself. Kevin." Then, "Hello, this is Glen. Remember our date for Thursday. Bye."

Drake wrote down the messages, then listened to the last one again. It was the tone rather than the message that disturbed him. Who was this Glen guy and what did he mean to her? How many more Glens were there? One thing was for certain, Cassie would certainly keep him alert. She kept an active social life and enjoyed her freedom in this sea of admirers. It would take a lot of strategy to stay on top.

Suddenly, the refrigerator began its strange vibrating dance, and he kicked it. It shuddered, then stopped. He'd worry about Cassie later. Right now he had to do something about that.

* * *

"Who's Glen?" Drake asked once he had returned. "He left a message on your machine." He waved the note in the air.

"Oh, no. I forgot about him," Cassie said, trying to snatch the note.

"Who's Glen?" he repeated.

"Glen Randall? He's a forty-year-old English teacher at—"

Drake shook his head. "That's not what I mean."

A slow smile spread on her face. "Are you jealous?"

"Insanely."

Cassie laughed, certain he was teasing her again. "Careful, I didn't ask you to check my messages." She waved a finger at him. "That's what happens when you snoop. You find out things you might not want to."

He hesitated then sighed. "I was trying to be helpful."

She nodded and her smile grew. "I know."

He nodded also, biting his lip. Though he didn't repeat the question, it still burned in his eyes.

"He's just a friend," she answered. "I'm supposed to go out with him to a poetry reading at eight-thirty on Thursday. Do you like poetry?"

"It seems to make Hallmark very rich." He handed her the note. "So he's just a friend?"

She quickly read the message and folded it in two. "You don't approve?"

"Oh, I approve. If he's anything more, it will give you the perfect opportunity to say good-bye."

"I'm not saying good-bye. He's a nice guy. It's comforting to be with a man with no hidden agendas."

Drake flexed his fingers. "I don't have any hidden agendas."

Cassie tapped the note against her lower lip. "Don't you?"

He took the note and tore it in half. "Actually, my agenda is quite clear."

She pursed her lips and sent him a coy look. "And just what would it be?"

"I plan to marry you."

She rolled her eyes. "You do know how to ruin a good flirtation, don't you?"

"I'm serious, Cassie."

She stared at him for a moment. "Was that a proposal?"

"Not yet."

"Good, I would hate to have to reject you right now."

He sat down. "I know you enjoy your carefree life—"

"I don't just enjoy it," she said firmly. "I treasure it. Being married to Timothy was the lonely hell of just being someone's wife and I don't intend to do that again."

Drake recognized any amount of discussion was fruitless. He nodded. "So he's just a friend?"

"I said yes."

He was quiet in consideration. "What's the name of the other guy you're seeing?"

"Other guy?"

"Yes, the one you're involved with."

She had forgotten about that lie. "Oh, yes. Right. He's out of the picture right now."

"If he ever was in it," he muttered.

She changed the subject. "Did I get any other messages?"

"Kevin has a hangover." He handed her the phone. "And I suggest you call Adriana. She's in a panic."

Cassie quickly dialed, knowing her friend was probably dreaming up horrible events of Cassie's demise since she hadn't heard from her.

"Where have you been?" Adriana shouted, after Cassie spoke.

She held the phone from her ear. "You don't have to shout."

She heard Adriana take a deep breath. "All right. I won't shout. So please tell me where the hell you've been!"

Cassie winced, sure that she had busted an eardrum. "I'm at Drake's place."

"Since the party?" she asked, amazed.

"Yes."

She heard the phone being dropped, a great big "Yes!" shouted in the background, and then the phone was picked up again. "I'm proud of you, but next time call. I was about to send a search party."

Cassie laughed. "It's not as romantic as it sounds. I got sick. And not heroine 'falling in a faint' sick."

Her enthusiasm faltered. "Uh, yes, that would put a damper on a romantic interlude. Are you feeling better?"

"Much."

"Good. Now you can jump his bones."

"Adriana!" she scolded.

"I'm serious. I was so worried you had lost him."

Cassie glanced at Drake and lowered her voice. "He's a hard man to lose."

"Still you shouldn't string him along without satisfying some curiosity. I mean aren't you curious how he is in bed?"

"Not anymore."

Adriana let out a little squeal, then drowned her with questions. "Was it good? Was he good? When did it happen? Where did it happen? Were you safe?"

"I can't answer that."

"Why not?"

"Because," she said delicately, "it's not appropriate."

Adriana began to laugh, understanding her friend's caution. "He's right there, isn't he?"

Drake was sitting next to her pretending to read a magazine, but she knew he was listening to every word. "Yes."

"I want to speak to him."

"Adriana," she warned.

"I'll be good, I promise."

Cassie reluctantly handed the phone to Drake. "She wants to talk to you."

He took the phone and listened gravely. Soon a smile touched his mouth. "Of course," he said simply. He handed the phone back to Cassie.

"What did she say?" she demanded.

He shrugged and returned to his magazine.

"What did you say to him?" she asked Adriana.

"None of your business," she said lightly. "Now are you two free for dinner in two weeks?"

"Perhaps, why?"

"I was thinking of a double date. You and Drake, me and Mike."

Cassie grimaced. "You're not seriously interested in that guy, are you?"

"He's fascinating."

She switched the phone to her other ear and turned away so Drake couldn't hear. "Yes, and so are butterflies. Unfortunately they have the same IQ."

Adriana let her statement pass. "His band is playing at the Colossal. We could have dinner afterward."

The thought was not at all tempting, but Cassie did not want to hurt her friend's feelings. She chewed on her lower lip. "I'm not sure Drake will be free. I will—"

Drake grabbed the phone. "I'm free," he said, winking at Cassie's stunned expression. "Uh-huh. We'll be there. No problem. Bye." He hung up, flashed a victorious smile, and returned to his reading.

Cassie stared at him, outraged. "You don't know what you just did."

"Yes, I do. I made a date. Now since you had me bring half of your apartment here you better find something to do." He caressed her cheek. "You can't expect me to keep you busy all day. A man can only do so much."

She slapped his hand away and began unpacking her things.

* * *

Cassie tried to work on her book, but her mind was still blank. When she ended up doodling more than typing, she abandoned the project and read a mystery novel. Unfortunately, the villain was so obvious, she hoped the inspector would be killed for pure stupidity. She tossed the book aside and read one of Drake's many food magazines, getting lost in the gorgeous pictures and descriptions of culinary treats.

Drake proved to be a comfortable companion. Since he felt no need to entertain her, she felt more like a resident than a guest. Soon dangerous thoughts of a more permanent situation began to fill her mind. She dismissed them.

Lunch was an uneventful affair. Chicken broth with apple juice. They ate it on the balcony, watching the people down below and guessing what they were up to.

"She is going to meet a man," Drake said, spotting a striking woman in a tailored black suit. "They're going to the National Theater, but first they'll have an early meal where she'll order the ostrich in red sauce and a Chardonnay."

"Very good, but how can you tell she's meeting a man?"

"No woman would glance at her reflection that often for a woman."

"You lead a sheltered life," Cassie teased. "She could be meeting a lady companion."

"I say it's a man." His comment was confirmed when the lady in question threw her arms around a man standing by a taxi.

"Lucky guess."

"No, pure observation. I've taught myself to try to understand people."

Cassie rested her chin in her hand and studied him. "If you understand people so much, why are you so awkward in crowds?"

"Socializing and business are two different mediums. I know how people like to be pleased. Since in my business I have to please them, it is helpful to know who my clientele is."

"And no doubt your clientele is the wealthy elite who can afford to spend the equivalent of a designer dress on a meal."

"You sound disapproving."

She hadn't meant to, but she'd attended a number of those types of restaurants with Timothy. Instead of being an enjoyable evening it turned into a battle with his ego as he spent extravagantly because he didn't want to be seen as cheap yet chastised her for every bite she took. "I'm not, but dining has not always been fun for me."

Drake lifted his glass and narrowed his eyes. "Well, I'll have to change that."

He wouldn't be able to, but she wisely kept her opinion to herself.

After lunch, Cassie returned to the computer, muttering curses under her breath as she tried to break through the emptiness of her mind. Drake stopped her from her self-imposed torture when he announced dinner.

He had turned the dining room into an atmospheric affair with golden candles, hand-painted china plates, polished utensils, and champagne glasses. All the lights were off.

"It's lovely," she said. "It's a shame it must all be wasted on broth."

He pulled out her chair. "Good presentation is never wasted."

The broth wasn't too bad either. She didn't know what he did to it, but it had a full, rich taste. She watched him eat—drink, she thought spitefully, eating involved chewing—his broth and guilt crept up on her. He was doing all this for her in spite of the way she had treated him before.

She put her spoon down. "I can't take it."

He glanced up, startled, the candlelight highlighting the golden specks in his eyes. "What?"

"I can't stand watching you eat something that looks like dirty water because of me."

"Now wait—"

Cassie waved her hand, dismissing any explanation he had. The candlelight flickered. "Drake, you're too big to survive on broth." She glanced down at the watery dish in front of her. "I promise I won't drool if you eat solid food. I'll pout and whimper a bit, perhaps burst into tears on occasion, but I won't drool."

He wiped his mouth with the cloth napkin and laid it on the table. "No, we're in this together. Besides, I've survived on a lot less."

"You've survived on less than beef broth?" Cassie asked, appalled.

"Yes." He stood, becoming part of the darkness. "Would you like to listen to some music?"

"Sit down. I'm not letting you get away with ignoring the issue. When did you have to starve?"

He looked decidedly uncomfortable, but Cassie wouldn't relent. She wanted to know more about him. "I didn't starve," he quietly corrected. He pushed in his chair. "It's not important." He reached for her bowl. "Are you done?"

"You know I can do a brilliant silent treatment when I put my mind to it."

"That's good. We all have our special gifts." He went into the kitchen.

"You are extremely aggravating," she said, meeting him at the sink. "You said you wanted a relationship."

"And I suppose that includes baring our souls?" He turned on the faucet.

"I told you about Timothy."

"Only because it affects the present. The past is something that should stay in memory. All that matters is now."

"The past is what makes you who you are."

He cut the faucet off. "Who I am is what you see," he said roughly. "My past is off-limits."

Chapter Nine

"If you're ashamed of your past, then you're a fraud in your present," Cassie argued. "It's like a tree looking at its root in disgust when that's what keeps it grounded and firm."

"Not all roots are so generous," he said in a low voice. "Some are weak."

"True, but they're still there or the tree would never have grown."

He rested his hands on the sink and studied her. "You really believe that?"

"Of course."

"Hmm, must be nice." He began to wash the dishes.

Cassie threw up her hands in surrender. It was clear he was not going to share anything. "You're right. It's not important." She returned to the dining room and cleared the table, then blew out the candles, encasing herself in blackness. The smoke danced for a while with the moonlight before it dissipated. She sat down and held her chin in her hands.

It didn't matter. Nothing about him mattered. He was a passing diversion like the smoke—something seen but intangible. He wanted a woman he could marry, someone to look good on his arm and in his restaurants. She did not want to be another man's wife again. Especially someone powerful and used to getting his way. Someone who was used to possessing things. He was doing her a favor by hiding his past. Knowing it would make him more real. A childhood and parents would make him whole with no room for fantastic thoughts—let him continue to be a sorcerer.

Tomorrow she would return home, Thursday she would go out with Glen, and then she would put her life back into perspective. She was vulnerable now and that's how Timothy had been able to catch her. She would not allow Drake to do the same.

She heard the chair in front of her scrape across the floor as it was pulled back, but she didn't look up to see its occupant.

Drake's voice cut into the black silence. "Do you like sitting in the dark?"

"Yes, on some level it makes everything clear." She let her hand fall to her lap.

"Hmm." He lit a cigarette. Cassie watched the end glow orange and burn its way to the center as he inhaled. "I became an orphan at sixteen," he said suddenly in a bored tone that gave no allowance for sympathy. Cassie opened her mouth to stop him, already feeling the tugs of understanding and sympathy wrap around her heart, but no words came out. "My parents came here for a better life and died instead. Mum worked in a factory and Dad on a boat. She got sick first; then he did. Our drafty apartment, filled with extra nightly companions, didn't help our hygiene situation." He tapped the ashes of the cigarette into the tray he'd brought with him. "When they were gone, I was left with a younger brother and sister to take care of. Eric was thirteen and Jackie seven. The courts wanted to split us up, but I wouldn't let them. I used someone as a bogus guardian, then disappeared out of the government's radar. I worked several jobs, making sure they were okay. I made sure they had sturdy clothes so that when they went to school, they didn't draw any attention. The housing wasn't the best and food was scarce, but I didn't want anyone to break us up."

"Of course. You didn't have a choice."

He nodded, glad that she could clarify what he had always felt. "Some called me a saint; others called me a fool."

"A fool?"

She heard the chair creak as he leaned back. "They thought that Eric and Jackie would be better in the care of the state where they would have a good home and meals."

Cassie sniffed, knowing that was luck of the draw. "So did they turn into juvenile delinquents?"

"No." She heard the pride in his voice. "Eric's a financial advisor and Jackie works at a not-for-profit organization, which I contribute to, and is also going to school."

"How did you come to own restaurants?"

Drake took a long drag of his cigarette. In the quiet she could hear the sibilant hiss of the flame eating the tobacco. "One night I was looking for leftovers behind a restaurant and a woman caught me. She was a small Swedish woman—Mrs. Larsen—with a loud voice and sharp green eyes. She asked me what I was doing and I said I was applying for a job. She asked me what I could do. I said anything. And that's what she hired me to do—anything. She and her husband owned the place and I was lucky because it was an upscale restaurant and I got to see how it was run from the inside out. I started in the back of the house and moved to the front. It was a new experience for me, the hustle of the kitchen, creating order out of chaos. I was able to taste new food. I'd never heard of lokdolmar or a breaker. Their son, Sveen, worked there and was perfect with the customers. I watched and imitated. They saw I had a knack for presentation, got on well with the customers, and had a head for business. I helped them run another restaurant and in turn they helped me get a degree in restaurant management. Finally Mr. Larsen helped me with the capital to open my own restaurant and here I am."

Yes. Here he was. The product of his own determination and tenacity, a man who had not asked for sympathy, but rather opportunity, and grasped whatever had come his way. His simple tale revealed more about him than many years of idle conversation could have. It wasn't what he said, but what he didn't say that exposed his character. He didn't talk about handling work and school, where he lived, or if there had been any family to turn to. He was a man who knew hunger, who spent his career feeding others; a man who knew poverty, who shared his wealth. They were alike in many ways. They had both overcome shyness to survive.

He was someone she could admire and love. And there again lay the danger that continued to lick at her heels. Her fists tightened, at the thought of loving him. She knew she could not bend to his will, he would be all-consuming if she showed a little weakness. A survivor like him knew nothing about love, only possession, and she didn't want to be another trophy on his journey to a complete conquest of a world that had been harsh. He had given her what she had asked for and now she didn't know what to say.

He stubbed out his cigarette and rose to his feet "I'm going to bed." It wasn't an invitation, just a statement.

Cassie sat still in the darkness until she heard the bedroom door close.

* * *

After a few moments of mindless typing, Cassie squeezed her eyes shut and resisted the urge to scream. She wondered if her publisher would let her out of the contract if she checked herself into an insane asylum. Her career hinged on this book and she couldn't even complete a solid first chapter. She stared at the notepad next to her, which was filled with doodles, then the paragraph on the screen and laughed at what she had typed. Why couldn't she focus?

She sighed fiercely, knowing the reason was sleeping in the other room. Drake was a definite problem. He was no longer a sorcerer she could relegate to her fantasies. He was a real man who had a past, who smoked when he was upset and made love when he wasn't. He had seen her at her worst and didn't care, but he wasn't safe. She knew that loving him would involve more than her heart; it would involve her soul, her mind, and before she could think, she would find herself married again. Feeling all the sensations a new marriage could offer before the novelty wore off and he discovered what marriage was about. That she wasn't always funny, that she could eat an entire pie without thinking. No, she didn't want to be present to see his illusion shattered as Timothy's had.

At first Timothy had been her perfect husband, her romantic ideal, but quickly all that charm had soured and she discovered the true man behind the extravagant gestures—impulsive trips to Europe, Asia, and the Caribbean. Gifts that made her head spin and events that were attended by notable personalities. In the beginning, he made her feel like a queen; by the end she felt like a servant. All that he had proposed to love before soon revolted him: her choice in clothes, her hair, the way the house was decorated, but most important the way she ate. He said he couldn't stand to watch her eat no matter how small the portions. After discovering his affair with Debra—casually discarded gift receipts and hotel reservations, seeing them in bed together— she knew her marriage was over. He had pursued her, then rejected her, and now he suddenly wanted her back. Was his ego so large that he hadn't expected his chubby little wife to really leave him and make it on her own?

She turned off the computer, dismissing the idea. Knowing Timothy, it wouldn't be something that deep. He was probably just bored.

This isn't wise, she thought, staring at Drake's dark shape in the bed, but right now she didn't want to be wise. She wanted to be held and enjoyed and desired. She changed into her peach satin and lace nightgown (no doubt Drake had scrounged through her cotton pajamas to find this one), crawled under the covers, and stared up at the ceiling waiting for sleep to come. Drake gently tugged her toward him until her head rested on his chest. She lifted her head and kissed him.

She felt him smile. "What was that for?" he asked.

"Acknowledging your roots."

"What about you?"

She rested her head, melting into his warmth as he stroked her back. "What about me?"

"Tell me about yourself."

"I was born on the banks of the Mississippi to a Pentecostal preacher and his wife—"

"The real version."

She lifted her head. "But this one is much more interesting. I haven't even told you how many siblings I have."

"I don't care. I want the truth."

Cassie crossed her arms on his chest. "Okay, I was born in Pittsburgh, Pennsylvania. The middle child to Angela and Oscar Graham."

"How could you be the middle child when there were four of you?"

She paused, trying to understand who he was referring to. Then she remembered he'd seen her album. "Clarence, the eldest, was from another mother. He stayed to himself a lot." She didn't feel the need to mention how he used to walk them to school and help prepare their lunches or how much it hurt when he left at sixteen. "My father was a university professor, my mother a dress consultant. My older sister was homecoming queen three times in a row and graduated from Penn State with an attractive but useless degree in philosophy and is now married to a stockbroker. My younger brother made it into Texas AMU on a football scholarship and is now a sports commentator. He has yet to settle down. That's it."

"No, it's not."

"What do you mean?"

He yawned. "You have yet to tell me anything about yourself."

"I had the typical middle-class childhood and typical middle-child up-bringing. Nothing in my life stood out except me of course. Isn't that enough?"

His reply was a soft snore.

"I told you it would bore you," she muttered. She closed her eyes and tried to push away any worrisome thoughts. His warmth and steady breathing combined with the comforting sound of his heartbeat finally lulled her to sleep.

* * *

She was floating on a wave of syrup, rolling with butter on hot French toast, until she approached a waterfall of strawberries and melon balls. Cassie

sighed, waking from her dream with disappointment. She stretched and smelled the air that greeted
her with scents that made her stomach growl. She
grabbed her robe and ran to the kitchen.

Drake was at the stove, wearing worn jeans and
an apron, happily whistling to the rhythm of a xy-
lophone that came from the speaker, and the sound
of something sizzling filled the air. She watched
him check the oven, add lemon to a pan, then toss
something in the air and catch it in the pan. It all
looked like a dance. Not wanting to startle him, she
knocked on the wall.

He grinned as she approached. "Sleeping Beauty
has awakened. Are you ready to eat?"

"You never have to ask me that."

He pointed his spatula to the set table. "Sit
down."

"Oh, this is wonderful," she said, admiring the
fan-shaped yellow napkin that lay on the plate.

"You deserve it."

He placed in front of her toasted bagels with
tomatoes and ricotta cheese, seasoned scrambled
eggs, sable with dill sauce, sliced honeydew, and
mangoes. The smell of Jamaican Blue Mountain
coffee complemented the air.

She opened her mouth to tell him how wonderful it was, but he held up his hand and shook his head.

"Do not speak, madam," he said in the tone of a stuffy waiter. "Merely enjoy. That will be thanks enough."

Drake untied his apron and joined her at the table. Together they ate, listening to the light pelting of rain, the soothing sound of a flute over the loudspeaker, while a watery sunlight slipped through the windows.

* * *

He didn't allow her to thank him as she finished the meal or as he drove her home. She was glad to be completely better and now there was no other reason to stay with him. Although in her imagination she could think of a million reasons to. She watched Drake's car disappear into traffic as he rushed to get some errands done, then turned and stared at the dull red of her building. Their goodbye had been quick, almost anticlimactic. He had given her a brief kiss on the forehead, 'Whatever that meant,' smiled, and left. No "Good luck," no "Take care," not even "I'll call you." Not that she expected him to. She was glad to be back to get on with her life. Glad that he finally recognized that it was best to leave things as they were and not expect more. Her mind was keen on the idea. Her heart, however, was heavy.

She stepped into the elevator, determined to get hold of her mixed emotions, and saw Glen buried in a book: *Finding Love after Divorce.*

"Good book?" she asked.

He hastily closed it and moved it out of view. "Not really, I was just curious. Perhaps I'll write a book of my own someday." He tapped the cover. "Doesn't seem hard."

"Famous last words. What's that on your wrist?" she asked, noticing a purple rash.

"Food allergy."

She made a face. "Ugh. Food can really be a nasty beast, it either makes you fat or gives you a rash. I hope the meal was worth it."

"Unfortunately, I'll probably do it again. So where have you been? I've missed you at aerobics." He flexed a muscle.

Cassie gave it an appreciative squeeze. "Very nice. I was at a friend's place."

"And from that vague reply, I'd say it was a male friend." He quirked a brow, looking very much like a professor. "Sounds serious."

"It's not. I wasn't feeling well."

"Sorry to hear that. Are you feeling better?"

"Yes, thank you."

"Are we still on for the poetry reading?" he asked as the elevator doors opened on her floor.

She smiled at him as she stepped out. "Definitely."

At least she had something to look forward to. Something else to occupy her mind. She turned the corner and saw Timothy about to knock on her door. Her good mood left. "What are you doing here?" she demanded.

"I need to talk to you."

She heard the door creak open next door.

"Hi, Mr. Gianolo," she called. "I'm fine."

There was a grunt and then the door closed.

She pushed Timothy aside and opened her apartment door. She held out her hand when he began to follow her inside. "You can't come in."

He frowned, confused. "Why?"

She placed her bags down. "Because this is a Timothy-free zone."

His handsome face creased with worry. "Cassie, I really need to talk to you."

She folded her arms, unmoved by his expression. "To put me down or ask me back?"

"I'm sorry about the other day. You looked so good, I was jealous. You know I say horrible things when I'm jealous."

"Or upset, or hurt, or annoyed, or confused, or—"

"I know I wasn't always the best husband. But I've changed. A lot has happened to open my eyes." His voice softened, his eyes pleaded. "Cassie, I need you right now."

She sighed, feeling herself weaken. Not from concern, but curiosity. "Why?"

He hung his head. "My father's dying."

* * *

She shouldn't have come here, Cassie thought, watching Timothy order two snow cones from a street vendor.

The summer air was cool, the sound of kids playing Frisbee and the loud flux of tourists rushed past. Here she was sitting on a bench waiting for Timothy—her ex-husband. The situation had an odd, disquieting feeling. She knew why she had fallen for him. It was not only because he was handsome, although that had been a deciding factor in the beginning. He had been so attentive then, flooding her with compliments with his smooth deep voice. She hadn't felt the need to constantly be "on." He had wanted a friend and she had been one. At that time she would have been anything he asked.

"Strawberry," Timothy announced, handing her the cone.

"My favorite, you remembered."

"Of course." He sat, his voice deepening to an intimate level. "I remember a lot about you."

She held up her hand. "Hold on. I feel a line of bull coming."

"I'm serious. Remember when we used to come here to help you break through your writer's block? We'd stretch out on a blanket and watch the crowd and brainstorm."

"Yes." She had been her happiest then. She'd enjoyed being married, having someone to listen to her ideas and care about her success, but there was so much more to marriage than that. "While I do admit that we had some good times together, they obviously weren't enough to keep your attention."

"Debra meant nothing. You were so busy and I needed someone there for me. I didn't want to bother you so I strayed. But I did it for us."

Cassie bit into her snow cone and frowned. "You had an affair to save our marriage?"

"In a way, yes. I've heard affairs can make a marriage stronger."

She held her forehead. "Damn, I am so sorry. I didn't realize that sleeping with another woman and spending nearly twenty thousand dollars on her was a purely selfish—excuse me, selfless—act on your part to save our marriage. If only I had known that sooner, then perhaps I could have found my own lover and our marriage would have been as strong as ever."

Timothy furrowed his brows as he watched a group of kids. "Why can't you be serious?"

"I can be, but not when I'm shoveling myself out of crap."

He sighed and bit into his melting snow cone.

"So tell me about your father," she said, eager to change the subject.

"He's dying," he said.

"Yes, we've already established that, but don't expect me to coddle you. You never liked him."

"I know but he's still my father."

Cassie stared at him, unmoved by his sentiment.

His voice changed to normal. "Okay, I admit I'm worried about inheriting the business."

"Right, that means you'll have to work. That must be a scary prospect." She patted his knee as she would a little boy. "Don't worry, you'll be fine."

"I know." He rested his arm behind her. "I would just like to have someone by my side during this time. Someone I could trust."

"Your mother's still alive, isn't she?"

He touched her shoulder. "Cass, I need you."

She moved away. "My name is not Cass. Despite the fact that I like some of their music, I am not a former member of the Mamas and the Papas."

Once they had gone to a costume party and Cassie had dressed up as Cass Elliot and been a hit. Timothy remembered this and began humming "Monday, Monday."

"I'm not going to dance so you might as well stop humming."

He stroked her cheek. "Cassie, I know I hurt you. I've always been a selfish bastard, but with you I really tried. I tried to give you whatever you wanted: jewelry, trips, parties. I realize it wasn't enough, but I can learn. What we had was special."

"You're just scared. If you relax, you'll be fine." She stood.

He frowned as she walked away. "Where are you going?"

"To get another snow cone," she called over her shoulder.

He followed her, his face a tight mask of disapproval. "Don't you think one is enough?"

"No." She approached the vendor. "One strawberry cone please." She turned to him. "Aren't you glad you're not married to such a pig ? Oink, oink."

"You're not a pig. You just need to watch your weight."

"Sort of hard to watch it when you're wearing it." She took the cone and paid the vendor, then began walking.

"You're pretty, you know." He shoved his hands in his pockets, examining her profile. "You'd be prettier if you lost a few pounds. Just exercise and watch what you eat. When you get upset eat a cookie or something."

"Eat a cookie?" She laughed. "That's like eating a peanut or a grape. Sorry, but there are certain foods that must be eaten by the handful."

"You can joke all you want, but obesity can lead to many health problems like diabetes or heart disease."

Cassie threw her head back. "Oh, so now I'm not just fat, I'm obese! Soon you'll be calling in the cranes."

Timothy's lips thinned. "I'm just giving you the facts. You're not obese yet, but you could be. Cassie, I only say this because I care about you."

There was that nasty word again—care. Instead of making her feel good it made her feel guilty. It seemed to give people permission to toy with her feelings.

"Thank you for caring about me. I do exercise and try to stay healthy. Is that okay for you?"

An arm snuck around her waist. He pulled her close. "I love you, Cassie."

She wanted to believe that. She wanted to believe that their marriage had been based on more than his need for a wife. That his love for her had mirrored her own. Did one ever get over a first love?

She looked at his appealing earnest face, feeling comfortable in his familiar embrace, and sighed, suddenly feeling impulsive. At least he wasn't dangerous. "Let's go to a movie," she heard herself say.

* * *

If she knew she'd have so much fun with him, she would never have gone. They laughed through a slapstick comedy, took a bus ride around the city, then ate in a Georgetown restaurant. Timothy ordered a salad for her, but she didn't mind because she knew he only did so because he cared. They talked about old friends, old times, and vaguely about the future. When Timothy kissed her at her doorstep a rush of emotion filled her— excitement, pleasure, dismay, shock—but none of it was love. She smiled at him as he waved good-bye, knowing they could never go back to what they once had. He could never enthrall her again because she wasn't the woman she had been. He would never be the man she had thought he was. Feeling renewed, she went inside and went straight to bed.

* * *

She was glad to wake up in her own place, free from the men who tried to shackle her with their "care." She had been vulnerable to both Drake's and Timothy's charms, but now she was back on her turf and could begin to think rationally again. She showered, then headed for the kitchen, avoiding the computer monitor in the corner that seemed to be sneering at her.

The phone rang.

"Hello?"

"Cassie? Hi, Patricia Rodgers. How's the book coming?"

She winced. Although she enjoyed her editor's southern drawl hidden behind an acquired New York accent, she always regretted hearing from her if she didn't have good news. Patricia was always optimistic and full of energy. Cassie had no desire to deflate that energy by telling her the truth—that being stabbed would be less painful than writing this book. "Oh, it's coming along well."

"I'm glad to hear that. Just wanted to make sure we're on schedule."

"Completely," Cassie assured her.

"You realize this book is important?"

Her career breaker or crusher. "Yes. Don't worry."

"Great. Talk to you later." She hung up.

"Hopefully much later," Cassie muttered, replacing the receiver. She went into the kitchen ready for brunch, but stopped at the sight of the big white object in front of her. She stared at it in dismayed fascination, then dialed Drake.

"What is this thing in my kitchen?" she asked, pointing to the object, as if he could see her.

She heard him yawn. "I have no idea what you're talking about."

She let her hand fall. "You replaced my refrigerator."

"So?" He yawned again.

"Stop yawning. Didn't you sleep well?"

"No."

"Why not?"

"Missed you."

She tried to ignore that, but her face still grew warm. His voice sounded extra sexy when he was sleepy. "You shouldn't have replaced my refrigerator."

"Why not?"

"It was mine. You had no right to replace it."

"But it moved."

"It worked."

"Cassie," he said patiently, "I don't know if you realize this, but appliances aren't supposed to move."

"And what about my cutting board?" she asked, spotting a new one near the sink. "And knife block?"

"You don't like them?" He sounded surprised. "I got top of the line."

"That's not the point." She opened the fridge and nearly dropped the phone. "Drake!"

"What?"

"It's filled with food!"

"You're kidding!"

She closed the door. "Don't be funny."

"You couldn't expect me to give you a fridge empty of food."

She opened the freezer, then began pushing buttons on the outside panel. "This must have been expensive."

"It gives me peace of mind. I don't have to worry about your refrigerator attacking you at night. As for the stove—"

She rested a hip against the counter. "The stove stays."

"It's not self-cleaning."

"It stays."

He sighed, resigned. "Fine. I hope you're as loyal to me as you are to broken-down appliances."

"They aren't broken down."

"Okay." He yawned again.

Cassie wrapped the cord around her hand. "I'm going against my better judgment in thanking you, but this in no way means I encourage such arrogant behavior."

"Certainly."

"Thank you."

"You're welcome. So when's your date with Greg?"

She unwrapped the phone cord. "His name is Glen."

"Like it matters."

She would always blame his smug teasing tone for her next comment. "I went out with Timothy yesterday."

His voice didn't change. "Did you have fun?"

"Surprisingly, yes."

"He didn't hurt you?" he asked cautiously.

She suddenly regretted bringing up the topic. She didn't know how she had expected him to respond, but this wasn't it, "No. It was fine."

"What did you do?"

"We went to see a movie and then he took me to dinner." She told him the name of the restaurant.

"Good place. What did you have?"

"He ordered a nice green salad."

There was a pause. "And?"

"That's it."

"If that—Timothy can't afford to spend more, then he shouldn't have taken you there."

"It wasn't the price, it was a... precaution."

"A precaution?"

She rolled her eyes. She wished she didn't have to always explain things to him. If Timothy knew the statistics she'd think he would too. "You know an obese woman is susceptible to many diseases."

"So is a malnourished one. Fortunately, you're neither." His voice deepened with regret. "He did hurt you again, didn't he?"

It had been subtle, he had wrapped it in the guise of caring, love, and affection, but he had hurt her by making her weight an issue, by ordering for her as if she didn't have the mental capacity to order a sensible meal. "He doesn't mean to," she said, beginning to feel depressed. "He's too self-focused to know that what he says and does hurts." Her voice lowered. "I had two snow cones," she confessed like a naughty child.

"So don't have two today. Cassie, there is nothing wrong with you."

She closed her eyes, wishing she could believe him. Wishing she could imagine what he saw in her. "Drake?"

"Hmm?"

"How do you see me?" Her voice was a whisper as if the subject were taboo. "Truly?"

"I've already told you. I think you're beautiful."

"Beautiful." She repeated the word, but still could not apply it to herself. She was cute, sweet, but far from beautiful. She looked down at herself.

Especially with a body like this. "But what about my size? I'm not exactly model material."

"No. They like to choose weird-looking women." He yawned again. "I'm happy with the real thing—true beauty."

She laughed. "I wish I lived on your planet."

"Give me time and I'll take you there."

"Get some sleep."

"I'll try."

She put the phone down and scowled. Damn the man, he always made her feel good. She knew she deserved it, but at what price—marriage? It was impossible. She couldn't risk her freedom no matter how good he made her feel.

* * *

"Was that Cassie?" Eric mumbled into the couch cushions where he had fallen asleep last night.

"You weren't supposed to be listening."

"Blame it on my ears." He stretched and reached for his glasses on the coffee table. "Timothy sounds like a real jerk."

"He is." Drake sat and ran a tired hand down his face, pensive, "I don't like him bothering her."

"I'm sure she can handle herself. If you're not careful you'll end up the villain."

"How do you know?"

"Experience," Eric said smugly. "There was this girl— excuse me, woman—I really liked who was dating a jerk. I had a little face-to-face with him and she told me what a creep I was and promptly fell into his arms."

"Hmm."

He stretched his legs out. "When are you going to see her again?"

"Not sure. She's got a date on Thursday with a guy named Glen. A poetry reading," he added, his voice full of disdain.

Eric nodded. "At Baden's. I heard James Sheffield is reading there. He's great. I helped him through some financial trouble." He narrowed his eyes. "Why are you looking at me like that?"

Drake began to grin. "You like poetry, right?"

He straightened, his tone cautious. "I have a healthy appreciation, but that's all."

"That's good enough."

"Whatever you're thinking, don't."

Drake grabbed a pad and pencil. "I want you to help me write a poem and then ask Sheffield to read it."

Eric scowled at the objects. "I'm not a damn poet. I work with numbers, not words." He rubbed his forehead. "Wait... I did do an excellent poem on logarithms once, but that's it. You're not listening to a word I'm saying, are you?"

Drake scribbled something down on the pad. "Raspberries have to be in it because that's what her lips taste like."

Eric briefly shut his eyes. "I don't want to know this."

"I think I've got the first line. Her raspberry lips capture my heart. I love it when she spreads her legs ap—"

Eric snatched the pad. "This is supposed to be romantic, not erotic. I'm assuming you want this poem to rhyme."

"Of course. Don't all the great poems rhyme?"

"No, but let's not get into that. So her lips are like raspberries."

"Sweetened," he added.

Eric sent him a curious glance, then wrote it down. "Right."

"It was raining outside on our last day together. Mention that. And—"

Eric held up his pen. "Hold on. A poem is not like a recipe. You don't throw in a few words and hope you come up with something." He began scribbling some lines down, then scrunched the page up and tossed it aside. "Leave it alone," he growled when Drake bent to retrieve it.

"But it might be good." He picked it up and began to smooth it out.

"It's not. Leave it or I won't finish."

Drake dropped the paper and sat back. "Poets are such moody people."

Eric worked on the poem for about a half hour.

"Yuh no done yet?" Drake complained, slipping into patois.

"Leave mi nuh. This is crucial." He wrote for a few minutes more, then handed the pad to Drake, who made a few changes and then declared it perfect.

"It will do," Eric reluctantly agreed. "I'll give it to James and hopefully the audience doesn't laugh him off the stage."

Drake grinned triumphantly at the paper in his hands. "It will all be worth the expression on her face."

* * *

The current expression on Cassie's face was disgust. She'd gone through an entire loaf of bread and avoided her computer most of the day. She punished herself by eating nothing for the remainder of the day until she began to feel light-headed and images of Drake occupied her thoughts. Twice she jumped for the phone, wondering if it was him asking to see how she was doing, but the first call was a wrong number and on the second no one replied. She knew Glen was her only chance to break an unhealthy pattern.

* * *

Unfortunately, Glen seemed to be a hard pattern to begin. She tried to hide a yawn as she sat next to him in the cozy bookstore. She couldn't focus on the mournful words of the world-weary poet in front of them. His head hung low, his voice was soft, his long dark hair covered his face. Only a straight pale nose stuck out. She couldn't wait until James Sheffield approached the stage. She wished that the event had been televised so she could have taped it and fast-forwarded to someone interesting.

At least Glen was enjoying himself, tapping the rhythm of the poem on his brown trousers. She was glad she came with him. He was a calming presence. None of the disturbing feelings of attraction arose when he was near; his touch was soft and pleasurable like rice pudding, nothing like the sinful rich chocolate caramel sensations Drake raised in her.

She glanced at Glen and saw him blink back tears as the poet talked about death of beauty and spirit in the wake of society's hold on our emotions. She tugged impatiently on the yellow tunic top she wore. Frankly, she wasn't impressed. Wasn't there anything in life to be happy about? Couldn't they talk about flowers, rain, love? Did true poetry have to reflect such doom and gloom? She shrugged, she cared too much. She was happy to be here with Glen. Timothy would have fallen asleep by now and Drake... no, she would not think about him.

"Are you enjoying yourself?" Glen asked when there was a break for refreshments.

"Immensely," Cassie said, trying to conjure up an enthusiasm she didn't feel. Why did she feel so bored, so restless? This was what she wanted, right? "I noticed that some of the poet's words impressed you."

He popped a grape in his mouth. "Reminded me of my ex-wife."

"A dead spirit?"

He looked shocked by the suggestion. "No, a prisoner of society."

Cassie sighed, remembering Adriana's words. "You're still in love with her, aren't you?"

"No. I just miss her. I miss what we had, or at least what I thought we had." He lifted her chin. "I have no regrets, Cassie. I'm right where I belong."

Cassie felt her heart flutter and a sense of rightness greeted her with eager cheer. She was right where she belonged too.

She was happily munching on a pineapple slice, when James Sheffield approached the podium and read a poem that nearly had her choking on it.

Sweetened raspberries have been my victory
The gift my lover bestows
For in my arms she lays till morning
Her head against my pillow
Outside the rain tapped and cried
Upon the world below
While patiently I waited
To end her nightly doze
At last, I greet her with a smile
And she replies with a kiss
That reminds me of sweetened raspberries
And a soft, gentle mist.

It couldn't be, she thought when the crowd burst into applause. It was too ludicrous, too narcissistic to consider. Yet...

"Are you okay?" Glen asked, taking her hand.

"I'm fine." She forced a smile. "I'm just digesting the words." They were so powerful and had the hint of a sorcerer's spell, casting their magical tentacles around her heart. She stood. "I'll be right back."

He reluctantly let her hand go. "I'll be here."

Cassie made her way through the seats and the people captivated by the next poetry selection and headed for the restroom. She had almost reached her destination when a hand shot out from behind a bookshelf and grabbed her arm.

"Looking for me?" Drake asked, pulling her to him. She smelled the sweet summer evening on his jacket.

"What are you doing here?" she demanded, ignoring the thrill creeping up her spine.

He dismissed her outrage. His arm slid around her waist. "You look beautiful. Did you like my poem?"

"You didn't write it. You don't even like poetry."

"I admit I had some help." His thumb climbed up her spine, sending electrical chills through her body. "But we both know who inspired it." His mouth captured hers for a brief wild moment.

"It was lovely," she allowed, not wanting to encourage him, but unable to pull away. "But you shouldn't be here."

"You know I've waited all evening to see you tell your friend good-bye."

"I'm not telling him good-bye."

"Why not?" He glanced around the bookshelf and stared at Glen with a frown. "He keeps crying."

"That's because he's touched."

"In the head?"

"The poems remind him of his ex-wife."

"How can he be thinking of his ex-wife while sitting next to you? Seems a little off."

She scowled.

He outlined her lips with his finger. "Forgive me, I can't help being unkind to the competition."

She pushed his hand away. "He's not your competition."

His eyes lit up with the confidence of expected victory.

"He's not?"

"No," she said coolly. "You're not even in the running."

The expression in his eyes turned flat—a dull bronze. His arms fell from her waist. For a long moment he didn't say anything, just stared at her in

his intense unreadable way. "At least you're honest," he said eventually, his voice neutral. He
shoved his hands in his pockets and turned.

She was ready to see him go, but something else
made her call his name. "Drake—"

He spun around, his eyes spitting fire. "What?
Do you wish to soothe me by telling me it wouldn't
work? How you'd like to remain friends?" He
pointed a finger at her. "Erase it from your mind.
Now go back to your drippy friend and do not
waste my time or yours. I will not be one of your
toy boys." He turned on his heel and stalked away.

Cassie stood riveted, waiting for the feeling of
freedom to come crashing over her. Instead a sense
of overwhelming loss crawled over her skin, leaving
her feeling raw and vulnerable. The sorcerer was
out of her life, gone forever, leaving her to the
world that was familiar. Why did forever seem
more like a sentence than a gift? Tossing aside practical thought, she ran after him. But she was too
late. The night had taken him. Life continued.
People pushed past her, cars drove by, the stars
twinkled above, and she was alone—free. Blinking
back tears of frustration and emptiness, she went
back inside the store.

Chapter Ten

"*A*w, hell," Eric muttered when he saw his brother's face as he entered the cafe.

Jackie turned in her seat and said something even more colorful. She looked at Eric. "I guess things didn't go according to plan."

"Yes, the fact that Cassie isn't here says it all."

Drake was supposed to bring Cassie to the cafe so they could meet her and treat her to dessert, but it was obvious that wasn't going to happen.

Drake sat down and reached for the cigarettes inside his jacket pocket.

"This is a nonsmoking section," Eric mentioned as Drake raised the cigarette to his lips.

He sent him a cool glance. "Why would you get a table here?"

"Because we don't smoke."

"And we want you to stop," Jackie added.

"Well, it won't be today." He lit the cigarette.

Jackie snatched it away and stubbed it out while Eric asked for a table in the smoking section. Once seated, Drake lit up another cigarette and stared out at the crowd. "I don't want to talk about it," he said, feeling their eyes on him.

"But you have to," Jackie said. "Perhaps we could help you."

"I don't want or need help."

"You shouldn't have written her a poem." She rested her elbows on the table and shook her head. "What do you two know about poetry? She was probably offended."

He slowly exhaled, watching the smoke float upward. "It wasn't the poem, it was me."

"But what did you do?"

He glared at her. "I don't want to talk about it."

Eric lifted a menu. "Let's at least order something while we slowly die from secondhand smoke."

* * *

"I should give this Cassie woman a piece of my mind," Jackie said as she finished her pecan pie.

Eric studied the bill. "What would you have left?"

"Shut up."

"Don't worry about her," Drake said. "It's over." He tossed some money on the table. "That should cover me."

Eric handed him back the money. "I'm paying."

Drake ignored him and stood. He zipped up his jacket, glanced around the cafe, then looked at his brother and sister. "Don't call me tonight." He pointed a finger at Jackie. "I mean it. No badda mi."

She nodded. He left.

"If I ever get my hands on that Cassie, I don't know what I'll do," Jackie grumbled as she watched Drake leave. "She really hurt him."

Eric shrugged, shuffling through his wallet. He would return Drake's money later. "He'll live. He's been hurt before." His voice dropped below his sister's hearing. "We all have."

* * *

Dread fell on Cassie as the elevator ascended to her floor. She didn't know how to end the evening without hurting Glen's feelings. She knew he'd want to come in to talk, perhaps share a drink, but all she wanted to do was get rid of him.

"I had a wonderful time as usual," she said, stepping out on her floor. She inwardly sighed when he followed.

He rested a casual arm on her shoulders. "I'm glad you enjoyed yourself."

"Oh, yes," she said, trying to resist the urge to shrug his arm away.

Door 712 creaked open. "Have a good time?" Mr. Gianolo asked.

Cassie forced a smile. "Lovely."

"Where did you two go?"

"Baden's to hear a poetry reading."

"I hope you had a nice nap." He chuckled at his own wit and closed the door.

Cassie turned on the lights and watched Glen make himself comfortable on the couch. "I'm really not in the mood to entertain," she said.

"That's okay, I won't stay long."

She put down her bag, resigned. "What would you like to drink?"

"Juice is fine."

She opened the fridge. Boy, was she hungry! She bit her lip at the sight of a barbecued turkey leg, at the thought of making deviled eggs, or wrapping apple slices in cheese. She grabbed grape juice and closed the door. She'd indulge once Glen left. It took her nearly twenty minutes to get rid of him. He discussed the poets while food called her from the fridge. The stove begged for the smell of sweet blueberry muffins, the toaster asked for a nice crisp bagel, a bag of chips and a box crackers shouted from the cupboards. When he finally stood she nearly wept with joy. Once she'd shut the door behind him, the binge began—when it was over she did cry. She felt like a weak-willed slob. Why had she done that to herself? It was Drake's fault of course. If he hadn't come into her life, she wouldn't be stuffing her face now. But no, that was wrong. She had always done this when she was upset and she was definitely upset, but she'd get over it. She would exercise tomorrow and make up for today.

A week passed and she felt much better about the binge. She had lost five pounds by sticking to a strict low-calorie diet and exercising twice a day. Her book was coming along—slowly, but at least that was something.

She had just flipped on the computer to begin a day's work, when the doorbell rang. She glanced through the peephole, then rested her forehead against the door, gathering her strength. She finally opened it.

Adriana stepped inside. "You haven't returned my calls," she accused.

"I've been busy. I'm working on a book, remember?"

Her friend sat down, smoothing out her white shorts. "How is it going?"

"Fine."

"Liar." She crossed her legs and sat forward. "So how was your date with Glen? I hope you brought enough tissues for the sob stories."

"I had a lovely time."

"Lovely?" She opened her compact and touched up her lipstick. "How boring. So how is Drake doing?"

"I don't know." She headed for the kitchen, ready to avoid the subject. "Would you like anything?"

"No." Adriana snapped the compact closed and narrowed her eyes. "What have you done?"

Cassie folded her arms. "Why do you assume I've done anything? Perhaps he just got tired of me."

"I know this is your fault because you're Ms. Sabotage."

Cassie flopped down onto the couch. "Oh, please."

"Remember Nick Terrel?"

"No."

Adriana waved a finger at her. "He liked you in our freshman year, but you never gave him a chance."

"He was a frat boy."

"What's your point?"

"It wouldn't have worked."

"We'll never know that." Adriana crossed her legs and swung her foot. "So what did you do?"

"I didn't do anything." Cassie stopped—that was a lie. "I really liked him but he wanted more than I could give him and I wanted to save him any heartache." She rested her head back. "He wrote me a poem for heaven's sake."

Adriana stared at her, stunned. "What?"

Cassie sat up. "And had it read at the poetry reading I went to with Glen. Talk about gall!"

"You mean he had the gall to publicly display how much he cares for you?" she said with mock outrage. "That bastard."

"I know," Cassie agreed, missing her sarcasm.

Adriana rested her head back and threw an arm over her eyes. "You could drive a friend to drink," she moaned.

"Why can't you see this from my point of view?"

"I'd be afraid to. Drake was perfect for you. A perfect remedy after a virus like Timothy."

She bit her lower lip. "Actually I went out with Timothy a couple of weeks ago," she confessed.

Adriana sat up and shuddered. "What for?"

"His father is dying. He wanted someone by his side."

"Tell him to get a psychiatrist, he can afford it."

"We had a really nice time," she said, thoughtful.

Adriana rolled her eyes and stood. "Let's go shopping."

She looked at her, confused. "Why?"

"Because it will make me feel better."

* * *

"This is an expensive way to raise your spirits," Cassie said, reading the price tag on the blouse Adriana was admiring.

"Be quiet and pick something. I'll buy it for you."

Cassie adjusted the hat and sunglasses she was wearing. She hated clothes shopping. Nothing she liked was ever in her size. "No, thanks. I don't feel like searching in the big and beautiful section to-day."

Adriana pointed. "Then check that rack for me. I need to find a silver blouse."

Cassie began searching through the rack and picked up a grayish blouse. She held it up against her to see how the color would look against her slacks.

"Excuse me, ma'am," a sales clerk said. "If you would like to find designer clothes in your size I could direct you to our women's section."

The fact that the clerk was a coiffured older woman with a sweet smile and good intentions didn't quell Cassie's desire to wring her neck.

"I'm looking for a friend," she said in a tight voice.

"Oh." The sales assistant took a hasty step back. "Okay. If you need anything, I'll be right over there." She pointed to the checkout table.

Cassie tried to smooth her sneer into a smile. "Thank you." She put the blouse back and tapped Adriana on the shoulder. "Come on, let's go. I've been spotted as an outsider."

"What are you talking about?" Adriana asked, running her hand over the soft material of a blouse.

"Never mind." She glanced around the store, eager to leave. "Are you ready yet?"

"No. I can't feel better unless I buy something."

"Then I'll be in the bookstore next door."

"Fine." She put the blouse in her cart and picked up another. She sent Cassie a sly glance. "Promise me that if you meet a wonderful handsome man you'll run in the opposite direction."

Cassie playfully bumped her with her hip. "I'll do my best."

* * *

She browsed through the fiction section, then headed for self-help. It was always good to see the competition and borrow some ideas. She was reaching for *1,000 Ways to Be Romantic* high on the shelf, when a large man behind her grabbed it.

"Is this what you wanted?" he asked politely.

She stopped. She knew that voice. She took a step back from the shelf and promptly trod on his foot. She turned to her present nightmare—Drake.

"I'm sorry," she said, making her voice breathy. She lowered her hat and pushed up her glasses.

Drake rubbed his instep. "It was my fault. I was standing too close. Is this the book you wanted?" He held it up.

She took it and held it close, affecting a demure smile. "Yes, thank you."

He took out a piece of paper. "I'm looking for Surviving Crowds. Could you help me find it?"

Leave, leave, leave, her mind urged her, but her body wouldn't move. "It's a rather dull book. What do you need it for?"

"Class reunion in about a month."

"That book is for people with real social dysfunction."

"I come pretty close," he said grimly.

"No, you don't. I mean I doubt it," she quickly amended when his face changed. She searched through the books and picked one. "*How to Please a Crowd.* It's quick and to the point."

"Thanks." He flipped through the pages. "Hopefully this will help, nothing else seems to."

She thought of his dog-eared copy of *The Fear of Ridicule* and winced.

"Hey, Drake, make a new friend?" a young woman, asked approaching them.

Cassie cleared her throat. "I guess I should be going." She was ready to make an exit. She didn't want to meet the new woman in his life. She was pretty and petite and looked oddly familiar.

He nudged the woman with his elbow. "This is my sister, Jackie."

"Nice to meet you," Cassie said, inching away.

Drake stared at the book, then at her. "What's your name?"

She glanced at one of the book displays. "Barbara."

"Thanks for the suggestion, Barbara."

The way he said her name made her swallow. He seemed to caress the syllables of her name. He was definitely a flirt.

Jackie took the book from him and began scanning the chapters. "Do you know any good books on how to choose women? My brother could really use some help."

He snatched the book. "She doesn't care, Jackie."

She ignored him. "I mean this one woman pretended to like him, then stomped on his heart and cooked it."

He pushed her away. "Why don't you go find yourself a nice picture book to read?"

She shoved him back. "Let me finish, she'll like this story. Women love to hear stories like this." She turned to Cassie. "Both my brothers wrote this woman a poem and had it read by a famous poet and she didn't even care. Talk about a real—"

Drake covered her mouth and grinned sheepishly. "I made the mistake of encouraging her to speak."

Cassie nodded. "Well, good-bye." She turned and shoved her book in the arts section and left the store— her mind reeling. Was that how his family saw her? Was that how he saw her? She felt awful and thought of a nice place to grab a sundae.

* * *

Drake frowned at the cover of the book given to him, then returned it to the shelf.

"She seemed nice," Jackie said. "You should have asked her out."

"Sort of hard when you're driving her away."

"I wasn't driving her away. I was making her interested. Women like men who write poetry."

He gave her a significant glance.

"Right. Not all." She disappeared into the reference section.

Eric came up to him as he grabbed another book from the shelf. "Was that who I thought it was?"

He flipped through the pages seeing nothing. He wanted to feel anger, but couldn't ignore the layer of hurt. He kept his voice level. "Yes, that was Cassie."

* * *

Cassie almost stepped on the single yellow rose left on her welcome mat, when she returned from the gym the next day. There was no note attached, but she guessed who it was from—Timothy. She preferred it to the large bouquets. She smelled it as she opened the door, then dropped it in the trash bin on her way to the shower.

After her shower, she stared at her computer screen, her mind miles away from the necessity of completing her book. She had hurt him. That was what upset her so much. Not the fact that she had had to end their relationship, but the manner in which it was done. She finished her spaghetti TV dinner—it was supposedly low fat and tasted like it. She threw the tray away and stretched out on the couch. Why was Drake still buying self-help books? Didn't he know how wonderful he was? If she had been the type to settle down and marry, she would have snatched him up right away. She sighed. She hadn't done his ego much good rejecting him the way she had.

No, she had to fix things. She would fix things. She sat up and tapped her foot as an idea came into her mind. Perhaps she could give him confidence, help him through his reunion, and then once it was over he would discover that his desire for her came from a need, a lack of confidence, rather than from attraction. She knew all about transference of emotion and couldn't fault him. She was safe.

She sat in front of her computer once again. Perhaps they would end up as really good friends like she was with Kevin. Then she could feel happy knowing she helped someone reach their true potential, although getting Drake there wouldn't be too hard. She absently tapped her keyboard, watching a row of Es appear on the screen. The problem was how to convince him to take her back.

* * *

He couldn't focus, which was rare and a bad sign. Fortunately, his staff was competent and the business of the restaurant proceeded smoothly, allowing some lapses in the owner's mental capacity. He spent his time talking to Lance about deliveries and staff issues—namely Cedric's inaptitude—but he did so in an absentminded fashion that made the day a blur.

"Uh-oh," Monica, his pastry chef, groaned, shaking her strawberry-blond head.

Drake forced himself to concentrate on the sharp hazel gaze. "Uh-oh, what?"

"That's the second time you've called a dish nice. You've never called a chocolate soufflé sundae nice before, especially after you've tasted it."

"I apologize," he said humbly, taking another bite. "It is brilliant, creamy, with just the right amount of caramel. I have no complaints or suggestions."

"Thank you." Monica had soon gotten over her crush on Drake, but was curious as to what or who now occupied his thoughts. Unfortunately, getting him to open up was like trying to bite into steel.

"Henson, there's someone to see you," Lance called, whizzing through the kitchen.

"I don't have any appointments today." He rinsed his hands at the sink. "Make up an excuse."

"I've used three of our best ones, but she won't buy it."

He dried his hands on his apron. "She?"

"Don't worry, it's not Pamela. She's a cute little thing, you wouldn't think she'd be so stubborn."

Drake silently swore, annoyed with the abrupt speed at which his heart began to race. "You know where to put her," he grumbled, quickly untying his apron.

A few moments later he saw Cassie staring out at the city scene that the gallery dining lounge offered her. She stood in the middle of the arched window, a small figure dressed in a red blouse like a candle in the window of a great cathedral.

He took a deep breath, determined not to weaken first, though the sight of her reminded him of the precious nights they had spent together.

"Well?" His tone was curt.

Surprised, she turned and bumped into a table, causing the vase of flowers to tip over and soak the tablecloth.

"Oh, I'm sorry," she said, righting the vase.

"Never mind." He seized her hand as she tried to wipe up the mess with a napkin. "Why are you here?"

She sat down. "You have a beautiful place."

He shrugged. It was one of many. "Planning on doing a course here?"

"Would you attend?"

"If you recall, I'm not one of your success stories."

She glanced around. "I couldn't afford it anyway."

Her nonchalance drove through his patience. He clasped his hands behind him. "Cassie, what do you want?"

"Isn't it obvious? I want you."

Damn. Her words were like water eroding his resolve. He fought the dangerous impulse of grabbing her right now. Surrendering to her mercy. "Is that right?"

"Yes. I made a mistake before. I thought I wanted something else." She let her shoulders rise and fall, her butterscotch eyes melting into his. "But all I want is you."

Impulse won. He pulled her out of her chair and into his arms in one skillful swoop. His lips were on hers before she could speak. For both it was a homecoming. Their lips engaged in all the perfect eloquence that fevered passion communicates.

He drew away. "You didn't expect me to argue, did you?" he whispered, meeting her stunned gaze.

She could only nod.

He smiled, turning her insides to putty. "Isn't it nice to be proven wrong?" He captured her mouth again.

The hunger of his kiss shattered her calm. No longer would she deny him the truth of how he affected her. How his very lips drank in her essence, her soul. How the taste of him was better than any meal she'd ever consumed.

"I'm frightened," she gasped, pulling back from the intensity of emotion that gripped them both. She hoped she was doing the right thing. It certainly felt good.

"Of what?" He gently twirled a strand of hair around his finger. "That I howl at full moons? That I'll try to suck your blood?" He nipped the sensitive slope of her neck.

She shut her eyes, taking pleasure in being in his arms again. *No, that I'll fall in love with you and agree to marry you.* But she knew her fears could not be uttered aloud.

She shook her head. "I don't know," she said helplessly. "I just am."

"No worries, love," he said, his voice deepening into an island lilt that fell over her like cream. "Everything is perfect."

* * *

Cassie listened to the soft sigh of cotton sheets against Drake's skin as he moved against them. Some women needed lots of foreplay; for her the afterplay was becoming one of her favorite things. Drake was a thorough and compassionate lover and no part of her was ever ignored by his impatient, cunning fingers and hungry mouth. It was like a well-prepared dessert after a satisfying meal. Right now he was doing something to her ear that was probably illegal in some states. She lifted her foot toward his inner thigh.

His voice was hushed. "Let's turn on the lights."

Her foot fell to the bed. "Another time." Twenty pounds from now. Maybe never.

He sighed and rested his cheek against her chest. The night growth felt rough like a cat's tongue. "I just want to see you."

"You don't need to see me. Touch is enough."

He kissed one full breast. "Hmm."

She stroked his hair. "I'm sorry I hurt you."

"My shoulders are wide."

"Yes, you've said that. That's not the point."

"What's the point?" He lifted her hand and sucked her pinkie.

She pulled away, determined to do her duty. "You know you're wonderful, right?"

He stiffened. "Where are you going with this?"

"I just want you to know that you can get any woman you want."

"Good, because I have her right here." He buried his face in her chest.

She closed her eyes, moaning with pleasure. He was effectively distracting her. "Not just me. You don't have to be shy about..." Her words trailed off, because Drake had halted as her words sank in. A dangerous quiet descended.

He lifted himself on his elbows. She couldn't read his face, but his words fell around her like lead stones. "If this was pity sex to boost my self-esteem, I swear I won't be able to control my next actions."

She kissed the tip of his nose. "Calm down, it wasn't. I'm sorry I'm not making sense."

"Then stop talking," he ordered. And she did.

* * *

The doorbell rang early the next morning as Drake sat in the kitchen deciding what to make for breakfast. He raced to answer it before it woke Cassie. He opened the door halfway, knowing of only two people it could be.

"We brought breakfast," Jackie said, waving a plastic bag. Eric added, "And coffee."

"I won't be able to join you," he said, trying to sound regretful, but failing.

Jackie frowned; Eric began to smile.

"Who is she?" he asked.

Jackie stared at her brother's smug grin. "Who is who?"

Eric's smile widened. "Can't you tell he has company?"

"No." She tried to peek around Drake. "Where is she?"

Eric took a sip of his coffee. "Better yet. What's her name?"

Drake rubbed the back of his neck. "She's sleeping." He hesitated. "It's Cassie."

"You took her back!" Jackie screeched.

Drake covered her mouth. "Keep your voice down. You won't like me if you wake her up."

She removed his hand. "But you're taking her back after the way she treated you?" She stomped her foot like an angry child. "That's not right."

Drake looked at Eric, knowing he would understand. "She comes into the Blue Mango wearing this hot red blouse. I ask her why she's there. She says because I want you."

"Enough said." They hit fist over fist.

Jackie was not convinced. "The woman says 'I want you' and that's enough? No pleading, no begging?"

Eric adjusted his glasses. "I'm sure the sex made up for it."

"Is that all you guys think about?"

Eric was silent; Drake flexed his fingers. "Food comes in a close second," he finally said.

Jackie rolled her eyes in disgust and marched to the elevator. Eric quickly saluted and followed.

* * *

He was happy to have Cassie back in his life. Although he was beginning to discover some of their differences. "Are you sure this will look good in my kitchen?" he asked, staring wearily at the elaborate wooden bowl Cassie had persuaded him to buy.

"Trust me. It has the same feel as your kitchen. Look at the intricate wood burning. It just screamed out at me."

He put the bowl back in its bag. "You know I worry about your close relationship with inanimate objects."

Cassie laughed. He reached for her hand but she pretended to dust something off her jeans. She didn't want to draw too much attention to them by looking like a couple.

"I think I'll buy you a new pair of jeans," Drake said.

She frowned at him. "Why?"

"Because that's the fourth time you've brushed them off. Unless it's a nervous habit."

"Partly nervous. I feel awkward being affectionate in public."

He raised a brow. "Holding hands is too affectionate?"

"Blame my mother. The only time she'd be affectionate in public was when she'd pick fuzz off my sweaters."

Drake was about to reply when a voice caught their attention.

"Mr. Henson!" Pamela called. "It's good to see you."

"If only I could say the same," he muttered. Cassie hit him. He cleared his throat. "How are you doing, Pamela?"

"Just fine." She flashed an impish grin, tapping one of her large earrings. "I would be doing better if I got a position at a certain culinary establishment."

"Hmm."

She looked at Cassie, making her the new focus of her charm. "Hi, Mrs. Henson." She grabbed Cassie's hand and enthusiastically shook it. "I'm sorry. I haven't introduced myself. I'm Pamela Watkins...." She then went on to describe herself and her present and future goals and talents.

"You sound very experienced," Cassie cut in when the girl took a breath.

"That's not all," she said, sounding very much like a late-night infomercial. "I can also cook. You've got to try this." She dug into her backpack and pulled out a container. She lifted the lid and revealed cream pastries. "Take one."

Cassie took one; Drake watched a passing cyclist.

"This is delicious," she said, amazed. "Drake, taste one."

He glanced at the pastry Cassie held out to him. "I trust your judgment."

"Tell me this isn't the work of a future pastry chef," Pamela said.

Drake shrugged. "I wouldn't know."

She clasped her hands together. "Please give me a chance, Mr. Henson."

He shoved his hands in his pockets, reluctantly impressed by the young woman's tenacity. He had always felt that persistence should be rewarded somehow. "I'll think about it."

She let out a little squeal and grabbed his arm. "Oh, thank you."

"I only said I'd think about it," he grumbled.

"I know, that's a big improvement." She handed Cassie the container. "Enjoy." She rushed off.

Cassie watched her go, thoughtful. "I wonder why she called me Mrs. Henson. I'm not wearing a ring."

Drake scowled. "Because she knew that would please me. The little brat."

She smiled. "Stop scowling. She's adorable."

"Like a little pit bull."

"Why won't you offer her a job?"

"Because she doesn't need my help. She comes from a good family and goes to a prestigious school. What good would my helping her do? She has plenty of opportunities."

"So?" she said, not completely understanding his logic. "That doesn't mean she won't work hard. These pastries are good."

"Great. Then she'll go to a fine culinary institute and make a good living. You don't have to worry about her. I try to help the underprivileged. My goal is—" He abruptly stopped.

Cassie followed the direction of his gaze and saw a group of teenaged boys hanging outside a store. She tugged on his jacket. "What's wrong?"

His voice was almost too low to hear, heavy with a layer of anger. "One of those boys is supposed to be at work."

She grabbed his arm before he went toward them. "Well, don't talk to him now in front of his friends."

His eyes blazed, but she knew the anger wasn't directed at her. "Why not?" he asked in a harsh tone.

"Because you'll embarrass him."

He smiled coldly. She immediately let his arm go. "Good." He walked up to the crowd. "Cedric, you're supposed to be at work."

Cedric sent him a bored look. "I'm there, man, in a minute."

"You don't have a minute. You either leave now or there won't be a job for you."

Cedric turned to his friends. "I'll check with you. I've got business." Once his friends were out of hearing he said, "Get off my back. You think you're my old man or something?"

"I'm your boss. The man who pays your salary."

Cedric flashed a superior grin. "Man, you ain't doing me no favors with your little restaurant job. I could make your salary and more in two months."

"True," Drake said slowly. "But would you live to spend it all?"

Cedric rubbed his nose and kept his smile. A smile that didn't reach his eyes. "We all gotta die sometime."

"I understand—"

His voice hardened. "You don't understand a damn thing. You've got your fancy car, money, your little restaurant." He glanced at Cassie. "And that—"

Drake's eyes turned to stone. "Whatever you say about her, you say about your mother." He measured him in one quick glance. "A woman I feel sorry for." He turned.

Cedric watched him, pushing down any feelings of regret with anger. He was glad to be rid of that job. Glad to become his own man. He could do better than cleaning up after other people and taking orders all day. Henson didn't know what the real world was about. It was about honor. And there was no honor in being a damn busboy. He turned to his friends, who were laughing at some old lady struggling with her bags as she crossed the street, her panty hose slipping down to her ankles. His first impulse was to go and help her, but he brushed the thought aside and joined in with his friends. Where would he be without them?

* * *

"Do you want to talk about it?" Cassie asked, watching Drake check his pockets and swear.

"I forgot my cigarettes."

"That's not what I mean."

"No. I don't want to talk about it." It made him angry. It angered him to see Cedric throw away all that he was offering. It angered him that he had failed.

She tugged on his sleeve. "You haven't failed him. He made a choice."

He slanted her a quick glance.

"The real issue is that you now have a position free for someone who will appreciate it."

Drake shook his head and walked numbly through the crowd. Suddenly, he felt soft fingers curl around his hand. He glanced down and felt some of his anger ebb as he faced the truth, then gave her hand a gentle squeeze.

* * *

"Do you want me to call Pamela for you?" Cassie asked once they'd reached his place.

Drake placed the new bowl on the dining table. "I don't have her phone number."

"That's supposed to go in the kitchen."

He picked up the bowl and moved it there.

"You do have her number," she said when he returned to the living room.

"Where?"

"She taped it to this container."

"Figures. If I'm not careful she might tattoo it to my— arm," he said, censoring himself.

She rested a hand on her hip and studied him. "You don't understand her persistence, do you?"

He shrugged.

"A good home doesn't automatically equal opportunity. Sure, things come more easily, but you still have to fight for what you want. I got into college with my parents' help, but didn't know what I was going to do until Mrs. Soughton told me I should be a speaker. If she hadn't been my mentor, I could have floundered like a lot of kids. The people who succeed are the ones who work at it. The ones who want an easy break, either rich or poor, are the ones left behind."

Drake pinched the bridge of his nose, stared at the phone for a moment, then dialed.

* * *

Cassie was right. Success came to those who worked for it and Pamela would definitely be successful. In only two weeks she had blended into the staff, secured three repeat customers, and elevated the overall of appearance of the restaurant.

"Have you told her what a wonderful job she is doing?" Cassie asked as they sat in his restaurant before the dinner crowd came.

Drake shrugged. "Why would I? She knows."

"Everybody needs an ego boost sometimes."

He rested his chin on his fist and watched the tables being set. "I doubt it."

"Since you missed my last class on social graces, let me show you the art and benefit of flattery." She turned. "Pamela, come here."

Pamela approached the table wringing a dishrag with nervous fingers. "Yes, Mrs. Henson?"

"Actually, I'm not—"

"She has something to say to you," Drake cut in. Cassie narrowed her eyes; he smiled.

"I just wanted to tell you what a wonderful job you're doing," she said. "You keep the customers happy and we adored your cream pastries."

Pamela loosened her grip on the rag and sent Drake a quick look. "I could make you some more if you'd like."

"We would love that."

The girl smiled and went back to her duty, completing it with extra care.

Cassie looked at Drake with triumph. "You can now thank me since you'll have an even more productive employee and free cream pastries."

He winked. "You're a true talent."

"It doesn't take talent, just common courtesy." She leaned forward and lowered her voice. "It doesn't hurt to be nice."

"I am nice." He straightened. "She has a job, doesn't she?"

Cassie stood. "I don't know why I try."

"I'll see you tonight."

"I might find somebody nicer and not come."

"Fortunately, I have many other talents." He clasped his hands behind his head and grinned. "You'll come."

* * *

Neither said anything when she arrived on at his place that evening. He just grinned knowingly and she frowned at him. Once inside, they snuggled on the couch and settled in for a pleasant evening watching TV. They were laughing at a sitcom when Drake's cell phone rang.

"Hello? Yeah, she's here." He looked down at Cassie, who was resting her head on his lap. "Sure, that sounds fine. Okay, see you then." He flipped it closed.

She glanced up at him, curious. "Who was that?"

"Adriana."

Cassie narrowed her eyes. "Adriana called your cell phone? How did she get the number?"

"I gave it to her." He reached over her and grabbed chips from the bowl on the coffee table.

"Why?"

He frowned. "In case she got lonely. Why else?"

She pinched him.

He rubbed his arm. "It's in case something happened to you, she could reach me."

"You're so sweet." She took some of his chips.

"I'm afraid I can't say the same," he mumbled, grabbing some more.

"Why did she call?"

"She wants to invite us out. Her boyfriend is playing at the Colossal." Cassie sat up, alarmed. "Oh, no, and you said yes?"

"Sure, why not?"

She fell back into the cushions. "Because we are going to regret this."

* * *

Her words were prophetic.

"I had a nightmare similar to this once," Drake said. "Of course I had the benefit of waking up then."

Drake, Cassie, and Adriana sat in the dimly lit room of the Colossal listening to a rock band screech its way to the crescendo of an unintelligible song. The Colossal was a known platform for people hoping to display their talents, or lack thereof, to a receptive audience either too bored or too drunk to boo them off the stage. The wallpaper was a metallic green that caused everything to shimmer as if one had stepped into the ocean, sipped the water, and started hallucinating.

Cassie had enjoyed coming to the place with Adriana when they were both in their college bohemian phase, but now looking around at the crowd that had more piercings than a voodoo doll and clothes that were most likely tattooed on, she felt too old for the place.

She picked up her tequila sunrise, unsympathetic to Drake's discomfort. "I had warned you."

"Mike's much better than this group," Adriana assured him. She could pass for a mermaid with her hair piled high on her head and falling down her face in ringlets. Her bluish gray top changed colors when she moved and her earrings resembled starfish. In contrast, Cassie wore a simple gold dress and teardrop earrings.

"That's not saying much." Cassie frowned. "That's like saying dirt tastes better than mud."

Adriana ignored her and clapped when the band finished.

Cassie nudged Drake as Corrosion of Sanity, Mike's band, entered the stage. He turned to her, curious.

She handed him two earplugs. "You will need these. Trust me."

He grinned and they both plugged their ears before Adriana could notice.

* * *

Mike approached their table at the end of his performance. Cassie and Drake pretended to drop something so that they could remove their earplugs. Adriana greeted him with a hug.

"What did you think?" he asked. He was a large man the size of a buffalo and the color of bark with small eyes that made him look as if he were constantly squinting. He had a shaved head and wore two silver hoop earrings, a brown leather vest, and jeans.

"It was wonderful," Adriana said, touching his arm in a light affectionate gesture.

His slitty gaze shifted to Cassie. "And you?"

Cassie hesitated. From behind his broad frame she saw Adriana mouth, "Be nice."

"It was amazing." She never knew music could sound so awful.

He nodded and glanced at Drake. "What about you, man?"

Drake took a long swallow of his drink and everyone held their breath until he set the glass down. "I think you could set a guitar on fire, but should leave the vocals to someone else." Preferably someone who could sing.

A stunned silence dropped like an atomic bomb, leaving everyone shell-shocked.

"You think?" Mike asked, his eyes narrowing to crescent moons.

"Yes."

Mike threw his head back in a shout of laughter and happily punched Drake in the shoulder. Cassie winced for him. Drake didn't flinch. "You really think I can rip, man?"

He nodded. "Focus your energies and you'll discover that your fingers are going to take you places."

Mike slapped him on the back. "Come on, man. I want you to meet the guys and tell them what you said. I've been trying to tell them to get a new sing-er." He headed toward the back room. Drake shrugged at the two speechless women and followed.

"What was that?" Adriana finally asked, feeling it was safe to breathe.

Cassie held her head. "God, for a second there I thought Mike was going to rearrange Drake's face."

"He sure took a risk by being honest like that."

"It seems Drake likes to take risks."

Still stunned, they hardly listened to the next band on the stage.

An hour later, Drake and Mike returned, looking like old buddies. Drake had his black jacket swung over his shoulder and his blue shirt hanging out of his trousers while Mike walked with a hand on Drake's arm, his vest open.

"Where have you two been?" Adriana asked.

"They've been drinking," Cassie said. She watched in disgust as Mike pulled out his chair as if it were a monumental task.

"I'm afraid only one of us has," Drake said, steadying Mike before he slid out of the chair.

"What have you done to him?" Adriana demanded as her date began to make a pillow out of napkins.

"Adriana," Drake said with the patience of a knowledgeable older brother, "he's a great guy and a lot of fun, but you and I both know you deserve better."

Cassie grinned and nudged him. "Go on," she urged. "Give Mike the lecture you gave Kevin, except mention the drinking."

"What lecture?" Adriana asked.

"Never mind. Cassie's about to get one of her own. Thanks for the experience." He dragged out Cassie's chair and pulled her to her feet. "Let's go."

Once they were outside, Cassie shook her head in frustration. "I knew this night would be awful."

Drake cupped his ear. "What?"

She raised her voice a fraction. "I said, I knew this night would be awful."

"What was that?"

She glared at him, catching his joke. "I suppose I could resort to sign language. How could you say those things to Mike?"

He shrugged, unaware of the mortal danger Cassie believed he had avoided. "The man has more passion than talent and in this world that's what counts. There are a number of brilliant starving artists and stupid millionaires."

She sniffed. "You've definitely got the stupid part right, but did you have to make him drunk?"

"It's not as if I poured the drinks down his throat."

"Adriana is going to think I made you embarrass her date." She sighed with regret. "I never liked him."

He squeezed her arm. "No, she's smart. She knows the truth."

Someone rested a hand on their shoulders. "Can a third party join this cozy twosome?" Adriana asked behind them.

Drake held out his arm and Adriana looped hers through his. Cassie teased them about looking like a couple, but their mutual glare quickly ended the attempt.

At least Drake liked her, Cassie thought. Timothy and Adriana had never gotten along. Of course, the fact that Timothy was a selfish bastard was a factor. He liked to keep Cassie to himself.

They walked down the sidewalk crowded with people who enjoyed and thrived in the night. The city lights bounced off the buildings in a burst of raucous colors. At Adriana's insistence, they stopped in a music store to look around. Adriana headed for alternative music, Cassie to light rock, and Drake to classical. They met in the world music section discussing the various attributes of different artists, then raced to capture a free headset. Cassie won, doing a little victory dance.

After Drake paid for their items, they headed to a restaurant to get something to eat. They were teasing each other about their bad taste in music when Kristin and Eric approached the table.

"Drake!" Kristin said loud enough for a few patrons to turn their heads. She wiggled toward the table in a purple tube dress. "It's so nice to see you laughing and now I know why." She glanced at Cassie, then Adriana. "Eric told me you were seeing someone and she's captivating. Malcolm was wrong. She isn't fat. God, he made her sound like you'd harpooned a whale. If only all woman could carry curves that well." She held her hand out to Adriana. "It's nice to meet you, Cassie."

For the real Cassie, the world stopped, allowing her to hit reality with a sickening thud. She had gone through the night feeling beautiful, forgetting what she looked like, how others perceived her. Now, like an unexpected slap, she knew the truth and it hurt so much that she quickly blinked back tears.

"You've made a mistake, Kristin," Eric gently scolded, sliding into a seat next to Cassie. "My name's Eric." He held out his hand, offering her a smile and serious brown eyes that were kind and understanding behind round, golden frames. His gaze was perceptive to her present feelings and so full of sympathy that she had to swallow in order not to burst into tears.

She decided to laugh instead and make light of the humiliating situation. She shook his hand. "Nice to meet you. My name is Shamu, but most people just call me Cassie."

Kristin looked devastated, all color leaving her pretty face. "I'm so sorry."

"Not as sorry as Malcolm will be," Drake promised.

Eric caught his eye, warning him not to lose his temper or embarrass Cassie by making a big deal out of it.

Kristin continued to stumble through an apology. "I didn't mean. I... I... mean you're pretty too."

Drake picked up his drink, saying nothing. And since both he and Adriana looked as if they wanted to skin Kristin, Cassie smiled at the woman. "Don't worry about it. I've been called worse, but I'll leave the names to your imagination. I'm a big woman.

When people can spot you from a hundred miles away, you stop being shy about it."

"Yes, well, that's a good attitude to have. I—uh..."

Eric took some money out of his wallet and handed it to Kristin. "Why don't you treat yourself to something?"

Kristin eagerly took the money, knowing this was her best chance to escape. "Thanks. Nice to meet you." She wiggled back to the counter.

Cassie glanced at the quiet group. Drake was staring into his mug. Probably wishing he had a cigarette instead. Adriana was watching Kristin like a vengeful spouse studying "the other woman" and Eric was staring at Drake with a solemn look. She knew she had to be the one to clear the air. "So anyone in the mood for seafood? I can eat my weight in shrimp."

"Cut it out," Drake said, in no mood to entertain her humor.

Silence fell; tension hovered.

"So," Eric began, trying to think of how to remedy the situation. "How has your evening been?"

"We came from the Colossal," Adriana said, as willing as he was to change the subject.

Eric grimaced. "That bad, huh?"

"It was wonderful actually," she defended.

"Right," he said, doubtful. He took a small piece of cloth from his pocket and began to clean his glasses. "So which band did your boyfriend play in?"

Cassie bit her lip in order not to giggle at the stunned expression on Adriana's face. "Corrosion of Sanity," she replied coolly.

Eric returned his glasses to his face. "Aptly named, no doubt."

"Now wait a minute." She tapped a blue nail against the table. "They're great. Some people can't understand hard rock."

"Yes, the mutilation of good sound is hard to understand. At least you have a better taste in friends than in music."

"Now wait—"

"We can argue about that later. Right now I have a pretty woman to impress." He suddenly grabbed Cassie's hand with surprising familiarity and stood. "I want to show you something. Don't worry, Drake, I'll bring her right back." He led her to the checkout counter and looked up at the chalkboard. "Pretend to look at the menu."

She did.

"I'm Drake's brother," he explained.

"I know. He told me about you and your sister."

That revelation gave Eric pause for a moment; then a secret smile touched his mouth. "You're supposed to act surprised and say 'But you look nothing alike.'"

She looked at him, confused. "But you do look alike. You're both very good looking." To her surprise a tint of red touched his honey skin. She turned away to hide a smile.

"Yes, well. Anyway." He cleared his throat and adjusted his glasses.

"I didn't mean to embarrass you."

"You didn't embarrass me." He flashed such a wicked grin, Cassie instantly knew he could be just as dangerous as his brother. "I just figured out something."

"What?"

"Why Drake's always such a lucky man." He changed the subject. "Since we didn't have much, it forced us to take value in the things that mattered, find beauty in things others might ignore." He scratched his cheek and pointed vaguely at the menu. "Do you understand what I'm trying to say?"

"You're saying beauty is in the eye of the beholder."

He shook his head. "No." He placed his hands behind him and rocked on his heels. "I'm saying we've seen ugly things and you're not one of them."

"I know I'm not ugly."

He turned to her. "But you don't know that you're beautiful."

She patted him on the shoulder. This one was more serious than Drake. "You don't need to worry about me. What your friend said didn't bother me. Besides, Drake and I are just friends."

His brows furrowed. "But I thought—"

"That we were something more?" she interrupted, not wanting him to name what they were. "No, that's not possible. We're from two different planets. I'm from Earth and only you know where he's from."

Like Drake, he didn't smile at her humor. Instead, he softly swore. "So you're not interested in him?"

"Of course I am. I enjoy his company, but we both know the type of woman he deserves."

Eric adjusted his glasses and swore again.

"You know, that's a bad habit of yours."

"Don't worry, I have plenty of others." He studied her for a moment. "So you're just friends, huh?"

She didn't know why he kept repeating the fact. "Yes. Close friends."

He swore with feeling.

She nudged him when an older woman stared at him in shock. "Stop that."

"Sorry. Come on, we'd better return before Drake decides to get us."

He deposited her in the seat, glanced at his brother as if he wanted to say something, and then his eyes fell on Adriana. "Who are you anyway?"

"Adriana."

"That's what I thought." He spun on his heel and left.

She looked at him speaking to Kristin. "What the hell did that mean?" Adriana grumbled to no one in particular.

"What did he have to show you?" Drake asked.

Cassie shrugged. "Just the pastry section."

He frowned, but said nothing. His eyes watched her.

"What a dreadful bore," Adriana muttered. "I don't know what he's doing out with that bimbo. I bet he reads the dictionary for fun. He's got intellectual written all over him."

"Sinful man," Cassie teased, feeling Drake's eyes on her, but trying to ignore them.

Drake abruptly stood. "Let's go home."

He offered to drive her home, but Cassie said she preferred to return with Adriana.

"You're trying to punish me for what Kristin said, aren't you?" he asked.

She quickly denied that, not wanting him to see her as shallow. "I just really need to work on my book. It's going nowhere. I've been distracted, happily of course. But now I have to get to work."

Drake nodded, accepting the explanation. "All right. I'll see you later."

For some odd reason, she felt as if they were saying good-bye.

Chapter Eleven

"What a load of crock," Adriana said, shutting the door to her spiffy blue Acura.

Cassie snapped her seat belt. "It's not."

"I know." She pointed at Cassie. "And you know that you would be at his place right now if it hadn't been for that woman."

"Her name is Kristin."

"I don't care what her name is." She checked her rearview mirror, then pulled into the street. "Something that wiggles that much should be kept in a box."

"What about her friend?"

Adriana shivered. "He should be dusted once a week. A dull, analytical, left-brain who has to analyze everything before it can be enjoyed. What did he mean by 'That's what I thought'?"

"He's just thinking aloud."

"He should try thinking quietly like the rest of us."

"Shame he's so good looking," she said, wondering if her friend had noticed.

"I'm afraid that the glare from his spectacles blocked my view."

"Oh, so you didn't notice his light brown eyes?"

"They were dark brown."

"Oh, right," Cassie said, trying to keep a straight face. "Must have been the glare."

Adriana laughed at herself. "All right, you caught me. I admit he's good looking, not as good looking as Drake of course, but that's all I'll admit. It's completely wasted anyway." She changed the subject. "How's the book?"

"Dead on arrival."

"You're still stuck?"

"Like a pig in a doggy door."

"That says something." But she didn't say what.

* * *

Cassie tried to believe that Kristin had nothing to do with her decision to come home, but the woman's words kept repeating in her mind—fat, fat, fat. As big as a whale. She'd probably dream about Drake with a harpoon in his hand. She was fat. That was the truth and that's how people would see her. She tried to use Eric's words to calm her stormy thoughts. Both he and Drake didn't see her that way and that was something she could cling to. But it didn't help. It was Drake's fault women saw her as competition and felt the need to tear her down. It happened with Timothy. She would have to make sure she didn't appear as a threat and that's how she would maintain their relationship until the reunion.

She suddenly felt chilled and shut the window. She secured the latch, then stared at it, confused. How had it opened? She was positive she had locked it before she left. She shrugged, dismissing any sinister thoughts. The building was old anyway and nothing had been touched. She secured the window with a stone and headed for the computer.

* * *

Two days later, Drake hadn't heard from Cassie and figured she was busy. So he found himself watching an action film with Eric. "Heard Lance was singing your praises because of Pamela," Eric said, staring at the TV.

"She's a good kid. Cassie instantly took to her."

Eric nodded, then began muttering prime numbers.

Drake tapped his leg. "You don't like her, do you?"

"I don't know Pamela."

"Cassie," he corrected.

"Sure I like her." He slouched lower in his seat. "She's fun."

"But there's a problem."

"Why do you say that?"

"Because you start muttering prime numbers when you have something to say but won't." He sent Eric a smug look. "You're not the only one safe from Henson predictability."

Eric shifted in his chair. "I saw Malcolm the other day. He has a black eye."

"It wasn't me." He flexed his fingers. "I didn't have time to get to him."

"I know. He walked into my fist first."

Drake stared at him, shocked. "That's not your style."

"I know." He glanced at his swollen knuckles. "He said a few things that sort of set me off."

Drake didn't ask what because he knew his brother probably wouldn't tell him.

Eric pushed up his glasses. "As you can probably guess we're not friends anymore."

"Hmm. What about Kristin?"

He shrugged, nonchalant. "Gone."

"You don't seem sorry."

"I'm not. I never make a big investment in people." He cleared his throat. "You should do the same."

He paused. "Why?"

"Makes life easier."

Drake clasped his hands behind his head. "If you have a point, make it."

Eric hesitated. He hated getting involved in other people's relationships, but Drake was his brother after all. "I think you see your relationship with Cassie in a different way than she does."

"I know she's hesitant about marriage, but in time she'll come around."

"So you don't mind being friends?" he asked cautiously.

He frowned. "Friends?"

"That's what she says you are."

"Like buddies?"

He nodded.

Drake let his hands fall. "She said that?"

Eric nodded again. "I know she likes you, but I don't think she's serious. You've already told me she has other guy friends. How do you know she doesn't sleep with them too?"

"She doesn't." His voice was ice.

"Fine." Eric was in no mood to argue. "So you are the only one she sleeps with. Do you really think that's enough to make you different?"

Drake stared at the TV.

"I'm not saying you should dump her. I just think you should lighten up, perhaps get some girlfriends of your own."

Drake dismissed the idea. "She's just confused." A malicious grin swept across his face. "Fortunately, I know how to make it clear for her."

* * *

Cedric pulled his cap lower as he watched the girl come out of the restaurant. She really bugged him— always looking so good and cheerful. He wouldn't admit it aloud, but he missed his job. He'd liked wearing a uniform and being part of a team. It hadn't always been fun, but it was better than hanging with his boys all day. They were getting old and some of the stuff they did made him nervous. If Henson hadn't tried to show him up he would still be there. He hadn't even been given a second chance because *she'd* taken it from him.

"You think you're something, don't you?" he sneered when she passed him.

She ignored him; he followed.

"You know this used to be my job. You don't have to act like all that. I know how much you're making and could make a lot more."

Pamela stopped and stared at him. "You're not bad looking for a stalker."

He gazed at her, stunned. "What?"

"Although I guess stalkers don't have a certain look, do they? I'd have to say I'd rather have you stalking me than someone else. You don't look scary, just angry."

"I'm not stalking you."

"Then why have you been watching me after work all week?" She suddenly smiled. Cedric blinked. The girl was crazy, but cute. "I know why," she said. "You're afraid to ask for your job back."

She was supposed to be angry or defensive, not grinning at him as if he were her new best friend. He had come for a fight and she was ruining it for him. "You have my job."

"No, I don't. You quit." Pamela lowered her voice. "Bad move. You had it made. I bet you know that now. Fortunately, you're in luck. We need a new dishwasher. The hours are good and I know Mr. Henson can make the work fit into your schedule when school starts." She dug into her backpack and handed him a card. "He's at his main office right now. I wouldn't wait."

Cedric stared at her, amazed. Girls like her never talked to guys like him. Let alone gave some advice. He knew that he probably looked like an idiot. But he didn't know what to say.

She smiled shyly. "Well, bye."

"Why are you being nice to me?" he asked as she turned.

"I had a cousin like you." She hesitated. "We buried him three months ago." Pamela lowered her eyes, but he already saw the building tears. He had a strange urge to comfort her, but instead buried his hands in his pockets and watched her walk away.

* * *

Drake had to stop himself from rubbing his ears in disbelief when his assistant announced that Cedric had come to see him. He thought for a moment, then called him in.

Cedric came through the door wearing a cap low on his eyes and an extra-large T-shirt. "I want a job," he announced.

Drake leaned back in his chair, quickly remembering why he had gotten rid of him in the first place. "So?"

"I heard that you needed a dishwasher."

He nodded. "That's right."

"I could do it."

Drake straightened his tie and watched him.

Cedric came toward the desk. "Come on, man, give me a break."

Drake rested his elbows on the armrest and placed the tips of his fingers together. "What's my name?" he asked quietly, his eyes unreadable.

"What?"

"Oh, I forgot." He let his gaze fall. "Hearing loss comes with an attitude problem."

Cedric sighed. "Mr. Henson."

He looked up. "Yes?"

"I want a job."

Drake leaned forward, resting his arms on the table. "I don't care what you want I'm a businessman. What can you give me?" He smiled coolly. "I've already seen what you can do and haven't been impressed."

Cedric shifted from one foot to the other, feeling awkward under the intense gaze. "I messed up big time and I was wrong."

"Tell me something I don't know."

"You don't have to be so hard, man."

Drake rubbed his chin. "The door is right behind you."

Cedric threw up his hands—frustration, anger, and helplessness evident in the gesture. "Man, I don't need this." He stormed out, slamming the door.

Drake sighed and returned to his work, fighting a small amount of guilt. Perhaps he'd been too hard. But then again life wasn't kind.

"Mr. Henson?" He glanced up and saw Cedric peering from behind the door. The smug arrogance was gone from his tone. "I really need a job. I'm a good dishwasher, I wash all the dishes at home. I'll arrive on time and everything."

"Why should I give you a second chance?"

"Because you won't regret it."

Drake held out his hand, wanting to smile with pride but frowning instead. "You make sure I don't regret it or you will."

After Cedric left, he lifted the phone to call Cassie, but immediately replaced the receiver. Cedric wasn't the only one who needed to learn a lesson. He buzzed his assistant and scheduled a business trip to Florida instead.

* * *

Cassie slammed down the telephone. Nearly two weeks and Drake hadn't returned her calls. Kristin must have changed his mind about her and he had chosen the coward's way to dump her. Damn him! She had thought about calling his cell phone but didn't want to appear desperate. She would not bow to him again. She would not allow him to handle her emotions this way. So it was over, huh? Good riddance.

The doorbell rang expectedly. She had invited Adriana over for a serious session of male bashing. She opened the door and in a fit of anger, lunged at the person standing there. "Get out of my sight!"

Door 712 swung open. "What's going on out there?"

"We're fine," Drake said in a quiet voice. He removed Cassie's grip on his shirt.

"We're not fine," Cassie countered. "I want him to leave."

Mr. Gianolo glanced from Drake to her, then back to Drake again. "Seems like everything is under control." He shut the door.

"Men," Cassie said, disgusted.

Drake frowned down at her. "Why are you so upset?"

She hit him in the chest. "You don't call for nearly two weeks and you ask me why I'm upset?"

"I was busy. I had to travel to Florida on business."

She held up her hand in the shape of a phone. "And you couldn't call to tell me this?"

"Well, I—"

"I would have understood," she cut in. "But no. You didn't have the decency to call. One moment you're everywhere I turn and then poof, you're gone."

"Things got crazy. I rehired Cedric."

Her anger subsided into surprise. "You did?"

Drake nodded. "He came to my office and asked for a job. At first the staff wasn't pleased to see him again, but he's doing very well."

"I'm glad. I know how much—" She closed her eyes and shook her head. "Wait. That's not the point."

He rested against the door frame and shoved his hands in his pockets. "I also had to meet with a new delivery service since our old one is under new management. There was a menu change and a new assistant manager to break in, plus a big catering affair. I didn't think I needed to call you. We're just friends after all."

Cassie narrowed her eyes, suspicious. "What are you up to?"

Drake pushed himself from the frame and walked into the apartment. "I'm not up to anything, babe."

She closed the door and glared at his back. "Don't call me babe."

"Sorry, buddy. You liked it when Kevin did. What do your other male friends call you?"

"They call me Cassie. Now listen here—"

He sat. "How's your book coming?"

"Fine." She sat next to him, determined to get answers. "Why didn't you return any of my calls?"

He yawned. "Are we back to that? I explained that I was busy. Besides, I didn't think it was urgent since you didn't call my cell phone." He leaned forward. "I'm not staying long. I just came by to say hello and see if you'd be free for a bazaar later this week."

A bazaar was too public. "How about a movie?"

"Are you free?"

"I don't know."

He stood and patted her on the shoulder. "Call me when you do."

"Drake, stop acting like this," she demanded, annoyed.

"Like what?" He rested his hands on the back on the couch. "A friend? I thought that's what I was."

"You know you're more than that."

He looked surprised. "Do I? You told Eric we were just friends."

"He misunderstood me."

"He misunderstood 'We're just friends'?"

"Okay, I admit I sort of misled him," she confessed with shame.

He sat down, "Why?"

Cassie let her shoulders slump. "It seemed a good idea at the time."

"Why?"

She shrugged helplessly. "I don't know."

"Yes, you do," he insisted.

She shook her head. "No, I don't."

His voice was hard. "Yes, you do."

"I was humiliated, okay!" she admitted, feeling all the hurt of that evening rushing back. "I couldn't stand his pity. He felt so sorry for me that I wanted to make him feel better and I didn't want him to take me seriously. I didn't want any of you to take me seriously." Tears welled in her eyes. "I wanted to laugh about it, but you all refused and made me feel worse."

His voice softened. "We didn't mean to make you feel worse, but what happened wasn't funny. We couldn't even have forced ourselves to laugh if we tried."

She covered her face, her thoughts as jagged and painful as Kristin's words had been. "But it was so embarrassing. How could you not have been embarrassed to be seen with me?"

"The only person who should have been embarrassed was Kristin because what she said wasn't true."

Cassie shook her head, wishing it were as simple as that.

Drake removed her hands, forcing her to look at him. His amber eyes were tender. "What she said was not true."

She squeezed her eyes shut, but a stream of tears still escaped under the lids. Drake let out an audible breath and held her close. His lips brushed her forehead. "Why didn't you tell me she hurt you this much?"

"You were so angry and ashamed," she whispered miserably.

"I wasn't angry at you and I definitely wasn't ashamed." He rubbed his cheek against her hair. "I could never be ashamed of you." He briefly shut his eyes, battling the anguish her tears caused. He should have known how much Kristin had hurt her. How her flippant attitude was just a mask. He should have been there for her. "Can you forgive me?"

"You didn't do anything."

He shook his head, disgusted with himself. "I know." He held her face and wiped away her tears, then gently kissed her. Her lips were salty and sweet. "Open your eyes, Cassie."

She opened her eyes and saw such tenderness reflecting in his she had to turn away. "It's no big deal really," she said, needing to make light of it all. "I'm okay. I just... wished you'd call."

"I'm sorry I didn't call."

She turned to him and blinked. "Are my eyes red?"

"As a mango."

She rubbed them with the back of her hand. "Now you see why I prefer laughing to crying."

"Well, the next time you need to cry, let me know," He placed a finger on her lips to keep her from smiling and making light of his words. "Do you understand?"

She buried her face in his chest and nodded.

"You feel like crying again?"

"No." Her voice was muffled against his shirt. "But I feel a giggle coming on."

He sighed, knowing she was ready to change the subject. He tossed a package on the table.

She lifted her head. "What's that?"

"Never mind." He lifted her chin. "Kiss me again."

She brushed her lips against his. "Now what's that?"

"I think you're beginning to take me for granted," he said dryly.

She lifted the package. "This had better not be food."

"It's not."

She flipped it over. "What is it?"

"Open it."

She eagerly opened the package and smiled. "Pictures!"

"I thought since you showed me your family, I would show you mine. There isn't much."

"It's enough. Are there any naked baby pictures of you?"

"No. Why would you want to see me naked then when you can see me naked now?"

She made a face. "It's not the same."

He lifted a brow. "I should hope not."

She looked through his handful of pictures with the same reverence he had given her album. "Are these the pictures of your parents?" she asked, staring at a young couple.

"Yes."

She brought the picture closer and studied the happy pair. "They look so in love."

Drake stretched his arm the length of the couch. "For all the good it did them."

Cassie turned to him, hearing the disgust in his tone. "What do you mean?"

"When my mother died, you would have thought my father's soul had been ripped from him. There wasn't a day that passed that I didn't hear him crying." He shook his head in irritation as if trying to rid himself of the memory. "We had to take care of him—a man who had been my hero. I think he succumbed to illness just to be with her, leaving us to fend for ourselves."

"You blame him for dying?"

He shook his head. "No, I blame a love that was all-consuming, a love that could make a grown man weak. He once told me that my mother was his heart. I believed him because once she died his heart stopped. Unfortunately, his actual death took longer." He stared out in the distance, his voice quiet. "That won't happen to me. I lost the people I loved and it made me strong, not weak. It was the enduring love of family that strengthened me—not romantic love."

Cassie bit her lower lip, choosing her words carefully. "Yes, the love of family is important, but so is the love between a man and a woman. Family is built on the very foundation of that love. As crazy as they were, my parents' love for each other kept us in balance, made us feel safe. It was the glue that bonded us."

"And the axe that split my family apart." Drake stared at the black TV screen. "What good is a father so in love with his wife that he can focus on nothing else? What good is a mother who smiles through pain just so that her husband won't worry? It leaves the children as spectators."

Cassie cupped the side of his face, feeling the tense muscles constrict on his jaw. "With so many kids growing up in single-parent homes, your parents stayed together. Doesn't it make you proud that you were the product of such a love?"

"No."

"It wasn't love that killed your parents. It was surviving in a new world, a new culture, fighting poverty and disease. It was love and hope that brought you here."

Drake absently stroked her neck, but said nothing.

She decided it was a subject better left alone. "Are you hungry?"

His eyes raked over her. "Only for one thing."

"I'm afraid I'm all out of hot sex on a kitchen table."

His fingers left a sensuous trail down her neck, disappearing into her shirt. She felt one bra strap being removed from her shoulder. "How about cool sex on the living room floor?"

She stood, unbuttoning his shirt. "No, I think I can make sweet sex on a mattress much better."

He tossed off his shirt. "Sounds good to me. I've brought my own utensils." He held up a condom.

She grabbed the lapels of his shirt and walked toward the bedroom. "Let's get started before you lose your appetite."

"That's not possible. I've developed a mighty big one."

The doorbell rang.

Drake scowled. "Who is that?"

"Adriana," she said, chagrined.

"If you have an appointment we can make this quick," he said, tugging on her blouse.

She slapped his hand away. "That's not necessary." She opened the door and smiled at her friend. "There's been a change in plans."

"What change?" Adriana demanded. "Drake's no longer a jerk?"

He came to the door wearing only boxer shorts. "That's right and now we're making up. She'll call you." He shut the door.

Cassie stared at him. "I don't think you changed her opinion of you."

He grabbed her hand and pulled her toward the bedroom. "Yours is the only one that matters."

* * *

Drake nudged her awake the next morning. "Would you like to join me in the shower?"

The thought was enticing and in her sleepy state she almost said yes. But her mind soon cleared. Even in her fantasies she couldn't imagine standing naked in front of him with the harsh bathroom light exposing all her faults.

"No, thanks." She turned, ready to go back to sleep. "Enjoy yourself."

He sighed with exaggerated dismay. "I'll try."

When she woke up again, he was gone.

* * *

Two days later, Cassie stifled a scream of frustration as she deleted a line of rubbish she had entered on the computer.

"Just a minute," she called when the doorbell rang.

She quickly threw away her muffin wrappings and donut boxes and answered the door. Timothy stood there with a smug smile on his face. "Hi."

Cassie didn't return the expression. "Hi."

"It's been a while," he said, his smile dimming a bit.

"Yes. How's your father doing?"

"He's hanging on."

She nodded.

He hesitated, then took a step forward. "Aren't you going to invite me in?"

She shook her head.

His smile disappeared. "How long are you going to punish me for one mistake?" His eyes filled with agony. "I need you, Cass—Cassie. I go home and there's no one there for me."

"Get a dog. Timothy, I can't help you." She started to shut the door. He stopped her.

"Is it me, or didn't we have a good time a few weeks ago?" he asked, confused.

"We did."

"And that doesn't matter?"

She suddenly grinned, pleased. "You're beginning to catch on." She tried to close the door again but he stopped her.

"You're not going to get better than me, Cass," he said, all warmth and agony gone from his eyes.

"No, the fact is you're not going to get better than me and you know it. You know you're going to have a hard time finding someone who truly loves you—not just your face, your money, your name or career, but you." She poked him in the chest. "Someone who idolizes you and lets you get away with cruel remarks and spiteful attitudes. You're terrified of being alone because you're scared the next woman you meet will be as shallow as you are. Fortunately, that's not my problem."

"Perhaps you're right." He hesitated. "Perhaps I'm afraid to lose something special that I know I've lost. But why are you afraid to give us a second chance? Are you afraid perhaps that you still have feelings for me? That what I've said is true, that I have changed?" Tears glittered in his eyes, his voice was a whisper. "I love you, Cassie, please believe me. I married you, didn't I? Out of all the women who wanted me, I married you. That has to mean something. I loved you then and I love you still. I always will."

For a second she did believe him—her ego was eager, and a wounded part of her needed to believe he had loved her, that he still did. But the reality of how he had treated her made his words hollow. He could choose to believe them, but she couldn't afford to.

"Timothy, I loved you once. That's why I became your wife. But we also made promises on our wedding day and you broke yours. So now it's over. We're over— forever."

The tears disappeared as his voice grew harsh. "You're making a mistake."

"Then I'll deal with the consequences."

"You'll regret this. You'll look back on this day and wish that you had taken me back. You think you have other men, but they just see you as a diversion. You're a lot of fun but that doesn't last. I know and I was willing to settle—"

"Bye, Timothy." She slammed the door, barely missing his fingers.

Timothy jumped back and swore. He couldn't believe he had failed. He had failed. It left an awful feeling in his gut. He felt bad now, but she'd feel bad later. She would regret her decision one day. He stalked to the stairway door. He halted when he saw a big man, twirling an unlit cigarette between his fingers, blocking his path. He was about to ask the man to move, but piercing amber eyes left him speechless. The man did not have to speak to let Timothy know he had been waiting for him.

"You can have whatever you want," Timothy said, reaching slowly for his wallet lest any sudden movements set the man into action.

"I know that," he said simply, as if that were common knowledge.

Timothy swallowed, his Adam's apple bobbing up and down in a nervous twitch. "Then what do you want?"

"I want you to stay away from Cassie."

Timothy paused, trying to comprehend the un-expected request. "What?"

The man stared at his cigarette. "You don't live in this building, do you?"

"No, but that's—"

The man met his gaze. "Then there's no reason for you to be here."

Who the hell was this guy, anyway? "Listen, you can't tell me what to do."

His gaze didn't waver. "I can and I have."

Timothy began to grin. "You think you can fight me? She used to be my wife. I've had her in ways you'll never know, never comprehend. You're one of many, but I was her husband. She belonged to me." He held up his hands in mock surrender and chuckled, shaking his head. "Now if you want to fight over my leftovers that's up to you. Just remember I—"

The man cut off his windpipe. His large hand fastened around his neck like a noose. "Let me try again," he said slowly, "since I don't seem to be making myself clear." His hand tightened a fraction. "Stay away from Cassie."

Timothy made a gurgling sound in response and the man let him go. Gasping and wheezing, Timothy glared at the stranger's dispassionate expression. "It's up to her who she wants," he panted. "She's the one who has to make a choice."

The man opened the door to the stairwell. "Not if I make the choice for her."

Timothy sent him a dirty look, then left. He stormed down the stairwell and opened the door to the ground level, halting for the second time when he saw another large man standing by the front doors. Sharp dark eyes and a hard mouth greeted him. He held up his hands in ready submission, then let them fall when he recognized him. "She's all yours. You don't have to worry about me anymore. She doesn't know what she's lost."

The man said nothing, but his expression said, Not much.

Timothy smoothed down his hair. "You never liked me but now you've got some other guy to deal with and he's not as friendly as I am."

He shrugged.

"She's not worth the trouble."

The man didn't blink. Timothy cleared his throat and headed for the exit, feeling the man's gaze.

* * *

Drake shut the door behind Timothy and sighed, wondering what damage Timothy had done to Cassie's self-image and how much injury he would have to undo. He knew she needed space, but he had just wanted to see her. He was glad he'd come. He'd been curious to see the ghost that kept them apart—a scrawny, egotistical playboy. Drake had been a little sorry when he'd spotted Timothy, he had hoped to have a more worthy adversary.

He heard the familiar creak of Mr. Gianolo's door. "Get rid of him, did you?"

"For now."

"He's wrong. Cassie is a good girl. She doesn't have a lot of men coming and going."

"I know."

"Have you asked her yet?" he demanded.

"No, not yet. You'll be the first to know."

"Don't wait too long. I'm not as young as I look." He closed the door.

Drake knocked briskly on the door, running over in his mind the excuse as to why he was here. Then he remembered the box in his jacket and concluded that was reason enough.

When Cassie opened the door, he was surprised to see that she was okay. Instead of the red eyes, droopy mouth, and wary expression he had expected, she looked rumpled and frustrated like a kid whose Lego castle refused to stay up.

"Why are you grinning like that?" she asked.

"I'm happy to see you." *And happy to see that your ex no longer affects you.* Their relationship had reached a new level.

Cassie impatiently drummed her fingers on the door. If she didn't get rid of him soon he'd become a pleasant diversion and then she would never get anything done. "It's nice to see you too, but I'm really busy."

"Of course." He handed her a plastic container.

Cassie groaned. "Tell me it's not something sinful."

"Food can't be sinful."

She shot him a glance. "Spoken like a true non-believer."

He took the container and opened it. "Go ahead and try one."

She tugged on her sweatshirt. "Do you see this shirt? Do you want my body to resemble this shirt?"

He ignored the question, holding out a pecan praline.

She should be furious with him. She used to hate when Timothy gave her food, knowing that eventually he would tease her about it. But since she knew that for Drake giving food was the highest honor, it didn't annoy her. It wasn't like Timothy's gift or her father's absent-minded treats. It was a well-thought-out present that always made her feel special and cared for.

Resigned, she took a bite, letting the crunchy, sweet taste fill her mouth. She met his eyes, which reflected warmth and the pleasure that he could make her happy. "Delicious."

He nodded. "What's this?" he asked, picking up a shiny, silver card.

"Another invitation from Kevin. Would you like to go?"

His glare was eloquent enough.

"He's not as bad as you think."

Drake folded his arms.

"Very well. I'll say no." She pushed him toward the door. "Now leave. I have to get some writing done."

He spun around her and went to the couch. "Your book's not going well?"

"It's not going, period." She sat down next to him, facing defeat.

"Let me see what you have." He took a praline. "Perhaps I can help you."

"That's a joke, right? Mr. Unromantic wants to help me write about keeping love alive."

"I'm not unromantic," he said, offended. "My entire job is about creating environments where romance can flourish. Remember your broth dinner?"

She handed him her outline. "Fine. Try."

Drake quickly scanned it, then tapped the paper. "I can already see your trouble."

She leaned over his shoulder. "What?"

"You're not focused. In order to keep your book together you need to have one underlining theory on how to keep romance alive."

"But there are plenty of ways."

"Let other books discuss them. What could you focus on?" He munched on another praline, then suddenly snapped his fingers. "Food."

"Is that all you can ever think of?"

"Just listen. Don't they say that a way to a man's heart is through his stomach?"

"And the way to a woman's heart is through his wallet. What's your point?"

"You could have recipes and blend them with narrative ideas about why certain foods are considered an aphrodisiac. Or what they mean in some myths or love stories. For couples who are married with kids, you could use recipes families can do together. You could call it *Ingredients for Love*, *A Taste of Ecstasy*, or *Recipes for Romance*."

Cassie chewed her lip, reluctantly impressed. "Damn, that's a good idea. Why didn't I think of it?"

"Because you're not a Henson yet."

She made a face.

They brainstormed for two hours, went to a movie as a break, then brainstormed some more.

When Cassie thought she had enough information, she banished Drake from her place until the book was done.

* * *

The air was too humid. He hated summer, especially in the city. Give him the icy breath of winter, the chill of autumn. Why the hell did Cassie have to choose DC? He ran his fingers over the selection of flowers the little shop had to offer. He hadn't expected Henson to last so long. It made him wonder if Cassie was getting serious.

He had underestimated him, and that had been a mistake. Henson was cunning and could be charming even if his coarse edges showed most of the time. Plus he had a temper. The thought made him smile. It might come in handy.

He picked up a yellow rose and smelled it. Henson wouldn't get rid of him. He stroked the petal of the rose, then broke it off, crushing it between his thumb and forefinger. First, he had to do something about these.

* * *

It had only been a few days and Drake was feeling restless. When would Cassie call him? How long would it take to type up the book? He opened the door of the Blue Mango just as Pamela stormed out with the energy of a woman on a mission. He grabbed her arm as she passed him.

"Where do you think you're going?" he demanded.

"That bastard left me a three-dollar tip!" She pointed to a well-dressed man stepping into a Mustang.

He tugged her inside the door. "Come on."

"No. I want to have a word with him. He's some hotshot lawyer who demanded everything, but did I complain? No. I was the most pleasant I've ever been and he spent a hundred and fifty dollars and gave me this lousy tip." She waved the money.

"Follow me." She wisely recognized the tone and followed without protest. He led her to the back office.

"Just ignore me," Eric said when they entered the room. "Because I'm not going anywhere."

Drake didn't spare him a glance. He pointed to a chair and Pamela sat. He took a deep breath and rubbed the back of his neck. "Don't ever do that again."

Her mouth fell open at his anger. "But I—"

"I know why you did it, that's why I'll give you another chance. But don't let me see you doing it again. Image is important and I can't have my staff chasing after customers that upset them."

"But he—"

"Gave you a lousy tip." Drake shrugged. "So what? Perhaps he's not a nice guy. You can't expect to be loved by everyone." He turned away. "Now get back to work."

Pamela pushed herself out of the chair, still shaking from an indignation she was trying to control. Drake watched her head for the door and he shoved his hands in his pockets.

"Pamela, sit a minute."

She opened her mouth, then shut it and sat.

He took a deep breath and stared out the window. He wasn't used to explaining himself. He drummed his fingers on his leg and turned to her. "I'm impressed with your work."

Her eyes widened and her mouth fell open.

"I'm not flattering you," he added quickly. "I'm just stating a fact. You're punctual, diligent, and smart. An excellent asset to the staff. That's why I can't allow you to make the mistake you did today. Rude customers are part of our business. Trust me, I've had my share, but you must understand the power of networking." He lowered his voice to a conspiratorial tone. "That lawyer is a bastard, but he knows a lot of other people who are great tippers and recommends this place highly. So we have to tolerate him. Do you understand?"

Pamela could only nod, stunned that he had complimented her let alone spoken to her at length.

Drake grew uncomfortable under her awed gaze. "Get to work," he said with a dismissive gesture.

She jumped to her feet "Thank you so much, Mr. Henson. You won't regret giving me another chance. I just love working here and I—"

"Goodbye, Pamela."

She smiled happily and darted out the door.

* * *

"What are you grinning about?" Cedric asked her as she made her way through the kitchen.

"Mr. Henson gave me a compliment."

He sprayed a dish. "So what?"

"It made me happy."

She was the only person he knew who could continuously be in a good mood. She always had a smile or a friendly word for him as she headed to her duties, leaving the sweet smell of her perfume as a reminder. "You're always happy," he grumbled.

"And you're always a sourpuss."

Cedric set the plate down. "Sourpuss? I didn't know normal people used words like that."

"See what you learn when you crawl out of the gutter?"

Instead of taking offense, he grinned. "I didn't crawl, baby, I leaped."

Pamela straightened his collar. She had an odd habit of doing that; he didn't mind. "Yeah, I know." She laughed as she pushed through the doors and Cedric found himself whistling.

Later that day, Drake and Eric went to the Red Hut. When Drake saw his manager, Patrick, he knew the day would not go smoothly. Patrick had that look in his eyes.

"This is my best idea yet," he announced, eagerly approaching them.

Drake silently groaned.

Patrick took his silence as a cue to begin. "Because Tuesdays are our slow days, why don't we close the kitchen and restaurant and advertise dancing to Motown hits?"

"No."

Patrick's face fell. "Why not? We could have different groups come and perform."

"You're forgetting about our Tuesday night dinner patrons. They are our most loyal group and it would be foolish to lose them. We need to be consistent. If people want to dance they can go to a club."

"We could become a supper club."

Drake glanced around the room, ready to end the discussion. "No."

"You're always shooting down my ideas," he said bitterly. "You didn't want me to hire Lesage when we both know he is one of the best chefs around. He's been on TV, in movies and magazines."

Drake looked at him, fighting a battle with his patience. "I explained to you that I didn't want a prima donna with knives cooking in my kitchen."

Patrick tapped a pen against his palm. "You know the owner of Martin's likes my work and my ideas. He asked me if I'd like to work for him."

"I see." Drake nodded. It was to be expected. "Well, I can't make up your mind for you."

Patrick turned. "I think it's already been made up."

Drake sighed, shoving his hands in his pockets. "However, I'd hate to see you go."

He glanced over his shoulder, unconvinced.

"You're a strong manager, you keep up staff morale, you're creative and full of ideas."

"Ideas that you constantly reject," he said with resentment.

Drake rubbed the back of his neck, trying to choose his words carefully. "Because they don't fit the place doesn't mean they're not good. You just need to focus. Think about what would make the Red Hut more successful by building on what initially made it a success. If you had a house, you don't need to knock it down and start all over again. You think of changes. You see its strong points and build from there. I think you're on the right track by focusing on our slow Tuesday night. How would you improve that without losing our loyal customers?"

Patrick thought a moment. "What about a dinner club?"

Drake folded his arms and thought for a moment. "Put the idea together and present it to me."

Patrick slapped him on the arm, triumphant "Looks like you're stuck with me."

"Hmm. Keep up the good work."

Patrick grinned and walked away. Eric stared at his brother.

"What?" Drake asked, annoyed.

"Do you have any extra compliments up your sleeve? I'm beginning to feel undervalued."

Drake walked toward the kitchen.

"First Pamela, now Patrick," Eric said in disbelief. "Are you starting a new trend? Actual civility?"

"Shut up."

"You've changed. I know it's Cassie's influence. No one else could work such a miracle. It's nice to see."

Drake pushed through the kitchen doors. "If you don't shut up, you won't be able to."

Eric adjusted his glasses and did.

* * *

Three weeks of self-imposed exile, except for one presentation, and she was finished. Done. Completed. All before schedule. With artistic flourish Cassie hit the Save icon and made up a little cheer. She sat back, exhausted but exhilarated. Her reputation was saved. She stretched the kinks out of her back and neck and mentally patted herself on the back for a job well done.

She turned the ringer back on her telephone and checked her voice mail messages—the usual from Adriana, one from Kevin and Glen, then two strange delayed hang-ups where she could hear breathing. She erased the messages, wondering what to do next. She glanced down at her shabby T-shirt and jeans and thought a shower would suffice, but first she had a call to make.

Her fingers trembled with anticipation as she dialed Drake's number. She was eager to hear his voice again.

"Hello?" a decidedly female voice answered.

Cassie paused, a hot pain shooting through her heart. She took a deep breath, catching hold of her thoughts. Perhaps she'd dialed the wrong number. "I'm sorry, I was trying to reach Drake Henson."

"He's not in. May I take a message?"

Her first instinct was to decline, hang up, and forget Drake had ever entered her life. Her mind repeated Timothy's betrayal like a film reel in Technicolor, carrying all the emotions with it. She had just finished *The Fear of Ridicule* only to discover she was the biggest fool of all. Timothy had said she hadn't been there for him. Would Drake use the same excuse? If he had someone else, she wanted to know. "Just tell him that Cassie called."

"Cassie!" the woman cried as if she were hearing from an old friend. "It's so good to hear from you. Drake's told me you're working on a book."

"Yes, it's completed now," Cassie admitted proudly.

"Congratulations. Hey, why don't you come over and we can celebrate with a strawberry smoothie?"

"All right," she said, catching the woman's enthusiasm.

"Okay, see you in a while." She hung up before Cassie could ask her name. It had to be his sister, she guessed. She must have changed her opinion about her. The one in the bookstore was less than flattering. Of course meeting his sister presented a small dilemma—what to wear. She picked up one of her "hope" dresses, a yellow satin-cotton mix. She had bought it on a buying binge when she'd promised herself to lose weight. She hadn't been able to wear it yet. She shoved it to the back of the closet with the rest and chose a maroon shirt and jeans.

An hour later she was riding the elevator to Drake's condo, with her manuscript in the bag, trying to perfect the smile she would use, wondering what Drake had told his sister and if she would prove to be a shock.

The door was already open when Cassie reached the floor. She was embraced by a petite woman with big eyes and a full grin. She felt like a gigantic blob next to her.

"Come in, come in," the little elf said, pulling Cassie inside with a remarkably strong grip. "It's so good to finally meet you."

Thank God she didn't recognize her from the bookstore. "And you as well, Jackie."

Her smile took up her face. "So he has talked about us. I'm glad." Jackie turned and headed for the kitchen, but continued talking. "He rarely shares anything about us for some reason, so you must be someone special. Sit, sit. This won't take long."

Cassie sat and watched Jackie toss a bowl of strawberries, milk, and ice cubes in a blender, then turn it on. Later, she poured the mixture into two long-stemmed glasses and garnished it with green leaves. She had the same quick efficiency her brother had.

"Delicious!" Cassie said, after taking a sip.

Jackie straddled the chair, her eyes flashing with impish delight. "I'm glad you like it. I was mad at you for a long time, but how can I hate a woman who makes my brother so happy?" She rested her chin in her hands. "It will be nice to have a sister." She grimaced at her own indelicacy. "Forgive me. I sometimes talk before I think."

Cassie nodded in understanding. Unfortunately, once the topic had been introduced Jackie wouldn't leave it.

"But if he did ask you to marry him, you'd say yes, right?"

"I'm not sure I'm the right one for him."

"You make him happy and few people can do that. Case closed."

She was a woman with the guile of a child. Cassie found herself being honest. "I had a bad first marriage so I'm not eager to rush to the altar again."

"No wonder. The word 'altar' always has me thinking of some sort of sacrifice. That's all right. We can have the wedding here." She changed the topic before Cassie could argue. "Drake's been busy at the Red Hut. It's going to be featured in the Washingtonian magazine." Cassie shared her surprise and the conversation followed that innocuous track until they heard a key in the lock. Jackie leaped out of her seat and whispered, "Stay here" before she left.

"I got you some-ting," Drake said, greeting his sister in a playful tone.

"I got you some-ting too and I bet mine's betta dan yours," Jackie teased, glad that Cassie had arrived when she did. Only she would notice the drawn look in his eyes despite the genuine smile.

"Here you are, you little nuisance." He handed her a box. She lifted the lid and inside sat a glass figurine of a deer among purple tissue paper. She could add it to her collection. She kissed him soundly on the cheek. "Oh, thank you." She grabbed his arm. "I have a surprise for you."

He easily disengaged from her grip. "Mi haffi shower first."

"But—"

"It can wait. If it's something that will spoil, put it in the fridge." He patted her on the head. "Don't screw up your face like that, I won't be long."

* * *

"I'm sorry," Jackie said to Cassie, falling into a seat. "He decided to take a shower first."

"That's okay."

Jackie rested her chin in her hand, drumming her fingers against her cheek when suddenly the impish expression entered her eyes again. She surged to her feet. "I'm leaving. Wait for him."

She grabbed her things from the couch and pushed Cassie in the direction of the bedroom. She waved a quick good-bye and dashed out the door.

Not knowing what else to do, Cassie entered Drake's bedroom. It greeted her with a comfortable familiarity, its large mahogany bed and dark-accented furniture unchanged, but the flood of emotions that swept around her was anything but familiar. She was too afraid to try and understand them. She sat on the bed and ran her fingers over the shirt he had casually thrown across the bed. Her head snapped up when the bathroom door opened.

Chapter Twelve

A cloud of steam drifted out, curling around the air in the room. Drake emerged like a magician appearing from a cloud of smoke.

"Jackie, I'll be ready for your surprise in a minute," he called.

He didn't see her since he was drying his face with a hand towel. A large blue towel clung around his waist, while his body still wet from the shower had streams of water sliding over the contours of his chest. Cassie chewed on her lip, fighting the urge to jump on him.

He tossed the rag away and glanced up. Startled amber eyes collided with her own. "Tell me I'm not dreaming," he said. He'd meant to sound casual, but it came out husky.

She laughed breathlessly. "You're not dreaming."

He leaped on the bed like a skilled jungle cat bouncing on his prey, and gathered her close. "Yes, you are real," he whispered, his hands exploring every part of her.

"You're getting me wet."

"I like you wet." He tugged her panties down and explored the liquid heat between her legs. "Especially when you're ready for me."

"I'm ready," she breathed, burying her head against his throat, eager to have him inside her.

"I should make you wait."

She nipped on the soft, sensitive part of his ear. "You wouldn't dare."

He traced an S pattern from her neck to her stomach. "Are there dire consequences for that?"

"Yes." She yanked off his towel, feeling the hardness of his erection against her thigh. She wiggled suggestively against him.

"I don't think I'll risk it." He rolled on a condom, then entered her with the enthusiasm of a novice deep-sea diver looking for a lost world.

Cassie's nails bit into his back.

"Careful, woman, or you'll leave me with scars."

"That's okay, then everyone will know who you belong to."

His lips hovered above hers. "They already do."

He kissed her. She tasted of strawberries and smelled like vanilla. He held her close, his heart pounding in his ears. Twice she whispered his name, but no other words were spoken. Their bodies speaking for their hearts. When it was over, they lay still as if any movement would shatter their joy and reveal that everything had only been a dream. Outside they heard a squirrel race up a tree and a pigeon land on a branch rustling its leaves.

"I never want to do that again," Drake said with feeling, his head buried in the pillow.

Amazed, Cassie lifted herself on her elbow and stared down at him. "I thought it was pretty good."

"I don't mean the sex." He turned on his back and rested an arm over his eyes. "I mean being away from you. I missed you." He suddenly scowled. "And it was annoying." It was also frightening. He wasn't sure if she was keeping him at arm's length for another reason besides the book, but he didn't want to seem untrusting. Or appear like the type of man that didn't give a woman space to be a professional in her own right. But it had been hard not seeing her or hearing from her. He felt as if a vital organ had been ripped from him, causing an aching gap. It felt too much like how his father had expressed losing his mother. It was ridiculous of course. He was nothing like his father. Fortunately, he didn't have to worry anymore. She was here.

Cassie toyed with his flat nipple, still in awe that this beautiful man was hers to claim. "I missed you too, but I had to finish my book."

"Is it safe to assume it's finished?"

"Yes." She briefly held her hands together. "Thank God. Your sister told me the Red Hut is going to be featured in the Washingtonian. Are you nervous?"

"Why would I be nervous? The food is excellent, as well as the service, location, atmospherics, and —"

She kissed his nipple. "Forgive me, your lordship," she said humbly. "How could I have made such a suggestion?"

He tenderly stroked her arm. "You're forgiven. So did you bring your manuscript with you?"

"Yes. I don't know why. I usually don't let anyone but my editor see it."

"You can make an exception." He slapped her playfully on the bottom. "Go get it for me."

Cassie sat up, gathering her knees to her chest, unsure.

"I'm waiting."

She reached for her clothes.

"You don't need those."

"I'm not walking around naked." She pulled on her top.

He sighed, disappointed. "Shame."

* * *

Cassie busied herself with a crossword in the newspaper while Drake read. She always felt awkward to be around when someone read her work. It was like having a seat next to the teacher's desk while he graded an exam. She hoped Drake appreciated the acknowledgment she had added, telling her readers that most of the recipes were inspired by the Red Hut and the Blue Mango, two fine restaurants in northwest DC. It was an unnecessary plug since he probably didn't need the extra publicity, but it was her gift to him.

When Drake turned the last page, a tense silence enveloped the room as Cassie awaited the verdict.

"It's great," he said simply.

"Do you really think so?"

He sent her a cool glance. "No, I just said that for effect."

She slapped his arm. "Don't be facety."

"Sorry, but I've always been poor at gushing."

"Try."

Drake rested his head back and then a sly grin spread on his face. "It's excellent, marvelous, magnificent, stupendous, except..."

She stiffened. "Except what?"

He turned to her. "You could do better."

Cassie's stomach dropped as her skin tried to recover from the sting of criticism.

"It's very well written," he continued, unaware of how his words hurt. "But there's a lack of emotion."

"This is a self-help book, not a romance," she said, anger clipping her words.

"I know, but I've read your other books and there was an honesty that I don't sense here." He flipped through the manuscript and set it aside. "In *The Fear of Ridicule* I felt that you knew how it felt to be awkward or shy, but here I don't get the feeling that you believe what you're writing. If I didn't know you better, I wouldn't think you believed in romance or even love."

"Of course I believe in love."

He tapped the manuscript. "Then prove it."

She snatched it and shoved it in her bag, then pulled on one shoe.

"You're angry with me," he noticed, surprised.

She searched the room for her other shoe, fighting back tears. "You have no idea how hard I worked."

"I can tell. I didn't say it was bad. I just said—"

"I know what you said," she interrupted, glancing under the bed. She spotted her shoe and pulled it out.

"Cassie," he said gently, "it was just an observation. It's nothing serious."

"It's nothing serious to you. You don't have a career worthy of being flushed down a toilet. I'm a joke, you know. My book sales and popularity have gone down since my divorce. Oh, sure, I can fill a classroom, but I haven't been asked to be a guest speaker in a year. This book is my last chance. If it doesn't work, then my publisher will drop me. And now you tell me the book I've been working on, in spite of my ex-husband's distractions and the up-and-down relationship with my current lover, is dull."

"I didn't say it was dull."

She didn't hear him. "And maybe you're right. Perhaps I'm a fraud. Perhaps like you I don't believe in love and romance. I think relationships are constant chains we happily attach on ourselves."

"You're not a fraud and you're missing the point."

"And what would that be?"

"In the pressure of worrying about book sales and lecture tours you've forgotten why you write in the first place. You inspire people to dare to step out into the world and make their presence known. There's someone out there who's starting a new relationship and wants it to work. You have the tools to help him or her."

Cassie bit her lip. "I don't think I do."

"That's the whole problem. You're thinking too much. As you romantics like to say, 'Write from the heart.'"

She stared at the manuscript.

"It's good," he said.

"But not good enough."

Drake stood and began to change. "You have two minutes to feel sorry for yourself and then we can try out one of the recipes. Excellent selections, by the way."

"Thanks," she grumbled.

"I feel in the mood for chocolate caramels."

She pushed down the need to sulk and managed a small smile. "Okay."

"I'm not sure I have all the ingredients." He tucked in his shirt. "We'll have to go shopping."

* * *

"Who taught you how to shop?" Drake demanded, taking a bottle of corn syrup from her and replacing it on the shelf.

"Nobody had to teach me. You just pick up what you want."

"But you have to know which type to get. Certain brand names have different flavors."

She shrugged. "It doesn't matter."

He slanted her a harsh glance. "I'm going to pretend you didn't say that." He grabbed a name-brand corn syrup and placed it in the basket.

Grocery shopping turned out to be more enjoyable than either could have guessed. Cassie teasingly picked up whatever seemed handy while Drake put it back and got what they needed. She rested against the cart as Drake studied the label of a new olive oil. An older woman draped in a long yellow knitted shawl peered into Cassie's cart, then looked at her.

"You aren't doing your figure any good, honey, picking up those items," she said.

Cassie was ready with a witty reply, but Drake spoke first. He glanced up, his voice soft, but his tone loaded with steel. "Are you implying that there's something wrong with my wife's figure?"

The woman seemed to visibly shrivel under his stare. Cassie came to her rescue. "She didn't mean any harm."

Drake's eyes didn't leave the woman's face. "Then she should learn to keep her opinions to herself."

The woman hurried away.

Cassie watched the woman dart around the corner, then looked at him. "Don't you know to respect your elders?" she scolded.

"Sure, when they're worth respecting." He walked to the next aisle. "Let me show you how to choose walnuts."

"Drake, you can't..." Her voice trailed off.

"What?"

Be my protector, she silently finished. He couldn't take issue with every person who made a comment about her size, but he'd learn that eventually. "You can't show me how to choose walnuts."

"Just watch me."

* * *

"I'll wait for you outside," she said when they had finished selecting items. "Unless you want to show me how to pay for the items as well." She batted her eyelashes and smiled like a naive school-girl.

Drake pulled out his wallet, his expression the perfect caricature of a staid professor. "That will be another lesson."

She clapped her hands in feigned delight. "I am full of anticipation."

Once outside, Cassie rested against the redbrick wall of the building, staring at the traffic and people rushing in and out of shops. Those trying to walk at a leisurely pace were effectively pushed aside.

"Hey, Cassie! Long time no see!"

She turned her head at the greeting and saw two women—one was short in a bright purple pinwheel hat; the other medium height with a necklace that looked like a dog collar: Tanya and Nanj. She had met them through Adriana in college. They were friendly enough, but she didn't want them around when Drake showed himself. They would probably wonder what he was doing with her.

She pushed herself off the wall and walked toward them. "Yes, I've been busy," she said vaguely.

Tanya adjusted her hat. "One should never be too busy for friends," she said, her smile bright and genuine against her pale skin. She wore a dress that looked identical to Cassie's "hope" dress. Cassie saw how it hugged her slender frame and decided she would donate her dress to the Salvation Army.

Nanj frowned. The expression made her face look extra fierce. With a habit of wearing harsh dark eyeshadow, which contrasted with the light gray of her eyes and spiky black hair that made her olive skin look almost chalky, Nanj already looked intimidating. "How are you handling your divorce?"

"I'm a pro now."

"I broke up with Marco a week ago."

"Oh, I'm sorry," she said lamely, wishing her ready wit was at hand.

"We're going to have a cleansing ceremony if you're interested," Tanya said. "Adriana has all the information. We're going to rid her place of his memory."

"I'll check my schedule. I've been really busy working on a..." Her words trailed off as she watched their faces change.

She could feel Drake's presence even before he rested a friendly hand on her shoulder. "I'm done."

"Good." She smiled at her friends. "It was nice seeing you again." She began to turn.

"Aren't you going to introduce us?" Nanj asked.

"Another time. We're in a hurry."

Drake challenged this by stepping from behind her and stretching out his hand. "The name's Drake." He shook both their hands.

"Nanj." She pointed to her companion. "And that's Tanya."

Tanya wiggled her fingers. "Pleased to meet you. We knew Cassie in college," she explained. Her eyes darted between them. "So are you two..." She trailed off, leaving them to fill in the blanks.

"We're just friends," Cassie said.

"That happen to sleep together," Drake added.

Cassie stared at him, horrified. Tanya laughed; Nanj grinned. "Well, that explains a lot," she said. "See you around. Hope to see you at the cleansing."

"How dare you!" Cassie said in an angry whisper once they were a good distance away.

"How dare I what?"

"Imply that we're sleeping together."

He blinked. "Hell. Have I been sleeping with another woman?"

"No, but that's none of their business." She jerked a thumb at the pair.

"At least I didn't say I planned to marry you."

"You're not marrying me and you can't change my mind about that. Not with your looks or your money, so don't even try."

"Is that all you think I have to offer?" he asked quietly.

She didn't reply. She didn't know how to.

They walked in silence until he asked, "Why didn't you want to introduce me to your friends?"

"It just didn't seem important. I wasn't thinking. We're not close anyway."

He didn't believe her, but would accept the explanation for now. "All right." He reached for her hand; she pulled away.

"I don't like being affectionate in public, remember?" she said.

He tightened his grip on the grocery bag. "I just want to hold your hand. I don't think that counts as a lewd act."

"I explained this to you before."

"You let me hold your hand last time."

"That's only because..." She stopped.

"Because you felt sorry for me," he finished grimly.

"Let's not ruin this day by arguing."

His jaw tensed. "Fine," he said in a clipped voice.

At home, they made the chocolate caramels as if they were two colleagues instead of lovers. Drake barely uttered words that required more than one syllable. Later, they watched a movie since the caramels had to sit overnight, then went to bed with the fight still between them. Cassie felt miserable, knowing he had felt slighted. She squeezed her eyes shut and swore as the truth hit her. She couldn't face anyone judging their relationship. It meant too much to her. Being friends was so much safer, it didn't allow for any scrutiny. But they'd passed that threshold long ago and she knew she could never go back. A deep part of her didn't want to. She had been trapped into what she had been running from. She had set out to befriend the sorcerer with his compelling eyes and tender heart and he had won. Damn him. She punched him in the shoulder.

"Ow!" He sat up and turned on the lights. "What the hell was that for?"

"What you did was arrogant and inexcusable, but I apologize for not introducing you."

He was quiet for so long she wondered if he would continue to ignore her.

"Why didn't you want to introduce me?" he finally asked.

She rested her hands behind her head and stared up at the ceiling. "I just like keeping you to myself, I guess."

He turned off the lights and she heard the sheets shifting as he turned away from her.

"I still feel awkward about us," she admitted in a rush. "You should have seen the look of shock on their faces when I married Timothy. They couldn't believe it. I just didn't want to see that expression again."

"Is that why you keep me at arm's length in public?"

"I don't keep you at arm's length."

"If I brush up against you, you snap at me."

She rolled her eyes. "That's not true."

He turned to her and rested on his elbow. "Except for our first night, I haven't been allowed to kiss you, hold your hand, or touch your face in public. I feel like I'm having an affair with a married woman."

"That would include dark hidden places," she teased.

"How many times have we gone to the movies, or sat in the dark corner of a cafe?"

She sighed. He had a point. "I'm still getting used to us," she said. "Being part of a couple again."

Drake lay down and gathered her close. She rested her head on his shoulder, glad the wall between them had crumbled. "My reunion is next week. You had better get used to 'us' fast."

"Why?" she asked sleepily.

"Because I plan on introducing you as my wife."

* * *

The woman was crying. He slipped on his shoes and tossed her a tissue. He'd learned early that some women liked to cry. Liked to find some man to give them grief. His sister had shown him that, choosing any bad boy with a trigger fist she could find.

He looked at the woman. Her dark frizzy hair covered her face; her skinny knees came together like a triangle over the side of the bed. She'd known he wasn't going to stay but she hadn't believed him. Too bad. He glanced at his watch. He had to go by Cassie's place. Being at a distance was beginning to get to him.

He was annoyed when she wasn't home. Where was she? She shouldn't be out this late. He heard 712 open. He shook his head. The old man was pathetic.

"You might as well leave her alone," he said.

He grimaced. The man's voice made his skin crawl.

Mr. Gianolo continued. "I tell her who's good and she doesn't need you or want you anymore. She's got a real man now."

He only smiled. He didn't want to upset him. The man was as harmless as a little barking dog tied up in a yard. But he had no idea the dangerous game he was playing.

* * *

She was going to be Drake's wife. It was even worse than being his girlfriend. She could just imagine the people's faces when he introduced her. She had argued with him in hopes of changing his mind, but he was adamant and she had ultimately succumbed. She was to be his support and if having a wife made him feel more comfortable at the reunion, then she would do it. Besides, it would be a role she would play in front of people she would never see again. The major question was, after the reunion where would they go from there?

"This is your last chance to change your mind," she warned as he parked the car in front of a crumbling cement barrier.

Drake shut off the car and unlatched his seat belt. "I don't plan to."

Cassie glanced at the ring that shone on her finger. "How were you able to guess my size?"

He lifted her hand and kissed it. "I suck them often enough, I should know them by now."

"Drake," she said, embarrassed by his honesty.

He shrugged and opened the door. "What? It's the truth."

They walked up to the building. It was formidable even in the warm glow of the setting sun—angry redbrick walls sported graffiti and dull windows stared sightless. Inside was no better, although clean. The lockers were a pale green against the peeling white walls.

"They've fixed the place up nicely," Drake said. "That was a joke."

"I sincerely hope so," Cassie said seeing something scurry into a hole in the wall.

He took her hand. "We're married now, remember?" he reminded her when she instinctively began to pull away.

"I remember."

They entered the gymnasium. Gold and black balloons complemented a stream of ribbons of the same colors. Drake received his badge and frowned at it.

"Do you recognize anyone?" Cassie asked, studying the crowd—a sea of love handles, receding hairlines, and cosmetic surgery.

He briefly looked up, then returned his gaze to the badge. "Yes."

"Aren't you going to say hello?"

He flipped the badge over. "No."

"Why not?"

He glanced up. "They wouldn't know who I am. What am I supposed to do, go up to them and say, 'Remember me? No, of course you don't, I was invisible'?"

"I doubt you could ever be invisible."

He held up his badge. There was a blank box with a line through it where a picture should have been.

Cassie smiled sheepishly. "At least you have nothing to hide. Point to someone you recognize. Or do they all look different?"

He surveyed the group for a moment, then nodded to a man near the wall with a model-like wife. "Voted Most Popular." He glanced to their right at a woman surrounded by men. "Voted Best Dressed."

"Not for long."

He smiled, then told her of others.

"You remember a lot," she said, surprised.

He pushed his badge in his pocket. "It's amazing what you notice as an outsider."

"You're supposed to wear your badge. It's only one night and people will be able to read your name. I'll pin it on."

He reluctantly handed it to her. "I hate badges."

"You'll survive. Do you see Brenda Timmons anywhere?"

He raised his brows, impressed. "You remembered her name?"

"Of course. Have you forgotten? I was an outsider too. She's why we're here, right?"

"Partly," he said absently. "Would you like a drink?"

Before she could respond, a woman with large glasses came up to them dressed in a green outfit with ruffles that threatened to choke her. She squinted at Drake's badge. "I don't believe it. Drake Henson?"

"Yes," he said cautiously.

She smiled. "You haven't changed a bit. You still look like you'd rather be somewhere else."

"Bad habit of mine."

"What's your name?" Cassie asked.

She touched her badge. "They misspelled my name. I'm Greta Rodgers. It's all right if you don't remember me."

"I remember you," he said, offering her a warm smile. He also remembered that Eric said she was his first. "Physics whiz and played the clarinet."

She blushed with pleasure. "That was me. I'm a physicist now. If the rumors are true, you're a successful restaurateur. Not too bad for our class."

"I didn't do it alone. Cassie's been my rock."

Greta's glow dimmed. "Cassie?"

He rested a hand on her shoulder. "Yes, my wife," he said proudly. "She helps me with the recipes, design, and a number of other projects and she still keeps up her job as a speaker. You should attend one of her seminars. They are amazing. That's how we first met. Actually—"

Cassie nudged him to stop; Drake stared at her, confused.

"Nice to meet you," Greta said.

Cassie tried not to look sympathetic, understanding the woman's disappointment. "Likewise."

"Figures you would still be married. I'd hoped with all the divorces you'd be one of them. It was nice to see you again."

Drake frowned. "You don't have to leave. I could get you two ladies a drink and—"

"No, thanks. I'd better go see who else I can recognize."

He shrugged. "Okay." He turned to Cassie. "Why did you nudge me? I was trying to be sociable. Did I do something wrong?"

"You don't talk about your wife to a woman who is obviously attracted to you. It's bad enough you're married; you don't need to rub her nose in it."

He stared at her, amazed. "What are you talking about?"

"Why can't you tell when a woman is attracted to you?"

He cupped her chin. "I thought I was doing pretty well in that department."

She stepped back. "Someone besides me," she said, irritated.

"Well, you're the only one that counts."

For now, she thought. What would he be like when he saw Brenda? Cassie watched Greta, her heart heavy. She knew every emotion the woman was going through. "Poor woman, it must be dreadful to carry a crush this long."

"Sounds sick to me."

She poked him in the arm. "Hey, remember why we're here. Her name begins with a B." They ate some appetizers and Cassie continued to watch Greta, who was talking to someone near the punch bowl. "You know, if she changed her glasses and that ridiculous dress, she would be much more attractive. Maybe if she stood a little straighter and—"

"I see her," Drake interrupted.

Cassie's heart began to pound at the eagerness in his voice. "Brenda?"

"Yes." He gestured to the main entrance. "She just walked in."

Cassie switched her gaze to the door. She expected to see an average woman in her late thirties—what she saw was a knockout. She was tall, slender, sophisticated, slender, striking, and of course slender. She had an air of confidence that could rival Drake's. A striking turquoise dress complemented her rich maple skin and devastating physique. No wonder he had been attracted to her.

"Let's go meet her." He was halfway to the door when he realized Cassie wasn't with him. He turned to her, frowning, as she tugged off his ring.

He seized her wrist. "What are you doing?"

"This is your big chance. She came in alone. This could be like the prom you never had."

Drake stared at her for a moment, his face unreadable. "If you don't stop being an adorable romantic, I'm going to have to kiss you." She gaped at him; he smiled. "That's better, let's go." He took her hand and dragged her to where Brenda stood talking with two other women. Their heated conversation stopped when Drake approached.

"Hi, Brenda, I'm—"

Gorgeous sable eyes drank him up. "I know who you are," she said in a smooth voice. "I just can't believe it." She hugged him, then drew back, her hand still on his arm. "You look almost the same."

"The gray gives me away."

"It works on you." She ran a hand through his hair. Cassie blinked at her boldness. They must have been closer than she thought.

He introduced Cassie and the women exchanged pleasantries, and then he and Brenda began talking about old times, work, and life. They were undoubtedly the most successful of their class. Brenda was a millionaire, having created her own weight-loss empire. She had a home on both coasts and traveled extensively. Cassie suddenly recognized her from one of the many workout tapes gathering dust on her bookshelf—*Brenda's Boot Camp.*

She watched the pair as the other two women left. She thought about how she could escape too, but Drake kept a solid grip on her hand. The two former classmates talked as if no one else existed, and she couldn't blame them. Seeing the dull building that was in stark contrast to the bright state-of-the-art design of her high school, proved that they had worked hard to achieve their goals. They had both come through life the hard way and succeeded.

Physically, they made a magnificent pair and it was evident by their warm tones and easy teasing manners that they meant a lot to each other. Drake was a complete gentleman, cool, calm, and best of all civil. No abrupt remarks or bored expressions, he was the man she had met that hot summer day months ago. This was what she had wanted, right? She had succeeded in training a rogue. Her triumph was mingled with heartache. She had helped him and now she had to let him go.

She glanced around the crowd, feeling a sense of alienation crawl up her spine. She was being forgotten in the presence of someone more attractive and more interesting, and more successful—again. She felt as if she were fifteen, standing against the wall because she had no more jokes to share, no other way to keep people's attention.

When Drake released her hand, she discreetly made her escape. She went to the table and stared at a tantalizing row of desserts. She resisted the urge to gather a few and stuff her face in the corner. Instead she rushed into the hallway and looked down the long corridor—patches of light followed darkness. She traced her fingers along the cold metal lockers, then slid to the ground in front of a classroom door. She loved him and it hurt to admit it. She had tried to run from it, ignore it, but now it stared at her just when she faced losing him.

She squeezed her eyes shut and took a deep breath until the need to cry left her. There was no need to cry. Tonight she was Cassandra. Cassandra could love them and leave them, right? Cassandra was bold, sexy, and fearless. She definitely didn't let a roomful of strangers intimidate her or the loss of the man she loved get her down. There were plenty more men out there, much more fun to be had. She stood, took a calming breath, and gathered her courage before returning to the gymnasium.

An attractive woman in a cream dress came up to her. "Cassandra Henson," she said, reading her badge. "I don't seem to recognize you."

She smiled wearily. The night would take a long time to end. "I'm just a wife."

"Lucky. You don't have to get on the bragging bandwagon. I'm Frederica."

She shook her hand. "Nice to meet you."

Frederica looked around the room. "Whose wife are you, so I won't make fun of your husband?"

"Drake Henson."

She frowned. "I'm not sure I remember him."

"He said he was invisible."

"That explains it then." She narrowed her eyes. "You know, you look oddly familiar. That's the real reason I came up to you. Have we met before?"

"I don't think so."

The woman was insistent "What's your maiden name?"

"Graham."

Her eyes widened. "Cassandra Graham!"

Cassie stepped back as the woman's enthusiasm struck her. "Yes."

"You changed my life." She gave Cassie a fierce hug. "I went to one of your seminars and was never the same. I am so honored to meet you. You must do a session for young girls. It would help my twelve-year-old a lot."

"I'll definitely consider it I'm glad I was able to help you."

"You didn't just help me. You transformed me. I wouldn't have met my husband if it wasn't for you." Her voice lowered. "I'm sorry about your divorce. I know some people said nasty things, but you showed them, didn't you, keeping your marriage secret and all? You're truly an inspiration."

"No, it's people like you who inspire."

"Please consider doing something for young girls. Here's my card. Please call me. I could give you ideas for the new seminar."

"Sounds great." She watched the woman return to her table, then smiled down at the card, her spirits renewed.

"Cassie, right?" a cultured female voice asked behind her.

She pushed the card in her purse and turned to Brenda. "Yes."

"I seem to have lost track of your husband," she said with an ironic little laugh. "He left before we could exchange phone numbers. He wanted me to call him. I was hoping you could give it to me."

"Certainly." She rattled it off.

Brenda jotted the number down, then glanced up, studying her. "You're exactly what I expected Drake's wife to look like. He had it so rough it figures he'd marry a sweet... motherly type."

Cassie smiled. "Yes, like all mothers I cook his meal, tuck him into bed, then sleep with him."

Her eyes hardened. "You're a lucky woman, Cassie."

"I know."

"I didn't expect much from tonight, but I'm glad I came. Seeing Drake again has changed my life and by the look of things it's changed yours too." On that enigmatic note, she left.

She wants him, Cassie thought, watching the predatory sway of her hips as she approached a small group. The question was, did Drake want her too? From her hint the answer was clear. Cassie glanced toward the dessert table suddenly feeling ravenous. She headed in that direction, but was ambushed by Frederica and her cohorts. They riddled her with questions and for a half hour her worries were forgotten.

"Are you ready?" Drake asked behind her. It was the male equivalent of "let's go."

"Oh, don't drag her away yet," a woman protested. "We're just getting started."

Cassie laughed. "It's past his bedtime, but it was wonderful speaking with you. Good-bye."

* * *

"So did you have a good time?" she asked as they rode the elevator to his place. He'd been quiet and restless on the drive home. No doubt trying to reevaluate his feelings for her. She had expected him to drop her home; at this point she would have preferred it, but he hadn't. He'd driven straight to his place. She wondered if he even remembered she was there. Here she stood next to him, her heart trembling, waiting for the big blow.

"Yes, I did." He opened the door and Cassie followed him inside. "Would you like something to drink?"

"No."

He turned on the kitchen lights. Cassie took a seat.

He opened the fridge. "Something to eat?"

"No, I'm full."

He shut the fridge and wandered to the sink. "The food was okay. Except the chicken had too much..." He searched for the word.

"Cilantro," they said and shared a smile.

"And the rice?" he asked.

"Overcooked. The wine wasn't bad."

"It was as appetizing as sewage."

"Drake," she scolded.

He grinned. "I only said it to shock you. You seem a little tense."

She loosened her grip on the table. "I'm not."

He sat down in front of her and drummed his fingers against his palm. "So."

"So."

He stared down at the table. "Cassie, you know I'd never intentionally hurt you, but seeing Brenda again—"

A cold knot formed in her stomach. "You don't have to say any more," she cut in.

His eyes met hers. "Yes, I do. It will be gnawing at me if I don't."

Let it gnaw, she silently pleaded. *Let it eat you up inside, just don't say it. Don't make me have to hear the words.* She bit her lip to keep from speaking.

"This is hard for me. I don't do this."

Lucky her. She abruptly stood, her mouth as dry as paper. "I think I'll get a drink."

He stood behind her as she poured herself papaya juice. "Cassie, this is important. I need you to look at me."

Why did people always want your attention when they were going to hurt you? "Just let me finish my drink." She took a long swallow, placed the glass down, then turned to him.

His voice was low, his eyes intense. "Cassie, I'm sorry, but I don't think—"

"You're right," she readily agreed. "And though it hurts I understand. These things happen. We've had a good time and perhaps we could stay friends. You know, Brenda is a..." She broke off, unable to think of a positive attribute. "And you deserve someone like her. I hope you're happy." She smiled bracingly although the need to cry tightened her throat.

Drake looked as if she'd slapped him. "You want to break up with me just because I failed?" He hit the counter with the flat of his hand. "Damn it, I tried. Doesn't that count for anything? I know I didn't do my best with Greta but I didn't do too badly with Brenda. I even mingled. I know that's nothing big to you, but that's monumental for me."

"I know that."

"But that's not enough. You still want your flash man so out I go."

She hesitated. "What are you talking about?"

"You think a man doesn't recognize when he's being dumped?"

She patted her chest. "You're dumping me first."

"Why would I be dumping you?"

"Because you've fallen in love with Brenda."

Drake fell into a chair, resting his head on his arms, and groaned. "Cassie, Cassie, Cassie."

"What?"

He glanced up. "How did you come up with that?"

"You said you didn't want to hurt me."

"That's right because I don't think your social method worked for me," he explained patiently. "I used *Surviving a Crowd* as a reference."

"But you said 'I don't do this'—"

"I don't ask people to rate me. You're always teasing or scolding me about my manners and I wanted your opinion of tonight."

"You were wonderful."

"Obviously so wonderful you thought I was in love with a woman."

"She's very attractive," Cassie said, sheepish. "And she liked you a lot."

He shook his head, tired. "I can never convince you that you're the only one I want."

She unbuttoned the top of his shirt. "I'm up for a little persuasion."

His eyes smoldered. "Fortunately, I'm in the mood to persuade."

* * *

The phone rang early the next morning. Cassie reached from under the covers and answered it.

"Hello?" she grumbled.

"Hi," a familiar female voice replied. "Could I speak to Drake?"

"Sure." She rubbed her eyes. "Who is this?"

"Brenda."

Her eyes flew open. "Oh, one moment."

She put the phone down and nudged Drake's sleeping form. When he didn't wake, she pinched him. One fierce amber eye glared at her. "What is it?"

"Brenda's on the phone."

He closed his eye and groaned as if in pain. "I gave her my home phone number? Was I drunk last night?"

"No," she said, chagrined. "That was my fault. I'll explain later. Here."

Drake growled and took the phone. "Hi, Brenda. What? I can't. Another time. Right, right, uh-huh.

Good. Bye." He handed Cassie the phone. "Why did you give her my number?"

"She asked me for it. She was your first love, how could I refuse? I assumed you had forgotten to give it to her. She said you changed her life."

He drew her close. "So how many other women did you give my number to, you little romantic?" he grumbled.

"I thought one was enough."

"At last we agree," he said and they both drifted into sleep.

* * *

Cassie woke to the sound of rushing water and muted Calypso music. Her first impulse to join Drake in the shower was followed by doubt. She pushed the bedclothes away and sat up. She knew it was time to take the relationship to another level if this relationship was to have any sense of permanency. She loved him and if they were going to stay together, he would have to love her too—all of her.

She gathered her courage, wrapped a towel around herself, then crept into the bathroom. Steam rose like a fragrant mist and moistened her skin. The white and black tile floors were cool beneath her feet and her eyes fell on the sunken tub and separate shower stall.

She grasped the handle of the shower door, then stopped as doubt assaulted her again. Perhaps she could try this little test another time. Twenty pounds later. She took a step back. Suddenly, a hand reached out and pulled her in.

"It's about time you joined me," Drake said, smiling down at her, his wet eyelashes clinging together, surrounding a warm amber gaze.

"My towel's getting wet!"

"Then take it off."

"But—"

"Having a hard time?" He didn't wait for a reply. "Let me help you." He yanked off the towel and tossed it over the side. His appreciative eyes traveled from her feet to her breasts. His gaze was as tangible as a touch.

She covered her chest. "You're embarrassing me."

He stared at her with bewilderment. "Can an art collector embarrass a Rodin, a sommelier a Pinot Noir?" He grabbed a bar of soap, a wicked smile touching his mouth. "I'm going to enjoy this."

Who enjoyed it more was debatable. Drake's hands roamed over every part of her with masculine deliberation—not one part of her cocoa skin was missed and Cassie surrendered with pleasure. She later returned the favor, creating a soapy path up the muscular form of his chest and down the solid column of his legs. Showering took up the best part of an hour.

"We should do this more often," Drake suggested, shaving in front of the mirror.

Cassie sat on the rim of the tub and watched him—the quick, sure movements of his razor, the final fragrant splash of aftershave. She felt more intimate with him as he completed this simple morning ritual than at any other moment. She had never watched Timothy shave or even brush his teeth. Once he closed the bathroom door, no entry was permitted until he left it. Being with Drake was so natural. He welcomed her into every aspect of his life. Why couldn't she just accept that? Why couldn't she accept what he felt for her? Her eyes involuntarily strayed to the weight scale in the corner, her unconscious answering that crucial question.

"Don't bother. It's broken," Drake said.

Cassie stared at him. "Can you read minds now?"

He winked at her in the mirror. "Only when they're obvious."

She made a face and left to change.

* * *

"I want you to move in with me," Drake announced as he sliced tomatoes for breakfast.

Cassie shook her head as she set the table. "No."

"Why not?"

"Watch your fingers," she admonished him when he cut with extra vigor. "If you're not careful you'll cut them off."

He put the knife down. "You haven't answered my question."

"I don't want to move in." She straightened a fork. "I like my place."

"We can make this place work." He glanced around the kitchen. "Or get another one and decorate it together."

She placed coffee on the table and sat. "That sounds too much like people engaged."

"Is there a problem with that?"

She sent him a warning glance. "You know how I feel."

He put the tomato slices on the cheese and toast. "Cassie, life involves risks."

"I already took that risk. I don't want to get married. I'm sorry, but you came too late."

"I'm not asking you to marry me. Just move in with me." He placed the breakfast on the table and sat.

"It will be the same and I'll lose my freedom."

"I have no desire to take your freedom."

She looked at him. "Then why do you want me to move in?"

He scratched his chin, feeling awkward. "I like having you around."

"I'm not going anywhere," she said lightly.

He sighed. "Cassie."

"Drake," she said, mimicking his tone.

He took a bite of his food. "You drive me crazy."

She laughed. "That's been my plan from the beginning."

"At least give it a chance."

"No. Now let's not argue, it's bad for digestion."

They both happily changed the subject and ate heartily. When they were through, Cassie volunteered to wash up. "Where do you keep new sponges?" she asked, throwing the old one away.

Drake motioned to the counter. "In the drawer."

She opened a drawer and saw a pile of snack bars. "What is this?"

"Breakfast. It's what I eat when I'm by myself."

She lifted one and frowned, disgusted. "That's terrible."

"It's healthy."

She turned it over and read the label. "Aren't you worried that you can't even pronounce any of the ingredients?"

He shook his head. "Not really. I haven't dropped dead yet."

She tossed the bar back in the drawer and shut it. "The operative word being yet."

"If you stayed with me, I'd promise to eat better. We could have breakfast like this every day."

She pointed the faucet hose at him. "The answer is still no."

He held up his hands, admitting defeat, then grabbed a dishrag.

* * *

When Cassie returned to her apartment, she was surprised not to hear the familiar creak of Mr. Gianolo's door as she placed her key in the lock. Her surprise immediately turned to worry. It was uncharacteristic for him not to make an appearance. Perhaps he was sick. He couldn't have traveled, because he always asked her to watch over his place when he did. She went inside and checked her answering machine to make sure he hadn't left a message. He hadn't.

Maybe he had gone out or was taking a nap, she reasoned. But none of her thoughts could quell a sense of uneasiness. She would have to make sure everything was fine. She knocked on his door; there was no reply. She used the spare key he had given her and entered the apartment. She was greeted by an eerie stillness followed by a violent stench that assaulted her nose. She pinched her nose and went to the kitchen, wondering if something was rotting in the garbage. It was clean. A large pot sat on the stove and the remains of chopped vegetables lay on the counter. "Mr. Gianolo?" she called. "It's me, Cassie."

She headed into the bedroom, and saw the bed in violent disarray. The sheets and bedspread had been tossed about as if the occupant had struggled to free himself. Then she saw the light trail of vomit. She covered her mouth and followed the ominous path to Mr. Gianolo's body lying on the bathroom floor. She didn't remember screaming, didn't remember calling out Mr. Gianolo's name, checking his pulse, or wiping his mouth. She vaguely remembered a neighbor calling 911, the sounds of the ambulance and the police. Even when everything seemed to be over, the nightmare continued.

* * *

He had been poisoned. Poisoned. The police said he had accidentally poisoned himself by cooking a bulb of chrysanthemums thinking it was an onion.

She stared at the traffic below her balcony, disgusted that horrible changes happened in life. The day was warm, but all she felt was cold. A cold that pierced her bones and nothing—not sweaters or tea—could soothe it. She buried herself in her jacket as the autumn wind blew past. It wasn't real. He would live, he couldn't die. He would be okay. He had to be.

She watched the wind rip the brown dried leaves off a skinny tree and push them down the sidewalk where people trampled on them. A death that no one noticed. She turned away and headed for the kitchen. Mr. Gianolo wouldn't be like that. He couldn't be. She called Drake to tell him what had happened. She planned on being matter-of-fact, on sounding hopeful. But when he answered, she burst into tears.

She was later bombarded with visitors. Glen was the first to appear and read her poetry. He lifted her spirits with Emily Dickinson's "Hope," but dashed them with Christina Rossetti's "Remember." Adriana bought her a new blouse and CD, and Kevin offered to take her to his cottage in Maine. When Timothy arrived, she grudgingly invited him in and allowed him to offer his sympathies. But in this stream of people her rock and strength came from Drake and as time passed she felt at peace.

Good news arrived on a crisp autumn morning as a pigeon cooed on her balcony railing. Mr. Gianolo's daughter called and told her he would live. Cassie visited him in the hospital until he was released to his daughter's care. He was tired, and their time together was brief, but she was glad to know he would be okay.

She was so happy that the sight of three yellow roses that met her on the doorstep at first didn't bother her. They had the loveliness of velvet sunshine and a sweet fragrance, but slowly the sight of them filled her with trepidation. A shiver of fear swept through her. They didn't represent a man in love, but a man determined to reclaim a possession he had lost. She refused to let them frighten her.

She tossed them in the trash bin as she had all the others.

* * *

Drake shifted awkwardly in front of 712, wondering what had urged him to visit a sick man. Atonement, maybe, for the times his father had lain sick in his bed and he'd avoided his room? He didn't belong here. Why would Mr. Gianolo want to see him anyway? He turned to go. The door opened and a woman around his age appeared with a knowing grin. "My father said you were standing out here. Come in."

"I brought soup." He held out the bowl, feeling uncomfortable.

"Thank you. He's in the bedroom waiting for you."

"Hmm." He walked to the bedroom and stood in the doorway. Mr. Gianolo looked small and weak surrounded by huge pillows and layers of blankets. Fortunately, the smell of death didn't linger in the air. He would be okay.

"Good to see you," Mr. Gianolo said, his voice still strong.

"Same."

"Sit down."

Drake closed the door behind him and sat in a chair, placed near the corner. He glanced at the TV. "Good game?"

"Horrible. An old woman could play better."

"I brought you soup. I... gave it to your daughter."

"From the Blue Mango?"

"Of course."

"Thanks." Mr. Gianolo ran a restless hand across the bedsheet. "I didn't do it," he said urgently. "I didn't poison myself. I would remember."

"It was an accident."

He clenched his hand, grasping the bedsheet. "I don't make accidents like that."

"What do you think happened?"

He leaned forward. "I made one of them angry. One of Cassie's playboys and poets."

It sounded far-fetched, but Drake decided to listen. "Which one?"

"He's black, tall, with dark hair."

He frowned. "Hell, you just described me."

"Except for the gray."

"There's nothing that sticks out?"

"I think I'd know his footsteps." Mr. Gianolo rested his head back and sighed, looking suddenly worn. "I can't seem to focus somehow and I know

I'm not good with descriptions, but I know he's not right."

"How do you think he did it?"

"I get my soups from Mrs. Hill next door. She leaves some in the hall for me. He could have put something in it. I know a chrysanthemum from an onion. I didn't do it."

"Hmm."

"You don't believe me. Nobody does and now they want to put me away like some useless old man." His voice crumbled and tears swam in the pale blue eyes.

Drake expected to be embarrassed by the tears, remembering the many times he'd turned away from his father's. But strangely all he wanted to do was comfort him. He dragged his chair closer and lowered his voice. "Maybe I could convince your daughter to get a caretaker."

His mouth became a straight line. "I don't need anyone."

"Just for a while," he urged. "Until you prove your independence. We always end up proving ourselves somehow in this world."

Mr. Gianolo shook his head. "A caretaker costs money."

Drake hesitated, wanting to phrase the offer in a manner that didn't sound like charity. Every man had his pride. "Taking care of Cassie is a lot of work. You've done a good job looking out for her and being a friend. Cassie is special to me and it's only fair I take care of those special to her."

He turned away. "It's too much money. I couldn't let you."

For a moment the room was quiet but for the sound of a crowd cheering on TV, the curtains swaying from the breeze blowing through a vent Drake absently reached for his cigarettes, then clasped his hands together. "When my dad died, I hated him," he said suddenly. "I thought it was because I believed him weak, believed that he had given up and left us. But that wasn't why." He took a deep breath. "It was because I couldn't do any-thing for him— there's a feeling of helplessness that can torture a man's soul. I know how you feel—the weakness, the lack of hope—but it doesn't have to be so. Think of it as a contract. You continue to look out for Cassie and I look out for you."

Mr. Gianolo kept his head turned, but reached out and seized Drake's hand in a surprisingly strong grip. "It's rare that people make an old man feel useful," he said in a rough voice. He looked at him. "You're a good son. Your father understood."

Drake tried to ease the tightening of his throat. "Hmm."

Both men were relieved when the door opened, easing the strain of emotions hanging in the air.

"Mr. Gianolo, how are you?" Cassie asked, entering the room. She halted when she saw Drake. "Isn't this a surprise?"

Mr. Gianolo grinned, his face a lot more animated than when Drake first entered. "My friend's visiting me."

"I see that." She put her gift near the window.

Mr. Gianolo pulled Drake's collar and whispered in his ear, "So have you asked her?"

"What?"

"The big question."

"No, I—"

He released his grip and sat back. "You're going to have to. She's no longer safe in this place."

"But I—"

Mr. Gianolo patted the bedsheets, in no mood to debate the issue. "Sit down, Cassie, Drake's got a proposal to give you."

She narrowed her eyes suspicious. "It's not—"

Drake nodded, resigned. Now was the time to ask the question he'd waited months to utter. "Yes, it is. Will you marry me?"

Chapter Thirteen

"You asked her to marry you?" Eric asked as they walked to Drake's office the next day. "What did she say?"

"She said she would think about it," Drake said.

Eric cringed. "It's better than no."

His jaw tightened. "You try it sometime."

They entered his office and sat.

Drake's assistant peeked his head inside. "Hey, did you two pass her in the hallway?"

"Who?" Drake asked absently as he sorted through his messages.

"She said her name was Cassie."

His head shot up. He turned to Eric, then back to his assistant. He rose to his feet and came from behind the desk. "Did she leave a message? Did she say what she wanted? How long ago did she leave?"

"She didn't leave a message, but she did give me this." He handed Drake a large paper bag.

"Looks like the booby prize," Eric muttered.

His assistant held up his hands. "I'm just the delivery boy," he said and closed the door.

Drake set the large paper bag on his desk and stared at it.

"You have to open it at some point," Eric said.

He pushed it aside. "No, I don't."

Eric reached forward. "Then I will."

Drake snatched the bag away. "You won't either."

"You can't just stare at it," he argued, pushing up his glasses. "We already know what the answer is, why deny it?"

Drake scowled at the bag, then opened it. Inside he found a thermos marked *hot chocolate*, a can of whipped cream, and various containers: an omelet, a fruit salad, and a bagel: she had made him breakfast.

He stared at the containers of food with a mixture of emotions engulfing him: fear, pleasure, astonishment, and something he couldn't yet analyze. She had cooked him breakfast—no one except his mother and brother had ever cooked for him before. This gift meant more to him than any gold cufflinks or silk ties others had given him. To a man who in the past had to do without breakfast and lunch most of his life, it was almost sacrilege to eat it. He ran his hand over the containers as if they were sacred artifacts.

"She made you breakfast," Eric said in awe.

His voice sounded far away. "I know."

Eric picked up the fork. "Can I have a taste?"

"No."

Eric lifted the lids, knowing his brother needed a little urging to begin. "Aren't you going to eat it?"

Drake met his brother's gaze, still stunned, but unable to articulate his feelings. "I'm not sure." Since his mother's death he hadn't been greeted with a homemade meal. He even remembered what she'd last prepared for him—saltfish with scrambled eggs because there was no ackee. He stared at the puffy yellow of the omelet as the cheese and green peppers peeked through the soft layers. How would he remember this moment? Why wasn't she here with him to enjoy it?

Eric handed him the fork. "You would be shaming her if you didn't eat it. Not to mention wasting a good meal. At least try it."

"Right." He took the fork and twirled it between his fingers before tucking into the omelet and taking a bite. He pushed a container toward Eric, handing him one of the plastic forks he kept in his drawer.

Eric took a bite, then rested his head back and closed his eyes. "We have to convince her to marry you."

"Hmm." He didn't want to damper the moment by thinking about that.

Eric glanced in the bag for napkins and saw a note. He held it up between two fingers. "I think your answer is here."

"Throw it away." He turned back to his messages.

"At least read it."

"I know what it says." He didn't care that she wouldn't marry him. For now this was enough.

"Can I read it?"

Drake nodded.

He tried to work as Eric read, but instead listened for a sign of his brother's response to the note. He heard him softy swear and tear it up. Drake felt his last hope crumble to his feet.

"I'm glad you didn't read it." He stretched his legs out. "The woman tries so hard not to hurt your feelings that she doesn't get to the point."

"Hmm."

"I mean she goes on about how much she loves you and the reason why she'll marry you, but doesn't—"

Drake leaped out of his seat and grabbed Eric by the lapels of his jacket. "And you tore it up?"

"I thought you didn't want to read it," he challenged.

"I could break your fingers." He returned to his seat and pointed at him. "You'd better not be lying to me about what she wrote."

"I wouldn't do that. Here." He tossed the note on the table. "Read it yourself."

Drake glared at him. "Bastard."

Eric shrugged good-naturedly. "Sorry, I couldn't resist teasing you."

Drake read the letter, then placed it down almost afraid to believe the words she'd written. She'd said she loved him and would marry him. At last she would belong to him.

* * *

She should have said yes in person, Cassie thought, staring at the phone as if she could make it ring. Why hadn't he called yet? Had he changed his mind now that he had what he wanted? Maybe the day had given him a chance to think as well—to change his mind. She had not been able to sleep last night, her mind running with all the reasons to say no to his proposal. A failed first marriage, her need for space, her convictions, Drake's feelings about love. Yes, she was certain to say no, but somehow this morning as she had prepared breakfast she thought of Drake munching on one of his disgusting breakfast bars. Before she knew it, she had his breakfast in hand and was heading to his main office.

She could have waited to see him, but a part of her was still unsure that he knew what he was doing. Now that he had achieved his goal, would the prize lose its potency? She couldn't sit and wait anymore. She went into the kitchen, grabbed a bag of oatmeal cookies, and indulged. Of course the phone rang when her mouth was full. She raced to it and picked it up on the second ring.

"Hmph?"

"Cassandra, I hope you're not answering the phone with your mouth full."

Cassie fell into the couch like a lead doll and tugged on her shirt like an awkward teenager. She swallowed and said, "Hello, Mother. How are you?"

"Just wonderful. I went to the spa yesterday and treated myself to a delightful mud bath. So how are you doing? Are you seeing anyone?"

Just what she needed, her mother prying into her life and injecting it with her negativity. How could she tell her mother she was planning on marrying a man she'd known only a few months? That she loved him but that he might be a big mistake? Thankfully, someone knocked on the door, giving her the needed reprieve. "Just a moment, I have to get the door." She put down the receiver, prayed that it was some sort of emergency—a fire per- haps—and opened the door.

Her big mistake was leaning against the door frame like a sexy rogue, dressed in a black turtleneck and trousers, his amber eyes lazily sensuous and his smile even more so. "Hello, Mrs. Henson," he said.

"I'm on the phone," she replied stupidly.

His smile grew. "Don't let me stop you. I'll be in the kitchen."

Drake piled the containers in the sink. He planned to go look at engagement rings once she got off the phone. He had been able to squeeze in an appointment for them that afternoon. Breakfast in the morning and ring shopping in the afternoon. His patience had paid off. It was a good day. He tried not to listen to Cassie's conversation, but found himself eavesdropping anyway. He wanted to make sure it wasn't someone bothering her.

Just when he was about to turn on the tap, he heard Cassie say in a low voice, "No, I'm not seeing anyone special, Mom. Of course I'd tell you. Adria- na said what? Uh-huh. Yes, well, he's not important. He's just a close friend. Uh-huh. No, he's not like Timothy." A heavy sigh. "I know you liked him, too bad you didn't marry him. No, I'm not trying to be facety. Uh-huh. That's right. No one. Talk to you later. Good-bye." She hung up.

Drake felt ice spread through his stomach, then shatter as if someone had kicked him. Had he misunderstood her? Had he misread how she felt about him? He took out the note he had carefully folded and tucked in his pocket. He reread the words he had begun to memorize. She had said she loved him, and for a moment he had let that mean something even though he knew she was just being romantic. But her words had been a lie. He crumbled the note in his fist.

"Whew. I'm glad that's over," Cassie said with evident relief as she entered the kitchen. She halted when she saw him. She'd never seen such a look of anger floating in his eyes before. "What's wrong?"

He gestured to the phone. "That was your mother, right?"

"Yes," she said slowly.

"Why did you tell her you weren't seeing anyone important?"

She dismissed his concern with a wave of her hand. "It's just a ruse. If she knew you and I were close, she'd start asking questions and then want to meet you."

"Would that be so bad?" he asked in a quiet voice.

"It would be dreadful. Trust me on this one." Cassie knew her mother would spend the entire time comparing him to Timothy or ask him what he saw in her daughter.

Drake shook his head as if finally solving a riddle that should have been obvious. "You really had me fooled." He laughed without humor. "I actually believed that your insecurities about weight was what kept us apart, what kept me from meeting your family, having you introduce me to your friends, or kept me at a distance in public. But now I know the truth." His intense eyes held her still. "You're ashamed of me."

Cassie glanced skyward. "Don't be ridiculous."

His eyes flashed but his voice remained level. "You really expect me to believe that you didn't want to introduce me to your family and friends because *I'll* be embarrassed to be with you?" His accent thickened his words. "I used to be that stupid, but now I know it's the other way round. You're scared people will ask about my background or that I'll do something to make you ashamed. I'm good for the back room, but not the front. I don't have Timothy's elegance and polish."

"That's not true. I said I would marry you, didn't I?"

"Through a note. Heaven forbid you would tell me in person where someone else might hear."

She walked toward him, her eyes pleading. "You don't understand."

He stepped back. "I'm tired of going through hoops for you."

"I don't expect you to go through hoops for me."

He walked to the door. "This isn't working."

"I never expected it to," she muttered to his back.

He whirled around, pinning her with his eyes. "Yes, that was the problem from the start. No matter what I did, I was never good enough for you. You never expected me to be around for long and that's why you didn't want to marry me." He stormed to the door.

She grabbed a rolling pin and followed. "You're not leaving until I get a chance to explain."

He opened the door. "I am tired of your explanations."

"You're not leaving."

He lifted an eyebrow in challenge. "How are you going to stop me?"

She slammed the door shut and held up the pin.

He sent her a cool, dark glance. "What are you planning to do, Cassie? Roll me into submission?"

"I'm planning to make you listen," she hissed. "And I don't care how. I won't have you leave thinking that—"

He opened the door again; she closed it. He took a deep breath, fighting a losing battle with his patience. "I'm not in the mood for games and you know I can't hurt you. Let me pass."

"I spent all morning preparing that breakfast for you because I wanted you to know what you meant to me." She threw up her hands. "Didn't it mean anything to you?"

His cold glare left her face and focused on an area above her head. His reply was a whisper. "It meant everything."

"Then is it just me or don't we have something worth fighting for?"

"What exactly do we have? I can't even hold your hand in public and I am continually introduced as your friend even when we're supposedly engaged."

"Let me explain. I—"

He held up his hands. "I don't want an explanation. All you give me are words. You have an explanation for everything."

"If you don't want an explanation, what do you want?"

"I want you to call your mother and tell her that you want her to meet your fiancé."

Cassie shook her head. "That's asking too much. You see—"

"Yes, I do see. I tried to prove myself at the reunion. I tried to show you that I could be cordial and civil when needed. That I wouldn't humiliate you in social situations, but that wasn't enough, was it? I'll never be good enough for you. You tried to warn me, but I was too stupid to listen. So now I'm listening. You wanted to get rid of me from day one. Congratulations, you've succeeded." He bit his lip as if stopping himself from saying more, then walked out the door.

Mr. Gianolo peeked his head out as Drake headed for the elevators. "So when's the wedding?" he asked.

"There isn't going to be one," Drake replied and headed for the stairs.

Chapter Fourteen

*H*e was back where he had started. In Eugene's Bar with a half-empty mug of beer, the background buzz of voices and the enthusiastic shouts of a sports announcer on TV. He inhaled his cigarette, feeling the smoke burn his lungs.

"You can't keep this up," Eric said. "Since your breakup I haven't seen you without smoke coming out of your mouth."

Drake slowly exhaled, lifting his beer. "What's your point?"

"You need to talk to her. Okay, you've ignored her calls and notes for over two weeks; she's been suitably punished, now mend things."

"I have another date with Brenda tomorrow night."

"Brenda isn't the marrying type."

He tapped his cigarette against the ashtray. "That's fine because I'm not interested in marriage."

* * *

Drake's eyes trailed over the informal elegance of the restaurant. The evening had been pleasant as usual, but for some reason he just wanted it to end. He shouldn't have come... the ghost of Cassie seemed to float around everywhere.

"This place is everything you said," Brenda gushed.

"Hmm."

"The food was fabulous."

"Hmm."

"And the atmosphere—"

"You don't have to go on. This isn't my restaurant."

She smiled and touched his hand. "I know. I'm just so happy that we've had the chance to become reacquainted. I'm sorry about your impending divorce."

Drake inwardly winced at the lie. For some reason he hadn't been able to admit the truth.

Her finger made a slow circle on the back of his hand. "You know I have a place in San Diego where you could relax for a while."

"I—"

She raised the finger to his lips. "Don't say no yet. Just think about it." She glanced up briefly at something, then leaned forward and kissed him—

softly but effectively. She wiped her lipstick from his lower lip and stood. "I'm just going to the ladies' room."

Drake paid the bill, then glanced around the restaurant. His eyes stopped on a large crowd listening enraptured to a woman dressed in a cream sweater and red scarf—Cassie. His heart began to race and his fingers itched for the feel of a cigarette. He hadn't brought any with him since Brenda couldn't stand smoking. He turned away, but his eyes involuntarily slid back to her.

She would be here, he thought, mentally kicking himself. This was the same place she had taken his class. The place where he'd flirted with her like a schoolboy with a crush. His eyes fell on one guy who mirrored what his expression had once been. He tapped his fingers against the table trying to forget the feel of her scarf or the warmth of her skin. He had been a fool to think he could claim her when he had been one of many. He scowled and turned away.

* * *

"Cassie," Adriana whispered urgently when the class broke up.

"Yes, I know," she said with a resigned sigh. "Drake's here."

"Don't you care?"

"Should I? He broke up with me. And now he's happy."

"How can you tell?" she demanded.

Cassie pushed papers into her bag. "A sixth sense of mine. I can feel my heart breaking."

Adriana drummed her fingers against her thigh. "Be serious."

"I am being serious. He's with his first love. Brenda Timmons the aerobics guru. They were kissing."

"So?"

If her friend didn't understand, she wasn't in the mood to enlighten her. "I really don't want to talk about this."

"You're unhappy."

"At least he's not. I want him to be happy."

"And I want you to be happy. He should be with you."

Cassie let her bag fall to the floor, annoyed. "Adriana, we can't have both. I have tried to reach him, but he ignores my calls and my notes. It is obvious he wants nothing to do with me. So will you please drop the subject?"

"You haven't done enough to give up yet."

Cassie sat and held her head in her hands, defeated. "What do you expect me to do? Run over hot coals proclaiming my love, lie naked on his windshield—no, that might scare him."

"You teach people to be bold and go after what they want, but you won't do the same."

Cassie's voice was muffled but firm. "I have succeeded in all that I've set out to do."

"Yes, driving away the man you love because you're too afraid to admit that you deserve him."

She lifted her head and stared, incredulous. "Where do you come up with this? Haven't you heard a word I've said? I've tried to get him back. He doesn't want me. Do we need a translator?"

"Just listen for a minute. The first day I met you, your mother came to pick you up. She wore this stunning black and white polka-dot dress and big round sunglasses like a movie star. When I asked you if that was your mother you said she was your aunt."

"Okay, so I was a liar."

"No, you were ashamed that you couldn't measure up. It was the same with Timothy, that's why you let him stray. You didn't expect him to treat you right."

"Well, that's a good argument for infidelity. Actually it coincides with his statement that he did it to save the marriage."

"You're not listening. You love Drake and you deserve him. He belongs to you. He's yours, don't let some other woman take him away."

Cassie stared at her for a moment "I'm waiting for a point."

"He doesn't believe you love him. So you have to prove it."

"If you don't get off my back I can prove how fast a friendship can end." She grabbed her bag and headed to the ladies' room. She saw Brenda coming out and stopped.

"What a surprise," Brenda said.

"I see you're here with Drake."

"Yes."

"I hope you have a good time."

"Don't worry, I know how to keep my men."

Cassie watched her go, anger shooting through her veins. Brenda might have Drake, but she'd make his complete surrender difficult.

* * *

Drake felt Brenda's fingers inching their way up his thigh as he drove home and he knew it wasn't going to work. Instead of feeling aroused he felt annoyed. He hadn't changed much, he still didn't like people enough to be civil longer than necessary. For all her intelligence and beauty he always found that he wished to be elsewhere. He would have to end it. It might be a relief to her; he wasn't the most exciting guy to date, hardly responding to any of her invitations. She might even be eager to end the evening.

She smiled at him and whispered, "I'm not wearing any panties."

Then again he'd never been able to read women well.

* * *

The chilly air was invigorating—perfect for his morning jog. He loved the smell of fall mornings, the color of the changing leaves, the sound of the city beginning to wake. A week had passed since he'd seen Cassie in the restaurant and he was doing fine. He was completely over her. Although at quiet unwanted moments he did miss her face, the way she would poke him when making a point, the delicate way she ate. He swore, fiercely trying to control his wayward mind.

"So what did you say?" Eric ordered, breaking into his thoughts. "You don't just stop a story at the point where a woman mentions she's not wearing panties."

"I said then she must be cold and turned up the heat."

Eric pushed up the glasses sliding down his nose. "Are you joking? That's the first thing that came to your mind?"

"No, not the first," he admitted. "But that's what I said."

Eric let out a breath. "I was worried about you for a minute. So you admit you still care for Cassie?"

"I'm over her."

They continued the last lap of their jog in silence. Drake looked at his building and groaned. Great, now he was hallucinating. Cassie was standing right in front of the glass doors with one of her determined looks.

Eric squinted. "Isn't that—"

"Yes."

He spun around. "Talk to you later."

"You don't have to—" But Eric had already jogged away.

Drake slowed his jog to a walk and headed for the door.

Cassie spoke up as he passed her. "I know that I messed up, but I'll do whatever it takes to get you back."

He stopped with his hand on the handle. "Why?"

She stared at him as though the answer was obvious. "Drake, I miss you. I love you."

She loved him. Why the hell did those words mean so much? "Today maybe." He ground his teeth, fighting the need to believe her, and opened the door. "I don't have time for this."

"So you and Brenda are together."

No. "Yes."

"She may have you, but she'll never love you like I do."

He looked at her, his eyes sharp. "I don't want her to love me. I don't want you to love me. I want you to stop being ashamed of me. Ashamed of who I am or how I act. I want you to give a damn that I'm in your life. Brenda may not love me, but she's made me feel better than you ever did. Romantics like you use love as a weapon because you know how much guys like me—" He turned away.

"Drake, you have to let me explain."

He grabbed her shoulders and shook her. "I've told you that I've had enough of your explanations. I haven't returned your calls or responded to your notes. In case you haven't noticed, that's a hint that I don't want you in my life." Even as he said the words he hated them, hated how cold they sounded, but he wouldn't be hurt again. "I don't want to see you or hear from you. I want you to go away." He threw a hand in the air. "Disappear. Pretend that we never happened."

"I'm not ashamed of you." She grabbed the front of his shirt, desperate to make him understand despite how his words hurt her. "Give me another chance. I'll show you how much I love you. I'll prove it to you. No more words, just actions. I promise." She smiled weakly. "I haven't sung yet, so this show can't be over."

He seized her wrist, loosening her hold. Her butterscotch eyes were wide and soft and slowly melting into tears. For a moment he let his lips brush against her forehead, inhaled the sweet scent of her. He abruptly pulled away. "How can you love me, when you don't even like yourself?" He turned and went inside.

Cassie wrapped her scarf tighter and stared at the intimidating glass doors. He had every right not to want her. She didn't deserve another chance. He'd already given her one before and that was more than she'd given Timothy.

He was right. For a woman in love she'd done a poor job of showing it, her own insecurities shadowing her true feelings for him. She had introduced him as a good friend for the last time and ultimately pushed him away. As a gentle wind blew her hair, the magnitude of what she had lost hit her. She felt the soft stream of tears down her cheeks. Brushing them aside, she slowly headed down the road.

* * *

How could you love me when you don't even like yourself? Those words echoed like a church bell in an empty cathedral over a week later. At first they made her sad, but she soon became furious. Who was he to judge her when he wore his background like broken armor? Soon her anger led to an eating binge. How dare he criticize her! He didn't love her. He only wanted what she could give him—the prestige of a good background and a few kids that she would raise while he set out on his next conquest. He'd done her a favor by leaving. He didn't even like her work. She grabbed her manuscript and threw it in the air, letting it scatter like large snowflakes.

She went to her closet and grabbed all her "hope" dresses and tossed them on the bed. He'd said she was beautiful, then why did he leave her to date one of the most fit women in all of America? Why had he pretended not to be interested, then suddenly started dating her? Perhaps they'd been seeing each other all along? It didn't matter. He was gone. And since he wanted her to like herself she'd show him just how fat and happy she could be. She didn't need anyone.

She snatched all her diet books off the shelf and her health and beauty magazines and dumped them in the trash bin. Then she seized the diet videos. Her eyes fell on Brenda's beautiful face and gorgeous figure. She had everything Cassie had ever wanted—a successful career, a beautiful body, and now even the man she loved. As quickly as her anger had come it fled and she crumbled to the floor in tears.

It was late afternoon when she was able to pull herself together. She cleared up the mess she'd made and briefly considered calling Timothy, thinking anything was better than feeling this alone, this unwanted. Fortunately, she quickly dismissed the idea, considering someone else.

* * *

"You look sensational," Kevin said as they sat in the sunroom where Cassie had convinced him to take her.

She shifted closer to him. "Thank you."

"So where's—"

She crossed her legs, brushing her thigh against his. "Gone. I told you he was in training."

"Right, I remember. I got the sense he was a lot more than that."

She took his drink and set it down. "Not anymore. I'm completely free." She kissed him.

He drew away. "Cassie, don't."

Heat filled her cheeks. "But I thought you wanted this."

"No, not—"

She jumped to her feet, her humiliation making her furious. "You're all alike. You, Timothy, Drake. You all say you want me, compliment me, give me gifts, but once you have me you couldn't care less. The novelty has worn off and you can move on to the woman who you've had your eye on all the time. I'm like a strange rite of passage. Date a big woman and then you've arrived."

Kevin grabbed her arms and turned her to face him. "That's not it. I do want you."

"You have me."

"No, not the way I want."

"I don't understand."

"That's the problem. Don't you know when a man's in love with you?"

Shock choked her words. "Not you. You have beautiful women all around you. You'll never settle down."

He grinned boyishly. "A man has to keep up his image. I'm shallow, vain, spoiled." His voice fell. "But to my surprise I have a heart as well and you walked right into it. No, don't feel sorry for me. I know you don't feel the same. You never will and... I've dealt with that. I've found it bad practice to start wanting things you can't have. So I'm over it. But I doubt Drake will recover as quickly. You have no idea how you effect men. It's attractive and a little scary."

"He doesn't love me. He thinks I'm ashamed of his background."

"Be patient, babe," he said, making them both smile. "He'll come around."

* * *

Stunned amazement followed Cassie home. Kevin had loved her? Suddenly her eyes became clear. She had been so self-absorbed she hadn't even seen how others felt. She had been so tied up with feeling bad about herself she'd never noticed anyone else. Drake was right, how could she care for anyone when she treated everyone as badly as she did herself? Unexpectedly, words began to fill her mind and she knew exactly what she needed to say in her book. That evening she typed until her back ached and her fingers started to cramp, but she didn't stop flooding the manuscript with the emotion Drake had once said it lacked. She did believe in love and that anyone could grab it and hold it. Everyone was the master of their own bright future.

* * *

Pamela flew into the kitchen and grabbed Cedric's arm. "Oh, my God! Kevin Jackson just walked in."

Cedric frowned. "Who's Kevin Jackson?"

"Only one of the richest, most handsome black men on the East Coast."

Cedric rubbed his chin. "He can't be that handsome with me living here."

Pamela ignored him and dragged him to the door. "Let's see what he orders."

"But I don't—"

She peeked around the corner and pointed. "There he is." They watched Drake approach the table. "I heard that he came in especially to speak to Mr. Henson. I wonder how he knows him."

"It's a woman," Cedric said.

"How do you know?"

He watched Drake ignore Kevin's outstretched hand as he sat. "Because they hate each other."

* * *

Neither of the men would have put his feelings in such broad terms, they would settle on mutual dislike.

"What do you want?" Drake asked.

Kevin smiled slightly. "We have a problem. You hurt a friend of mine."

Drake began to stand. "My relationship with Cassie has nothing to do with you."

Kevin's smile hardened. "That night you stood up for her you made it an issue. If I had known what you were up to, I wouldn't have made it so easy for you to take her."

Drake sat back down. "What do you mean by that?"

"I have money, I was born with it. I went to good schools, eventually Harvard—it's expected. I've never had to struggle a day in my life. I've been to places you've never even heard of, could debate literature and recall mathematical equations you couldn't even hope to understand with your level of education. I knew Cassie before you and could offer her anything she'd ever wanted... and yet she chose you." His eyes turned to ice. "But guys like you are dangerous. You wear your past poverty like a badge of honor, always ready to take the offensive. Always ready to maintain that you're the only ones who've ever suffered. I've never had to scrape my knuckles on the bottom of a trash can or sleep out in the cold, but I've seen hell confined in the beauty of a marble mansion and felt pain echo off a crystal chandelier. Even shallow guys like me recognize true beauty. I'm giving you a second chance. But if you hurt her again, we'll see whose fist is kissed first."

* * *

Cassie called Adriana once her book was completed. "I feel like going out," she said when her friend answered.

"I don't think we have anything to talk about."

She knew Adriana was probably still annoyed with her, but she knew the best way to get past it "I thought about calling Timothy and I tried to seduce Kevin."

Adriana's curiosity was piqued. "I'll meet you at the Golden Diner in an hour."

Hurt feelings were mended with laughter and Drake's name was never mentioned. Cassie was in a relaxed mood when she returned home. Then the phone rang.

"I'm going to be at the Memorial Church at four on Thanksgiving," a familiar voice said. "If you want to talk, see me there." She didn't dare move or breathe in case it was a dream.

"Cassie?"

"I'm here."

"Do you want directions?"

She bit her lower lip. Just when she was beginning to recover from his spell and the hurt of his leaving, did she want to go back? They'd hurt each other so much, was it worth it? "I don't know."

"I don't know either. That's why we have to talk." He gave her the directions, then hung up.

* * *

The basement of Memorial Church was bustling with activity when Cassie arrived. People draped the tables with red and orange tablecloths and set up streamers and balloons on the walls. There was the clank of pots in the kitchen, the loud squeak of metal chairs being opened and set on the white tile floor.

"Oh, good, I'm glad you could make it," Jackie said, coming up to her. She grasped her hand and led her toward the far wall. "You'll be serving food." She handed her a plastic cap and apron.

Cassie stared at the items. "I've never done this before."

"Just make sure the food hits the plate and you'll be fine." She hurried away.

Cassie put on her cap, but had trouble tying the back of her apron.

"You look great," Eric said, tying the back for her. He came from behind and studied her. "You'll fit right in."

She looked at his worn jeans and sweater. "Where's your apron?"

He shrugged, nonchalant. "Don't need it, I'm working with the kids."

She stared at him, waiting for the punch line. Waiting for his solemn face to split into a grin. It didn't. "You're serious."

"Yes." He turned toward the kitchen. "They're bringing out the food, I'll talk to you later." He smiled. "I'm glad to see you here."

She spotted Drake at the food table, uncovering the biscuits. Despite her best efforts, her heartbeat accelerated as she approached him and for an instant she felt like a school wallflower approaching the school bad boy. Her sneakers padded across the tile and her corduroys made a soft zip, zip sound as she walked. She'd gained five pounds. Would he notice?

She stopped and watched him. It had been only two weeks since she'd last seen him on a cold autumn morning when he'd hurled angry words at her. Words that had forced her to look inside herself. She gazed at the man she'd once wanted to hate. A man whose wealth and physical beauty made him seem unattainable. Yet as she watched him direct one of the volunteers and carefully set out the food she remembered his tenderness and knew he was only a man. She walked up to him and took a deep breath. "Hi."

It was the only word she could manage before he kissed her—driving away all doubt, all fears, all worries. She would have expected such an impulsive action to be hard, almost aggressive, but his mouth was surprisingly gentle, his hands upsetting her balance and all rational thought. When he at last pulled away she stared, speechless.

His eyes were intense. He cupped her chin and rubbed her lower lip with his thumb. "Sorry, but I had to get that out of the way."

"What was that?"

"An apology." He let his hand fall. "I'll never forgive myself for what I said to you."

"But you were right. I needed to hear it."

He caressed her cheek. "I missed you."

"I missed you too."

A hand darted between them, snapping its fingers. "Okay, enough, you two," Eric said. "You can make up later. We've got work to do." He walked away.

Cassie frowned in his direction, concerned. "Do you realize Eric is going to work with the kids?"

"Yes."

"Do you think he knows what he's up against?"

"He's fine. He does it every year."

"He doesn't seem the type."

Drake sent her a sly glance. "Still misjudging people, huh?"

She folded her arms. "Oh, come on. Look at him. He looks like he's ready to give a lecture on the importance of economics."

"If he decided to they probably would listen. He's good with kids."

"Wonders never cease."

He headed for the kitchen. "We'd better get this table set up before our guests arrive."

* * *

She didn't expect to enjoy herself, but every toothless smile, warm greeting, and "God bless you" she received made the day special. She used her humor to provoke a smile from a solemn old man and a tearful young woman; heaped the plates of a pregnant teen and her boyfriend. She watched Pamela carry a plate for an elderly woman and saw Cedric let an old man use his arm as a cane. The smell of turkey and mashed potatoes mingled with the scent of moth-eaten coats, old shoes, and the streets, but it didn't bother her and she began to see what Eric said about seeing beauty—not one of the disenfranchised looked ugly to her. She saw Eric wipe the nose of one child while he held another on his lap, the others eating with their eyes fixed on him. Jackie rushed back and forth making sure everything ran smoothly and Drake handed out the food, saying something under his breath that seemed to make every guest smile. She felt beauty all around her.

"Glad you came?" Drake asked as they tied up the large trash bags.

"I'm thrilled I came, but I'm starving," she said, struggling with one of the bags.

He took it from her and expertly tied it. "We'll pick up something afterward."

She hesitated and stared at his hands as he worked. "What about Brenda?"

"She won't be there."

"You know what I mean."

"That ended a while back."

"I suppose you still want to meet my parents?"

"Yes."

"I need you to do me a favor first."

He lifted the trash bag over his shoulder. "What?"

"My parents will be back in town in about two weeks and they want to meet you because I told them about you. If you help me lose twenty pounds, that will be really helpful."

He let the bag drop to the ground. "Twenty pounds! Are you crazy?"

"I'll be doing something for you and you'll be doing something for me."

"You cannot lose twenty pounds in two and a half weeks."

Cassie folded her arms and lifted her chin. "I can and I have. I just need help—support really."

"You've lost twenty pounds in two weeks?"

"Yes."

Drake took off her plastic cap and his. "Hmm, and I bet you lost your hair and had about as much energy as a sloth."

Her arms fell. "How would you know?"

He flexed his hand. "Let's just say that I know a little something about malnutrition."

"I don't want to meet my mother looking like this."

"Looking like what? You look fine."

"But I don't feel fine and that's what matters, right?" She rested her hands on her hips. "Will you help me or not?"

He thought for a moment. "Make it three pounds and you've got a deal."

"Three pounds! That's nothing. I could spit that off."

He held out his hand. "Great, then we have a deal."

She slapped it away. "No."

"I'll help you gain muscle."

"Make it fifteen."

"Five."

"Twelve."

"Seventeen," Eric said. "What are you two arguing about?"

"She wants me to help her lose twenty pounds," Drake said in disgust.

"I'm visiting my parents in two weeks," Cassie added.

Eric frowned. "So?"

Drake nodded. "Exactly. Even though I'm against it, I said I'd help her lose five."

"Twelve," Cassie argued.

"Make it ten," Eric suggested.

They looked at each other, then Eric. "Fine, ten," they agreed.

He bowed. "Glad to be of service."

Drake lifted the trash bag. "You'll have to move in with me. So I can keep an eye on you."

"You're just adding that as a bonus."

He suddenly smiled. "I'm glad you see it that way."

"Okay."

He wrapped an arm around her waist and pulled her close. "We'll have to seal this deal with a kiss."

She held a hand against his chest, glancing at the people as they swept past "Wait a few pounds."

"You either kiss me now or we don't have a deal." He saw her hesitation and sighed, annoyed. "Cassie, we kissed before."

"That's because you caught me off guard."

He glanced around. "It's safe. Nobody's watching."

She suddenly felt foolish, understanding how he would have thought she was ashamed of him. Her voice was a whisper. "I'm sorry I hurt you."

He met her eyes, his gaze holding her still. "Then kiss me and make me feel better."

She kissed him, then whispered. "That's just the Band-Aid," her tone suggesting a much more complete healing later on.

His voice was husky as he lifted the trash bag. "We'll be eating at my place."

She smiled and watched him go, feeling nothing but joy, but a sliver of doubt settled in her thoughts —after all they've been through, did he still want to marry her?

Chapter Fifteen

*E*ric stared out Drake's balcony window with a pensive expression. "When is Cassie arriving?"

Drake glanced at his watch. "Soon."

"Since you and Cassie are now back together, Brenda is out of the picture, right?"

"She's been out for a while."

He paused. "How did you do that?"

"I made it clear that I was only interested in being friends."

He pinched the bridge of his nose, looking pained. "Are you sure Brenda got the message?"

"Yes." He looked at him, curious. "Why?"

"Because she's on your balcony."

"What!" Drake flew to the window. He saw Brenda climbing over the balcony railing. He opened the sliding door. "What are you doing?"

She smiled. "Seeing you."

"How did you get here?"

"I know people in high places."

Drake leaned over the balcony and saw a fire truck driving down the road. He turned to Brenda. "You have to leave. I'm expecting a guest."

"I don't plan to stay long." She cupped his face. "Of course that all depends on you." She opened her trench coat. There was nothing underneath.

Behind him Eric softy swore; Brenda snapped the coat shut.

"You know, those breasts look vaguely familiar," Eric said. Drake glared at him. "But of course that's not the point."

She studied him. "Who are you?"

"Doubt you would remember me."

"He's my brother," Drake said.

"Ah..." she said, remembering. "Still trying to measure up?"

Eric flushed slightly and took a step back. "I'll leave you two."

"Excuse us," Drake said, following his brother to the door. He seized Eric's arm before he could escape. "Did you sleep with her too?" he asked in a harsh whisper.

"No, she just let me see her breasts."

"For how much?"

"It was free."

"Did we attend the same high school?"

"She felt sorry for me," Eric admitted. "If you survive tonight I'll tell you about the student teacher." He dislodged Drake's grip and made his escape.

"Good," Brenda said. "I thought he'd never leave."

"I thought I explained—"

"What you said and what you wanted to say were two different things." She traced his lips with her finger. "I know you're shy, so I'll do all the work."

"I'm back with Cassie."

She smiled, smug. "That's okay. I know you're loyal. Your type usually are. I don't mind being the other woman." She licked her lips, grasping the front of his shirt. "It's less stressful anyway."

He grabbed her wrists, debating whether to toss her out the door or through the window. He was certain she would just turn into a bat and fly away. "I'm—" She pushed herself up against him. He moved back, disgusted. "Brenda—"

"Wait right here. I have a surprise for you." She disappeared into the bathroom.

He pounded on the door. "I'm not interested in your surprises." She just laughed. He considered bursting in when the buzzer rang. He squeezed his eyes shut, debating whether to pretend he wasn't home. When the ringing continued he pushed the button to open the front door and paced, trying to figure out a good excuse for Brenda's presence. He pounded on the door again. "What are you doing in there?"

"Patience."

Someone knocked on the front door. He took a deep breath and opened it, blocking her entrance. "Cassie, I'm in a jam right now. Could you come back in an hour?"

"But I brought my bags," she argued, holding up the objects. "At least let me drop them off."

He took the bags and tossed them on the floor. "There."

"Wait, what's the rush?"

"Drake, are you ready for your surprise?" Brenda called out. It was a statement rather than a question because she gave him no time to reply.

He turned and saw her wearing red stiletto heels with chocolate and whipped cream spread all over her body. "I hope you're hungry." Her mouth fell open when she saw Cassie, then smoothed into a grin. "Oh, you have company."

Drake turned to Cassie, ready to explain. She wasn't there. He found her at the elevators. "It's not what you think."

She pushed the elevator button with extra force. "You have no idea what I'm thinking right now. Of course now I understand why you need an hour to get out of your... situation." She quirked a brow at him. "Forty minutes wouldn't give you enough time to get through all that whipped cream and the chocolate should take at least twenty minutes."

Drake began to explain, then stopped. He'd seen Cassie upset before and this wasn't one of those moments. He rested his hand against the wall and scowled down at her. "You think this is funny, don't you?"

She bit her lower lip and pushed the button again.

He folded his arms. "This is what you get when you're nice to people."

She laughed at his disgust. "You must have been very nice."

His scowl deepened. "It's not funny. She climbed over my balcony wearing just a trench coat. You can ask Eric. I told her that I wasn't interested, but she thought I was just being shy. Stop laughing."

Cassie sucked in her lips, but her chin trembled at his look of outrage.

"I told her we were back together and she offered to be my mistress. The next thing I knew she disappeared and came out... like that."

"She's very attractive. If I were a man—" His fierce glare stopped her. She flashed a wicked grin. "Do you want me to help you get rid of her?"

He spun on his heel. "I can get rid of her, but I doubt I'll be nice about it."

Cassie jumped in front of him, holding her hands out to stop him. "I'll take care of this. Take off your shirt."

"What?"

She wagged a finger at him. "Don't ask questions, just do as I say and follow me."

They returned to the apartment and Drake took off his shirt and threw it over the couch, while Cassie slipped out of her shoes and unbuttoned her blouse.

"You're beginning to worry me," he muttered as he followed her.

"Good."

They both stopped in the bedroom doorway where they saw Brenda lying seductively on the bed. Her creamy brown body looked like the topping on a sundae. Cassie nudged Drake's paralyzed form. "Stop drooling and try to breathe." She stepped forward and took off her blouse. "Brenda, I am so happy you're here to join us. We weren't expecting you of course, but the more the merrier. Drake is so... fond of you."

"You can't compete, Cassie."

"I don't plan to." She sat on the edge of the bed. "Fortunately, with you here we can get started before the others come."

Her superior expression faded a bit. "The others?"

"Yes. Marie, Debbie, Tawana." She turned to Drake. "Who else was there, dear?"

He blinked. "Uh—"

She smiled at Brenda and shrugged. "We've had so many we've lost count."

Brenda's eyes widened, horrified. "Are you telling me that you have other women come and—"

"Not just women. Men too. We believe in equal opportunity." Cassie lowered her bra strap. "So do you want to start with Drake or me?"

Brenda leaped out of the bed. "This is sick! Being a mistress is one thing, but what you're talking about is immoral." She grabbed her trench coat and backed out of the door, staring at Drake as if he were about to attack her. "I hope I never see you again."

They heard the clicking of her heels as she ran and then the front door slammed.

Cassie ran a hand through her hair and fluttered her eyelashes. "Well, don't I deserve a thank you?"

Drake began to grin. "Why didn't you just tell her to get out?"

"Because she might come back. I had to give her a reason not to."

"What if she had said yes?"

"With that ego?" she scoffed. "There is no way she would want to be one of many."

"You know, that little bit you did with her gave me some ideas...."

Cassie narrowed her eyes. "I will not sleep with another woman."

He sighed with mock disappointment. "A man can dream." He frowned at the bed. "She got chocolate all over my sheets."

Cassie gathered some chocolate on her finger. "Yes, but she had the right idea."

Drake needed no more prompting. "I'll be right back."

She watched him go, then glanced at the chocolate-smeared bed and saw the ghost of Brenda lying there—Brenda's perfect slim body, perky breasts, soft curves.

"Is there a problem?" Drake asked, standing in the doorway with a can of whipped cream in one hand and a bowl of strawberries in the other.

She pushed the ghost of Brenda from her thoughts and grinned. "Not at all."

* * *

After lovemaking, they freshened up in the shower, and then decided to change the sheets. Drake snatched off the sheets and tossed them in a basket to be washed. "Thanks for believing me."

Cassie grinned as she removed the pillowcases. "I knew you couldn't be that imaginative on the spot. You know what this means, don't you?"

He stared at her, suspicious. "What?"

"When you find a naked man in my bedroom covered in massage oils you'll have to give me the benefit of the doubt."

He met her grin. "Don't worry. I'll never let that happen to you. The only naked man you'll have around is me."

She threw a pillow at him. "Where's the fun in that?"

"I thought I just showed you."

"Yes, but every now and then I'll need some convincing."

He laughed. "No problem. I'm here to serve."

"Speaking of which, what is my weight-loss regime?"

"You'll see."

* * *

He was such a nice guy, Cassie thought as she watched Drake jog in front of her. It was such a shame to have to kill him. She would plead self-defense. While their love-making last night could have made the record books, this evening he seemed bent on administering as much misery as physically possible.

Sweat poured down her face; her sweatband had long lost its purpose. It was now just a soggy piece of cloth on her forehead. Her legs seemed to move in slow motion and her lungs threatened to explode.

"How much...farther?" she puffed.

The wicked rogue threw a casual smile over his shoulder. "Just another two miles."

She stopped. "Two miles? Did you say miles? You meant meters, right?"

"Keep jogging! I told you that stopping suddenly will be a shock to your body. At least walk."

She did. "I'm sure dropping dead would also be another shock, but at least I'd be out of my misery."

Drake slowed down to jog beside her. "How can you be in misery when you have such great company?"

She threw him a cool glance. "Let me count the ways."

"Come on," he urged, poking her in the elbow. "At least give me a slow jog. Good."

"Don't congratulate me, it only gives me a terrible urge to slap you."

"Ha, you wouldn't be able to catch me."

That of course gave her enough energy for the rest of the jog.

She finally caught up with him as he approached the building. "Don't say a word," she ordered, sensing a verbal pat on the back.

"You'll feel better after a shower and a nice dinner."

Cassie made a face. This dinner would of course consist of birdseed and crackers. She walked into the kitchen after her shower and saw Drake put something in the oven.

"Hmm," he said, greeting her with a warm grin. "You smell much better. Set the table." He headed for the shower.

Cassie set put the plates and utensils out, wondering what kind of meal he had prepared: toast with peanut butter, rice cakes with cheese, chicken broth, hot lemon water. She grimaced. She wouldn't complain, they had a common goal. From the stove seeped a heavenly aroma that worsened her mood—the smell of his dinner.

Drake came into the kitchen looking pleased with himself and the table. He pushed her into a chair and put dinner on the table: grilled chicken, asparagus tips, and red potatoes.

"Where's my food?" Cassie demanded as he sat. "Oh, don't tell me I mean to starve."

His tone held a slight edge. "I would never do that to you." He held out his hand and she gave him her plate.

She watched, amazed, as he filled it "But I thought—"

"That I would give you bread and water? I don't believe in diets. Food was created to be both enjoyed and utilized. After a workout like ours you need to be rejuvenated."

Who was she to disagree with such logic? She was hungry. "Thanks for today."

"Don't thank me yet." His eyes gleamed with malicious delight. "Tomorrow we lift weights."

* * *

The man had hidden sadistic tendencies. After waking her up at 6:00 and feeding her a delightful breakfast, he began his campaign to ruin her good opinion of him. After sit-ups, push-ups, leg lifts, and aerobics he had put her on a contraption that could only be meant for torture.

"Eighteen, nineteen," Drake counted as Cassie tried to lift the massive weights with her legs. "Twenty." She let her foot drop; the weights crashed with a bang. "Only ten more to go."

She let her shoulders slump. For the first time in their relationship, she couldn't stand to look at him. Couldn't stand to look at that beautiful, perfect physique—the sculpted muscles of his bare chest and solid thighs. "I can't."

"Of course you can."

"Look at me. I'm only sitting here because I can barely stand." She could feel every muscle trembling.

"Ten more," he said.

"I've done everything you've asked," she complained.

"Ten more."

"You're supposed to be a support, not Attila the Hun."

He folded his arms. "Ten more."

"I think you're a low-down, arrogant, obnoxious son of a—"

"You can say that while your legs are in motion."

She gritted her teeth and finished the reps.

"Good, now it's time for a cooldown."

Cassie stood and collapsed on the floor.

Drake stifled a grin. "That's not what I had in mind."

"Oh, but it feels so good." She loved the cool feel of the blue mat against her face.

He pulled her to her feet. "Come on, you've got to stretch."

She snatched her hand away. "Could you just leave me alone!"

"You're the one who wanted to get into shape."

"No, dearie, I am a shape. I only need help to lose weight."

"And you will."

She shook her head, feeling perspiration sliding down her back. "Not this way. It will be easier to starve."

His jaw tightened. "Then do it yourself because you definitely won't get my help." He grabbed his towel and left.

She followed. "I thought this would be like when I was sick and you watched what I ate and fed me broth," she explained breathlessly. Did he have to walk so fast? "I didn't expect such a rigorous regime. This is not what I wanted. What's wrong with skipping a few meals?"

Drake stopped so suddenly she nearly crashed into him. "Starving to you may be some courageous accomplishment, but it's torture to your body and your mind. Denying yourself essential nutrients shouldn't be applauded when there are people who have to starve because they have no choice. I think you're beautiful just the way you are."

"Well, I don't."

He raised his hand in a dismissive gesture. "Then go and starve yourself on your own."

"People fast," she said quickly before he walked away again.

He sniffed. "So it's fasting now?"

"Look," she said gently, "I know it was hard for you growing up."

"Hard?" His voice cracked in disbelief. "It was more than hard. Do you know what it's like to dream about food? To dream about having your own shopping cart and going down the grocery aisles to pick up any items you wanted? Frosted

Flakes, Raisin Bran, Jiffy peanut butter, Ritz crackers, Campbell's soup. Why don't you ask Eric how good it felt to be sick every two months or to wake up screaming because your legs cramped up from lack of potassium? Ask Jackie how it felt being the smallest kid in class because your growth was stunned from malnutrition." He leaned against the wall, his harsh tone reflecting in his eyes. "I used to take ketchup packets, mix it with water, and heat it over the stove for soup. I would soak bread in milk, eat sugared toast for dinner, tried to make a can of baked beans last two days." He nodded in grim remembrance. "Yes, it was more than hard."

Cassie wrapped her arms around herself and lowered her eyes. "Well, why don't you ask me how it feels to look like this? To be known as the fat sibling, to get glares from other women when you enter the Dairy Queen line or order something from a fast food restaurant. Try making people laugh all the time because you're afraid you'll burst into tears if you don't. Try sitting with your family at holiday meals and watch them eat whatever they want while you get salad. When you look like me people think you're lazy, sloppy, and disgusting." She looked at him. "A diet shows discipline."

His expression softened. "I know that other people will look at you and judge you. Do you think I don't know what it's like to be judged? You should have heard the accent I had when I first came here. Not only was I poor, I was foreign." He rested an arm on either side of her, effectively trapping her beneath him. His amber gaze caressed her face. "Cassie, the weight is not the issue."

"It's not? Seems like a pretty big issue to me."

He put a finger over her lips. "You're afraid of how powerful you are." He continued before she could argue. "That's why you became Cassandra. A woman not afraid of her beauty, her sexuality, her intelligence...her power. She captivates audiences and has them mesmerized, her size is not a plus or a minus, it's who she is. You are Cassandra—Cassie—A. Graham, a woman with a dynamic career, wonderful friends, and—" He cleared his throat. "And an exceptional lover."

She rolled her eyes.

"You are a force to be reckoned with. Claim that."

"How long have you had that speech saved up?"

He wearily hung his head. "Cassie, have you heard a word I've said?"

She lifted his chin. "Every word." She leaned against him, feeling his chest hairs tickle her cheek. "I love you."

He wrapped an arm around her and held her close. "I know."

"Give me time. I know I'll feel happier when I lose a few pounds."

He continued to hold her, saying nothing.

* * *

The road to happiness was paved with obstacles: exercise that still seemed torturous and weight that refused to budge. But slowly as the week passed it grew easier and she felt free to enjoy herself, to like who Cassie—Cassandra—was with her round face and rounded figure. Her clothes felt a bit looser, but it was her spirit that seemed to float. And for the first time in a long while she decided to go clothes shopping.

Adriana was as stiff as a mannequin when Cassie entered the shop. She had never ventured into Divine Notions because the thought of lingerie frightened her.

"Are you really here?" Adriana asked, amazed.

"I felt like shopping. I can't believe I came here." She glanced wearily at a mannequin wearing a black bra and garter belt.

Adriana came around the counter ready to dismiss any of her doubts. She grabbed Cassie's arm and led her to a rack of garters. "You will not regret it."

"I may not, but my checkbook will."

"Think of this as an investment. Besides, I'll give you a discount."

Cassie was relieved the store had her sizes. She hated finding things she liked only to discover she couldn't fit them. She bought a black velvet robe with a matching silk and lace gown, two embroidered bras, and red panties.

Adriana handed her the purchases. "You are going to look fabulous. Drake won't be able to let you go."

"I hope so."

"So when's the wedding?"

"I'm not sure there will ever be one."

"Cassie, if you want a wedding, close the shop doors and you'll have a ring in no time."

Cassie laughed and waved good-bye, then stepped out into the cool sunlight.

* * *

He watched Cassie walk down the street with her purchases and his heart constricted. He so desperately wanted to say something to her it was painful, but the time wasn't right yet. Henson was still a problem and until that situation was handled, he couldn't let down his guard. Mr. Gianolo's poisoning had been a quiet threat they hadn't paid attention to. So he knew more had to happen before they listened.

* * *

Cassie had almost reached the metro when a black Lexus slid to a stop beside her.

"Cassie!"

She turned and saw Kevin gesturing to her from the backseat.

"There's no need to walk," he said, opening the door. "My driver will take you wherever you wish."

She got in the car and gave him the address.

Kevin studied her for a moment, then glanced at her bags. "You seem happier than when I last saw you. I always find that shopping puts women in a good mood."

"I would say my shopping is a result of happiness rather than the direct cause of it."

"I see." He dropped his voice to a mocking ominous tone. "The ex's revenge. There is no better way to vex an ex than to be happy."

"I can assure you that trying to irritate Timothy is not a source of happiness for me. Although I would agree that showing your ex you are happy without them is good revenge."

He said nothing for a few blocks, then, "So you're truly over him?"

"Yes, and I have been for a long time."

He read the label on the bag. "So you and the bully made up?"

"Yes."

"Am I looking at a June bride?"

"I don't think he's interested in marriage any-more. It's all right with me. I've done it before."

"If you want—"

"After all we've been through, I don't want something else to argue about."

"How do you know it's not something he wants?"

"He would have told me." The car stopped in front of her building. "Don't worry about me."

Kevin sighed. "Easier said than done."

She kissed him on the cheek. "Thanks for every-thing." She stepped out.

* * *

Cassie gasped when she saw a bouquet of yellow roses lying in front of Drake's door.

She cautiously picked them up and saw her name typed on a card. Could Drake have sent them? She frowned. He had never given her flowers before. She went inside and placed them on the counter. They looked so harmless, why did they fill her with such dread?

"Did you send me flowers?" she asked when Drake arrived home.

"No, why?"

"Because these were delivered to me today." She held up the bouquet. "Perhaps Timothy sent them."

He took the roses and examined them. "No, he wouldn't risk his life to send you roses."

She looked at him, alarmed. "What are you talking about?"

He put the roses down, choosing not to explain his encounter with Timothy. "Who else do you think they might be from?"

She chewed her lower lip. "A number of people."

"A number of people who want to scare you?"

"How do you know they are meant to scare me?"

"Cassie, there's no signature or note. This person wants to remain anonymous. Why? They send them to you at your boyfriend's place. That means they know where you are. Something is not right. Has anything else happened that seemed odd?"

"Strange phone calls."

He took a deep breath, trying to cool his temper. "Why didn't you tell me about this?"

"It seemed harmless," she said, defensive.

"Well, now it's a concern." He reached into his jacket and pulled out a cigarette. "I should have listened to Mr. Gianolo more closely," he said, annoyed with himself.

"Why?"

He lit the cigarette and inhaled. "Because he was worried about one of your admirers. We have to figure out who sent these flowers."

Drake's commanding presence pushed aside her feelings of dread. He was so safe and comfortable. It seemed so silly to worry about flowers. "I've got a surprise for you."

"I'm not sure I like surprises."

"You'll like this one."

"Can't it wait until we..." His voice trailed off when she pulled out her nightgown.

She wrapped the soft silk around his neck. "I believe the answer is no."

* * *

Cedric glanced at the box in his hand as he waited near the front of the restaurant. He hadn't bought her something because he liked her, he reminded himself. It was the holidays and it seemed like a nice thing to do, that's all. She'd been nice to him and she wasn't so bad when she got off her pedestal every once in a while. She probably hadn't gotten him anything, not that he cared. He just had to make sure his gift didn't look like a real gift, just something he picked up. He was sure she would like it—a case to hold her earrings.

He watched Pamela as she prepared to head home. She wrapped herself in an enormous coat and tied a blue cashmere scarf around herself until only her eyes showed.

"Hey, Pamela," he called.

She blinked at him. "Yes?"

He shoved the gift in her hands. "I, uh, got this for you. Thought you might need it."

Her eyes brightened as she lowered her scarf. "You got me a gift?"

He shrugged. "It's nothing."

"My first gift of the season." She opened the wrapping. "A makeup holder, thank you."

Makeup holder? "You're welcome," he said casually, his heart pounding with pleasure.

She smiled shyly. "Your gift's better than mine."

He felt his ears grow warm. "You got me something?"

"Yes." She pulled something from her backpack and handed him a knitted item. "It's a scarf," she said, saving him from guessing. "I notice that you never wear one and it's going to be cold."

"Not bad." He draped it on his shoulders and the two ends fell to the ground.

She grimaced. "It's kinda long."

"That's okay." He wrapped it twice around his neck.

She laughed. "You look like you're being strangled by a boa constrictor."

"Hey, be nice. My girl gave me this scarf."

She tilted her head to one side, her eyes twinkling. "You really see me as your girl?"

He shrugged again, trying to look cool. "Yeah, kinda."

She lowered her eyes. "Think we'll last?"

"Probably not."

"Good." She took a step closer and met his eyes. "Then there's no pressure."

"Yeah. No pressure." He bent his head and gently kissed her. It was nice and sweet, just like her. He took her backpack and rested an arm on her shoulder. "Come on, let me take you home."

Eric passed the new couple as they left the restaurant. He watched them for a while as they walked down the street, oblivious to the crowd that pushed past them. He shook his head, amused, and stepped inside. He found his brother ending a meeting with Lance.

"Love is in the air for the holidays," he announced, rubbing his fogged glasses on his sleeve.

Drake frowned. "Why do you say that? You met someone?"

He put his glasses back on. "I see a romance blooming between Cedric and Pamela."

Lance and Drake stared at him in disbelief. Drake said, "I urge you to get a new prescription."

He held up his hands in surrender. "Fine, don't believe me. Although I am the reigning king of observation." He waited for Lance to leave, then asked, "Speaking of romance, when are you and Cassie getting married?"

Drake straightened the papers on the desk. "I haven't asked her yet."

"Why not? She said yes before."

"I'm waiting until after I meet her parents."

Eric rested his hands on the desk and leaned forward. "Why?"

He didn't meet his brother's eyes. "Just because."

Eric glanced up at the ceiling, incredulous. "You're seeking their approval, aren't you? Like some old English gentleman, you're going to ask for their blessing."

He glanced up. "No."

"Then ask her to marry you now. Or are you afraid that if they don't approve of you, Cassie might not want you either?"

Drake impatiently tapped his pen against the desk. "You talk too much."

Eric's mouth quirked with a knowing grin. "You want to make sure you can measure up."

"Stop trying to figure me out."

"Why? It's fun." His smile widened. "You're in love with Cassie. Go ahead and deny it I know that's part of your nature, but it's true." He lowered his voice. "The thing is she loves you too and for women that's a big deal. Stop wearing the past like a dirty cloak." He sat down and crossed his legs at the ankles. "So we were poor and sometimes did shady things. So what?"

Drake frowned. "You did shady things. I cleaned up your mess."

Eric sat back and adjusted his glasses. "Let's not meddle with semantics. We survived and we're successful. That's all that matters. I loved my father, but it's no secret that you did a better job than he did. Jackie and I are fine now and it's time to be selfish. Travel, have some kids, and be happy. Live the American dream. That's why our parents brought us here."

* * *

Eric's words hung heavy in Drake's mind in the coming days. He pushed them away as the thoughts of a more pressing issue surfaced. A teenager who lived in his building had left the flowers for Cassie. He said a friend at school had slipped a note in his locker, asked him for a favor in exchange for a free pass. Unfortunately, Drake's search stalled after that. The teenager couldn't describe the friend and the flower shops had no information. His search for who had ordered the flowers was fruitless and that bothered him. It put him on extra alert. He barely noticed the joggers on the Mall, the sound of pebbles under his feet, or the feel of a warm December.

Cassie stopped walking and grabbed his hand. "Drake, look!"

Up in the sky toward the monument, which stood tall and white in the strawberry sky, a series of kites swayed in a dizzying dance.

She sighed happily. "I love kites."

Drake stood behind her and wrapped his arms around her waist; she leaned against him and they both watched the kites fly. He smiled to himself, amazed at how far they had come. A few weeks ago she would never have allowed him to hold her like this where everyone could see, and now it was the most natural thing in the world. He rested his chin on her head. She was his for good now and once he'd met her parents they would be married.

"Let's buy some pinwheels," she said.

"That's only for the summer."

"So is kite flying. Come on. I know of a place."

Cassie found a party store nearby and bought pinwheels that she later taped to the railing of his balcony. They watched them spin in the evening breeze before they went to bed.

* * *

He woke to the smell of home—a quick Caribbean breeze, the sway of palm trees, the hoarse sound of a bus rumbling past, the loud squeaky call of a vervain darting through the sky.

Drake opened his eyes, staring around his room. Where had those way-ward thoughts come from? Was it his talk with Eric about his parents? No, couldn't be. He glanced beside him and saw that the space next to him was empty. He stood and opened the door, and again the smell of home captured him in a warm embrace. He heard the sizzling of fish and the clank of utensils against a pot.

"Sit down," Cassie told him as he entered the kitchen. "I'll be done in a—hey!" she cried as he bumped her aside with his hip.

"Is this ackee and saltfish? My mother used to make this for me when I was a boy." He bent over and inhaled the scent. His eyes trailed to another pan. "And callaloo and dumplings." He kissed her on the cheek. "Boonoo-noonoos!"

She kissed her teeth. "Come, nuh, man, you haven't tasted it yet."

He grabbed some pineapple juice from the fridge. "Come on, let's eat."

They filled their plates and ate in the breakfast nook listening to the traffic below. He wanted to ask her to marry him, but his lips wouldn't open. He wanted her to be sure. Wanted to see how she'd respond if he was brusque with her mother or rude to her father. He'd try not to be but sometimes...

"You don't like it?" Cassie asked, worried.

"I wouldn't be eating it if I didn't like it."

"Then why the frown?"

He pushed food around on his plate. "Just thinking."

She placed her fork down and rested her arms on the table. "Are you ready to meet my parents?"

"Sure."

"You don't have to if you don't want to."

His gaze grew intense, full of suspicion. "Don't you want me to meet them?"

"Of course, it's just...how should I introduce you?"

"As your boyfriend. What else?"

A fiancé perhaps? Cassie sighed. Maybe she had blown it, he had become accustomed to what they had now and didn't want anything more. She had lost her allure. She rested her chin in her hands. At least he had figured it out before they were married.

The next day she didn't care. She had to be in a nightmare. A terrible, horrible, never-ending, heart-crushing nightmare. Cassie stared at the new steel-gray weigh scale as if she were confronting the magic mirror, which was showing her she was the fattest of them all. She'd lost five pounds. Five pounds! All her work for a lousy five pounds. All that nonsense of feeling lighter and looking better had been in her head. Now she would see her mother again and face her disappointment. She felt like wringing Drake's neck. He had the misfortune to walk into the bathroom right then.

He grinned at her. "Good morning."

"Don't good morning me," she snapped.

He glanced at the scale and scowled. "Get off that damn thing."

She pointed to it. "Five pounds."

"What?"

"This damn thing says I've lost five pounds."

"Hell, it talks?" He pushed her aside and stood on the scale. "Hmm," he said when it remained silent. "It must only work for you."

She looked down at his weight and groaned. "With a little work, I could weigh as much as you do."

His arms circled her waist. "Do you want to start right now?"

She pushed away from him. "No."

"We have to have those kids sometime."

"Right. Then the place will be filled with diaper bins."

"Toys," he challenged.

"The sound of banging pots."

"Songs from *Sesame Street.*"

She folded her arms. "Crying."

He did the same. "Laughing."

"Shouting."

"Singing."

She couldn't help smiling. "Now who's being the romantic?"

He turned to the mirror and picked up his razor. "You must be rubbing off on me. We have to think of names."

She felt honored that he wanted her to be the mother of his children, but wondered if it would be without the benefit of a ring. She turned away from him. "We're seeing my mother today."

"I know it will be fine."

"Said Custer to his troops; said the captain of the Titanic."

"It will be fine," he repeated slowly.

She shrugged, suddenly nonchalant. "I know."

"How do you know?"

She winked at his reflection. "Because I have you."

A few hours later Drake wished he had her confidence. His stomach was in knots. Today was the ultimate test—one he could not fail. The mother of all proving grounds. He had to impress Cassie's parents.

"Stop fiddling with your tie," Cassie whispered as they walked up to her parents' home.

He glanced down, surprised. "Didn't realize I was."

"There's no reason to be nervous," she assured him, her classy sling-back heels clicking against the walkway. "Apoplectic perhaps, but not nervous."

"I'm fine."

She didn't believe him. He had taken special care with his clothes, ironing any wrinkle or crease in his dark trousers and gray shirt, polishing his shoes until they gleamed. If she had just met him she would have thought him vain, but she knew that wasn't the case.

He stopped and stared up at the house. "I thought you said your family was middle class."

"It is."

"Your house has pillars," he said, unable to disguise his awe.

She nudged him forward. "It's a regular colonial."

"With tall, white pillars like you see at the White House." And numerous windows, a manicured lawn, and a cobblestone walkway lined with lights.

"This isn't the White House. It just looks big, it's really average." She noticed him tugging on his tie again and grabbed his hand. "Drake, you look great and I don't care what my parents think. I'm glad you're in my life."

He blinked. "Thanks, but I already knew that."

She dropped his hand. "You are so unromantic. You could have pretended to be impressed."

"Forgive me. I'll try to swoon once the night is over." He lifted his hand to knock. "A butler better not answer the door."

The door swung open and a woman in a maid uniform appeared. Drake shot her a glance. Cassie grinned sheepishly. "She's new."

The maid led them into the formal living room. On an elaborate white sofa sat Angela Graham. Near the bar Oscar Graham fixed himself a drink.

"It's about time you two got here," Angela said, uncrossing silk-clad legs.

Drake watched Cassie greet her parents. It seemed almost appropriate that Cassie's mother was wearing a leopard-print blouse, a black skirt, and earrings that looked like spider webs. She was a predator and when she smiled at him, he could envision teeth sinking into his neck. The challenge to outwit her consumed him.

"Did you find the place okay?"

Drake transferred his gaze to the quiet man in a tweed jacket and gray trousers, shaking a brandy snifter. "It was fine," he said.

Cassie spoke up. "Dad, I was with him, remember?"

"Oh, right. Of course."

"You have a beautiful home here, Mrs. Graham," Drake said. "I see where Cassie gets her good taste."

"Thank you. So from what part of Jamaica are you?" When he told her, she nodded in cool disdain. "Oh, yes. I could tell by the accent. How unfortunate."

Cassie spoke up. "Mom, I think—"

"I'm not criticizing him, Cassandra. I'm just making an observation." Angela stood and took Drake's arm. "Let's go into dinner so that you can tell me all about yourself."

In the back of his mind a bell rang. Let the games begin.

Chapter Sixteen

"*I*'m sorry," Drake said with regret, breaking the heavy silence that permeated their drive home.

Cassie noted the tense lines of his jaw that the passing city lights lit up with harsh accuracy. His large hands swallowed up the steering wheel in a vicious grip. "It's all right." She patted his knee. "You tried your best."

The simple gesture eased the tension coursing through him, but it wasn't enough. He needed something more. At the stoplight, he lit up a cigarette and angrily inhaled. "She's awful," he muttered, still shocked that such a woman existed.

"And now she knows it. You told her so in no uncertain terms."

He silently swore, vexed with himself. "I didn't mean to."

"I know."

He sighed. The evening had started out fine. He didn't mind Angela Graham turning her insolent honey-colored gaze on him and quickly exposing him for the street urchin he used to be. He wasn't bothered about the questions about his work, his parentage, or his schooling. He didn't care about the pointed remarks that smacked of prejudice. He could understand her viewpoint; those who had never been poor rarely understood what it was like and somehow thought that those in poverty deserved their fate.

She later congratulated him on his success although, she pointed out, she would have preferred it in another field. Throughout this inquisition, Cassie squirmed and tried to soften her mother's remarks, but her opinion ultimately meant little to him. The evening would have continued to go smoothly if Angela hadn't made a mistake—she attacked Cassie.

She despaired of her daughter's clothes, her job, her hair, her friends, but then she clinched it by mentioning her weight. To everyone else it was an innocuous, casual remark. Cassie could easily have turned it into a joke, but Drake stared at Angela with such anger she nearly choked on her food.

"Did I say something wrong?" she stammered, wondering what she had done to become the recipient of such a fierce gaze.

"I suggest you start your apologizes now, ma'am."

Cassie nudged him. "Drake, it's okay."

"It's not okay." He placed his utensils down in controlled anger. "My parents are dead, Mrs. Graham, and for a long time I didn't appreciate them the way I could have. Parents are wonderful people. I now see that I succeeded because of them while Cassie has succeeded in spite of you. In spite of your bitterness, your vanity, and your acrid wit. You wouldn't care if she dropped dead tomorrow, would you?"

Angela held a hand against her chest, horrified. "Of course I would."

He pounded his fist on the table, rattling the fine china and glasses. "Then act like it! I for one know that we don't have every day to tell our family that we care about them, or make them feel good to be alive. And every day you squander your chances. Every chance you get, you tell her how little she means to you. How would you like to have the words you have just spoken be the last words she'd ever hear?"

"I think that's enough," Oscar said.

Drake redirected his glare. His voice was low, dangerous. "No, I haven't talked to you yet."

"But I—"

"You think your silence is neutral? You think that watching this drama only makes you the audience?

You're the stage that allows the drama to continue. Your silence is as painful as your wife's words. I didn't come here to hurt either of you. I'd actually hoped..." His eyes fell. "Forget it. I only say this to protect my family. I want to make sure our kids have a safe place to come to. A place where their grandparents are their champions, a mountain of strength they can rely on in this harsh, cruel world. And, boy, do I know how cruel it can be! I will not allow my children in this house until you start treating your daughter with the dignity and respect she deserves." He stood and held his hand out to Cassie. It was a silent test of where her loyalties lay. She glanced at his hand and then at him, her butterscotch eyes unsure.

For a moment, he felt his throat close as the possibility of failure clawed at his heels. But she did not let him suffer long. She rose and took his hand.

Drake inhaled, feeling the smoke burn his lungs. He wasn't sorry about what he'd said, just how he'd said it. He could have been more subtle, more refined. Instead he'd left her mother in tears and her father in shock. Not the best way to endear yourself to the woman you wish to marry. He angrily stubbed out his cigarette. He had blown his last chance. She might be by his side, but she'd never belong to him.

"Your parents love you," he said quietly.

"I know."

He gripped the wheel until his palms burned. "Why are you staring at me?"

"Because I'm so proud of you."

He glanced at her, trying to read her mood. "You're proud after I... I..."

"Stood up for my honor, my pride, my dignity?" she finished. "Announced that you are my protector and champion? It was so romantic I nearly clapped."

He stared at the road and shook his head, hurt that she could make a joke out of it. "You're making fun of me."

"No." She rested a hand on his sleeve. "I have taught a lot of people about social graces—small talk, flattery— but I could never teach anyone what you have in buckets. Integrity. Something beyond class, beyond wealth, beyond intelligence that makes a man truly great. Yes, I'm proud of one of my best students for showing others what grace truly is. I'm proud of the man I hope will always be in my life."

He was too moved to speak or even look at her. Cassie wisely stared out the window.

* * *

Drake dropped Cassie's bags near the door. "This is illogical," he said, glancing around Cassie's apartment. "You liked staying at my place, you're over there often enough, and we get along well."

"I love my little place. I like my freedom." Besides, moving in with him wouldn't be enough. She wanted to be married. She laughed at herself. She'd never thought she'd feel that way again.

"Cassie, you wouldn't be losing your freedom."

She put a finger over his lips. "Let's not have this conversation."

He felt restless and frustrated. He hated knowing that she thought she was losing her independence by being with him. "You can still have your friends. You'll have your own study to work in."

"I know."

"You wouldn't regret it."

She shook her head.

"Mr. Gianolo says you're not safe here."

"He's overreacting. It's probably a student with a crush."

"I don't like it."

"I'll be fine." She kissed his frown. She wondered if she would have to ask him to marry her. She would have to think about it. He cared about her, but she wasn't sure he loved her. "I love you."

"Hmm." He sighed, defeated. "I'll be back tomorrow."

"Okay," she agreed. Then she closed the door.

She was glad to be back in her apartment. She liked seeing the signs of the Cassie she used to be. A desk filled with unfinished outlines, a Rolodex of acquaintances, but she also saw Drake's umbrella still sitting in the corner. That's how life with him would be. He'd be a wonderful accessory to a complete life. She just had to convince him to make it permanent, and then she would seduce him into loving her. With that thought, she went to bed.

* * *

Drake decided to stop by the bookstore. It was no use going home since every nerve ending seemed to hum with a certain restlessness. Cassie said she was proud of him, that she loved him, but would that be enough for her to marry a man her family disapproved of? He didn't have much of a family to offer her. Just Eric and Jackie. Would that be enough on holidays? He aimlessly searched the aisles until he saw Cedric in the poetry section.

"You surprise me," he said. "I never would have thought you enjoyed poetry."

Cedric grimaced. "I don't. I'm only here because of her." He moved and revealed Pamela peering at the lower bookshelf. She angrily shoved a book back and grabbed another.

Drake watched her, worried. "Should I ask why?"

Pamela straightened. "Because that archaic, old fogy Mr. Randall gave me a C on my paper. And I'm going to prove to him that I deserve an A."

"Archaic?"

Cedric raised his hands. "Don't argue."

"Yes, archaic," Pamela said. "He belongs in the Middle Ages. He thinks women are too free now and that romantic love has suffered for it. I'm going to prove him wrong."

"Randall... that name sounds familiar. I think Cassie knows him. A teacher, right? Glen Randall?"

"Yes."

"Hmm. Cassie doesn't seem to have the same opinion as you. Personally, I think he's a drip, but she told me that's because he's divorced."

Pamela snapped the book shut and stared at him, confused. "Divorced? His wife is dead."

Drake's cell phone suddenly rang. "Henson."

Gianolo's voice came through in an urgent whisper. "I heard the footsteps go to Cassie's door...."

Chapter Seventeen

*I*t was the whispered words along with the distinct feeling that something was wrong that woke her. Something about the air being too still, a faint familiar smell that didn't belong there. She felt Drake's arm around her, but somehow it felt different. The cotton of his T-shirt felt coarse against her skin and his grip was unusually tight. She turned to him and realized why. It wasn't Drake at all.

Glen covered her mouth before she could scream. "You don't want to do that."

She nodded and he slowly removed his hand.

She had an unnatural desire to laugh. The whole situation was preposterous. "What are you doing here?" she asked, trying to understand the punch line to this joke.

"I've been a very patient man, Cassie." He softly touched her hair, then her cheek. "Don't you think it's time I got to be with you for a change? After all those times you've teased me and kept me just out of reach?" His beautiful booming voice shook with pain, his eyes making it clear that this was no joke.

In the moonlight she could see the serious contours of his face.

All humor disappeared, replaced by a rush of fear. Fear that the man she had called a friend was not a friend at all. Had never been one. "What are you talking about?"

"Don't act coy." His gentle caressing became painful, a mixture of desire and anger, causing hot friction against her cheek. "You knew how I felt about you and you used it against me, always calling me a nice guy while you went out with Neanderthals. I thought you were different, I thought you liked class, sophistication, tenderness; but like most women you like the challenge of taming the beast. So here I am willing to be tamed. I'm not going to be nice anymore. I'm going to get what I want the way other men have, by taking it."

She smelled the stale stench of whiskey on his breath. "You've been drinking."

"Only to clear my thoughts." He pressed wet lips to one cheek and then the other. "I've been thinking about this—about us for a long time. You've hurt my feelings a lot."

"I'm sorry," she whispered.

"You're always sorry. It was your fault Mr. Gianolo nearly died. He insulted me. I couldn't have that, now, could I? A man's pride is everything and he threatened mine. He thought he knew what was best for you, but he was wrong. He knew it was me. Therefore, I had to keep him quiet. I slipped a bulb in his beloved soup."

"You poisoned him."

Glen traced her brows and shrugged. "The same way I poisoned you. It's amazing, the power of flowers."

"That night—" She remembered not smelling the onions for his minestrone.

"That night you got sick after the party you dumped me for. Yes, that was me. The particular bulb I used takes about six hours to get the effect. I wanted you to attend the party, but I had to make sure you didn't enjoy it too much. After all, I wasn't there with you like I am now." His eyes filled with tears. "You forced me to do it. I was going to make it up to you, but you didn't follow the plan. I called you, but you weren't home. You were supposed to come home and let me take care of you. I told you that you and I were part of a different time, but you had begun to stray. Just like Rita with her extravagant hair, clothes, and love for rock music. When I met her at college she was much more conservative than that. But society changed her, changed her from the woman I loved. The woman who adored and catered to me. You're luckier than poor Rita. I let you live."

Cassie swallowed. "Why the flowers?"

"It was the perfect way to portray my feelings as any man would in the 1800s. I had given you fair warning of how I felt with the carnation. Oh, how you teased my poor heart! The yellow roses were eloquent enough, although you chose to ignore them. I made it clear that I was jealous of your unfaithfulness. It wasn't hard to get them delivered. I had plenty of students who would do anything for a no-homework pass."

She firmed her voice, determined to talk reason. "Glen—"

He grabbed her chin and squeezed so tight she thought the top of her head would shoot off. "Don't Glen me. You can't fight me on this. You can't manipulate me any longer. You wanted friendship and I gave it to you. You wanted space and I gave it to you. The least you can do is give me what I deserve. I'm much stronger than you and I'm not going to be nice about it."

"What you deserve isn't legal anymore."

He let his hand glide down her arm. "Sounds interesting."

She drew away in disgust. "You won't get away with this."

"Oh, yes, I will."

"Are you going to spout poetry to get me in the mood?"

He pulled out a knife from under the pillow. It winked cruelly in the glow of the moon. "I think you'd better rephrase that."

Cassie bit her lip.

"That's better. I prefer silence. Women are just too full of opinions nowadays. See how complacent I can be even when annoyed? Much more civilized than the other men you choose. There's no need to tremble, darling. I'll make sure that it's good for both of us."

She licked her lips, her mind leaping back and forth to find a new strategy. She shut her eyes as he lowered his head to kiss her—she felt as if a fish were sucking her face; his long, cold fingers felt more like a squid than a hand. She opened her eyes and saw the knife. She grabbed it.

"Oh, God!" she screeched, hysterical. "I've cut myself!"

"Relax, Cassie."

"I can't stand the sight of blood. I wanted to take your hand, but grabbed the knife instead. Oh, I think I'm going to pass out."

"It's just a little cut, dear. You women can be so irrational." He chuckled, pleased by her demonstration. "Don't worry, I'll take care of things."

He left the room. When she heard him running the water in the sink, she raced to the front door. She grasped the handle, but Glen seized her from behind and pulled her back.

"I knew I couldn't trust you." He yanked her head back and trailed his finger across her neck. "You like getting cut? I'll make sure I indulge you." He squeezed her wounded hand, dragged her back into the bedroom, and pushed her on the bed. He covered her like a tsunami. "Go ahead and cry. I'd like to hear you cry."

"Not for long," a voice said from the shadows.

For a moment Cassie wasn't sure what to fear. Glen or the anger that crept into the room from the familiar figure standing in the doorway. Unfortunately, Glen did not sense the danger she did.

"This is not about you, Henson. I've already had her. The woman is a damn whore. Do you think you're the only man in her life? Do you think you're somehow special? You're not. None of us are. She toys with us. But men rule the world, not women, and this one needs to learn her place. You can have her when I'm finished."

"You're finished now."

Glen lifted the knife and held it close. "Take one more step and I'll finish her completely."

With Glen focused on Drake, Cassie knew this was her last chance. She jabbed him in his Adam's apple. He grabbed his throat and dropped to the floor. She rolled away, but felt his fingers clutch the hem of her nightgown. They loosened when Drake leaped on top of him and squeezed Glen's neck until the other man's eyes rolled to the back of his head. Cassie's sense of relief was shattered when she realized Drake didn't plan to let go. She grabbed his arm, feeling the rage that strengthened him.

"Let go, you'll kill him!"

"He raped you." His voice cracked in anguish. "I saw the blood."

"He lied. I'm all right." She waved her hand in front of him. "It's from the knife." She shook him, trying to slacken his grasp. "Please. He's not worth it. Please."

"She said let go," a deep, threatening voice said behind them.

Drake released his grip and Glen's limp body collapsed to the bed. They both stared at the shadowy figure in the doorway. He stepped into the light. Cassie gasped, then ran to him.

"Clarence! What are you doing here?"

Clay held her tight. "Looking after my little sister as always." He pulled away and looked down at her. "I suggest you call the police."

She nodded, then turned to Drake, who was swinging Glen's limp body over his shoulder. "What are you going to do with him?" she demanded.

"Hand him over to the police with a few souvenirs. Don't worry, I'll wake him up to make sure he enjoys them."

"But—"

"Call the police." He disappeared out the door into the darkness of the hall.

Clay let her go and turned to follow. "Don't worry. I'll make sure he doesn't kill him. I have a few parting words myself."

* * *

Once the cops and medics had left, Clay explained his presence. "I was hired to check up on

Glen by a family member of one of his girlfriends whose death was considered a suicide."

Cassie looked at her brother, curious. "Hired? What do you do?"

He smiled blandly, a hint of his Manchester accent coming through. "Let's not worry about the details, love. Basically, I was hired to watch him and learned he's a nasty piece of work. Been transferred from school to school because of his views of women, and his track record with wives and girlfriends haven't been great either."

"Wives?"

He nodded. "When I discovered he was in your building I nearly went mad. He had a pattern with the ladies and you seemed to fit his type. Unfortunately, I was right."

"But why didn't you come to me?"

"I wasn't sure how I'd be received." He rubbed his knuckles against his chin. "I'm not exactly a family man and you know I don't get on well with Melody and Lewis."

She wasn't close to her brother and sister either. "Join the club."

"Besides, with Drake in the picture I didn't let myself get too worried. Although I wasn't quite sure of him either."

She studied her brother for a moment. It had been years since she'd seen him, yet he still looked the same—remote, distant, unsure. "I used to be angry at you. I thought you'd abandoned us, abandoned me," she clarified. "But now I understand. You had to escape."

His voice tightened. "I couldn't tolerate that woman one more day. You weren't the only one she..." He shook his head as if to rid himself of the thoughts. "When you were old enough I left. But I couldn't stay away. After Simone's husband knocked her off I kept thinking about you and worrying about you, hoping that you wouldn't be the same. I wasn't too keen with your first husband and let him know it. I've kept a steady eye on you, wanting to be close, but not knowing how."

Cassie squeezed his hand. "I'm glad you're here now."

He glanced at Drake, who was pacing the balcony and smoking. "I think you chose yourself a decent bloke this time. I don't have to look after you anymore."

"No, but I'd like to keep you around. Mom doesn't like him either."

"Then we'll definitely get on." He kissed her on the forehead and left a number where she could reach him, then left.

Cassie immediately took a shower. When she was through, she found Drake sitting on the couch still smoking.

"What is so wrong that you need to puff away like a ganja man?" she asked.

He flashed her a glare so fierce she coiled away.

"I know. Stupid question, but you can't be blaming me for this."

"I'm not. How do you feel?"

"I'm fine. Considering." She stood behind him and leaned against the couch. "You know, for such a romantic guy, Glen is a terrible kisser."

"Cassie," he warned.

"Please, Drake, don't make me take this seriously," she pleaded softly. "Not tonight. It's too awful."

It was the tears brimming in her eyes that stopped him. He took her injured hand and kissed the bandage. "Okay, not tonight, but tomorrow."

She nodded.

He glanced around as if the very sight of the place offended him. "Don't you have an ashtray?"

"No, I don't smoke."

"Of course you don't." He grabbed a saucer from the cabinet and tapped his ashes into it. "If there were no law, I would have snapped his body in two. Unfortunately, your brother is very persuasive."

"You once said the world was full of rogues, but you forgot about heroes."

He abruptly laid the saucer down. "Gather some of your stuff, you're staying with me permanently."

"Well, I—"

"Don't argue, just do it."

"I wasn't going to arg—"

"Why aren't you packing?"

Cassie quickly gathered her things, no longer feeling indulgent. "You know, you can be such a bully sometimes—stubborn, unyielding. I'm afraid I may have to revoke your hero status."

He took her bags. "That's okay. I'm not a hero, or a gentleman, or a rogue."

She grabbed his umbrella from the corner and opened the door. "Then what are you?"

He began to smile. "A man who loves you."

"Drake!" She threw her arms around him, her heart overflowing with joy.

Door 712 opened. "Is everything all right?" Mr. Gianolo asked.

Cassie sighed, her eyes fixed on the man she loved. "Yes. Everything's perfect."

* * *

They walked to his car with the fresh scent of cold in the air and the promise of holiday festivities engaging the city. Miniature white lights draped trees; menorahs, wreaths, and candy canes vied for space in shop windows, and people loaded with packages rushed past. Cassie remembered another night similar to this when wizardry seemed to course through the air and she'd kissed a man with abandon during a warm summer rain. She thought of how she had tried to push him away in an effort to remain free, but in time he'd taught her how to be free of her thoughts and her fears. She felt something cold and wet drop on her nose. She glanced up and saw that it was snowing.

Drake held out his hand and let a snowflake melt in his palm. "Do you love snow as much as rain?"

She grabbed his face and kissed him among a few shouts and whistles of a passing Gothic crowd and odd stares of others trying to figure out the odd pair. She didn't care. "No. I only love you. And the answer is yes."

Drake frowned. "Yes?"

"Yes, I will marry you."

He abruptly dropped her bags and spun her around until she pleaded for him to stop. "You'll hurt your back," she scolded.

He didn't hear her. The happiness he felt was almost terrifying. At last, she would belong to him and he to her. He had succeeded. "My middle name is Marcus," he confessed, lifting her bags.

She stared at him. "What? You told me you didn't have a middle name."

He grinned wickedly. "I know."

She narrowed her eyes. "How many more secrets do you have?"

Her beloved sorcerer just laughed and together they walked toward a bright and exciting future.

Epilogue

"*I* can't believe my mother is paying for the entire wedding," Cassie said as she, Drake, Clay, Jackie, and Adriana ate lunch at the Golden Diner.

"She's trying to make up for a lot of years," Adriana said, picking through her chicken salad, too excited to eat.

"And she can afford it," Clay grumbled.

Drake stole a grilled shrimp from Cassie's plate and popped it in his mouth.

"Stop eating my food," she warned.

"Then stop worrying and eat it yourself," he argued.

Cassie made a face and took a bite.

He patted her on the head. "Good girl, and don't forget your vegetables."

She swatted his hand away. "I can't believe how eager she is for me to marry you after what you said."

Clay and Drake shared a quick glance. Neither would mention the little chat they had at the Graham house that resulted in Angela's Graham sudden enthusiasm.

"I told you that your parents love you."

"I know that, but clothes shopping is a different matter. I don't want to end up looking like a walking marshmallow. "

"But I like marshmallows." Drake took another shrimp before she could slap his hand away. "Whatever you wear, you're going to look beautiful."

Cassie moved the dish out of his reach. "Thank you."

Adriana watched the exchange and sighed happily. "I'm so glad you two worked everything out." She rested her chin in her hand. "If I didn't love you, Cassie, I'd be jealous." She looked at Drake. "You don't happen to have any brothers, do you?"

Jackie and Clay turned away to hide their smiles. While behind her, Drake and Cassie watched Eric enter the diner, flash a wicked grin at a harried waitress, and point in their direction. They shared a look, then turned to Adriana.

"Well, as a matter of fact..."

Sneak Peek

Turn the page for a sneak peek at
GAINING INTEREST
Dara Girard's second book in the
Henson series

Chapter One

Eric Henson listened to the loud crack of a tree snapping, its limb an unfortunate victim of the harsh October weather settling over the city and slapping a crisp wind against his office window. The tree's destruction echoed in his ears. He had to remind himself that the sound wasn't his patience snapping in two.

He stared at Adriana Travers across the broad mahogany desk. She didn't meet the disbelief reflecting in his serious, speculative gaze. She was too busy buffing her nails, casually tapping her foot. He wasn't angry, he reminded himself, letting his gaze fall to his desk. He didn't let himself get angry. She had obviously misunderstood his suggestions.

It was perfectly understandable that she be confused about his recommendations regarding her finances. She didn't seem the type to take much interest in financial matters. The dreadful state of her books was a good indicator of that. He wanted to help her, but doubted he had the fortitude to do so. Most times he hoped he would glance up and she would disappear like a bad dream. However, she was real and in his office looking as out of place as two commas in a tax return.

She had the color and vibrancy of a hummingbird and was completely incongruous with the serene gray of his office. Her curly black hair fell around her face in a crazy array that seemed to suit her carefree personality. A long purple skirt draped her legs while thick-heeled black boots peeked from underneath. A shimmering jacket completed the look, but her silver earrings caught most of his attention. They constantly twirled and he couldn't understand what law of physics allowed their continuous motion.

He pulled his gaze from them and focused on the problem at hand. He was a professional and needed to handle the situation in a calm and tactful manner. He would not insult her intelligence and put her on the defensive. He was used to her type. He'd met a few in his line of work and knew they required a patience his other clients didn't need. He sat forward and clasped his hands together, ready to address and dismiss any of her concerns.

"Did you hear what I said?" she asked, clearly annoyed by his silence.

"Yes. What do you mean by 'no'?" His voice was soft, laden with a hint of steel. Usually his tone gave a person pause. She, however, presented him with a brief, disinterested caramel glare and continued to buff her nails.

"It means that I disagree with you," she clarified. "It means that I think your suggestions are poorly thought out and most of all illogical."

Eric adjusted his glasses, a small bit of temper beginning to claw around him. He prided himself on being logical. He was always logical. What did she mean he... He loosened the grip on his pen and took a deep breath. She did this on purpose to provoke him. In the three years he had known her they had never been able to speak without annoying each other. He had thankfully seen her only a few times since her best friend had married his brother. They were usually spared the aggravation of being in each other's company. Until now.

When he had heard she needed financial counseling, he had wanted to help. So for once in all his practical years he had—in a moment of temporary insanity—done something he never did. He'd been impulsive. He had called her up and offered his services. To his surprise she had accepted. He glanced at her now as she wiggled her fingers in front of her. He was too tired to kick himself for that brief lapse in judgment.

"What did you find..." He searched for words. "Unacceptable about my suggestions?"

She leaned forward, took the budget from the desk, and tapped each item. "No, I will not eat regular nameless foods, cut down my visits to the salon, stop my cable, or put my cat to sleep."

He blinked. "I never suggested that."

"You probably would if you knew how much I spend on cat food and kitty litter."

Eric sat back and folded his arms. *Patience*, he reminded himself. "I think your cat is a necessity, an essential part of your life. You probably consider it a family member as many pet owners do." He paused, thoughtful. "Ultimately, the cat likely serves some purpose. I've read that it's healthy to have a pet. Usually they refer to dogs because they force you out on daily walks, but I'm sure cats offer some sort of healthy regime." He shook his head. "No, I would never suggest you get rid of your cat."

Adriana crossed her legs and tapped the buffer against her knee. "How generous of you," she said in a dry tone. "I was completely unaware of my cat's many benefits until I met you. She's not just a beautiful, friendly, and furry companion, but she's also a good health investment."

The brown eyes flickered. "There's no reason to be sarcastic."

Adriana hid a tiny grin. She was beginning to get to him. She didn't know why the thought cheered her, but it did. It was nice to know the unflappable Eric Henson had a temper. Perhaps he had a heart as well.

He was eerily too much like his office. Cool, elegant, and intimidating. There were no pictures on the wall, not even a plant to give color to the gray decor. Just a pathetic vase of plastic lilies that sat high on a bookshelf, turning gray from the gathering dust. She measured him in one quick glance, wondering how often he needed dusting. The dark blue of his tie and shirt complemented the brown of his skin. It was an unremarkable light shade with all the dimension and warmth of a piece of cardboard.

She would not call him handsome. His face was too serious for such a clichéd label. His features were firm, undeniably male in structure with eyes as warm as petrified wood, offset by round, gold-framed glasses. He didn't have a mouth that entertained a smile or laughed very often and his hair was pitch-black and cut almost cruelly short.

She didn't know why she was here. She inwardly groaned. That was wrong. She did know. She had been impulsive. It was a terrible fault of hers and usually landed her in trouble. She remembered when Eric had called her one late afternoon while she was flipping through a *Victoria's Secret* catalogue. After overcoming the shock of hearing his voice on the other end, she heard herself saying yes to his seemingly reasonable offer, forgetting whom she was saying yes to.

The beginning of the meeting had been cordial until he started taking charge of her spending habits like an overzealous hospital nurse. He had angered her by treating her as if she had no common sense. She knew his type—a pulse-free intellectual who thought he had the sole monopoly on brain function. Yes, she liked to tease him. She wanted to show him that he was human and emotional like the rest of the ordinary world.

"Do you have a pet?" she asked.

"No."

"Not even a cold, dull goldfish swimming dizzyingly around in a bowl on your windowsill?"

"No."

"Remind me to get you one. A tiny one so that it won't be too much of a bother to you."

He glanced out the window. "As I was saying, your cat Elena —"

"Elissa."

"Right. Elissa is part of regular household expenses. However, the other items I listed are easily dispensable. For example, you could do without going to the salon."

"No, I could not."

He met her gaze. "Then go to a cheaper one."

"Would an owner of a Mercedes send his car to a Saab dealership for repairs?"

"We are not talking about cars."

"No, we're talking about me. My skin, my body."

Ah, hell, now why did she have to mention that? Eric tried to keep his eyes from the satin beauty of her dark coffee skin. He knew she thought of him as an automaton, but he was a male automaton.

"My visits to the salon are part of my monthly maintenance," she continued.

He waved the receipts. "Only a person with severe physical deformities needs to spend this much money on maintenance." And she had absolutely no physical deformities from where he was sitting. She was not a beautiful woman but her caramel eyes were captivating and she had a full mouth that on more than one occasion occupied his mind with purely male distractions. He put the receipts down, gathering his thoughts, when he found himself staring at her lips.

"It's part of my job."

He wanted to laugh. Now how was she going to explain this expenditure as a necessity? He leaned back in his chair instead. "Explain this to me. I can't seem to make the connection."

She spoke slowly. "I can't sell my merchandise if I look unkempt. I sell a fantasy and I have to look the part."

"At these prices you'll have to sell a lot more than a fantasy. You spend over a hundred dollars every visit and you go twice a month."

She ignored the implication. "Going to the spa relaxes me."

"Find a hobby."

"It is a hobby."

"I thought your hobby was club hopping."

She narrowed her eyes at his tone. "That's under entertainment."

"Isn't that Keith's role?"

"That's none of your business." Her voice was ice.

Eric shook his head, pushing his glasses to the bridge of his nose. He knew he was treading on dangerous territory, but he liked the feeling. A part of him liked the whisper of warning that came with risk. He didn't care if she got angry as long as he made his point. "You have spent nearly three thousand dollars on him. That is my business."

"Don't make it sound so vulgar," she snapped. "He's an artist and needs supplies."

He rested his chin in his hand and studied the list of supplies for a moment. He looked up at her and raised one eyebrow, softly mocking. "Seventy-five dollars for one brush?"

"It's of excellent quality. Haven't you ever wondered why paintings are so expensive?" She glanced around his bare walls. "No, I guess you don't. The fact is Keith is really very good and once he's made his big break he'll pay me back."

"His big break," Eric murmured. He shut his eyes for a moment. Adriana was more naive than he thought. He hated Keith's ability to capitalize on that. She was flighty and vexing, but she was kind and he would not let her get used.

He softened his tone, trying to sound indulgent. "Has he displayed his work?"

"Yes." For the first time that afternoon, she actually smiled at him, excited by his interest. "Actually, I'm wearing one of his prints now. Would you like to see it?"

He nodded. Inside, his gut clenched. He hoped Keith showed some marketable talent.

She opened her shimmering jacket, displaying a black dress shirt with splatters of red, yellow, and pink—like one would find on a baby's bib— accentuated by white dots.

He squinted at the design. "What is that supposed to be?"

"It's not supposed to be anything. Keith says it's just a conveyance of emotion. Anger versus despair versus hope."

Eric lost his patience."Why don't you get him a paint-by-numbers set and invest in him when he learns how to draw?"

Adriana glared at him. She shoved the buffer in her handbag and stood. "Thank you for your advice," she said stiffly.

He silently swore. He had pushed her too far. "Sit down, Adriana," he said. "I'm not finished."

"Yes, you are." She rested her hands on his desk and leaned forward. "All you've done is waste my time and insult me. I'm not a complete half-wit although you have done your best to make me think so. You've insulted my lifestyle, my job—"

"I never made fun of your job."

"No, you just smirked. My lingerie boutiques are excellently run and very profitable."

He nodded. "Yes, I agree you make a handsome income."

There it was again, that arrogant, condescending tone that showed his surprise at her fortitude. She'd had enough of him, his unreadable dark eyes and cool, mocking voice. She had made a mistake, but she would not make it again. She turned on her heel and headed for the door.

Eric was there before she could open it. She gaped up at him, surprised. For his placid, calculating ways she hadn't expected him to be so swift or so large. His size always came as a shock. One wouldn't expect a mathematical robot to tower over six feet with a powerful, intimidating presence. She looked at his pressed shirt, amazed at how it clung to his wide frame. While not overly muscular he was anything but scrawny and moved with a sinewy, catlike grace. He leaned against the door looking mildly regretful. "I apologize."

She shrugged, mollified by his apology. "What for? It was my mistake for coming here."

"No, it wasn't. It was bold of you to come and I haven't made it easy for you." He stared at the floor. A tiny frown formed between his brows. He was trying to be gentle. She found the attempt endearing. The soft whisper of a Jamaican lilt accented his words. "Talking about money is always difficult. It represents much more than our financial status; it reflects our habits, our personalities, our fears, our goals... It takes a lot for my clients to be as honest with their spending as you have been. People feel more comfortable talking about their sex lives than debt."

"Would you rather talk about sex?"

His eyes captured hers. "Are you offering?"

Her heart began beating an odd rhythm. He was quick for a nerd. "No."

He pushed himself from the door and took her arm. The grip was loose, but she knew escape was impossible. "Sit down. Let's see if we can come to an agreement."

Adriana sat and stared at him in wonder.

"What?"

She rested back, impressed. "You're very good."

He frowned.

"I was prepared to storm out of here, bristling with indignation, and somehow you convinced me to stay. Amazing."

"It's because you realized—"

"No, you're just very good at reading people." She tilted her head to the side, trying to read his dark eyes. "Pull any cons when you were a kid?"

He gathered some receipts. "About the spa—"

She sighed. Why did she even try with him? "I like to go," she cut in. "I like being pampered." She looked at him. The poor man was trying, but he still didn't understand. Before he could argue she said, "Isn't there something you like to do? Something that relaxes you and makes you feel so good that you couldn't imagine life without it because it's part of who you are?"

His dark eyes flickered with genuine amusement. He nodded. "Good argument. Okay, once a month."

She let out a breath in relief, then frowned. What hobby couldn't he do without? She couldn't even picture him with a hobby. What would he find entertaining? *Business Week*, CNN, a scientific calculator? She knew it was no use asking him. What he didn't offer he wasn't willing to share.

He wrote something down on a Post-it. "Let's see what other adjustments we can make to this budget."

The phone rang. Eric glanced at his watch and answered. "Henson."

Adriana watched in amazement as his face softened. Not into a smile, but something close. She knew at once who was on the line: her best friend, Cassie.

"Thank you. Yes, I got them." He nodded and glanced at her. "Yes, she's still here. Would you like to speak with her?" He nodded again, then handed her the phone. "It's Cassie."

"Hi," she said as she watched Eric discreetly leave the room. Once he closed the door she asked, "How do you do it?"

"Do what?"

"Get the statue to soften."

Cassie sighed. "How many times do I have to tell you that your opinion of him is all wrong?"

"Until I believe you, I suppose."

"He is one of the sweetest, most gentle men I know."

She reached for the Post-it note he had written, but his handwriting was too illegible to read. "You're just biased because he's your brother-in-law."

"If he's so horrible, why did you ask for his help?"

She pushed the pad away and toyed with his pens. "I didn't ask for his help, he offered and I accepted out of desperation. Believe it or not I would really like to get my finances in order."

"Well, Eric can definitely help you do that."

"So why did you call?"

Cassie hesitated. "He didn't tell you?"

Adriana straightened. "Tell me what?"

"I guess it's his business. He doesn't have to share if he doesn't want to."

"Share what?"

Cassie sounded annoyed with herself. "Never mind, it's not important. I'll call you tomorrow to find out how everything went."

"Cassie, are you going to let me die of curiosity?"

"You won't die. Besides, you'll figure it out soon enough."

"Cassie—" she began, but her friend hung up.

Eric came into the room soon after. Adriana briefly wondered if he had been listening by the door, but quickly remembered he wasn't the type.

She watched him walk to his desk, her mind brimming with curiosity. What was Cassie talking about? What wouldn't he want to share? There didn't seem to be anything different about him. "Are you feeling well?" she asked.

"I'm fine, thank you." It was a nice polite response that offered her nothing. She pushed her curiosity aside. Why Cassie had called him was none of her business. It was probably something dull anyway.

After another half hour of debating, they finally settled on a budget.

"It's going to be difficult at first," Eric said as he handed her the final plan. "But the end reward will be worth it."

Adriana folded it and pushed it in her handbag. She hated it already. She felt as if the fun and freedom that were an integral part of her life had been taken from her. Eric wouldn't understand. He wasn't the sort to indulge in simple pleasures. Unfortunately, he was to be her saving grace. She had come to him for help and she would do what was necessary to get out of debt. It was difficult to fly on the wings of fun and freedom with debt chained to your ankle.

"Thank you." Her voice came out muffled.

"Sometimes the word 'budget' scares people."

Or makes them ill.

"Try to think of it as a spending plan. It is not set in stone and is flexible for your needs. It's just a guide to help you achieve your goals. For example, money for your parents' care."

She had given him that financial goal just to impress him. She knew that if she had told him the truth he would have scoffed at her.

He rested his arms on the desk and clasped his hands. "However, we still have one thing we need to address."

Oh no. "What?"

"I want you to write down everything you spend for an entire week."

"No."

"Either that or only use a checkbook."

No plastic? "Why?"

"Because even though you gave me a detailed list of your expenditures I know that money is running through your fingers. We need to know where it is going."

She swung her foot, annoyed. "You don't need to put it like that."

"I find honesty very helpful. You're an impulsive shopper."

"I like to shop. I wouldn't call it impulsive."

"You could make shopping an Olympic sport."

She grinned bitterly. "Thank you. I always go for the gold."

"You would have a lot more in your savings or more to invest if you would use only cash in stores and wait a day before you purchase something that catches your eye. Especially sales."

Time out. He'd overstepped the line. Sales restrictions were off-limits. "You've helped me with my budget. I don't need any more of your advice."

"If you buy it on sale and you don't need it, it's not a bargain."

Adriana tapped her foot and blinked.

Eric leaned forward, his voice lowering to a coaxing tone. It had an unsettling effect on her. Only he could get excited over money like this. "Give me just a thousand to invest for you and I can show you how it will grow."

She grabbed her bag, ready to leave. "No, thank you."

"Listen, Adriana—"

He stopped when the door flew open. A young woman dressed in a dark winter coat with hood and blue knit scarf entered the room.

"Are you Eric Henson?" she asked in a high New York accent.

His reply was flat. "As it says on the door. Why?"

"Because I've got a message for you." She turned to Adriana. "Don't worry, this won't take long." She pulled a music player from inside her jacket and place it on the desk. Suddenly, raw, raunchy strip music filled the tense air. A light flashed; the woman's clothes dropped to the floor. She began dancing in front of Eric, dressed in a red, sequined bikini that glittered and shook with each gyrating motion.

Adriana managed to pull her eyes away from the display to stare at Eric. Her mood went from shock to amusement to dismay. The poor woman was wasting her time. Eric wasn't even impressed. He rested his elbow on the desk and watched her with the same interest as a scientist observing a research participant. Even as the woman wrapped a scarf around his neck and let her blond hair cascade around him he didn't even flinch.

Her dismay turned to disgust. Wouldn't he even smile at her? Cool the stone in his gaze or soften that hard mask on his face? He was completely inhuman. Any healthy male would at least show some interest in a beautiful woman dancing solely for his pleasure. Even she, as a female, was amazed by the woman's shapely form and awe-inspiring moves. She glanced at his granite profile, waiting for even the barest of emotions.

She was about to look away when he turned and winked at her. Adriana gasped, the soft sound drowned out by the music. In that one fleeting moment she knew that he was very male and could be very dangerous to any woman who underestimated him.

She pushed the thought away. Her flare for the dramatic was taking over her common sense. Eric was a dull, ordinary intellectual. She must have imagined his wink. She stared at him again. His impassive mask was firmly in place, confirming her suspicions.

When the music stopped, the woman kissed him, leaving bright red lipstick on his cheek. "Happy birthday," she whispered. She gathered her clothes and left.

Adriana stared at the closed door, then said, "I guess we all splurge once in a while."

He wiped his cheek and frowned at the red smudge on his fingers. "I didn't pay for that." He grabbed some tissues and wiped his hand. "My sister will, however."

"Jackie sent her?" She turned to him and laughed.

He began to clear up his desk.

"So today's your birthday, huh? How old are you?" She held up a hand. "No, wait, let me guess. You're not a day over a hundred and four."

He disappeared behind the desk. "A hundred and ten." He peeked at her, his serious eyes teasing. "The lack of gray tends to fool people."

Adriana smiled. The guy was definitely quick. She wanted to see how he would respond to a few more harmless taunts. "So how are you going to celebrate? Dust off a couple of dictionaries, read the financial expenses of a nineteenth-century household, or organize the soup cans in your kitchen?"

She heard the sound of the bottom drawer closing. He straightened. "Actually, at the stroke of midnight I'm going to ask Lynda to marry me."

She dropped her handbag, spilling the contents on the floor. She didn't notice. "I don't believe you."

He came from behind the desk and began gathering her things. "It's true."

She kneeled down and stared at him as if he were a Gucci bag marked 85 percent off. Why was it just when she thought she had him figured out, he did or said something unexpected? "But that's so romantic."

He picked up her bag and flashed a wicked grin. "Surprised? Don't be. The reason is practical." He handed her the bag. "It has to do with midnight and when I was born."

About the Author

Dara Girard, an award-winning, national bestselling author of more than forty novels, from romance to suspense, loves telling stories.

Born in the US to immigrant parents, Dara enjoys pulling from her Jamaican, British, Nigerian heritage and exposure to various cultures to bring what reviewers and fans call "vivid emotional stories" to life. She is best known for her popular Henson Series, the mysterious Clifton Sisters, and the fun Black Stockings Society.

You can write her at:
contactdara@daragirard.com
or
PO Box 10345
Silver Spring, MD 20914

If you'd like to receive a reply, please send a self-address stamped envelope.

Visit www.daragirard.com to sign up for her newsletter and get sneak peeks, monthly updates on new releases, and special offers.

CPSIA information can be obtained
at www.ICGtesting.com
Printed in the USA
LVHW110025130919
630868LV00008BA/1109/P

9 781949 764307